To Catch a Dream

Born the thirteenth child of fifteen to a middle-class mother and an East End barrow boy, Mary Wood's childhood was a mixture of love and poverty. This encouraged her to develop a natural empathy with the less fortunate and a fascination with social history. Throughout her life Mary has held various posts in catering and office roles, and in the probation service, while bringing up her four children. Mary now has numerous grandchildren, step-grandchildren and great-grandchildren. An avid reader, she first put pen to paper in 1989 whilst nursing her mother through her last months, but didn't become successful until she began self-publishing her novels in the late 2000s.

BY MARY WOOD

The Breckton novels

To Catch a Dream
An Unbreakable Bond
Tomorrow Brings Sorrow
Time Passes Time

Proud of You

The Cotton Mill saga

Judge Me Not

To Catch a Dream

Mary Wood

PAN BOOKS

First published 2013 by Books By Mary Wood

This edition published 2015 by Pan Books
an imprint of Pan Macmillan, a division of Macmillan Publishers Limited
Pan Macmillan, 20 New Wharf Road, London N1 9RR
Basingstoke and Oxford
Associated companies throughout the world
www.panmacmillan.com

ISBN 978-1-4472-6744-7

1 3 5 7 9 8 6 4 2

A CIP catalogue record for this book is available from the British Library.

Typeset by Palimpsest Book Production Ltd, Falkirk, Stirlingshire
Printed and bound by CPI Group (UK) Ltd, Croydon, CR0 4YY

Visit www.panmacmillan.com to read more about all our books
and to buy them. You will also find features, author interviews and
news of any author events, and you can sign up for e-newsletters
so that you're always first to hear about our new releases.

For my husband, Roy.
You stand by my side.
You prop me up if I falter.
Your love is my life.

Acknowledgements

To Louise Buckley, my editor at Pan Macmillan. Louise, you have helped and guided me every step of the way. Your insightful editing of my work brings clarity where I may have muddied the waters. Thank you, Louise. Every author should have an editor like you.

To all the Pan Macmillan editorial team, especially Laura Carr for her help with the line edit and timeline of *To Catch a Dream* – we got there in the end, Laura. And to the publicity and sales teams, the cover artists and models, and everyone who has worked on my book – thank you.

A special thank you goes to my agent, Judith Murdoch, who is always there for me. Having known of you and your work for many years, I still have to pinch myself to think that you actually represent me! Together with Louise, you have made my journey and first year in traditional publishing much smoother, as well as one of the most exciting in my life. Thank you.

My grateful thanks go to Julie Hitchin, Stan Livingstone, Rebecca Keys, Patrick Fox, Pam Howes and my colleagues at Blackpool, Lancaster and Fleetwood probation offices; many of you read and reread early versions of this novel – the list is too long to mention you all, but you know who you are and how grateful I am to you for the help and encouragement you have given me along my journey. In my self-publishing days you were my editorial team, my cover artists and my mentors, and still are, above all, my most valued friends.

Thank you, too, to my readers. I value you all. Many of you have become my friends through my Facebook page and the interaction I have with you is a source of great support to me. Your love and loyalty means the world to me and I give mine to you.

As always, my heartfelt and most important thanks and love to my wonderful family: my lovely supportive husband, Roy; my amazing children, Christine, Julie, Rachel and James – with a special thank you to James for all the help you gave me with the proof of this novel. To my adorable grandchildren and great-grandchildren. To my Olley and Wood family. All of you are there for me when I need you and all of you are my joy and inspiration.

PART ONE
Ultimate Betrayal
1873–76

1

Bridie

County Cavan in the north of Ireland, 1873
Confusing conflicts

'Will you shut your mouth, woman? Haven't I enough on me plate without your constant whining?'

Fear tickled the muscles in Bridie's stomach and tightened her throat. The eruption of her pappy's anger grated in the already tense atmosphere that coated the walls of their home.

''Tis as I'm worried to the heart of me, Michael . . .'

'Whish, woman, you'd drive a man insane, you would. Would you have it any different? Would you have that traitor free to do further damage? It has to be done. Sure, the cause depends on it. We must rid ourselves of those who would betray us.'

Torn between staying to see that her mammy was all right and delivering the loaf she'd been told to, Bridie hesitated, but she knew her disobedience would only add to her pappy's agitation.

The argument taking place in her parents' bedroom quietened. Her prayers begging for her mammy not to keep protesting at whatever Pappy referred to seemed to have been answered, though she knew that if her pappy came out and found her there, listening, it could all start again. She couldn't risk that.

'Is that yourself, Bridie?'

''Tis, Mrs Finney. Mammy sent me with some bread for you.'

'Aye, that's good. Your mammy is kindness itself. Is she keeping better?'

'She is. She's been grand these last weeks.' It wasn't easy to keep the tremor from her voice, but Mrs Finney didn't seem to notice it.

'Come away in, then, my wee lass, and let me get a proper sight of you.'

Disturbed from his peaceful grazing, the piebald tethered nearby snorted. His nostrils flared. His cream, silky mane fanned out with an annoyed movement of his head. 'Whish now, Ginger, 'tis only me.' One more defiant huff and he settled down.

Catching up the hem of her muddied, rust-coloured skirt, Bridie climbed onto the ladder. The familiar creak of the Vardo steps enhanced the excitement in her. She loved it when the travellers arrived. They visited her pappy's farm twice a year: once in springtime to help with the planting and, as now, in the autumn, to lift the potato crop and turn the soil ready for winter.

Going into the semi-darkness of the interior blurred her vision. It took a moment to adjust after the bright sunshine outside. Once she could focus, she saw Mrs Finney lying on the bed at the back of the caravan, her swollen legs supported by a block with a soft fleece thrown over it. The old lady peered at her and said, 'You've grown. Is it fourteen you are now?'

'Yes, I'm not for having to go to school any longer. I left just after your last visit at Easter time.'

'And is it you have to work at the castle like the rest of the girls around here?'

'No, the priest tried to get me a place in service, but Pappy would have none of it. He says there is enough for me to do around here.'

'Aye, Michael's always looking for the cheap labour, so he is. But you should be finding yourself a fella by now and settling down. All my girls did by your age. They've all caravans of their own and are off around the country. Some have even crossed the water.'

'You know that isn't our way, Mrs Finney.'

'Aye, we have our differences. Put the loaf on the shelf next to the tea chest, my wee one, but wrap it first. Use one of those cloths from the pile in the corner.'

The aroma of fresh-baked bread as Bridie wrapped it in the crisp, white muslin mingled with the smells of the small wood-burning stove, the canvas of the arched roof and the sheepskin rugs. This, and the clinking of the jars containing jams and preserves as she slid them along the shelf to make room, settled a feeling of homeliness in her and calmed her tangled nerves.

The brass key of the small, wooden tea chest – a legacy from the days when it had lived in a much grander place – swayed back and forth, as if to remind her that it had once locked out anyone not allowed to touch its contents. Now it no longer housed expensive *real* tea, but a blend of herbs and nettles. These brewed into a delicious, refreshing hot drink and held properties to heal you of all manner of illnesses.

5

Bridie didn't give a thought to how it came to be here, or how any of the rich-looking jugs with funny faces and the inlaid boxes found their way into the Finneys' possession. She just liked to admire them, adorning the shelf around the interior of the Vardo and arranged amongst the colourful plates that she had watched the gypsy girls paint.

'Sit yourself down.' Mrs Finney waved towards the trunk opposite the stove. 'Just look at you, Bridie! Sure it is you are turning into a beauty. In just these short months you have blossomed into a young woman.'

Bridie blushed, but her embarrassment was tinged with a little pride. She too had noted the changes in her body. And her mirror reflected the truth of what everyone said: 'Now, don't you know that it is you that features your mammy, Bridie.' Her unruly, long red hair, falling into ringlets around her face, and her large blue eyes, replicated those of her mother, as did her height and shapely figure. Already she had breasts bigger than all the girls of her age from the nearby town, and most of the older ones too, as it happened. Not that she found this something she admired or wanted. For weren't they the cause of her attracting stares from the lads, and looks of envy from the girls? These she coped with, but the way older men leered at her repulsed and disgusted her. Sometimes, when going into the town, she would resort to tying a band from one of her frocks around herself to flatten her chest, and pinning her shawl in such a way as to cover herself.

As if reading her thoughts, Mrs Finney said, ''Tis, Bridie, as you'll be for having problems with the menfolk. God made you for them, so He did. And you will find a burning need in you for what they have to offer. But don't be giving into it, my wee Bridie, as it will be your downfall.'

The tone of caution lay heavily on the dread still lying

within Bridie concerning the worries of her pappy, and she was glad as Mrs Finney's voice changed and made light of the warning.

'So, mind you take care, but don't be for hiding behind your cape. 'Tis their sin, not yours, if they have bad thoughts at the sight of you. Hold yourself proud and give off an air of *You can look, but don't be touching*. That should sort them out.' Her cackle of laughter held a naughty insinuation as she said, 'That is, unless it's your choosing to have them touch!' She laughed louder at this and the sound filled the space in the Vardo.

Bridie stared at the one tooth hanging at the front of Mrs Finney's open mouth, but the embarrassment she'd felt at her words dissolved as the laughter got to her. And though she hadn't been for understanding what Mrs Finney had said, her easy sense of fun had Bridie giggling until the tears rolled down her face.

But then Mrs Finney sobered Bridie and nudged the trepidation inside her as she changed the subject. 'Eeh, it's good, so it is, to have the crack. Now, will you be around when the stars are up, as we plan on having a sing-song round the campfire? That is, if Seamus gets home from the dealings your pappy sent him on.'

'Do you know what it is Pappy asked Seamus to do, Mrs Finney?'

'No, he didn't tell me, as is the way of it with the menfolk. Why, what has caused the powerful look of concern you have on your face?'

'I hear things, Mrs Finney. Pappy has visitors, and they hold their meetings in our parlour. He doesn't know it, but sometimes when they rant and rave their voices come through the wall to my bedroom.'

7

'And what kind of things are you hearing?'

'I know Pappy is a member of the Fenians and, from what they are saying, I think they have a hand in some of the bad goings-on. Not the killings – to be sure Pappy could not take part in those – but the torching of buildings and the movement of weapons. And last night Seamus attended—'

'Aye, well, don't be worrying. These are troubled times, but as daft a job as the men will make of it, we women have to leave the politics to them. Besides, that grandson of mine can take care of himself, so he can. Now away with you and leave me to me rest.'

This sudden dismissal came with an odd, intense look, which shuddered through Bridie. 'Are you out of sorts with me, Mrs Finney? Is it as I have . . . ?'

'No, you haven't done anything. 'Tis me all-seeing eye troubling me. I need to have time on me own. Will I see you the night?'

'Aye, you will, Mrs Finney.'

'Good, and Seamus will be here, to be sure. But, Bridie, afore you go, listen to me. You have to let go of how everything used to be. Don't be for hanging onto how things were when you were little. You are a grown woman now. What you dreamed of as a child must remain that – a dream. Are you getting my meaning?'

A blush crept up from inside Bridie's chest. Unable to hold Mrs Finney's gaze, she said her goodbyes and left.

Taking care to avoid the water-filled ruts the wheels of the gypsy caravans had gouged, she picked her way along the muddied lane leading to her home. The uncomfortable, prickly feeling visited on her by Mrs Finney's words remained with her as she realized that her inner secret had been seen by others. But then, it was the way of Mrs Finney to be knowing of all things, so she would not have missed the adoration Bridie had for Seamus.

As a child she'd spent many hours playing with the traveller children of her own age and following the bigger ones around, especially Seamus. Seven years older than herself, he'd fascinated her with his knowledge of the land and the animals. When she tired, he'd lift her up, calling her his little red-haired girl. She would fall asleep on his shoulder, twiddling his dark curls between her fingers.

Sometimes she longed for those days. Now Seamus had other things on his mind, and on the last couple of visits had spent little time with her. At twenty-one, he'd become one of the main men of the clan and had serious duties to attend to. She didn't like to think of him mixed up with her pappy's lot. And, like her mammy, she wished her pappy would leave things alone, too.

Although her parents tried to shield her from the politics of Ireland, she understood more than they thought, and knew where her pappy's sympathy lay. When in drink, he always toasted the bravery of Michael Barratt, a lad from the next county who had gone to the gallows for trying to blow a hole in the wall of Coldbath Field Prison, over in England. Her pappy expressed condemnation of Michael's public hanging and spoke of him as a hero for trying to release the Fenian prisoners.

Mammy always said Pappy had changed after that event. He'd started going off on his drinking bouts. He'd be gone for days and they had to cope on their own; but, worse than that, on his return the rows would start. Many days went by with her mother not leaving her room. Muffled cries of pain sent hurt and loneliness through Bridie, and she'd squat in a corner, curl up her body and cover her ears with her hands.

But Pappy would say it was just one of Mammy's turns, and off he would go again. An end would come suddenly and without warning, signalled by the whistling. Pappy would come in, heralded by a cheery tune and without a care in the world. He'd send Bridie off on some errand or other, but she never minded, for on her return home he would be there again, and Mammy would greet her, looking beautiful, smiling at Pappy and snuggling into him while he teased her and planted kisses in her hair.

A tenanted farmer, her father had a lot of worries: how he would meet the rent, how to get the fields hoed when he couldn't afford the labour, and what would happen if Gladstone didn't get amendments to the Irish Land Act. And what would happen if he did.

All of it confused Bridie. It seemed there was a need for an Act to restrain the landlords from putting up the rent, but her father talked as though this wouldn't happen. She'd heard him say to one of his friends, 'The British government won't interfere in matters of private property, to be sure they won't.'

When she approached their small cottage built of grey stone, her mammy stood in the doorway, broom in one hand and holding her back with the other. A different worry crept into Bridie. Her mammy suffered from many bad pains, and her body seemed to bend over more every day. And yet her radiant beauty returned the moment she smiled and, like a miracle running through her, the life of her came back into every part of her. That transformation came about as she caught sight of Bridie and called out, 'You didn't stay long, Bridie. You needn't have hurried back. I have everything done now.'

'No one was about, Mammy. No Petra or Rosalee . . .'

'Oh, that's right. Didn't they say as they may have their

10

betrothal in the summer? It must have happened. Did Mrs Finney not tell you?'

'No, she only talked about the changes in me, and it wasn't long before she seemed eager for me to leave her. Mammy, are you for thinking she can see things?'

'I don't know. She's a funny one. She did predict the blight back in '45, when my own father was alive and running this farm. But then, 'tis the way of things, as travellers pass through many counties and she could pick up on things along the way. Why is it you are asking?'

'She knew a secret I had held, and she had an awful look on her just before she said she needed her rest.'

'Aye, I know what it is. Haven't I had the dread in me at times, when she gives me one of her looks? Don't be worrying, me wee lass. She's only getting her fun at our expense.'

'Well, I wish she wouldn't. Anyway, they're for having shenanigans tonight, and I said I would go.'

'Oh, that's good. 'Tis just what we're all needing – a little fun and laughter in our life. Now, away with you. Go for a walk and see if there is anyone around to chatter to. Pappy has gone to the village, so he has, and there's nothing to keep you here.'

'Is it sure you are, Mammy? That would be grand. I might meet up with Amy; she should be leaving the castle just now.'

With a lighter heart, Bridie waved to her mammy. It wasn't often she had the freedom to roam. When she did, she gave way to the child still lurking inside her, for more often than not the confusion of growing up left her unsure of which person she wanted to be: the one with longings that she didn't understand, or the carefree, full-of-fun young girl.

The night, crisp and moonlit, turned into a swirl of colour and fun, dampened only by the knowledge that Seamus and his grandmother had made a hasty decision to move off on the morrow. No one would say why, and her father verged on anger with Bridie when she asked. In an effort to try to put it out of her mind, she let the excitement take her and threw herself into the moment. She danced as well as any of the traveller girls. Her bright, emerald-green frock, made by her mother from some old curtains that once hung in the dining room of the castle, and bought at the jumble sale, swished around her feet. The fitted bodice showed just a hint of her cleavage, but enough to suggest a passion burning inside her. Like a princess, she captivated everyone's attention. The concerns of earlier drifted away from her. The rhythm of the mouth organs and the fiddles filled the air, and she twisted and twirled in the heat of the bonfire.

'For sure, you are a regular travelling lass, Bridie.'

She stopped dancing and fell against Seamus, laughing up at him. 'I love it. It is so exciting.'

'It is as though you were born to it. Here, let me join you in a jig.'

He caught hold of her hand and together they reeled around, egged on by the younger ones enclosing them in a circle and clapping to the music. Seamus never took his eyes from hers, and the look Bridie saw in the depths of the dark pools of his enlarged pupils stirred feelings in her she couldn't understand, tightening her throat and sweeping a heat through her body.

Without warning, the world she'd allowed herself to enter splintered at the sound of her pappy's voice. 'Right, that'll be enough of that. Come on, Bridie. Your bedtime has passed this good hour since.'

Not wanting the moment to end, she begged of him, 'Not yet, Pappy. Sure the night is early and I am having a good time.'

'I said *now*! Will you disobey your pappy?' The music

stopped. His grip on her arm bruised her. 'Get yourself away, girl.'

Seamus stepped forward, but she saw the look on her pappy's face stay his protest. When he turned back to her, he'd become the Seamus she'd always known. The magic had gone. 'Do as your pappy bids, Bridie,' he told her.

'I don't need your help with the discipline of me daughter, Seamus. Come now, Bridie, I will see you to your bed meself, so I will.'

'Michael . . .'

Bridie held her breath as he looked round at her mammy. His face held a dark warning as he said, 'And you get yourself in, too. We'll speak of this later.'

Something about her father frightened Bridie more than she'd ever been frightened before. Once in her room, he flung her onto her bed, his teeth clenched in anger. He bent over her. 'You disgraced your mammy and me, flinging yourself around with that gypsy as though you were no better than them. I'll not stand for it. You remember: you're not the child you were!'

'Pappy, 'tis sorry I am. I did not know I did anything wrong. I—'

'You must think of the consequences of your actions. You cannot behave with Seamus how you were used to doing. He's a young man and his needs are different from what you understand. His kind have no respect.' His voice thickened. 'Bridie, Bridie, you're still Pappy's little girl . . .'

His stroking of her hair sent an unwelcome chill through her body. 'Pappy?' His hand stayed. His eyes bored into hers, then he turned and left her room.

2

Andrew

Breckton, Yorkshire, 1875
Changes afoot

The autumn colours enhanced the view Andrew Harvey had from the window of the sitting room of Tarrington House. Acres of fields spread out like a patchwork quilt before him to his right. In some he could see men with shire horses ploughing straight lines; in others, sheep or cattle grazed on the green pasture.

A thin spiral of smoke rose from between the trees of the bottom meadow, telling him that Seamus Finney still camped there. Funny to find an Irish traveller on his own. Seamus had appeared for the first time a couple of years ago and had been very useful, giving a hand with mending fences, digging out ditches and any other odd job that his own men hadn't had time to do. No doubt he'd be off soon. Seamus had once told him he went back to Ireland for the winter months, joining up with his own clan when they made camp in the southern counties.

The loud crack of a hunting rifle made him jump – the

gamekeeper, no doubt, busy culling the grouse. The estate had been overrun by them this year, and the August shooting parties hadn't lowered the numbers by anywhere near enough. The flutter set up in his heart by the sudden disturbance made it harder for him to calm the fear he held that one day all this might not be his. He turned away and faced his mother. She sat on the purple-and-gold striped chaise longue, placed next to the fire. For countless hours in his childhood, his grandfather – her father – had sat there with himself kneeling on the rug at his feet, enthralled by the tales his grandfather told and the pictures he drew. It hadn't mattered to him how many times they had gone over the same ground; he'd loved watching the piece of charcoal bringing to life the workings of the pit, and listening to his grandfather explaining how the mineral came to be in the earth, how his family mined it and what happened to it afterwards. 'One day, my boy, it will be your responsibility – just as it is your father's today – to see that everything runs smoothly and our fortune is protected,' he'd say, and then he'd go into detail of what the future held. What it didn't hold, Andrew knew now, was the great fortune he'd always been promised. His father's many mistakes had reduced their wealth.

His mother looked back at him with a steady gaze, holding her slight figure taut, as if ready to fight her corner. The extra hair she'd had woven in with her own beautiful golden locks gave her height. He had to look away. Always she presented herself as vulnerable and, even though he knew she wasn't, it undid him when he needed to take her to task.

Take her to task! God, how futile that was when she had her mind made up. And now he had to haggle with her over what should rightfully be his!

'Mother, this is awkward. Oh, I don't mean you shouldn't look for happiness, but – well, I mean . . .'

'Andrew, I know perfectly well what you mean. That is why Edgar is coming to dinner tonight. This isn't just one of his usual visits. I have only told you about his proposal to me so that you are prepared. I had hoped it wouldn't come as such a shock to you. After all, we have shown how close we are, and your father – God rest his soul – has been gone over ten years now.'

'Is Jeremy coming too?' It wasn't that he didn't like Edgar's son; he did. Even though Jeremy was older than himself by a year, they had played in the same sporting teams at Oxford and had become good friends. Their parents' liaison, or what-ever one would call it, had seen them acting like co-conspirators as they had poked fun. But this *marriage* Mother talked of . . . well, it changed things.

'Yes, he is. He has to hear what we have to say just as much as you do.'

'Mother, have you considered how everything you own will belong to your husband when you marry?'

'How could I not? It happened once before. I have never told you, Andrew, but your father married me because of my money and the mine, which I stood to inherit.'

'Mother!'

'I am not speaking out of turn, dear. It is the truth. Your father was a second son. His father before him had devoted his life to the Army, as his own father had done, and had little of the family wealth left. They had property, and some land, but no business to back it up or replenish it. So your father's prospects were to marry into money, become a vicar or take up the military life. He had no inclination or intention of going into the Church, and he kicked against taking a commission

16

in the Army, but as it happened he had no need to do either. My father and his were lifelong friends and a deal was struck between them. My father wanted me to marry into a good family line, and the Harveys certainly had that.'

Andrew couldn't believe what she was saying. He knew his Uncle Bernard – his father's older brother – had died, leaving very little to his children, and those who hadn't gone into the Army had worked for a living in the law or accountancy. But that his mother had been effectively *sold*, just to keep a good line in the family!

'Don't look so horrified, dear. Your father and I came to love each other dearly and rubbed along very well together. You children were born out of that love, and I miss your father still, but it happened. It is a fact of life for us women. Anyway, you can consider yourself lucky, as I do, that no other heirs of the male line were born before you in my family. If they had been, everything we have would have gone to them when your father died.'

'That is all very well, Mother, but you are putting one in the way of me now!'

'I am not. No one can take away what is yours. You in-herited the mine, and that is that.'

'But this place – this house and the land, the estate . . .'

'I hope you are not suggesting that Edgar is marrying me for what I own?'

'No, of course not. He could buy and sell us, I know.' *How could he not know? After all, Edgar owned everything one could see beyond their own estate, apart from the cottages and the farmlands to the west.* 'But, Mother, your marriage to him will mean that what is ours will become Edgar's too. And he has an heir who, I might remind you, is older than me and will take precedence . . . Oh, Mother, I can't bear to think of losing all of this! Grandfather would—'

'My father would not bat an eyelid, I can assure you!'

'He would. He . . .'

'I'm sorry, dear. Of course he would. You are a male and were the apple of his eye. I was thinking about me and what I owned, and how he married me off to someone with a good name to give me and nothing else! Well, not at first . . . Look, this is all pointless. What you fear won't happen. Edgar is seeing to everything. He thinks like you: he is fair-minded and he wants to make sure you are secure in the future. Please wait until you hear what he has to say.'

Rising, she walked towards the door. When she reached it she turned to him and said, 'Please don't spoil tonight, Andrew. Your sister is coming and, if she gets started, it will all be horrible.'

It shocked him to see tears glistening in her eyes. 'Of course not, Mother. I'm sorry; I didn't mean to upset you. I will listen to what Edgar has to say. Oh, and by the way, congratulations, old thing. I shouldn't have put my own worries before your happiness. I am pleased for you, really. I just . . .'

'Yes, dear, I understand, and thank you. I will be happy. I know I will. I know it is hard for you to think of it, but I love Edgar very much and he loves me. But I am not just thinking of my own happiness; I want you and Agatha to be happy, too.'

The door closed behind her, leaving a million questions hanging in the air. *Was Edgar going to live here, or was she moving into his much grander place, Hensal Grange?* Funny, that: the mine he owned, and which had been in his mother's family for years, had the title of Hensal Grange Mine. He'd once asked his mother about it, and she had said that some ancestor or other had lost the twenty-bedroomed mansion and moved his family to this smaller house. He'd kept some of the land, which they still owned, and hadn't changed the name of the mine. Neither had anyone else, down the family line. Once the mine had prospered again under her father, he hadn't seen the need for more land or a bigger house.

Not that this house was small, by any means. It had ten bedrooms, a large withdrawing room, a dining room and a study, besides servants' quarters and a more-than-adequate downstairs kitchen. It stood in its own grounds, with majestic beauty, but Hensal Grange boasted a ballroom and three grand drawing rooms, besides several dining rooms. Palatial in setting and with sweeping, mile-long drives, it came with acres and acres of land encompassing the small town of Breckton, a thriving place central for York and Leeds. The only part of the town remaining in Andrew's own family estate consisted of the cottages known as 'the Miners' Row', where his workforce lived.

Weighing it all up, he'd thought himself very fortunate and secure, but now his future lay in Edgar's hands. *What could Edgar's plans be? Oh, God! Why had Father invoked an ancient law that allowed him to leave the property and estate to his wife while leaving just the business to his son?*

Mother would always have had a home with him. Nothing would have changed for her, but now there was a threat that he should not have had to face. And what about Agatha? She had always hoped their mother would leave the house to her, saying that Andrew could sell some of the land and build a house on what was left. Even though she must know such a thing wouldn't happen, this new turn of events would really put her out. Married, with no issue and none looking likely, he doubted that with her mean-minded way she ever obliged her poor, long-suffering husband. But apart from that, her ambitions of living back in Tarrington House were ludicrous. Her lawyer husband, Teddy Wilmsmith, was a nice enough chap and had reasonable means. Agatha never wanted for anything, and mixed in the best of circles. She just hated living with Teddy's mother and didn't care enough for his ancestral home to want to live there for the rest of her days, or to fill it with heirs.

His irritation with his mother's plans and his sister's notions caused him to run his fingers through his dark-brown hair. 'Oh, bother it all.' He looked with disgust at his hand: the oil he'd sleeked his hair with now clung to it. Taking out his handkerchief, he wiped it off as he crossed the room to the hall, where a long mirror hung by the door. He stood in front of it trying to repair the damage, his frowning face staring back at him.

Thirty-two years old, with a degree in engineering and the arts, and owner-manager of one of the largest collieries in Yorkshire, he knew it was time he looked to finding a wife. Even that quest would be jeopardized by this new development. He was handsome enough, he thought, as he twiddled the ends of his fine moustache and turned his body to admire his trim, tall frame. His morning clothes of grey trousers and dark jacket, worn over a wing-collared shirt with a four-in-hand knotted tie, suited him well. All in all, he presented himself as a dashing, fashionable young man of the day, but what had he to offer?

Yes, he owned a mine, but it had problems and he needed to modernize. He'd recently complied with the law and provided wooden hats for all the workers, but he needed to install a steam winding engine and open up another seam – a project that would require money and take years of toil to complete. He had some investments, but the economy at the moment rendered them worth a lot less than when he inherited them from his grandfather.

Going back into the living room, he went over to the window once more. Feeling unsettled, he glanced out to where the roof of the stable block just showed above the high hedge surrounding it. With a sudden intensity, the urge took him to go for a ride. He had to clear his head, and he needed to do so before Agatha arrived. He called out to the butler: 'Granger, get a message sent to the stables to Henry. Tell him to have a ride ready for me in fifteen minutes, then come and help me change.' Poor Granger; in this house he had to do twice as many things as a normal butler, and acting as Andrew's manservant was just one of them.

The gentle trot of his grey mare soothed him; she always knew Andrew's mood and how he wanted to travel, without him having to prompt her. Riding at this pace across the fields, his body releasing tension with every step, he took in the scenery around him. Gentle hills gave way to more rugged ones, aspiring to mountainous heights in the distance. The stream snaking its way through the fields reflected the autumn golds and mustard-yellows, turning the area into a picture worthy of a Constable painting.

The crisp air refreshed his lungs and a sense of well-being came over him. He enjoyed the loneliness of it all. As he reached the flatter surface next to the road leading to the mine, he gave his horse free rein and let the rush of wind on his face blow away his cares.

Coming over the brow near to Carson's farm – one of his family's two remaining tenanted farms – he met a gang of miners making their way home after their shift. They took off their caps to him, their blackened, weary faces tugging at him. He pulled up and called, 'Good afternoon, lads. Everything going well?'

Mick Harman, the shift supervisor and usual spokesman, answered him, 'Aye, sir, we had a good shift, but I've been intending to speak to you. We could do with some more hurriers. Alfred Goodright and Toby Grossing have outgrown it, and I've moved them on to the lower seam. There's a couple of lads I know of reaching the age of twelve, both small for their age, so ideal. I've spoken to their dads, and they seem keen to get them started.'

'Well, have them brought to me on Monday. Are the fathers working down the mine?'

'One does, but the other is on the land. He works on your farm, sir.'

'And you say he is keen for his lad to go down? It isn't often that happens. Once a man has the taste of the open air, it's usually what he wants for his son.'

'He says he asked of the farm manager and nothing was doing. He needs the lad in work.'

'Yes, since they raised the age for lads allowed down the mine, there has been many more younger ones applying to work on the land who wouldn't normally. Well, see to it for me, Harman. I'll trust your judgement, but you know I like to see everyone before they are set on. By the way, how are things with you? I heard from Mrs Harman some time back that you had managed to get your daughter into service. Is it going well for her?'

'Oh, aye, she loves it. She works over at Hartington House as a cook. She's a good girl, is Issy . . . Isabella, I mean. She and young Denny Leighton have a fancy for each other, and I don't think it will be long afore he comes knocking and asking for her hand. In fact, we passed her a while back. She has a day off and was on her way to meet him off shift.'

'Well, she couldn't do better. He's a good lad. And if Isabella takes after her mother, who is the best cook we have ever had at our house, she'll do well. You're a lucky man, Mick. What about the rest of you?' Andrew looked at each of the men. He had no intention of keeping them long; he knew all they wanted was a good wash, a hot meal and a jug or two of ale. They didn't want to stand talking to a man they thought had no idea of how they felt.

Mick Harman spoke for them once again. 'Alf here has a chest. He could do with seeing the doctor, and Jimmy and Fred.' Mick pointed out each man to him, as if Andrew didn't know them, but he did. He prided himself on knowing all of his workers and most of their families. Mick finished by saying, 'They're doing all right.'

'Good, I'll get the doctor to see you all before your shift on Wednesday.' He nodded towards the men. Alf Cummings nodded back, but then went into a fit of coughing. The sound hacked at the peace of the lane and sent birds fleeing up into the trees. 'Cummings, you shouldn't be at work. You need to rest.'

'I have to, sir. I couldn't see me family starve . . . Sorry, sir, I spoke out of turn.'

'No, you didn't, man. How many times do I have to tell you – you can all come to me with your problems? Take a few days off. I'll get the doctor to come over to your cottage to see you. Your wife works in the kitchen at the house with Mrs Harman, doesn't she? Well, I'll get some supplies sent home with her. I don't want to see you in work until I hear from the doctor that you are fit. Now, good day to you all.

It has been nice to have these few moments with you, but I won't detain you any longer.'

Not feeling at all uplifted, Andrew turned the horse and rode away. He hadn't gone far when he saw Harman's daughter, Isabella, with Denny. They looked well together and were engrossed in each other's company as they strolled across the field. Thinking to have a bit of fun, he called out, 'And what do you think you two are doing?'

They jumped around. Isabella was a young woman in her late teens. He wouldn't call her beautiful, but she was very pretty, with her curly golden hair and huge blue eyes. She put her hands on her hips. 'It's more like what you think *you're* doing! You near frightened me out of me knickers.'

'Issy!' Denny sounded mortified. Andrew wasn't sure if it had been Isabella's crude language or the fact that she'd spoken to him in such a manner.

Poor Isabella's cheeks blushed as she dropped her indignant stance. 'Oh, I beg your pardon, sir, I didn't mean . . .'

'She didn't mean it, sir. You just startled us.'

Andrew's laughter rang in his own ears. It seemed Isabella had a turn of phrase to match her mother's, which was a source of great amusement to him whenever he visited the kitchens. 'Don't worry – I deserved it. Get yourselves home.'

Still smiling to himself, he cantered towards the bottom meadow. Seamus Finney sat by his fire, an unlit clay pipe hanging from his lips. He looked up on hearing Andrew approach and got to his feet, removing his cloth cap. 'Mr Harvey. Is there something I can be doing for you, sir?'

'No, no, I am just out riding, trying to clear my head a little. Has it been a profitable trip for you, Seamus? I see you have packed your wagon for travelling?'

'It has kept me going, sir, thanks to you and the other

landowners. And yes, I'm starting out on my journey before dark. Leeds first, then south to Liverpool.'

'Well, we will miss you. Mmm, something smells good. Your last supper, so to speak?'

'Aye, gamekeeper gave me a brace, so I have them in me stew. Not quite an Irish dish like me grandmother makes, but it will sustain me on me journey and for the fight tomorrow night.'

'Oh, you've entered the bare-knuckle contest in Leeds, then? I might come along and cheer you on. If not, have a good fight. Remember to keep your head guarded, and I hope you win the prize money.'

'Thank you. I am of the mind to have a good try. The purse is a good one and will see me through the winter. If not, there are a good few to have a go at on me route home, so there are.'

'And which way do you go? I could maybe pave the way for you. There is a hunt meeting next week, when men from many counties come together. I could have a word and get you some places to stay where you will be made welcome.'

'That's kindness itself, so it is, but I've not been for having any difficulties in the last two years since I've travelled back and forth. I go on from Leeds to Sheffield, then on to Manchester and follow the ship canal to Liverpool. In truth, I've built meself a fair reputation for me honesty, hard work and leaving a clean camp.'

For a moment Andrew envied Seamus. His life appeared carefree, with only the worry of his next meal to bother him – and even that didn't seem to pose him any problems. 'Very good, but I will be in the company of many a landowner on your journey's route, so will put in a good word just the same, or you can mention my name if you have any problems.

Goodbye, Seamus. I look forward to seeing you in the spring if I don't make it to the fight tomorrow.'

He turned his mount and set off at a pace. The smile in him deepened as he tried to picture himself leading a gypsy life. He knew it would never happen, but the prospect had its good points. Feeling much lifted by his two latest encounters, he felt ready – ready to take on whatever Edgar had to say, and in a much better mood to do so.

The table glistened with the silver settings gracing it. Andrew held his mother's chair until she had sat down, and he noticed that Jeremy held Agatha's and helped to seat her, instead of her husband doing so, as one would expect. Agatha looked up into Jeremy's face, a seductive smile hovering around her lips. *Good God, she isn't going to flirt with him, is she?* He had to admit that his sister was a good-looking woman. Like himself, she had sleek dark hair and charcoal-coloured eyes. Just this side of thirty-four, she held her age well and still had a youthful-looking, curvy figure. When it suited her she could charm a snake from a basket, but her real nature tended to the surly, with little time for anyone she thought of as a fool. Andrew suspected her husband came into this category.

Although he'd already greeted Jeremy, Andrew thought it prudent to engage him in conversation again to cause a distraction. 'So, how's things in the city, Jeremy? Are you still enjoying your life and work there?'

'Not as much as I first thought I would. I'm thinking of taking a commission in the Army. I've always had a leaning towards it and have several friends from my Oxford days who are officers and having a jolly good time of it.'

'Really, how interesting. Does your family have a military background?'

'No, I'll be the first, and it isn't going down too well.'

'I can imagine . . .'

A meaningful cough interrupted them. The first course of pigeon in port sat steaming in front of them. Andrew looked towards Edgar, who had cleared his throat in such a way as to draw their attention, and waited for him to speak. To his surprise, Edgar bowed over his plate and said grace. The custom had long left this house, and it made him feel like a child again as he lowered his head. The last 'Amen' said, Edgar went on to ask, 'I hope none of you minds us having a discussion of some importance whilst we eat?' He turned to Granger and addressed him: 'I would like it very much if you and your staff left the room between courses. If you would be so kind as to pass me the bell, I will ring when we need you, thank you.'

Andrew's indignation at this only half-matched that of Granger's, who looked towards him for confirmation. Edgar had shown bad manners by assuming Andrew's place as head of the household without even having the decency to ask. To save further embarrassment, Andrew nodded at Granger to indicate that it was all right for him to take orders from this *supposed guest*. As he did so, he caught Agatha's eye. She had an amused look on her face and was evidently enjoying seeing him usurped.

Not even bothering to apologize, Edgar continued speaking the moment the room had been cleared of staff. 'Now, I want us to discuss something of great importance. I have asked my dear Rosalind for her hand in marriage and she has humbled me by accepting.'

The sharp intake of breath from both Agatha and Jeremy told Andrew neither of them had had the benefit of the forewarning that he himself had. This annoyed him further. *Just who did this man think he was?* He wasn't as yet coming across as fair-minded, *and Mother had not even bothered to inform Agatha*! But then, to be fair, maybe she had expected Andrew to do so, instead of escaping into the countryside and avoiding contact until he had to.

'Yes, I know you are surprised,' Edgar continued. 'But I had hoped it wouldn't come as unexpected. You must have all seen how close Rosalind and I have become?'

Jeremy nodded, his body shifting from one position to another whilst his eyes remained on his food. Agatha looked like thunder and about to explode. He'd have to do something to save the situation.

'Of course we have. We have spoken of it between us. May I be the first to congratulate you both and to wish you much happiness together?'

'Thank you, Andrew.'

'Yes . . . Er, yes, of course it is very good news. My congratulations join those of Andrew.' Jeremy flashed a grateful look at him. Agatha remained silent.

'Well, whatever you all think, there is no argument about it. It is what it is, and you have to accept it. If you could do so graciously.' Edgar looked at Agatha and waited a moment.

'Well! It is just such a surprise. Mother, how could you let us hear it like this? Would it not have been better to have told us in private and given us a chance to get used to the idea?'

'Agatha, please do not blame your mother for that. It is down to me. I thought to give you the news and then tell you how it will affect you all. And I also thought that to do so all at the same time would be the best way of handling it. I have to say that my dear Rosalind felt differently about this approach, but I persuaded her.'

Andrew had a moment of feeling sorry for Agatha, who

looked as though she'd had the wind punched out of her. Her eyes found his. He tried to convey to her to take it on the chin by giving a little shrug and an expression that he hoped reassured her everything would be all right. It seemed to work, as she turned her attention back to Edgar and, with admirable composure, wished them both well, apologizing for her outburst.

'Good, thank you all. Now, I have to outline to you how your positions will alter. Rosalind and I have discussed all of this at length and have come to a complete agreement . . .'

All in all, the arrangement proposed hadn't been a bad package, Andrew thought as he waited for Edgar to join him in his study. It seemed that, apart from Mother making him her sole heir, which of course was a better position than he had been in, Edgar intended taking steps – if they were both in agreement – to adopt him and Agatha formally. This would make Andrew second in line to everything.

Edgar would secure Agatha's future by giving her a guaranteed inheritance of several properties he owned in London, and an undisclosed sum of money would be put in trust for her. Jeremy hadn't flinched at this, but then the wealth of the remains of the estate would not be jeopardized by losing this small parcel of the London holdings.

On reflection, Agatha might even do better than himself, as two deaths had to take place for him to really benefit – Edgar's and Jeremy's – whereas Agatha came into her inheritance on the death of Edgar, which was a much more likely, though not probable, occurrence of the nearer future. Not that he wished any of them such a fate, especially Jeremy, but his sister's elevated prospects rankled Andrew somewhat, he had to admit. As did the fact that Edgar had summoned him to this meeting in his own home, giving orders that they were not to be disturbed. Andrew's mind wouldn't give him the reason for this, unless Edgar wanted to find out whether or not everything had met with his approval.

Edgar's first words on entering the study dispelled this idea. Andrew was learning that Edgar thought anything he decided was acceptable, as his comment now testified: 'Now then, my boy, I think that went very well, don't you?'

This opening brooked no dissent. 'Yes, thank you. You have thought everything out very fairly, and with a generosity I am very grateful for. Thank you, Edgar. Please, take a seat. I have had brandy brought in for us both.' He motioned Edgar to the only comfortable chair, next to the fireplace. After serving him his drink, he stood leaning with one arm on the hearth.

'Thank you, Andrew. I am glad you are pleased. Now, there is another matter I want to discuss with you. I think you have made the acquaintance of my niece, Dvina Portland?'

'Yes . . .' *Oh God, what was coming?* Dvina was a horsey type, with a strong, manly figure that inclined to the plump. Her face missed being attractive because her nose not only crooked a little to one side, but stuck out to the extent that it seemed the only feature one saw.

'My brother-in-law is anxious to make a good match for her . . . No. Hear me out. Dvina is a wonderful girl: resilient and good fun. What she misses in the looks department she more than makes up for in her demeanour. She will make a good wife, skilled in running a home much larger than yours. She is educated and has an intelligent and engaging turn of conversation.'

'Are you trying to say that my offering for her is part of the deal?' Andrew could hardly keep the anger and disgust out of his tone.

'Not altogether, but I know you need both funds and a wife – not to mention an heir. This arrangement could give you all of them. My brother-in-law is offering a very substantial dowry – one that, if *you* take her hand, I will double. She is also his sole heir. And, as he owns Tacker's Mine, your nearest rival, and a huge estate to the north of it, you will be sitting in a very pretty position by agreeing to this match.'

'Oh, so I am to be sold to the highest bidder, am I?'

'That's childish, and you know it. This is the way we plan things. How else do you think we hold our positions in society? Love may come later, but if it doesn't, there can be a side-attraction, if done discreetly. Or you may have to wait, like your mother and me, for true love to have its way.'

Andrew took several deep breaths. The silence in the room suffocated him. Like a cornered animal, he backed away and sat down heavily on the only other chair in the room, a straight-backed one that he used for the purpose of sitting at his desk to work.

'Look, you don't have to agree now, but please say you will meet Dvina and give some thought to the proposal. I have invited you all to stay over at Hensal Grange for an official engagement party in three weeks' time. Dvina will be there. Dance with her. Talk to her, and then see what you think. But remember, your immediate future depends on the mine. That needs capital. I understand from your mother that she has very little left, and you have even less . . .'

The truth of his last statement hit hard.

But, Christ – Dvina Portland . . . ?

31

3

Bridie

County Cavan, 1875
A journey into the unknown

'Mammy, will you try to eat this?'

'What is it, wee one? Sure I'm not for having an appetite for anything.'

''Tis a gruel Mrs Finney made. She said it will be good for you.'

The skin on her mother's face resembled the fine, yellowed leaves of autumn. Her dark eyes, sunken and empty, looked back at Bridie. Her baby-bird-like fingers stretched out towards her. 'I'll try, so I will, but first a sip.'

As she crossed the room to the pitcher of cold water, Bridie thought with despair how rapidly her mammy's illness had ravaged her body. The pains she'd suffered these two years since had worsened, until nothing soothed them. The weight had dropped from her bones, and a lump had appeared on her neck. This last had seemed to hail the beginning of the end, for since then she had hardly lifted her head from her pillow. Even Mrs Finney had not been able to come up with any potions to soothe her.

Thinking of Mrs Finney, Bridie looked out of the window to where she could see the gypsy camp just up the lane. Smoke curled up towards the sky. Children played. Women worked in groups, no doubt making the lovely lace table-centres they sold in the town.

Further to the south, the men worked in the fields. Seamus wasn't amongst them. His grandmother, for the second year running, had come without him, and another of the grandsons had taken his place. Bridie knew her father still had contact with Seamus. She had heard his name in his conversations, but he never answered her questions as to his whereabouts.

She looked away, above and beyond the men. The low autumn sun glistened on one of Cavan's many lakes to her left, while to her right and on the horizon she could see Armagh against a backdrop of the mountains of Mourne in County Down and, below them, the forest she had explored with Seamus.

There they had listened to their voices echoing under the Cromwell Bridge and had dodged the keeper of the estate of Cabra Castle as they'd gone in search of the ancient Holy Well. After making a wish by throwing stones into its murky waters, they would find a vantage point from which to gaze at Sarah's Bridge. Seamus had told her the bridge, built in 1801, was in memory of a lady who had married into the Pratt family, landowners and residents of the castle. He would make up stories about Sarah, saying how beautiful she was and pondering on why she had died. And he would tell her of the bad things the landowners did to their tenants, pricing them out, so that they could regain the farms.

Shifting her attention, she trickled water into the tumbler.

Her thoughts wandered to how things had changed since she'd last seen Seamus, in the autumn of two years ago. Her pappy now lived in fear. He disappeared a lot more, but not to take the drink; he came back sober. He jumped at the slightest noise and often went out at night just to look up the road, as if he was for thinking someone would creep up on him.

'Bridie . . . will . . . you bring me – me drink.'

'Sorry, Mammy. Here it is.' As she held the water to her mammy's blue-tinged lips, a dread settled in her. 'Drink, Mammy. Try to take a sip.'

'Bridie . . . sit down . . . a wee while . . .'

The gentle tapping indicated she should sit on the side of the bed. As she did so, her mammy let out a small moan. Bridie jumped up, saying, ''Tis causing you pain to have the bed disturbed. I'll kneel next to you, so I will. There, I can reach to feed you.'

'Bridie, I have . . . something to say.'

'Hush, Mammy.'

'Listen, child. I haven't . . . long. This sickness is taking me . . .'

'No, Mammy, you will be getting better.'

'My precious one, 'tis as I cannot recover. Your pappy . . . he – he has to go. Go with him. He has . . . money . . . but . . .'

'Money? Pappy? He can't have. He . . .'

'He does. Tell him you know. Tell him, then he . . . he will have to see you right.'

'Oh, Mammy, stop talking. Save your strength. Don't worry. Pappy loves me, so he does. He will look after me. But I don't want you to die, Mammy. I . . .' Tears clogged her throat. Her heart weighed heavy with the realization that, no matter what she did or how much she pleaded, her mammy couldn't stay with her.

'Bridie, hold my hand.'

Bridie's heart sank. It seemed that with every passing second her mammy slipped further away, but still she tried to tell her things. 'Bridie . . . go with him, but . . . don't trust . . . don't trust—'

The effort had beaten her. Bridie watched the beautiful eyes take on an unseeing glaze. Through her tears she could only whisper, 'Mammy, no. Mammy, don't be leaving me.' But her pleas went unheard. A sigh expelled her mammy's last breath, and the face she loved fell into a waxy mask, smoothing away all the lines of pain.

The cold wind sweeping off the coast had a tinge of the coming harsh winter that the signs had promised, as it lashed the waves of the Irish Sea against the side of the ferry. Bridie clutched the rail to balance herself against the swell. The boat rolled and creaked from side to side. As the tears cooled on her cheeks, she brushed them away and tucked a stray, damp ringlet behind her ear. *Why had Mammy to die? And what did Pappy do that was so bad they had to leave so soon after she drew her last breath?*

The wind held no answers. It only further chilled the fear in her.

Knowing that Father O'Brian had given her mother the last blessing of her body and soul, and his assurance that he would see to everything, held no comfort. It only deepened the mystery. *Why would a priest be helping her pappy, if he had done something he had to run away from?*

Bridie looked ahead, her knuckles white with the effort of steadying herself. England stood on the distant horizon, teasing her into a new life. A life she had no understanding of and didn't want.

A screeching whine caught her attention. The door of the cabin she shared with her father opened and Michael O'Hara staggered out. A shudder that wasn't caused by the cold rippled through Bridie.

'Won't you come back in, Bridie? I have something I want to tell you.' The bottle he'd had to his lips for most of the last hour had only a quarter of the good Irish whisky left in it. 'Haven't I been occupied with your mammy being so ill this last year that I've had no time with you. Is it sixteen you are already?'

He swigged the neat whisky. The boat lurched. His unsteady feet, no match for the movement, caused his body to hurtle towards her. His hand reached out and clasped her breast. Alcohol breath fanned her face.

'Bridie – me own Bridie.'

'Pappy, don't . . .'

He removed his hand. 'I'm sorry, I didn't mean . . . I couldn't steady meself, Bridie. Bridie, will you listen? I'm sorry to the heart of me, I am.'

His touching of her hadn't been an accident and the trepidation she felt wasn't a new feeling. 'You should stop taking the whisky.'

The bottle whipped past her. Liquid splashed her face. 'Why do you look at your pappy in such a way, Bridie? Is it contempt you hold for me? I tell you I'll have none of it.'

She edged backwards.

'You will do as your pappy bids and come inside.' His hand caught her arm. Resistance proved futile, and he pulled her inside the cabin. 'I have things I must say to you.'

Leaning against the cabin wall, she stared at him. He didn't seem the same. His dealings with her had changed a few months ago. He'd said things, made remarks she didn't think he should be making to her, or in her presence. He would hold her too close and for too long at times, making her feel uncomfortable.

'What is it, Pappy? This swell is making me ill. I am better out on the deck. Can you not talk to me out there?'

'It is about your future. I cannot be sure to be around you all of the time. Things may happen . . .'

'What things?'

'I may have to be disappearing, and you will be fending for yourself. So in case I don't come back for a while, I want you to know there is money . . .'

Mammy had been right, then: he did have money. And she didn't have to wonder about where it had come from. Nor, as she listened to him, did she have to ask why he had to vanish, as it seemed everyone in Ireland was hunting him down – not least the Fenians – because, as he put it, he'd 'made a few mistakes'. But then neither did she care, as she waited for him to continue.

'Your Aunt Jeannie is to take you in. She has always wanted a daughter and will be good to you. I will visit when I can, but in case . . . Well, if it is as I don't, this is what you must do . . .'

She listened in silence. He told her of a bank in Liverpool where she should go and ask for access to the vaults. He gave her a codeword that only she would know, and assured her that the contents of the box they would give her would be plenty to take care of her every need. Then he staggered across towards her, his speech slurred. 'Here, this is the key . . .' A small silver key danced on the end of a pin. 'Come close, so I can fix it to your vest.'

His hands touched the flesh inside her bodice. He groped around, brushing his knuckles over her cleavage. She stood as still as she could, unsure what to do. Should she protest at the liberty he took? But then, he could just be trying not to prick her skin. Looking into his face decided her. His eyes had clouded over, and his putrid breath came in short pants as though he struggled to get air into his lungs. 'No, Pappy, leave it. Give it to me to put into my sack.'

His eyes held hers. She pushed his hand away, then extended hers. He gave her the key. A relief entered her as she turned away from him and took the key over to her luggage but, as she slipped it into a small pocket on the side of her bag, she could feel him close to her – too close – and her fear reignited. Before she could move away his hands grabbed her hips. 'Pappy . . . no . . .'

As she tried to pull away from him, a crashing wave hit the boat. The tilt it caused hurled them both to the floor.

'Bridie, Bridie . . .' His lips covered hers. His hands tore at her blouse. Her heart clanged with despair, and her stomach retched bile into her throat. *Jesus, Mary and Joseph, don't let this be happening to me!* 'Pappy . . . Nooo!'

Their struggle caused their bodies to sweat. Bridie's begging hung in the air unheeded. Clawing at him until her fingers and nails bloodied did nothing to stop the relentless tearing of her clothes. Her name, an ugly chant on his lips, assailed her ears.

By the time the chilled air touched every part of her, he'd positioned himself between her legs. His weight crushed the breath from her, and his free hand fiddled with his buttons.

A stretching pain seared her.

Terror strangled her pleas, but the foul knowledge that her pappy was inside her coiled a strength into her that she'd never possessed before. She arched her back and twisted herself in a movement that dislodged him. Before he could regain his momentum, she scrambled away from him. 'I hate you. I HATE YOU!' Snot mingled with her tears as the words rasped from her again and again. 'I – hate – YOU!'

With each grating, truthful word, his body shrank into the corner opposite her. They stared across the pit of degradation dividing them. Their sobs met somewhere in the middle and echoed off the cabin walls.

Bridie caught her breath as her pappy moved, afraid that he would try again, but his expression didn't tell of another assault. His arm reached into his case. The pistol he brought out glinted in the shaft of light coming through the porthole. 'NO – NO!'

The crack resounded around the cabin. His blood slapped every part of her. Her mouth opened, and her eyes seemed to stretch out of their sockets. The mass of burnt flesh where there had been a face she'd once loved became engraved on her soul, as darkness took her into its peace.

4

Will

Sheffield, South Yorkshire, 1875
Thrown into turmoil

William Hadler walked down the street towards his house.
The fresh autumn wind whipped around him. At nineteen he
had the height and stature of a full-grown man. Years of pit
work had contributed to this. He'd started at the age of six
as a trapper working twelve-hour shifts, opening and shutting
the trap to make sure air circulated along the shaft. Often his
candle lasted for only seven of those hours, and the rest of
the time complete darkness shrouded him. At the age of ten
he'd become a hurrier. Crouched low, he would drag the coal
in wheeled buckets by his shoulders through the tiniest of
tunnels to reach the stockpile. Now he mined the coal, chip-
ping away at the black wall, dust clogging his mouth and eyes,
but it was what his da had done before him, as had his grandda.
He knew no other life.

As he approached the turn into his street, Will wondered
how his da was. The coughing sickness had taken hold of his
lungs and this morning he had called Will over just as he was
about to leave the house, saying, 'Son, a word afore you go.'

Picking up his snap tin and his coat, he'd stopped by his da's bed, a shake-me-down in the back kitchen next to the fire. His da had taken his hand. 'Will, I haven't long. I'm sorry, lad . . .' A tear had traced a wet path down his da's cheek. His breath, laboured and rasping, had come in short bursts. 'Look out for your ma. Never leave her, Will . . .'

'You know I won't, Da,' he'd told him. 'I'll see her reet.' And then, as if their roles had reversed, he'd said, 'Now stop worrying, and concentrate on getting yourself well.'

Something had compelled Will to kiss the cheek of this man who'd given his all for him. He'd never done that before – hadn't thought it right for men to do such things – but there had been no protest. His da had given his hand a weak squeeze and closed his eyes.

Now, as he turned into the street, curtains closed and the women standing on their steps went inside without greeting him. The cobbles echoed the sound of his heavy boots. Dread gripped the pit of his stomach.

Across the road from his own house, Florrie Makepiece came out of the shadows. The lass showed an interest in him, but he had no return feeling for her. It was said she'd open her legs for anyone. He didn't know if this was true or not, and he didn't care. He felt sorry for her. She'd had a worse time than the rest of them round here. Most – with the exception of his own family and a few others – lived from hand to mouth, with what came in going on drink, leaving the young 'uns neglected and underfed. This was Florrie's fate, but on top of that she suffered beatings and abuse at the hand of her da. He called out to her, 'You alreet, Florrie?'

'Aye, I've no time to talk, but I wanted to say as I'm sorry . . .'

A screeching voice came from within the open door of her

house. 'Florrie, will you get in here afore your da comes home!' Florrie pulled her shawl over her head, bent over and ran towards him. 'I'm late, but I'm here for you, if you need help.'

'Eeh, Florrie, I'll be fine. You take care.' His heart, already banging against his ribs, dropped into his stomach. The look of pity Florrie had given him added to the eerie silence hanging in the air around him. It took a moment to move on a few steps to his front door.

A smell like he'd never experienced before hit him as he walked inside. Passing through the front room to the kitchen, he saw a white sheet covering the shape of his da's body. His ma stood with her back to him, looking out of the window. Sobs shook her shoulders.

'Ma . . . ?'

As she turned towards him it seemed that her small frame had shrunk into itself. Her sharp blue eyes were rimmed with red from the crying she'd done, and fresh tears still fell down her face. A strong woman with principles that didn't bend, if she thought others were doing wrong, she now looked broken.

Will took her in his arms. Brushing her grey hair back from her round face, he told her, 'It's alreet, Ma, I'm here. When did it happen?'

'Not long after you left . . .'

'You mean Da has lain there for more than twelve hours? Have you not sent word for Jackson?'

'No, I washed him, then covered him. I've sat with him since. Maggie came in, but I wouldn't let her do owt. I wanted you to find him at home.'

'Reet, let's get things sorted.'

Sitting down at the table an hour later, Will sipped the hot tea his ma had brewed. Jackson had been and taken the body to the chapel, and Ma looked a lot calmer, though her voice shook when she spoke. 'I've done me grieving this last while, Will, but the thought of you – just a lad, and with no da to take you for your first pint or see you married with a family of your own – broke me.'

'I know. We knew as it were coming, but things'll never be the same.'

'No, but we'll manage. I have a bit put by in the pot, and you're bringing in a good whack now you're mining proper.'

A good whack? The rent for their cottage and the food they needed took up most of what he earned. And his coal allowance only amounted to half what his da's had been. Even with both lots, they'd struggled to keep the cold at bay last winter.

'You needn't start worrying. Like I say, pot's full and'll keep us going for a good while. What you tip up will keep it almost topped up, and I've sommat else up me sleeve an' all.' When he didn't speak, she said, 'Timpson at the corner shop is looking to get someone in. He asked me a while back, as his wife's legs are getting worse, but with things as they were . . . Anyhow, he said he'd hold it for me, and he's been true to his word. He knows I've a bit more about me than most in this row. And honesty is one of the qualities he's noted about me.'

'Da wouldn't have you working. Thou knows that, Ma.'

'Aye, well, needs must. Drink your tea, lad. We have to pull together to get through. We have no choice.'

'Reet, but it's only until I get earning more. That should happen in a couple of years, when I'm twenty-one.'

'Eeh, your da will never be gone whilst you're alive, son. You have the look of him, and his ways. He were the better one of the two of us for you to take after, as me nature hasn't always made me friends.'

Will smiled. He knew she was right. His da had been a gentle man, tolerant of everyone and with never a bad word to say, whereas Ma could slice steel with her tongue at times. He took after his da in looks, too: big-boned, square-faced and dark-skinned. He'd heard that one of his ancestors had come from Italy, but no one knew the real tale of it to tell him. His piercing blue eyes were the only feature he'd taken from his ma. The girls around seemed to find him attractive, and some said the contrast of his eyes with his skin and hair marked him as different. Not that he had much time for them; he'd rather spend his time fishing.

This thought filled his eyes with tears. His da had taught him to fish, taking him out on the rare days they had off together to get some fresh air into his lungs. They'd had some wonderful times. By, he'd miss him. It were like a light had gone out. Mind, it had faded this good while. *Oh, Da . . . Da.*

'That Florrie Makepiece has been standing around outside again. I told her to bugger off.'

'Eeh, Ma, she ain't a bad lass . . .'

'I don't want you tied up with them lot. They're scum. Now let's get some food inside of you. I've some stew left. It's boiling away on the stove.'

He knew she'd seen his tears and sought to change the subject, but what she'd said grated on him. 'They're no different to us, Ma . . .'

'No different! Oh, yes, they are. Your da didn't drink every penny, and your ma keeps a clean house and pays bills up when they need paying. They . . .'

He let her rant on. Tonight was no time to get her going, but he had felt compelled to stand up for Florrie and her ma. It wasn't their fault their man drank like he did; but then, his ma could forgive that before she could forgive keeping a dirty house. At this moment he felt like going and having some of what Florrie offered. He'd heard tell how good she were at it. Not as though he would know; he'd never yet lain with a woman.

A bang on the door interrupted his thoughts. The sound made his stomach lurch – this wasn't someone calling with condolences. He opened the door. Light blinded him and the acrid smell of smoke choked him. 'What . . . ?'

Happy Harry, his trademark smile gone into a mask of horror, stood silhouetted against the glow. 'Fire . . . Fire . . . The Makepieces' house; and it's coming this way.'

Screams cut the air. The shrill sound shuddered through Will.

'My Florrie! She's in there! My Florrie!' Mrs Makepiece slumped to the ground, her blackened face demented and spittle running from her mouth. 'Help her, help her!'

Will grabbed his coat to shield his head and face. 'Where is she? Which room?'

One of the women shook her, saying urgently, 'Front or back, love?'

'The scullery, hurry! Oh, God . . .'

As he scooted back through his house, Will's feet slipped on the cobbles in the yard, which were always damp from folk spilling water as they carried it from the well. Florrie's back door gave in easily under his kick. Flames balled out, encasing him in searing heat. He fell back. Icy-cold water hit his body. 'Get up, lad, get away! You can't do anything!'

Others had followed him and one of them tried to drag him along the cobbles, but he resisted. *The front! He'd have to try to get in through the front*. Retracing his steps, he took no heed of his ma's protests as he passed her in their front room.

Breaking the front window to Florrie's house released billows of smoke. It stung his throat, but he choked out her name, 'Florrie? Florrie!'

A pain-filled moan came from the direction of the opposite wall. On the floor a heap of what looked like smouldering clothes moved. Keeping his head below the smoke, he made his way over to it. Now he could see the charred body of Fred Makepiece, but underneath him the source of the sound – Florrie – was trapped by the weight of him.

Pulling the lifeless body off to one side, Will swallowed the bile that was threatening to choke him and lifted Florrie. A million sparks spat from under the closed door to the scullery. They splattered onto his legs, but his thick work trousers resisted their attempt to reach his skin. From the scene before him, it looked as if Florrie's da had dragged her into this room and had tried to keep the fire back by closing it off. Will carried Florrie to the window and handed her out, before climbing through himself.

'You alreet, lad?'

Not knowing who'd asked, he just said, 'Aye, I'm not hurt.'

'Reet, grab a bucket. The womenfolk'll take care of Florrie and her ma. We have to stop it spreading to the other houses, and at the mo it looks like it's headed towards yours. There's lads attacking it from the back, and others making a chain from the well and through your house to here.'

The sound of steaming hot tea being slurped by an exhausted, blackened band of men disturbed the otherwise silent street a few hours later. Smoke still billowed from the burnt-out shell of the Makepieces' home, but no more flames licked the night air. Fred Makepiece's charred body had almost disintegrated when they'd carried it out.

Someone behind him said, 'Eeh, and they say as the lass is pregnant an' all. Happen she'll lose it after this lot.'

'Aye, and maybe that'll be a good thing, but at least she won't be taking any more beatings. Though Fred did right by her in the end, if what Will thinks happened is reet.'

A quieter voice, a whisper with malice, said, 'I think we can take it we now know who the father is.'

Will turned just in time to see Barry Watson nod in his direction. Looking around at the rest of the men, he saw them lower their eyes, one by one. His emotions choked him. He couldn't find his voice to protest. His limbs shook. Turning away from them, he went into the ginnel, a dirt path strewn with rotting rubbish that ran between the rows of houses. The stench of this and the communal bogs brought up the bile he'd swallowed down earlier. Vomit retched from him. When the bout had passed, he walked on unsteady legs a few more paces, trying to stem the huge knot that he held in his chest from breaking. He couldn't. He stopped and leant against the wall. His body folded, his knees gave way under him and huge sobs racked him.

'I'm not meaning to intrude on you, so I'm not, but you look like you could use a hand.'

Will looked up into a face not dissimilar to his own. It was crowned with hair just as dark, though tending to curl, whereas his fell straight from its centre parting. The eyes differed in colour, too. This man's were as black as a nugget of coal. He had a kind tone to his Irish lilt, and he spoke again before Will could answer. 'I was just after making my way over to the Miners' Social Club. I heard they had a bare-knuckle fight contest on in a few days, and I'm wanting to put me name forward. I changed direction when I saw the fire, but it looks as though 'tis under control. Was it your place as burned?'

Will cleared his throat and stood up. 'No, a neighbour's. The man of the house lost his life. The tragedy of it was a trigger to the greater pain I have had in me today. Me da passed away this morning.' As he said the words he wondered how it was that he could talk to this complete stranger, whom he was beginning to mark as a gypsy lad.

'That's fair sad, so it is. I lost me own pappy and me mammy when I was younger than yourself. They caught a fever. It took them and most of our clan. Well, I'm sorry 'tis as I cannot ease your pain. Grieving is a personal thing, so I'll be on me way and maybe I'll meet up with you again in better circumstances. Me name's Seamus Finney. I'm a travelling man from Ireland.'

'Will Hadler. And maybe we will meet again, as I have a friend – a fellow miner – who is a bare-knuckle man. He fights at fairs and in tournaments and I take an interest in his progress. But the one you have to watch out for is Bruiser Armitage, as folk round here have nicknamed him. He puts most of his opponents down in the first bout.'

'Aye, I've heard tell of him on the circuit. Have you a hint you could be giving me on how to tackle him? If it's not imposing of me at such a time?'

'Naw, it's good to talk on sommat else other than . . . well, you know.' Will wiped his face with his sleeve, and then blew his nose on a piece of rag he used to wipe the sweat from his brow as he worked. This reminded him that he hadn't yet washed and changed after coming in from the pit. He must look a sorry mess – even more so with the effect of the smoke from the fire, and the tears. They'd have streaked his face. He tried to put out of his mind how he must look, as he discussed

Bruiser's fight tactics. 'Anyroad, he's big – built like a brick shit-house – but he's slow, in my opinion. I reckon if someone were to tackle him by way of taking him by surprise, they'd have an advantage, but once you've gone in, yer to be quick about getting out of his reach. Dance round him a bit and tire him. I've said as much to me mate, but he's scared out of his wits of the man.'

'It is grateful I am to you, Will. From what you tell me and what has come to me notice, it sounds like a good way of tackling the man.'

'Glad to help, and thanks for stopping. You've reet taken me mind off things, and I feel as though I can cope now.'

Seamus offered him his hand. 'It is glad I am to have met you, Will. I'll be on me way now, and if you feel up to it I hope you will drop by the Social and give me your support.'

'Aye, I might just do that.' Will watched him walk back down the ginnel. A big muscle of a man, he had a swagger about him. A man to be reckoned with, he thought. Feeling strangely calm, Will hopped over the wall into the yard area where the communal well stood, hauled up a bucket of water and sluiced his vomit away. The action gave him back the last remnants of control, but with it came the feeling in his gut that he had a long way to go to lift the stigma some folk would put on his shoulders. And for it to have happened tonight, of all nights, when he could least deal with it. But even so, to walk away without so much as offering a protest . . . What had he been thinking of?

Seamus didn't spend long thinking about Will and his troubles. He had enough of his own to worry over. He needed to earn some quick money and get back over the water to find out what was happening. Coming runner-up in his bout in Leeds had meant he'd picked up only a quarter of the purse, and his earnings from the landowners hadn't covered his living these past few weeks. News should reach him soon of Michael O'Hara, the bastard that he was. If he double-crossed him again, he'd do for him as sure as God was in Heaven, so he would.

Not able to enter the north of Ireland for fear of capture, Seamus hated his lonely nomadic life. He missed the support of his family. At least he'd hooked up with them in the south of Ireland in the winter and had found out what was going on.

The thought of the last assignment he'd carried out for Michael and his followers shuddered through him. Michael had said, 'It's cut-and-dried, Seamus, so it is. You waylay him as he leaves the Green Emblem pub on Friday night. You tell him 'tis as we all know his leaning, and then you slit his throat and disappear into the night.'

Named as a traitor to the cause, the man he had to kill had given information to the English and the Protestants about the whereabouts of the Fenians' hideouts and ammunition hoards.

Seamus hadn't baulked at the task. But then, they'd said that unless he did this he'd find himself a corpse, to be sure. Now he knew the innermost secrets of the sect, they would see that he met his end as someone who couldn't be trusted.

Michael had given him a description of the man. He'd lain in wait. The target had left the pub, but as he did so a powerful arm had grasped Seamus around the neck and a hand had covered his mouth. He'd acted fast: his blade had sunk into his assailant's belly. Blood had squelched out as he withdrew it. By the time the crowd leaving the pub reacted to the terrible moan, Seamus had made himself scarce.

On returning to the farm, Michael had asked, 'What happened? A terrible mistake has occurred. 'Tis as we got the wrong man. Did John Sullivan manage to stop you in time?'

The mood had changed on hearing what had happened. Michael surmised that John would not have been able to shout out for fear of discovery, so he must have thought the best action would be to jump Seamus and cover his mouth to silence him. The horror of it put the fear of God into Michael, as his error had cost the life of one of their own. A man well respected; a brave man. The wrath of the Fenians would come down for such a disaster. Michael's life was in danger.

Seamus had learned that Michael and his men had denied any knowledge of why John had been in the alley near the pub. They had vowed to their leaders they'd find out who it was that had carried out John's murder, and had later given *his* name, saying he was a gypsy thief and had been seen running away from the scene.

Michael's only good deed was covering for Seamus while he escaped across the water. He'd promised that when it had all quietened down he would come over with enough money to help Seamus get to America.

On his visit to the south of Ireland last winter, his grandmother had told him that Michael had been over to England, and when he returned he'd told her to pass on the message that he was stashing money away in a bank in Liverpool and hoped he'd make his own escape before the next winter. He would meet Seamus in Liverpool. 'He said to tell you to go into Mick's Irish bar near the docks next November and ask for him. If he's across there, then there will be a message for you as to what to do next.' Grandmother Finney had warned, 'He's in deep, Seamus. His name is linked with a number of atrocities. I'd put a curse on him, so I would, if it didn't mean as you would miss out. But mark me, son: once you have your money and have crossed to America, he'll get what's coming to him. He'll die at the hand of travellers, and it won't be a death he'd be choosing for himself. They'll be able to smell his burning flesh for miles, but as his tongue will be cut out and his mouth stuffed with rags, he'll not be able to make a sound.'

Well, it was near November now, and him with two or three days' travelling ahead of him. But he couldn't be doing it on an empty stomach; he had to get money to buy some meat.

As he came up to the field where his wagon stood, his horse snorted a welcome. 'Good boy. Let me free you from that tree you're tethered to, so you can enjoy the grazing in that pasture. I'm thinking 'tis as you've had your eye on that grass all day.'

Setting the fire, Seamus sliced onions and potatoes, threw in a handful of hedgerow herbs and sat back with his pipe. Everything around him glowed red as the last of the winter sun sank behind the hills. He made his decision. After his stew he'd check his traps, and if he'd nothing in them he'd not wait to take part in the fight, but take his chances and move on.

It was as he thought: the traps were empty of prey. But then, hadn't a powerful disease hit the countryside in the months previous and wiped out most of the rabbit population? As he began to collect in his snares, he thought in desperation of taking his chance and breaking into a couple of the houses hereabouts. Nothing about them posed a problem as to getting into them, but he had built up a trust along his route and he thought better of it. If it was that the meet didn't go ahead, he'd want to come back next year.

Thinking of the meet and of Michael brought Bridie into his mind. Sitting around the dying embers of his fire he remembered the last time he had seen her. The image of her swirling skirt, laughing, joyous face and beautiful hair stayed with him as he drifted off to sleep.

5

Bridie

Leeds, Yorkshire, 1875
A friendship forms

'Bridie, Bridie . . .'

Bridie's heavy eyelids resisted her attempts to open them. No words would form to respond to the voice.

Pictures swam in and out of her mind. She remembered that someone had wrapped a blanket around her and dragged her out of the cabin. The wind had stung her back to full consciousness, but she'd been unable to utter anything in her own defence against the condemning voices of the group gathered around her. They'd spoken what they thought they knew to be the truth. Blaming her . . .

'Isn't it what I thought was going on? Didn't I say it wasn't right, the way they acted together? And them being father and daughter!' one had said. And a similar voice had answered, *'Yes, Mrs Lynch, you did that. Well, her behaviour has got her more than she bargained for! But then, didn't you know who he was? He was none other than O'Hara . . .'* Shock had registered in the voice of the first speaker: *'Be Jesus, Mrs Flynn! Michael O'Hara! Well, a man of his nature would be taken by the Devil*

54

*with a daughter giving him such attentions.' 'He'll be taken by
the Devil for more reasons than that. And she seems to have been
spawned in the same vein . . .'*

A strong-smelling cloth, like the ether the doctor had used
on her when she'd broken her arm as a child, had sent the
voices swirling above her and out of her reach, but not before
she'd heard the words 'correction convent . . .'

Part of her had become aware of being on a journey, lain
on a rough board in a conveyance. Her body had swayed from
side to side. Noises had come and gone – horses' hooves and
shouting – but always they had left her as she'd sunk back
into the black hole she could not release herself from. Only
those two words stayed with her, and now they screamed at
her from inside the cobweb of her mind. They gave her a fear
of where she was.

'Bridie, Bridie. Don't be thrashing about in such a way.
Come on, open your eyes. No one is going to hurt you.'

A sharp odour stung her nostrils. Her eyes watered and the
weight lifted from them. As she turned her head to avoid
the smelling salts, the black cloth of a nun's headdress wafted
her cheek. It shadowed the face bending over her.

'That's better. Now, I am Sister Rose and this is Sister
Benedict. How are you feeling?'

Bridie looked from one nun to the other. A filthy expression came to her mind, which contained a word she'd cringed
at in her innocence. But she wasn't innocent any longer. She
was . . . No, she couldn't give voice to those thoughts.
She tried to speak, but found she still couldn't. She couldn't
even blink her sore, staring eyes. *Why, Pappy? Why?*

'Dear, dear, I am afraid the child is losing her mind. We'll
leave her a little longer.' The nun turned as she straightened
herself. 'Elizabeth, you will remain with her, but you are

forbidden to talk to her. However, you are to fetch me immediately if she does speak.'

'Yes, Sister Rose.'

Bridie hadn't registered the presence of another person.
She looked over in the direction from which the Sister had
spoken. A young woman sat on a chair in the corner of the
room just beyond the door. She smiled. Bridie wanted to smile
back, but the click of the door took her attention. The hushed
voices of the departing nuns drifted over to her and found an
open part of her mind to penetrate: 'It'll be a miracle if she
comes through this. I will write to the aunt whose letters the
girl had in her belongings; we can only hope she will take her
in. Otherwise I have a feeling we'll have another Gracie on
our hands.'

'Is it to be wondered at, Sister, with what her father did
to her – and him being a murderer on the run at the time!'

'Shush . . . you know most of these girls ask for it.'

*Murderer . . . Pappy, wanted for murder! Well, they couldn't
have him . . . He . . .* Her inner self couldn't acknowledge the
truth.

She looked around the room. Small and with whitewashed
brick walls, it had no adornments other than a crucifix above
the door and a picture of the Virgin Mary – head leaning to
one side, a serene look on her face and with her eyes seeming
to see inside of you – hanging on the wall to her left. Bridie
felt no reverence for her or for her son. Instead she experienced
a bitterness towards them, which confused her and increased
her sense of loss.

Above her head a beam of light came through a small
window. It wasn't natural light, but from a gas mantle brighter
than the one inside the room. She was in a room within a
room! A prison? Her eyes shot over towards Elizabeth.

Though she didn't look more than about twenty, Elizabeth had a worn-out, downtrodden air about her. Bridie likened it to Mrs Rafferty's look. Mrs Rafferty was a neighbour back in Ireland who had to do everything her husband bade, or feel the might of his fist.

Elizabeth wore a kind of uniform: a plain grey day-frock with a navy-striped pinafore over the top. It was of the type you had to put your head through and tie at each side. With her dark hair pulled back, her elfin-like face shone in the lamplight. A mobcap sat on the back of her head. Her smile held kindness, and Bridie knew she would like Elizabeth. Some comfort seeped into her with this thought.

'Don't be scared,' Elizabeth whispered. 'I know what yer going through. You'll be reet.'

Reet . . . ? What did she mean? She supposed she meant *all right*, as that's the sort of thing that was said in these situations. She knew Elizabeth meant well, but how could she know how it felt, to be going through what Bridie was feeling? How could anyone know?

Elizabeth stood up, peeped through the window on the door, placed her finger over her mouth and then, bending beneath the window, came towards her.

'They say as your da raped you, before killing himself? I'm sorry for you, love. Me uncle was the one as raped me, only he isn't paying for his sin. I am. I were caught with a babby. He denied it all, and I were sent in here by the priest.'

Bridie struggled to understand Elizabeth's way of speaking. Was she saying her uncle had made her pregnant? She stared at Elizabeth and registered the pain in her face. She felt it curl around her own pain and intensify it, till she wanted to scream it out of her. But she couldn't.

'Me babby died in me before she were born. And I'm glad,

cos they'd have taken her from me, had she lived, and this way she will always be mine. Now I have to stay here until me so-called sins are atoned. But then, it's better than the workhouse. Anyroad, word is you aren't having a babby, so you're lucky in that, Bridie. And there's something to be said for being here: at least you're with girls as know.'

The heat in Bridie's head cooled. Tears moistened her dry eye sockets. The words she wanted to speak formed. 'Is it a girls' correction convent I am in?'

'Aye, it is. Though, like me, you probably don't need any correcting, but they'll work you hard to make you mend your ways.'

'I haven't got any – ways . . . I . . .'

'I know. I said, didn't I? I know how things happen. But be prepared, love, as the blame will rest with you.'

The unjust and filthy allegations of the crowd on the boat came back to clothe her in shame. Her spirits sank even further, but she could see this young woman believed her and that gave her comfort. Her voice shook as she asked, 'Is it Liverpool as this convent is in? 'Tis Liverpool the boat was headed to.'

'Aye, but I don't know exactly where. I'm from Leeds meself. Do you want to talk about what happened, love? It helps some.'

'No, only . . . only – why? Why did Pappy . . . ? I . . . I fought . . . I didn't let him.'

'Eeh, I know, lass, and I know the feelings as you have at one who is meant to love and protect you doing such a thing. I understand you not wanting to talk much about it. I was one as couldn't talk, not at first, not till after me babby died. Look, one of the Sisters is an Irish. Her name's Sister Theresa. She's the best here, and she'll help you. In fact, most of the

nuns are all right. Them two as have just been in are the
worst. They mind the sick, but are more likely to make you
sicker. Sister Rose can be cruel, and Sister Benedict just does
as Sister Rose bids her to.'

'Have you been in here long, Elizabeth?'

'Call me Beth. And, aye, I've been here just on six years.'

'Six years! Why is it they haven't let you out?'

'Me family don't want me back. Me da says as I enticed
his brother and made a sinner of him. But truth is, he can't
cope with me. You see, I'm second-hand goods, so to speak.
And with that fact and the scandal as was caused, well, no
man'd take me on. Besides, there's still eleven young 'uns
at home, and after four have already left to be married an'
all.'

'Do you have to stay here forever, Beth? Oh, God, what if
it is as my Aunt Jeannie won't be for taking me in?'

'Is that who the Sisters were talking about?'

'Yes, me pappy was taking me to her. She's a cousin of his,
but they brought me up to call her aunt. 'Tis as I haven't
met her, but she sounded kindly in her letters to me mammy.'

'Well, happen if she's not on with blaming you, she'll take
you in and they'll have to let you go. Mind, I'm not for
staying much longer. Me mate as got away last year is helping
me get out. She leaves notes for me in the hedge and I get
them when I'm on gardening duties.'

'Could you be taking me with you, Beth, if me aunt is not
for having me? I have money . . .'

'Hey, hold your clogs. I'm not sure as I could get two of
us out. And, well . . . look, me mate Agnes hasn't had it
good. She has to earn her living . . . well, you wouldn't know
the way of it. Anyroad, you'd not be able to bring your money

59

with you. If the nuns know as you have it, it'll be taken off you for your keep.'

'Pappy said I am the only one who can be getting it. He told me where it is, and a secret codeword I am to be using at the bank. He said he'd arranged it all in case he couldn't be fetching me from my aunt's house. I didn't understand at the time, but . . .'

'At least he did something decent by yer, then. Look, I'm on gardening the day after tomorrow. Sister Theresa sometimes gets deep into her meditation and doesn't notice what we're up to. I'll leave a note for Agnes. In the meantime, get yourself better, cos them as show signs of not being all there in their heads have it rough. You heard them say about Gracie? Well, she's not right in her head, and she's treated worse than if she were scum. You've to be strong and to find a way of accepting what happened. That's what I did. I don't let it – or anything – hurt me. I just think on getting out of here and doing whatever it takes to survive.'

'I will, Beth, but 'tis not easy. Just a short time ago I was for having everything, then my mammy got sick . . .'

'Look, I'm glad as you're ready to talk, but we'll have to leave it for now. I'm scared as they might come back. Best thing is, I call them and say as you've calmed down and want to speak to someone. You ask for their help, and be all humble and grateful; that'll get you out of here sooner and on to duties. Then if your aunt ain't for helping you, we'll sort sommat out. Agnes'll know what to do. But, Bridie, don't say as we've been talking.'

Bridie nodded. She felt less alone. She would do as Beth said and try not to dwell on everything. And not anything to do with her pappy. Her mammy was different; she'd never be forgetting her mammy. And she'd try to remember what she often used to say to her: 'Always have a dream, Bridie, and when that dream is near, be sure you are ready to catch it.'

The only dream Bridie had at the moment was to be free from this convent and her fears of the tales she'd heard about such places.

6

Andrew

Breckton, 1875
Meeting Dvina

A mystical, shadowy glow bathed the ballroom. The light from the gas mantles flickered on the wonderful silver adornments decorating every wall and picked up the sheen of the ladies' dresses and their immense amount of heavy jewellery: tiaras, necklaces and bracelets. As Andrew looked around, anxious to catch sight of Dvina, he thought the phrase 'dripping with gold' had an apt ring to it. Shivering, as much from nerves as from the cold he'd just come in from, Andrew thought that autumn giving way to winter reflected what was happening in his own life – how quickly the last three weeks had gone since the shocking announcement of his mother's enthronement and the awful proposal that he should marry Dvina Portland!

'Andrew, there you are. Come on, darling. Edgar has been engaging Dvina in conversation whilst we waited for you to arrive.'

'Really, Mother, was that necessary? This whole thing is going to seem so contrived.'

'Well, so it is. Oh, stop being so stuffy, darling. Dvina knows the score. She is fine with it and eager to meet you.'

As he followed his mother across the dance floor, several acquaintances stopped Andrew to greet him. Some, he thought, gave him pitying looks, embarrassing him in the extreme, as his fate had obviously been the topic of conversation.

As they neared the spot where Edgar stood, his heart thumped uncomfortably in his chest. There Dvina was, exactly as he remembered her. Standing almost as tall as Edgar, at around five feet seven, her heavyset body offered nothing for him to admire. Her laugh guffawed out, its deep tone a fraction of a decibel above that of a man, and in contrast to every other lady in the room she wore a linen dress with no glamour to it. No frills or bustle for her. Her dress looked expensive, but plain in the extreme, the only adornments being the pearl buttons running from the high neck to her waist. They bulged where they had to traverse her rounded, matronly breasts. Where they ended there was an unflattering V-shape from which the gathered skirt flared out, accentuating her robust thighs. Her hair, a sort of mousy shade, looked as though she had caught the brush in it, tangled it and simply tugged it out and shoved in a few hairclips to hold it up above her neck.

Edgar nodded over her head at him as he descended the stairs, causing Dvina to turn and say, 'Andrew, how nice to see you.'

Her well-scrubbed face lit up and her smile revealed her only redeeming feature: her white, even teeth, though too much of her pink gums showed above them. Two dimples appeared in her rounded cheeks, and her eyes disappeared into the creases of skin. Andrew's stomach lurched; he could see nothing to help him feel attracted to this woman. Too polite to show it, he stepped towards her and took and kissed her extended hand. It felt surprisingly cold, and it shook in his. Some empathy for her stirred in him as he realized that she, too, must feel nervous and afraid.

'May I have the honour of the next dance?'

Inclining her head in acceptance, she offered him her hand. Every part of him burned with embarrassment as he steered her towards the dance floor. A waltz struck up. His arms stretched around her. The feel of the soft padding of fat around her waist repulsed him. Her steps fell in with his, and in this at least he found her accomplished and easy to guide. After a few minutes he asked, 'I understand you know of the proposition put to me?'

'Yes, I do. Andrew, should you care to escort me to the balcony? I think some straight talking is needed between us.'

He hadn't expected this, and thought it bold of her to be the one to propose it. *Good God, this was going to be worse than I had imagined!*

They walked up the stairs he'd just come down. Feeling self-conscious, he concentrated on the ornate balustrade, the soft tread of his foot on the rich blood-red and gold carpet, the magnificent chandelier, the paintings that adorned the pink-white walls, and the luscious gold velvet curtains. Hensal Grange lived up to everything people said about it; and, he thought with a bitter twist, it could have come down the line to him. If it had, he would never be walking up these stairs to face the doom threatening his future happiness.

Agatha chose that moment to appear from the closet room across the landing. She caught his gaze and mouthed, 'Lamb to the slaughter', compounding his disgust at himself for even contemplating this match. He gave her a look that he hoped would wither her and turned his attention to Dvina. 'May I ask your maid to bring your cloak to you? I fear it may be cold outside.'

'Oh, Andrew, I am a modern nineteenth-century woman. I do not have, or need, a maid.' He would beg to differ on the need front, but again politeness prevented him saying so. Dvina, however, took the lead again, without any thought for propriety, adding, 'Look, if you will find the cold off-putting then let's go into uncle's study. I know he won't mind.'

Thank God! Going into the study seemed more business-like and had different connotations altogether from the balcony, which might be seen as a lovers' retreat. He nodded in agreement and called over one of the butlers in attendance. After instructing him to see that the study was unlocked for them and to bring whisky, he asked Dvina what she would like to drink.

'Whisky will do fine, thank you.'

Oh dear, it could get worse after all. In fact, it just had! A woman, drinking whisky!

What he had dreaded, the moment the door closed on them, didn't happen. Quite the opposite. Instead of an awkward silence, Dvina took a large sip of the whisky he'd handed her and launched straight in, saying, 'Andrew, I accept that I may only be a catch financially, but I do have feelings. I hope you mean to deal with me in a sensitive and kindly manner.'

'Of course. Can I take it you are in agreement then?'

'In principle, yes, but I will need wooing like any other girl. Are you up to it?'

He detected a note of humour in her reply, and a morsel of relief seeped into him. He laughed. 'Depends what you mean by wooing. I can do the flowers and the picnics – that sort of thing – but I wouldn't insult you by pretending to worship at your feet.'

'And I wouldn't expect it of you. I would like us to be friends, though. We could muddle along together very well, if we tried to do that at least. I would expect you to be very discreet with any . . . well, you know . . . extramarital activities – that sort of thing.'

He looked away to hide his horror. He'd never come across her like before. No *lady* of his acquaintance would ever broach the subject. Though he had to admit, her approach was refreshing, and welcome in their situation. It put the whole thing on the level of them entering into a legal agreement concerning everyday matters of business – which, he supposed, they were. Looking back at her, he saw that Dvina had a teasing smile hovering around her lips. What a minx! Against his better judgement, he found her humour attractive and felt bold enough to reply in the same vein, 'And what of *marital* activities? Are you thinking we should indulge in those, or is this to be a friends-and-money-only transaction?'

'I would hope you would treat me as a proper wife – children, maybe – and give me my social standing by your side at functions, et cetera. But I do accept that you cannot love me to the exclusion of all others, if at all. No one could.'

This hit a nerve, causing the heat to rise to his face. 'Not at all. Forgive me; I was taking your lead in placing all the cards on the table. I believe, after this, I can find a really good friend in you, someone I can talk to; and it is not unknown for friends to love one another. I promise to take your feelings into account at all times and to be very considerate towards you.'

'Well, Mr Harvey, I think we will do. I am willing to enter into this marriage if you are.'

'I am.' And he was. In fact he felt quite relieved, and the whole business had lost all its former dread. Instead of seeing his life as coming to an end, he thought it looked like he could continue in much the same way as he had up to now. But there was still the little matter of how he would be able to conduct himself in bed with her. As a friend she bode well, but as a lover . . . He shuddered.

'Please, Mr Harvey . . .'

'Call me Andrew. Mr Harvey is so formal and doesn't fit our situation.'

'Andrew, I saw you tremble after you said you were willing. Please don't enter into this with me if I repulse you. I could not bear that.'

'You don't. No, of course not,' he lied. 'It is just . . . well, I am afraid of how it will all turn out.'

'There is nothing to worry about. I won't expect anything of you on the intimate side of our union, other than to provide me with children, to make me look respectable in the marriage and to give us an heir. I am not an idiot. I know I am the least attractive proposition in that department that any man could wish to take on.'

'You speak very openly for a woman.'

'I'm sorry . . .'

'No, I was going on to say that in our situation it is helpful. But at the same time it exposes me, as if you will always know me and speak as you find me.'

'I probably will. I'm not one for pussyfooting around. And if you mean that I am practical over the intimate side of things . . . well, yes, I am. It comes from dealing with horses all the time. I take an active part in all the activities of my stud farm, so I have had a good grounding in how everything happens. None of it bothers me. Maybe it has taken away any sense of decorum I should have about such matters. I expect I am a little too forward, but I am a great one for truth and honesty at all times. I would like you to be, too. Up to a point, of course . . .'

At this she smiled up at him, her small eyes betraying a hint of fun-making. He liked her. He could not deny that. He just wished she . . . well, it wasn't that she didn't have some good points; she just didn't make the most of them. Maybe if she'd taken care to look nice tonight, chosen her attire to suit the occasion, perhaps spent money on having her hair done as the other women had, it might have helped.

As if she had read his mind, she strode across the room, poured two more whiskies and said, 'Look, I know myself well and don't expect too much, but I think that now we have settled things I will make more of an effort to look the part. For your sake, not mine. All the trimmings of being a woman are not me, but I would not like to be an embarrassment to you. I will employ a maid and . . .'

'Dvina . . .'

'Don't go into a lot of poppycock about not minding how I dress. I saw it in your face when you arrived. If these things matter to you, then they will matter to me. If you can agree to give me my rightful place and serve . . . I mean . . .' a guffaw of a laugh surfaced.

Good Lord, I thought for a moment she was going to say 'SERVICE' her. Though that might be an appropriate word for what she is talking of . . .

Her laugh continued until, against his will, he joined her. Somehow he thought she might be easy to deal with, like an old school friend. Once again his misgivings left him.

'Slip of the tongue, sorry . . .' Her giggling continued,

tears streamed down her face and, much to his chagrin, he couldn't stop either.

Their mirth fizzled out at the same time. A hush clothed the air in discomfort. But just then loud polka music seeped up through the floorboards, breaking the silence and giving Andrew a chance to ease the situation. He bowed. 'I believe you owe me a dance, Miss Portland.' He proffered his arm. Her gratitude smiled from her, but did nothing to allay his fear of the coming ordeal of walking her back to the dance floor.

They had to pass by a group of Andrew's friends, all members of the same hunt and local landowners. Guy Cantrum, a man who enjoyed fun at others' expense, called out to him, 'Andrew, come and join us.'

He hesitated, unsure for a moment. Dvina stiffened beside him. Glancing at her, he caught something of a plea in her expression. Leaving her now would be an insult to her, and she didn't deserve that. It seemed obvious, by how they acted, that his friends had a conspiracy to rescue him. He knew Dvina had sensed this too, and he couldn't do it to her. This realization shocked him; he'd have thought he would have been glad to be given a distraction to release him from her company. 'Thanks, but no. I have the honour of being with Miss Portland. May I present my future wife to you?' *I've done it, and God, don't they look shocked. Speechless in fact.*

'Dvina, this is Guy, Philip, Roland and Simon. We hunt together, so you will see rather a lot of them. Gentlemen, Miss Dvina Portland.'

Politeness stopped them from doing anything other than bowing to her and expressing how pleased they were to meet her, but more than one of them raised his eyebrows at him. *Oh God, this is going to be more difficult than I thought.* But then, as Edgar had said, Andrew wouldn't be the first to marry for money and position, so they would probably come to understand and respect his having to do so. What he couldn't stand was if any of them expressed pity for him or, worse, dropped him from their social circle. That would be too much to bear. He already had a job to keep up with them, as they spent money like water and had plenty of it.

'I do know these gentlemen, Andrew, in a business sense. Mr Bradshaw bought a horse from me just a few months ago, and my stallions have been engaged in husbandry to mares owned by them all. I trust my stable gave you excellent service?' Andrew saw her look boldly into each one's eyes before adding, 'Hunting, how marvellous! I ride to hounds myself and love it. I hope you will one day invite me to join you?'

'Of course.' Guy bowed. He took her hand as if it was contaminated and barely touched it with his lips.

Andrew glared at him. Roland stepped forward. 'Delighted to, Miss Portland, though I fear you may put us to shame. I have heard of your skill in the saddle.' He took her hand in a much more willing way and kissed it in the proper manner.

'We hope you will be very happy, both of you. May I be the first to congratulate you.' Simon followed Roland's lead. And as if his words had nudged the others, they all now offered their good wishes. Dvina's face flushed. Andrew suspected she had read the undertones – the barely hidden mockery in their response – but was glad she chose not to retort. Her actions were those of a true lady, and this gladdened him, as he saw she was capable of being such. Then he chided himself for even thinking she wasn't.

Andrew's head ached as he prepared for bed. Such a contradictory night! He'd contracted himself to a woman he didn't love and didn't even find attractive, then seen her in a different light and thought there was a hope of them getting along well together, then borne the embarrassment in front of his friends without being able to take them to task for their manners, though he would do so in future. On top of all of this, there had been the awful silence when Edgar announced their engagement, before decorum dictated a response and a slow applause started.

And, worse, he didn't think he would ever live down the obligatory dance. He'd stumbled around, treading on poor Dvina's toes and eliciting more than a few smirks behind silk-gloved hands. She hadn't helped by stopping the dance, curt-seying to him, then turning to the audience and saying, 'I think my future husband is a little nervous. I am of the mind to let him off, so please do join us.'

Oh, God! How the hell am I going to live with someone who seems able to dispense with social graces and make such fools of us both in public!

7

Will

The cage rattled Will's bones as it descended into the bowels of the earth. As the shaft of brightness from the gas lights in the foyer above disappeared, Will's cold hands struggled to light his oil lamp. The glow it eventually gave off illuminated a young lad squatting on the floor of the cage. He looked no more than seven years old, but Will knew he must have more years on him than that. Had to, these days, to go down. The movement of the lad's shoulders told of huge sobs racking his body, but his cloth cap shielded his face from Will.

'Hey, come on now. Nowt can be as bad as all that.' Will fished in his pocket for the nub ends of the candles he'd prised out of candlesticks at home. He'd had to do so before his ma caught him, as she liked to melt them down to form new ones. He knew he'd catch a lashing of her tongue, but it was worth it to help young trappers have a little extra time of the dim light they gave off. He'd never forget when he were a lad and did the job they did. Those last few hours of the shift, sitting in the terrifying, impenetrable blackness, still visited him and gave him nightmares. Mind, he'd been younger, but still. 'Make sure you light the first one just afore your allotted candle gives out, as you'll not get another chance.'

The lad lifted his tear-stained face. 'Ta, Mister.'

'Have you any snap with you?'

'Naw, me ma had no bread left. She tried to borrow some, but no one would help. She's allus borrowing and don't pay back. Not cos she doesn't want to, mind.'

'Aye, I know the way of it. I see you have a billycan, so that's good. Here, take this butty with you, but eke it out. A bite now and again, and ration your water an' all. Make it last. No good drinking it all and having to go ten hours with nowt, is there?'

The lad nodded. Will could see he had a job enough to swallow his tears back, without trying to answer.

The cage hit the bottom with its usual thud; 6 a.m. and a twelve-hour in front of him. A long time to give to his thoughts, because that's all he had down here: hard graft and mulling things over. There was never much time for talk. Not that he would welcome any today. This being his first shift since the funeral a few days ago, any conversation would be of condolences or slights about Florrie, and he hadn't the mind to take either.

It was easy to see how everyone had taken the wrong end of the shovel, by thinking of him as the father of Florrie's unborn. The evidence stacked up against him: Will always making time to have a word with her, giving her respect, not taking the rise out of her, like the others did; and hadn't he risked his life to save her? But then, with this last, anyone would have done that, wouldn't they? In answer to his own question he said to himself, *No, they wouldn't. They were too fond of their own skins to think of anyone else's.*

Mind, he'd have to talk to Florrie as soon as he could. Get her to tell truth of it all. Because if he let it go on, he might find himself landed with her and what she carried, and he'd not want that to happen.

There she was, as had happened on too many occasions of late, standing in the shadows, waiting for him to come home. It hadn't been so obvious before. But now, with her house gone and she and her ma living with Florrie's gran a couple of streets away, she had no other reason for being here. Will kept his head down and avoided looking at her as he passed her by.

'Will, can I have a word?'

'Florrie, you've got to leave me alone. You know what's being said.'

'I don't know who else to turn to . . .'

'Well, I'm sorry for you, lass, but I can't do anything, and I'd be glad if you'd put folk reet. You know what's in your belly ain't got nothing to do with me. If you thought of me as you say you do, you'd make sure as others knew it an' all. What if it got to me ma, and her only just having buried me da? I'm asking you now, Florrie, put the story straight. You know what will happen if I try to and you haven't spoken up: folk'll say as I'm a rat who shirks his responsibilities.'

'I know, Will, but I daresn't say. He'd kill me . . .'

'Who? Tell me who he is and I'll have a word with him.'

'You can't, Will. You're no match for him.'

'So where do we go from here? Couldn't you just tell folk as you're not saying who the father is, but you will say it ain't me?'

'I'm desperate, Will. We've got no money, nor fuel to light a fire at me gran's. We all went without food yesterday and the day before; we only had a bit of stew. Ma made it from scrounging in the waste tip for the outside cabbage leaves and potato peelings as folk'd discarded. At least when me da was here we had our free coal and we could keep gran's fire going with some of it. And, well, I had me earnings to help out, but that's stopped now. Bruiser won't help me, now me belly's up.'

Something in her look as she said this last gave him the thought that Bruiser could be the one she daren't tell of. He knew she'd worked on the game for him. 'Look, I could help you out with some coal, and I could ask me ma to bake you a pie now and then, but only if you tell the truth. Cos me helping you would only add fuel to an already blazing bonfire of rumours, and I'd be down as the father for sure.'

'I . . . I could make you happy . . .'

'No! No, Florrie, and I mean it. I don't want to marry you and I won't; nor do I want anything else you have a mind to offer. Now think on. Take me help in the only way I'm willing to give it, or not. It's up to you.'

'There is another way as you could help me . . . Will, please.'

He had turned to leave her, but the sob in her voice made him look back. Tears streamed down her cheeks.

She didn't have an unattractive face, but one ravaged by time and trouble. It gave her years beyond her age. As he stepped back towards Florrie and met her gaze, he saw in the dull darkness of her eyes a glimmer of hope as she stared up at him. Now closer, he could see she still had faint bruises on her cheeks – a legacy of what had happened to her at her da's hands just before the fire. Around her thin lips and neat little nose, red sores told of her many hours out in the cold wind.

'What is it? I'll do all I can.'

'I know this woman, only she charges a lot and I haven't the money.'

'What does she charge for?'

'She gets rid of it . . .'

This shocked him. He'd not heard of such a thing before. How? But then, he didn't really want to know. It sounded horrific. 'You mean, kill your babby?'

'No, it ain't killing. It ain't formed a proper babby yet. I've only just missed . . . I mean, it ain't even sure. Folk know cos me ma had a go at me, and then me da heard and he went mad and said sommat in the pub when he'd had a few.'

'You mean you've put me through all this and you're not even sure if you're pregnant or not? God, Florrie, you take the coal and the bucket with it. You have no right to stand aside whilst I suffer, and if it gets to me ma . . . Look, I've allus had you down as decent at heart, and as the stuff you do for money is cos you've no choice. But you do have a choice in this, Florrie, you do. And me offer still stands: clear me name and I'll help you in any way I can.'

As he went to turn away, he saw a couple of the neighbours' curtains drop back into place, and knew the fact that he'd been talking to Florrie again would be round all the houses by morning.

The houses in this street were two-up, two-down terraced properties. They stood in rows divided by narrow cobbled roads, the width of which only just accommodated the drays loaded with their weekly supply of coal or ale for the pub. Or, of course, the more unpleasant night-soil cart, which carried away the contents of the sewage pits under the shared bog-houses in the back yards.

The smoke belching out of the chimneys of the steel works, the silver-plate factories, the iron works and the mines had blackened the bricks and hung in the almost daily morning fog like a cloud of doom. They called Sheffield a prosperous town, but no one would guess that to look at it.

Its people had plenty of work, but they were profit-makers for others and saw little of the wealth generated. A proud lot, they had their own class system. Miners came a long way down the pecking order, but they stood by each other, and though they looked down on Florrie they still classed her as one of their own. Some said she deserved her lot – especially those whose husbands had been tempted. Others said her circumstances had led her astray. And they all had an opinion on who they thought responsible for her present predicament, and Will knew most had him down for it.

Florrie called his name again, but his ma opened the front door of their house and stopped him having to respond. 'Are you coming in, lad? Uncle Fred's here.' She stood just inside the door to let him pass, then moved her body into the open doorway. 'Get yourself away, you, and leave me lad alone. You're not fit to lick the soles of his boots. And don't let me see you round . . .'

'Ma! Ma, close the door and shut your mouth.'

'What . . . ?'

'Now then, lad, there's no need to talk to your mother like that. She has enough on her plate.' Uncle Fred had come through from the back kitchen. Will felt the shame of his words redden his cheeks. He'd never before spoken to his ma in such a way, and to do so at a time like this. 'I'm sorry, Ma. I just don't know what came over me.'

'No, I don't suppose you do, but to embarrass me like that. And she must have heard. She'll think you stood up for her against your own moth—'

'Leave it, Janet. You can see as the lad is upset, and if that's his young lady, I can understand why.'

'She's not, nor will be whilst I'm alive. She's a whore. She sells it to anybody, but somehow she seems to want Will. I can't stand by and let that happen.'

Will cringed inside. To think Uncle Fred had to listen to this. A defence of Florrie came to him, but he didn't voice it. Doing so would only fuel the awful situation. He'd talk it over with his uncle when his ma wasn't around. Perhaps he'd even find Uncle Fred could help with what to do about it all. Not that he wanted to burden him, but he had no one else he could confide in.

A bigger version of his da, but much younger, Uncle Fred extended his hand towards him. Will took it and found comfort in his words. 'I understand, and I'm here for you, lad.' This eased some of the pain he had in his chest for his da. 'Now then, Will, it goes without saying how devastated I was to hear of our John passing over.' He pulled a large white hanky from his pocket and wiped his eyes. His voice, though still Yorkshire-sounding, had a hint of the throatiness of the Liverpool dialect. This didn't surprise Will, as Uncle Fred had lived and worked as a fisherman there for as long as he could remember. His da had always spoken of going sea-fishing one of these days, and always talked with envy of his 'little brother', as he'd called Fred, who'd made something different of himself than following the family tradition.

Ma had gone into the back kitchen muttering something about making a brew. He could see that she seethed with hurt, but still he felt it best not to pursue things. Instead he thought to engage his uncle in conversation to try to ease the atmosphere. 'Thanks. It's nice to see you, Uncle. How long are you staying?'

'A few days. I wanted to see for meself you were both sorted. I'm sorry I missed the funeral. I didn't get your ma's letter until a couple of days ago.'

'We guessed that was it, but we couldn't wait, in case you were away on a long trip. But don't worry about us. We'll be reet. Ma's took it on herself to go out to work. I don't like the idea, but we will need the extra.'

'Well, maybe it'll do her good. It's been a long time since she did anything outside these four walls, what with tending to your da. What about you, Will? Are you still happy down pit?'

'I wouldn't call it happy . . . but there's nothing else I know.'

'It'd not take me long to teach you the ropes of sea-fishing. I've a new boat now and could do with a hand.'

'I couldn't uproot her, and I couldn't leave her, either.'

'Well, how about next time you're off? You come up and enjoy some leisure fishing with me.'

Will said he'd like to. At this his Uncle Fred went on to tell him all about his boat and his work.

'It sounds grand. Me da allus spoke of coming to see you. I'll do it for him. I'll check tomorrow when I've next got a couple of days between shifts . . .'

'Reet, enough of that talk, Fred.' Janet came back into the room. 'Will won't be going anywhere for a while. I need him here with me. He has responsibilities towards me now, him being the head of the house, so to speak.'

'Naw, Ma, you're still head of the house.'

'Not according to Fenshaw. He came round this morning and told me not to worry. With you working at pit, they'd not put me out. They'd just put the house in your name.'

Will seethed inside. Of all the rotten things for the miners' housing and welfare officer to do to her, and her only just widowed. Yes, he knew the rule that these houses were for miners and their families only, and he shuddered to think what would have happened to them both if he'd not been a miner . . . Still, that was a road he'd not go down. It hadn't happened, and there was plenty to occupy his mind that had.

8

Bridie

Leeds, 1875
A hope dashed

The brambles of the bare fruit bushes ripped at the skin on Bridie's hand as she pulled them apart and pruned them back. The pain added to that caused by the blisters she already had on her icy-cold palms, and drew her closer to shedding the tears she'd clamped away after her talk with Beth. The winter sun trickled a gentle warmth that penetrated her stinging cheeks as she looked over at Beth and tried to draw comfort from her matter-of-fact way of coping.

Five weeks had passed since she'd been brought here and still no word from her Aunt Jeannie or any communication with Beth's friend Agnes! What if Aunt Jeannie didn't come? The thought weakened her resolve. She swallowed hard and tugged the weeds with even greater determination.

If only the nuns were for allowing them to talk to each other while they worked. At least then her mind wouldn't clog with the filth of it all and the constant abrasion of asking over and over, *Why did Pappy do it?* And: *Who was he really?*

The horror of his death gnawed her into reliving the

nightmare, until she could smell his blood and had a need to pick at her flesh to remove the bits of him that she thought must still cling to her. How could she catapult the loving father he had been in her growing-up years into this monster that she knew nothing of?

'Bridie, Bridie O'Hara. Reverend Mother wants to see you.'

Bridie straightened up. She caught Beth's eye. Saw her glance at Sister Theresa and, seeing her with her head bowed, whisper, 'This'll be it, Bridie. Good luck, love.'

She smiled her thanks.

A tall girl stood on the edge of the path just outside the small wall that bordered this part of the garden, separating it from the flowerbeds. Bridie knew her as the secretary of the priests who occupied the house next to the convent and sometimes helped Reverend Mother with her bookkeeping. The girl beckoned with her finger. 'Are you Bridie O'Hara? Well, come on, hurry yourself.'

Entering the convent from the garden meant passing near the hospital wards. The gleaming polished floor led three ways: left to the classrooms, kitchens and the Reverend Mother's office; straight ahead and up the stairs to the dormitories; and right, through a swing door, to the wards. From this quarter, as often happened, she could hear cries of agonizing pain. 'Help me. Help me . . . I can't, I can't take any more . . .'

And then: 'Shut up! You should have thought of that before you lay down and committed your vile sin . . .' in the voice of the hated Sister Rose.

Bridie stood a moment, her heart telling her to run and help Enid. Hadn't it been hours now since poor Enid had started with her pains? And here it was, almost three in the afternoon and her baby still not born. *And to have that bitch of a woman tending to her. For sure, there'd be no mercy shown.*

The secretary's impatient voice broke into her thoughts. 'Hurry up. And take those gardening boots off. You'll have to walk in your stockinged feet. There's no time. You can't keep Reverend Mother waiting.'

Trying not to slip over took all of Bridie's wits as she followed the girl along the corridor. When at last she entered the office, fear took her. What would she do if her aunt wouldn't come for her? *Oh, Holy Mother Mary, could you not intervene on my behalf and make sure she does come?*

The office door creaked as it opened, to reveal the Reverend Mother sitting behind a large desk. She didn't acknowledge them. The girl bowed, announced Bridie and left.

To be sure, the swallowing of sand couldn't feel worse than this dryness of her mouth, Bridie thought as she waited for Reverend Mother to speak. In the silence, broken only by the rustle of paper, her hopes pounded her heart. When at last the woman spoke, her clipped tone could have cracked a frozen pond. 'Bridie O'Hara. Mrs Bottomley, your Aunt Jeannie, is willing to take you in, despite everything you have done. She is coming for you tomorrow. See that you have everything packed and are ready for when she arrives.'

A dismissing hand waved her away. Out in the hall and with the heavy wooden door closed behind her, a joy settled in Bridie. Breaking the rules she'd soon not be bound by, she ran along the corridor, laughing as she slid the last few yards towards her boots.

Beth looked up from her work, her face showing eager anticipation. One glance at Sister Theresa compounded Bridie's excitement. And to be sure she wouldn't have to keep the news to herself, as the nun sitting on a bench near the statue of Mary had fallen asleep. Now she and Beth could talk.

Brambles clutched at her skirt, but she didn't care. A robin darted out and chirped at her, as if annoyed at the disturbance she'd caused him, as she made her way onto the path and through the fruit trees. Beth clutched her hand when she came out the other side. Here they were no longer visible to anyone in the convent, but could still keep an eye on Sister Theresa. 'Well, did you get good news, then?'

'I did!' She told Beth what had happened, and Beth's expression drooped. 'Don't be worrying, Beth. I'll be coming for you, so I will, once I'm settled.'

'How? Agnes hasn't, and she promised. Oh, I know it ain't easy, especially for Agnes. How she has to make her living . . . Anyroad, don't worry about me. I know me time will come.'

'It will, I swear it will. Haven't I been for telling you: as soon as I can, I will be getting the money me pappy left for me and will come for you; sure we can find a place to rent and get work?'

'Thanks, Bridie. Oh, I wish I could walk out of here with you.'

''Tis me as is wishing that, too. I'll be thinking of you every day and doing all I can, so I will.'

Aunt Jeannie didn't look as she'd imagined. When spoken of, the image portrayed had been of a gentle, loving woman, someone to feel pity for. Bridie remembered hearing her mammy saying, 'Wasn't it a shame altogether that Jeannie couldn't have wee ones? Sure she would make a wonderful mother.' It had been the tone of this and other comments that had built the picture she'd held in her mind of her Aunt Jeannie.

But before Bridie, with her arms open, stood a tall, thin woman with black hair swept back into a bun and features that didn't tell of kindness. Her gesture of welcome looked forced. 'Bridie! Haven't I been out of me mind with worry for you? Look at you! You have the beauty your poor mammy had at your age. Maybe a tad smaller, but you have the look of her all the same. Come here and let me hold you.'

Bridie went into her arms, but felt no comfort – there was no honest giving of a welcome or of love in the hug. Being released from the bony hold brought relief. But, as they separated, her aunt's piercing blue eyes – the only thing about her, apart from her accent, that told of her Irish birth – searched her face. 'It is awful altogether what I am hearing happened. Did your mammy not tell you the way of things, and how a girl such as yourself can have an effect on the men around you?'

'I wasn't . . . I didn't do anything. Pappy was for forcing me . . .'

'Aye, well, 'tis what I was saying to Mr Bottomley; it never took much to get our Michael going, and if he had the drink on him he could get himself into a confusion as to who he was dealing with. What he did, once he realized it was you, told of that. He has paid dearly, God rest him. Now, let's leave it there and get you home.'

The gentle swaying of the coach did nothing to soothe the dread settling in Bridie as she watched the smart dwellings and business premises give way to grimy streets. Here, tiny, unkempt houses were built so close to each other that she was sure their occupants wouldn't have to cross over the road to knock on the door of their opposite neighbour. But worse than the sight of the rotting debris, hungry-looking, grubby children and skin-and-bone dogs and cats was the smell of fish. It clung to her nostrils until every breath became a fight not to heave up the contents of her stomach.

''Tis something you'll have to be getting used to, Bridie.

Your Uncle George works on the fish-gutting down on the dock over there, and he has a stench on him worse than this when he is coming in after his shift.'

Bridie looked over to the docks. Huge iron chains divided the area from the road. Ropes thicker than a stout man's waist lay here and there in snake-like coils on the muddied cobbles. Some men stood in circles mending fishing nets, while others threw fish into huge wicker baskets. Boats of all shapes and sizes bobbed up and down on the angry sea behind them. She looked away. The sight of the waves crashing onto the harbour had jolted the pain of memory back into her, but she could see beauty in the scene. Hadn't she seen the like captured in the paintings hung on the walls of the castle? Thinking of this brought Seamus to her mind, for wasn't it he who had lifted her high to take a peek? Her heart took on the extra weight of missing him and she wondered if she would ever feel happy again.

The driver halted the horses outside a building opposite the dock. Its doors stood open. The smell of alcohol and tobacco mingled with that of fish. Men's drunken laughter came to her, cementing her trepidation.

'He'll be in there, no doubt. I told him I'd be back after his shift finished, so your introduction to Mr Bottomley will give you a side of him that you'll become familiar with. He likes a drink, so he does. And I'm partial meself at times.'

They climbed out of the coach. Bridie caught her breath against the onslaught of the salty wind as it tingled on her cheeks and whipped her skirt round her legs. Her aunt shouted above it: 'Wait on the steps. I'll just be having the one drink and then we'll get you home.'

The chimes of a distant clock marked the passing of an hour. The cold had numbed every part of her, shivering anger through her. *Just who did the woman think she was? Sure you wouldn't be for treating an animal in this way.* Her temper had her barging into the pub.

Whistles shrilled the air in the smoke-filled bar as she stepped inside. A loud voice silenced them. 'Shut youse faces. Now then, hun, you can't come in here. You're not of an age. Besides, this bar is just for the men.'

'But me Aunt Jeannie was for coming in over an hour since. I'm fair freezing waiting out there for her.'

'What's her name? She'll be in the other bar, if at all.'

'Mrs Bottomley.'

'Right, hun, step outside and I'll give her the nod.'

Aunt Jeannie came out within a few minutes. 'What is it you think you are doing? Don't you ever be calling me out of the bar again, Bridie! You fair embarrassed me.'

'I'm sorry, so I am, Aunt, but I wasn't for standing the cold any longer.'

'Aye, well, cold it may be, but it is another lesson you have to learn. Did not Michael be telling you: a young lady does not go into a bar and fetch out her elders. Come on now, before your uncle comes out. He's raving, so he is.'

Bridie let the tear leave her eye and drop unheeded down her cheek. Loneliness shrouded her. During the few days she'd been in her aunt's care, it had been anything but clear as to whether or not she was welcome. One moment her aunt was full of the blarney, saying how good it was to have her, and the next telling her, ''Tis a hardship you've brought on us, so it is, Bridie.'

She put her head under the covers and wished she had a room separate from theirs, but this fisherman's cottage near the docks of Liverpool only had one room and it was the living and sleeping quarters for them all.

Her bed, a shake-me-down next to the iron stove, stood only feet from where her aunt and uncle slept in a curtained-off alcove. A sick revulsion settled in her at the memory of the noises she'd heard coming from there the night before. She tried to put it out of her mind and let her body relax into the sleep it demanded of her, but just as she felt herself begin to drift away a loud breaking of wind disturbed her. Her aunt's indignation came out in a high-pitched protest: 'George Bottomley, 'tis disgusting you are. Will you hold the blanket down and trap it in.'

'Shut it, woman! You do your fair share.'

Bridie's tears dried and she had to stifle a giggle at this, but what her uncle said next stiffened her body and had her straining to hear his whispered tones. 'Have you done anything about her yet? Cos I'm telling you, hun, if it weren't for what you say she has stashed away and the fact we'll be in for a piece of it, I'd have her out. With you being an Irish, folk are connecting her to that murdering cousin of yours. There's talk . . .'

'You watch how you are with her. I've told you enough times. Our Michael put plenty by. He was for putting me in the picture when he was over last. He said he had put a stash in one of the banks.'

'Aye, blood-money, I'd say, knowing him. But what I want to know is when we'll see any of it.'

'Be patient, and be leaving everything to me to deal with.'

'Just see as we do profit, Jeannie, as I'm telling you: if there's nothing up front soon, I'll have her out.'

'Oh, 'tis the big man you are now, is it? Go on with you, George Bottomley. Shut your fecking face and give us a cuddle.'

Bridie pulled the covers over her head once more, in an

effort to shut out the grunts and groans of her uncle and the sighs of her aunt that had replaced their conversation. Their words had put a new fear into her. Hadn't she known from the outset that she wouldn't stay with them long? But the knowledge of her money had helped – it had provided hope for her and for Beth.

Her instant dislike of George Bottomley had been stopping her offering to pay for her keep or even mentioning what her pappy had put by for her. A big man with a stomach that rolled fat almost to his knees and with the smell of his work embedded in his every pore, he repulsed her. And didn't the same fear she'd had of her pappy visit her every time she caught his eye? But now she had to contend with him knowing of the money, and it being his motive for having her here.

Trying to block out what was happening across the room, she held her hands over her ears and concentrated on the ideas she'd been mulling over for herself and Beth. She'd to find a way of sorting it all out without her aunt and uncle knowing.

A final groan, louder than all the rest, came from her uncle, then a giggle from her aunt as her uncle said, 'That shut you up, didn't it?'

'Aye, and you. Great lump of a man that you are, George Bottomley, you've still got it in you, so you have. Now get yourself away to sleep.'

Within moments snores reverberated around the room. Bridie curled up into a ball. Once more the tears threatened, but she swallowed hard and allowed the spirit in her to rise. For sure she couldn't be standing it here. She wasn't knowing what to do or how to do it, but she'd find a way. She'd not stay in this cottage a moment longer than she needed to.

9

Issy

Hartington House, 1875
The wedding event

Issy Harman stood with the rest of the staff of Hartington House listening to Mrs Baxdale, the housekeeper. There had been a buzz in the air ever since the announcement a few weeks back informing them of Miss Dvina's betrothal to Mr Harvey. And now here they were discussing the arrangements for their forthcoming marriage, and that of Mr Harvey's mother to Mr Eastland of Hensal Grange. It had taken time for it to sink in among them all, especially how someone as handsome as Mr Harvey could ever fancy their lovely but plain-Jane Miss Dvina!

'A marriage of convenience, if you ask me. And it will all end in tears for Miss Dvina, mark my words. Things ain't how they should be, thou knows,' Gertie had said at the breakfast table this morning. Gertie worked as an upstairs maid and saw and heard more of the goings-on of the household. She often repeated things she'd happened to hear or had speculated on with the other upstairs maids. You couldn't set store by a lot of it, but Issy thought there was some truth in this.

'Now, I am looking for volunteers to help out,' Mrs Baxdale continued. 'The venue for this double event is Hensal Grange manor. They need extra catering staff, dining-room staff and scullery maids for the dinner and ball that is to take place in the evening. Some of you are already familiar with the layout of Hensal Grange, as you have assisted at functions before. Isabella, I am hoping you in particular can offer your services, as I will need someone with your experience in the kitchen. There is a bonus payment of a shilling at the end of the month for senior staff, and sixpence for maids.'

'Of course, Mrs Baxdale. I could do with the extra, as I'll be planning me own wedding soon.'

Mrs Baxdale's eyes opened wide. Gertie dug Issy in the ribs and gave her one of her beaming smiles. Giggles and murmurs and oohs and aahs disrupted the proceedings, until Mrs Baxdale brought order once more with her stilted, 'Congratulations, I am sure, Isabella, but this is not the time to discuss your own private affairs.'

Issy allowed herself the good feeling of having won a small victory by knocking the stuffing out of Mrs Baxdale. Granted, she had a high position as housekeeper, but she thought herself better than the rest of them and had more airs and graces than the family did. It irritated Issy how Mrs Baxdale insisted on always calling her Isabella, while everyone else used her pet name, but nevertheless she thought it better to apologize. 'Sorry, Mrs Baxdale, I'm just so excited, I can't hold it in.' But she did manage to stop herself saying what came to her as a comparison to the feeling she had, and kept to herself the thought, 'It's like having me first kiss all over . . .', as Mrs Baxdale had pulled her up on more than one occasion for her coarse way of speaking.

Issy blamed her ma. She had some sayings, did her ma, and

they had sort of rubbed off on her. Something always popped into her head and came out of her mouth, no matter to whom she was talking. Look at the time Mr Harvey had surprised her and Denny as they walked across the field. She still blushed when she thought of it. Fancy saying a word like 'knickers' to him! Denny took ages to forgive her for that.

'Jane,' Mrs Baxdale now addressed the trainee lady's maid. 'You are to become Miss Dvina's personal maid. Mrs Portland has asked especially for you to take the position, as she was very impressed with you when you looked after her during Dorothy's illness.'

'By, you've got your work cut out, Jane. It'll be like trying to turn a pumpkin into a golden carriage . . .'

'Isabella, that is very rude of you, and the rest of you are no better, laughing at such an uncalled-for remark.'

This time, when she apologized, Issy really did feel mortified. She shouldn't have poked fun at Miss Dvina. You couldn't meet a nicer person, and she couldn't help how she looked. Though that wasn't true, not altogether, as Miss Dvina didn't care about such things. She always had second helpings at every meal, and often sent down to the kitchen for little snacks. And the chores she did alongside the lads in the stables! It was no wonder she had muscles on her in places she shouldn't.

The meeting over, Mrs Baxdale asked Issy to accompany her to her office. She stood just inside the small room waiting for a further telling-off, but apart from a short speech asking her to watch what she said, the housekeeper simply wanted to discuss the menu.

'Now, Isabella, Mr Eastland has asked for quails' eggs with ham. And pressed salmon and asparagus parcels with herb butter for hors d'oeuvre. Then beef consommé followed by game pie with root vegetables. After that there will be cheeses, fruit and biscuits, and finally a selection of hot puddings and trifles. It is these desserts that the Hensal Grange cook wants you to be responsible for. Oh, and the pastry for the game pie, and the biscuits for the cheese. So I would like a list of your suggestions as to suitable puddings to complement the other courses. And of course the ingredients you will need for them, as soon as possible. They are expecting three hundred guests to sit down for the meal at around six-thirty in the evening prior to the evening ball.'

'What's happening following the wedding, are the guests to be fed then?'

'There is to be a luncheon following the actual service, but for far fewer guests. They may need your assistance with it, but they haven't specified. But you will need to be in the kitchen very early anyway, so you can do as directed on the day.'

'I'll need more than a day to prepare all those puddings for three hundred folk.'

'Yes, it is thought you might incorporate a lot of cold puddings, and make them here in the days leading up to the event, so they can be transported over on the day. If this is the case, there will be an extra payment for you, as I have already mentioned. More pennies for your own planned nuptials, which you did not see fit to discuss with me before announcing!'

'I know I should have done, and I meant to, but all this talk of weddings set me off.'

'Very well. Just make sure you keep me informed of any further arrangements and discuss with me when you intend to marry. I need to make sure it all fits in with the house schedule. We will need to engage a new cook. I won't inform Mrs Portland until after the wedding. I can't have her concerned with domestic matters, with everything else going on.'

Issy bowed her head and went back to the kitchen. She hadn't really thought of having to give her job up, but she supposed she must. Married staff – well, the womenfolk anyway – could only really stay on if they wed others who worked for the estate. Then they had a cottage allocated to them.

Hartington House stood some ten miles from Breckton, making it impossible for her to travel over on a daily basis. She'd miss it, though. She enjoyed the work and the company of the others, and they could do with the money. Denny didn't make much, and the miner's cottage she'd have to live in wasn't up to much, either.

Standing on the edge of Breckton, all the cottages in the Miners' Row had one room downstairs. This served as a kitchen-cum-living room, and as a bedroom for the miner and his wife at night. Over this there was a sort of half-loft, a huge stone shelf reached by a ladder, where the young 'uns slept. Her ma had made theirs nice and cosy, though, with the rugs she'd made, and the pretty curtains for the window and a matching daytime tablecloth. Her da had whitewashed the walls and, being handy, had put up a rail across the beam supporting the loft, so Ma could partition off their bed with a nice thick curtain. Issy had many similar plans for the cottage she knew she and Denny were getting. They'd been lucky in that. Most young couples had to squash in with their parents until one came vacant, but as it happened, a couple stood empty at the moment. Issy had pondered on this, and the rumours it had caused of things not being so good at the mine. Usually, once someone left or died, a new man took the position within hours and his family moved into a cottage, but though her da had said they were stretched at the mine, no one had been taken on of late. Not grown men anyroad.

All of which gave truth to what Gertie had said about Mr Harvey marrying Miss Dvina for her money. She hoped not. She'd have liked Miss Dvina to find someone who loved her, like she had found Denny.

'Andrew, you *have* surprised everyone, you know. I mean, Dvina Portland! Good gracious, not a love-match, I'd wager. But, cash-strapped or not, you'd not get me—'

'I think that kind of talk is rather out of order and extremely insulting to my intended, Guy, not to mention unhelpful.'

'Well, you deserve it. I'm sorry, but it's clear you are marrying for money, so you don't get any sympathy from me. In fact, you get what you deserve: disdain. Your announcement at the ball the other week rocked us all to the roots, but having said that, of course I will stand as your groomsman and be honoured to do so, if only to support you through this dreadful mistake.'

'I don't know if it is such a mistake. Dvina is a good sort. Oh, I know she's nothing to shout about in the looks department, but, you know, she is honest. There is no double talk with her, and she can be very funny. I have enjoyed her company . . .'

'You sound as though you are reading from a script. All those things are good assets, and I have heard she has them in abundance, but what about when it comes to the bedchamber? Methinks you will still make regular visits to your whore, my good fellow, as I cannot see how lying with that great bulk could give you any satisfaction. The thought of having to do it, even as a duty, quite puts me off my lunch.'

This conversation, which he'd had a week or so ago with Guy, still haunted Andrew as he turned and saw Dvina walking towards him up the aisle. His mother walked in front of her on the arm of his brother-in-law, obscuring most of his view of his future bride. He smiled at Edgar standing beside him, who had leaned towards him and said, 'Here they come. Oh, look. Rosalind – I mean, your mother – looks beautiful.'

Andrew agreed. His mother wore a pale-blue satin gown, fitted at her tiny waist and flowing out to the floor in box pleats. Over it, and matching the colour of her veiled hat, a delicate, darker blue lace coat billowed out as she walked. He'd never seen her look lovelier. He hardly dared look over her head to see Dvina. When he did, he couldn't really make her out, as a veil of such close-knit, heavy lace covered her face that he wondered she could see through it.

The procession reached the altar steps. Edgar took the arm of Andrew's mother and steered her to the right of the altar, leaving Dvina and her father in full view. Andrew offered his arm and smiled. Though she presented much better than he'd hoped – her figure, he presumed, laced into shape by strong corsets – he hadn't yet seen her face.

Her long cream silk gown, with an organza overfrock ruffled into a bustle at the back, camouflaged her large rear effectively. He had to admit that it looked quite becoming and suited her tall frame, somehow making her appear much slimmer.

A sigh of relief came out louder than he intended. He coughed, smiled and said, 'Nerves, sorry. You look lovely,

Dvina.' She nodded her head, but he still could not properly see her face or her hair.

The vows of his mother and Edgar passed, and their turn came. Her veil billowed out around her mouth as she spoke hers in a clear, rather loud voice. His own voice shook as he repeated his, making him feel rather foolish.

'I now pronounce you man and wife.'

The words were hardly finished before Dvina flicked back her veil and proffered her lips for a kiss.

Shocked not just at the forwardness of this, but at the sight of her, he instinctively drew back. An uncomfortable murmur went round the church. Dvina's face reddened and she dropped her eyes.

He wished he could undo the moment. It hadn't been what it seemed. It was the difference in her that had taken him aback. He couldn't say that Dvina's rounded face looked beautiful, or even pretty, but it certainly looked a lot better than he'd expected. And her hair! Someone had done wonders with it, sweeping it back from her face into a mass of curls at the nape of her neck, leaving just a fringe and two ringlets each side. It suited her well.

Regaining his composure, he pulled her to him and kissed her lips. The softness of them stirred a feeling deep inside him, as did the sweet taste of her breath. He pulled away and looked into her eyes. 'My dear, I . . . I didn't mean to be rude. You . . . well, you surprised me.'

She smiled and whispered, 'That's the work of the maid Mother insisted I have. She has some very good tricks up her sleeve. I'm glad I passed, but don't expect me to look like this all of the time. It's jolly uncomfortable!'

He laughed out loud, then leaned forward. 'No, as long

as you are willing to some of the time, Mrs Harvey, just to please me,' he whispered back.

She grinned. Her gums showed above her teeth, her face creased and her eyes disappeared, but he didn't mind. For some foolish reason he felt very happy and relaxed, and none of it mattered.

The day had gone well, even to the point of Guy conceding some of Dvina's good points, but Andrew felt exhausted and not at all ready to perform his marital duties. The kiss they had shared when Dvina had snuggled up to him the moment he'd slipped between the sheets hadn't helped. The kiss itself had its merits, as once again her soft lips had given him pleasure, but the flutter of desire it had evoked had died when he'd pulled her closer. It was the feel of her. It reminded him of the nurse he'd had as a child and of the matron of his school: nice women, but motherly and plain, and not at all built for loving in a sexual way. The image had killed any hope he had of consummating his marriage. At least not tonight, and he wondered how he was ever going to.

Not wanting to be unkind, he held her close and stroked her hair, trying to invoke thoughts of Lilly, his favourite whore. Nothing worked. Dvina saved the day by saying, 'Please don't think you have to . . . well, you know. It's perfectly all right not to. I have had a wonderful day, but that laced corset pulling me in as it did has made me ache all over. Bloody things. They're like torture instruments.'

He laughed, more from relief than anything else.

'You may laugh, but it isn't funny. One day I'll rope you into one and you can see for yourself.'

They both laughed at this, and he found himself holding her even closer, but more in the way he would a sister or a friend when giving them a hug. He could love her as a friend, he knew that, but as for anything else . . .

'You had better stay with me tonight, though, Andrew. I promise I don't snore. Only it would look odd, and embarrass me, if you went to your own bedchamber on our first night.'

He kissed her again, lightly, on her sweet lips. 'I will. I'll never do anything to embarrass or hurt you, my dear. Thank you for understanding. Like you, I am exhausted. Goodnight, dear.'

A sound woke him: a quiet but unmistakable sob. The light from the full moon swathed the bed, highlighting the form next to him. Disorientated, he listened for a moment, and as he did the day's events seeped back into his memory, giving him the reason for there being a woman in his bed, and for that woman being Dvina. 'Dvina? Dvina, are you unwell?'

'No, I'm sorry. I couldn't sleep, and then I started to think what an awful situation we are in. You don't love me, and I don't suppose you ever could. Why should you? I have nothing to attract you or even to—'

'That's not true. I mean – well, I can love you. You are easy to love. Look, I'm sorry, I truly was very tired. Please don't be upset.' He reached out for her and once more she snuggled up to him. He lifted his head and kissed her eyes. Her arm came around his neck and their lips met. Her kiss didn't tell of inexperience; she probed his mouth with her tongue, sending shivers through him. He found one of her breasts and, though very large, it surprised him to feel how firm it was. Her nipple responded to his caresses.

Her soft moans told him she enjoyed the sensation, as did the way her body writhed. His throat tightened, and a familiar clutching of the muscles in his groin urged him to push against her. Nothing about her repulsed him now.

Somehow she discarded her nightdress, and her flesh, soft and silky, cushioned his body like feather pillows. He liked the feeling. His senses heightened to the warm, loving, giving of her, and to the absence of bony ribs, hard thighs and the demanding of pleasure.

Every part of her offered softness and sweet-smelling skin. He let his lips travel over her, tasting, sucking and gently nipping. Her cries of pleasure let him know she was ready for him, and he knew a moment when he had to hold back, so aroused was he that he feared coming before he had time to satisfy her.

As he entered her a moan echoed the pain she felt, but she didn't tighten up on him or resist him. It took him a moment to fully penetrate her, but as he did so he soothed her with gentle encouragement and words of endearment.

When at last he felt the depth of her, the feelings taking him almost made him forget to proceed with care. Never had he experienced an untouched vagina, and he couldn't match the feeling to anything he'd felt with the whores. Soon his thrusting became easier, and exquisite sensations pounded through him. Arched towards him, Dvina stiffened, and a plea for him to stop gasped from her. It took every ounce of his willpower to comply as the spasms pulsated, clutching him from deep within her, taking him to the brink. As her cry resounded around the room and she dug her nails into his buttocks, he could hold back no longer. His own juices released, and he was lost in an all-consuming wave after wave of rapture, bringing from him deep moans that he couldn't control. *My God . . .*

Sweat dripped off his nose onto her forehead. She looked

up at him and giggled. It wasn't the loud, horsey noise she usually made, but a girly giggle that he hadn't expected from her.

Easing himself from her, he lay back. His mind couldn't equate what had just happened with what he had dreaded having to do as a duty. A happiness surged through his veins, and once more he reached out for Dvina. 'My wife, my lovely wife, come here and let me cuddle you.' And he found he meant every sentiment of what he'd just said. He found cuddling her a wonder compared to what he had experienced earlier. 'I think I am falling in love with you, my wife. Yes, I think I am.'

Her voice, gentle and loving, answered him, 'I know I love you, Andrew, and have done since I first saw you.'

This surprised him, but he questioned why it should. Why had he and others always thought of her as a . . . a dollop of a girl, rather than as a woman with feelings and needs? Well, he knew now they had been wrong. For the Dvina he had discovered was a good, kind, funny and very sexy woman. Instead of life stretching out before him in an ever-increasing spiral of discontent, he knew just the opposite and held an anticipation of good things to come.

'Issy, eeh, it's nice to see you. How's things at Hartington House?'

'Hello, Jane. Nowt's changed, but then you've only been gone a couple of weeks. Have you settled into Tarrington House all right?'

'Aye, I have. I love working for Miss Dvina, or rather Mrs Harvey, as she is now. And thou knows sommat: she's reet happy. Gertie were wrong about it being a convenience marriage. Mr Harvey loves her, and she adores him. I'll tell yer, Issy, he ain't never left her bed to sleep in his own since their marriage and, between you and me, there were plenty of evidence on the sheets and her nightdress to tell of what went on that night an' all.'

'Oh, I am glad. I couldn't bear to think of her unhappy. Well, I s'pose as it takes all sorts, as they say, but them two I'd have never matched in a million years.'

'And what about you, you dark horse? How's your plans going? Have you and Denny set a date yet?'

'We have that, and you'll be invited. We're going to have a spring wedding: Saturday 14th April at 2 p.m. at St Gregory's church. I couldn't arrange it any sooner, what with the sudden arrangement of the double wedding we had to cope with and now Christmas being upon us. Besides, Mrs Baxdale is talking of getting a trainee in soon, so it'll take me a while to teach her the ropes of the kitchen.'

'Well, this might be of interest to you. I heard tell as Hensal Grange might be looking for a cook in the New Year, and they're only just up the road from where you're going to live. It could be just the thing for you, as I know you said as you'd miss the money when you gave up working. You should ask about it.'

'Ta, I will. Funny me ma ain't said owt. She usually has her nose to the ground, and she knows I want to work for a while until . . . well, thou knows.'

'She might not have heard as yet. I'm privy to a few things afore the others, as Mrs Harvey talks to me. And Mr Harvey discusses some things in front of me whilst I am tending to her an' all. I don't spread owt I hear, but it ain't as though this won't be common knowledge. I mean, Edna is getting on a bit.'

'Well, anyroad, ta for telling me. I'll talk it over with Denny, only I have to go. I've only got the day off and I want to meet him from work. I'll see you next time, eh, Jane?'

Issy turned into the ginnel, waving to Jane as she went. The news of a possible place at Hensal Grange had lifted her spirits some. She'd been pondering more and more of late how she and Denny were going to manage. Now she had hope. She walked the long way round to meet him. She wanted to go by the two empty cottages and peer into the window of the one Mr Harvey had allocated to them. She didn't care about the state it was in; just seeing it, she could dream about how they would fix it up and where she would put everything. And now it might be possible to spend more of their savings on the things they would need. *Eeh, I feel so happy I could do a little dance.*

10

Bridie

Liverpool, 1875
Taking control of her life

'There's no work round these parts for a young girl. You should try to get into service; there's a number of large houses in Birkdale.'

'Thank you. You have been kindness itself.' Bridie smiled at the shopkeeper, a small man whose head and neck were the only parts of him visible over his counter. 'Are you for knowing where they post their vacancies?'

'They don't post them; you have to stand on the corner on market days. That's every Tuesday, so that being tomorrow and Christmas only a week away, you could get lucky, as many will be looking to swell their staff for the festivities. Those who are looking to take on ride up to see if there is anybody suitable. Have your bags with you, mind, as they expect you to go with them there and then.'

Bridie's heart lifted at this. To be sure, nothing could be simpler. Getting out of the house with her things would be after posing her a problem, but she'd just have to think of something. Once established, she could ask for a position for Beth. Now to find the bank, and see how much money it was that her pappy had left her.

As she went to leave, the shopkeeper surprised her by asking, 'How long have you been off the boat, then? And who are you staying with?'

She answered his questions, but sensing his sudden disapproval of her, she was for leaving his shop as soon as she could.

'George Bottomley? You're a relative of his missus then, are you?'

With a quick nod of her head she skipped into the street, glad to be out of there, even if it did mean covering her nose against the smell of the dock.

Shielding herself from the ever-present wind, she walked round the corner. Here the huge buildings gave her a feeling of being swamped. Most seemed to be trading houses. She wasn't seeing anything that looked like a bank, and after the effect she'd had on the man in the shop she felt afraid to ask anyone. She stood a moment and looked around her. Then she saw it, and her relief lifted her spirits. The red-brick building just ahead of her had the words 'Liverpool Bank' carved into an arch above a heavy, ornate wooden door.

The clerk peered at her over his glasses; his eyes held a mocking, unsaid statement. Maybe she didn't look like his usual customer, but she had business here, so she lifted her chin. 'Please could you tell me who it is I am to see about accessing my safety deposit box?'

His look changed to one of astonishment, and his voice faltered as he said, 'Er . . . um . . . come this way, Madam . . . er, I mean, Miss.'

Bridie followed him, repeating to herself the codeword. She

needed to maintain her composure, and forgetting the code-word would look odd.

He led her into a room and indicated that she should sit down. Taking down a large ledger from a shelf, he asked, 'Name?'

'O'Hara. Bridie Mary O'Hara.'

The pages caused a draught as he flicked through them. Stopping on one, he ran his finger down the columns until it hovered over a name. 'We do have an O'Hara with a box registered, but . . .'

'That will be me pappy, Michael James O'Hara. He . . . he is dead. 'Tis as I am his heir.'

'Do you have proof?'

'I have his death certificate here, and a codeword I am to be giving you, so you will know right enough I am who I say I am.'

He took the crisp parchment from her and unrolled it, his head bent over, revealing a stark white parting in his flat, grease-slicked hair. She cringed at him reading 'Died by his own hand', but kept her head upright, hoping her dignity would remain intact. As he laid the document down and eased his glasses further up his hooked nose, his dark eyes looked at her, impassive and uncaring, as he asked, 'And the code-word?'

'*Ta suil fredom* – liberty and hope.'

His lip curled in an unpleasant half-snarl, as if those words confirmed in him something he already suspected. She knew the feeling might just be her own guilt at knowing that the money stashed away must have come from her father's dishonest dealings, but if that was so, she was for having no knowledge of what things. All she knew was that she needed it. She had to make a life for herself and, however much the box contained, that is what she would do with it.

The clerk's oily voice broke into her thoughts. 'I take it you have a key? There is no point if you do not have a—'

'I do.'

'Well, I have to say I cannot give you access today. I need papers giving you the right to it. A will or some such from a solicitor . . .'

'But my pappy was for telling me all I had to do was to give you the code. I do not have a will, neither is there one in existence.'

His stare at her outburst told of his disdain. 'That may be how you do business in your little country, but here . . .'

'Are you after being the manager?'

'No.'

'Then 'tis not for being your decision. Will you be getting the manager for me, please?'

Once again he faltered, and it seemed to her that he weighed her up and down before deciding. Then his chair scraped on the wooden floor as he rose and left the room.

When he'd gone, some of her strength left her. What was she to do now? Her pappy hadn't been for thinking the whole thing through, but then he hadn't expected to die when he set it up, either. If only he'd given her a note, something written down!

A large gentleman entered the room. His round face had a soft twinkle about it and his beady blue eyes looked at her in the way her grandpappy used to. 'Now, young lady, what is this I hear about you not taking Rothergill's word for the way our bank works and demanding I come from all the urgent business I have to attend to you?'

''Tis sorry that I am for being a nuisance, sir, but 'tis

important I access the mon . . . the box me pappy left here. 'Tis holding what he intended to be me way of taking care of meself. Me mammy is . . . she died, and pappy left me and . . .'

'You mean you have no one?'

'I do have an aunt, but I am not for staying with them. Their ways are not . . . well, it is independent I intend to be . . .'

'But you are a minor?'

'I am, sir, but I have someone who is of age who will be a guardian to me. It is just as she isn't of any means, and we need what has been left for me.'

'Well, we are not saying you can't have it, but we have to have everything legal. Now, don't be afraid of that. It is a simple matter to a solicitor.'

'But I'm not for having a solicitor.'

'I can sort that out for you. He will interview you, and maybe contact someone from where you live. A priest or businessman who can verify your identity. He'll maybe want the registration certificate of your birth, and the death certificate of each of your parents. Once he has done all of that, he will draw up an entitlement document for you.'

'Will all of that be taking a long time?'

'A few weeks, I imagine. Have you funds enough until then?'

'I'm looking for work. I intend to stand on the corner of the market on Tuesday.'

'You are a domestic?'

'It isn't that I have any experience, sir, as I have always worked at home. But me mammy showed me good house-wifery and taught me to cook, so I think I will fare well.'

A smile creased his puffy cheeks. Bridie liked him, and felt he was one man she could trust. She smiled back. He leaned back in the chair and studied her for a long minute. Her cheeks blushed under his gaze, but not from any discomfort as to his thoughts, just because she didn't know where to look.

'Have you had any experience with children?'

'Only as it isn't long since I was one, sir, so I have an understanding of their ways.'

'Ha! I like you, Bridie O'Hara. Look, I am not promising anything, but my wife and I are in need of a nursery maid. Our two children are cared for by my own nanny, but she is ready to go out to grass.'

Bridie giggled at this.

'Oh, we are taking care of her. She will stay on and oversee things for a while, but I think she will take to you, Bridie. And after she has taught you her ways and is happy with you, I am sure she will remain an advisor to you. What do you think?'

'I don't know what it is I should say. I just . . .'

'Have you any references?'

'No. Look, I . . . well, sir, me pappy did things – I don't know what, but they were for trying to arrest him. As soon as me mammy drew her last breath, he took me away and brought me to England. On the way, he . . . he shot . . .'

'Don't distress yourself, Bridie. I think I know what happened. It was well reported in the *Gazette*.'

'Oh. But it wasn't after being my fault.'

'No, I hadn't thought that for a moment. I am sorry you had such a terrible ordeal, but now I have met you, I can see you are strong enough to recover from it. However, it is better it is in the open between us. Obviously I took an interest in the story, as I do of any concerning our clients. Your father was an unusual man in the run of things – not the kind of person who would normally come to us for a deposit box. Therefore his profile drew our attention.'

'Are you for thinking the contents are—?'

'It is none of our business what a man puts in his box. And whatever is in his is now yours, I am sure. But I am charged with keeping records that will stand up to audit, so we have to go through the proper channels before we can release it to you. In the meantime, I think if you would like to consider the domestic post we have available, then a trial few weeks would be the best basis, until your papers are in order. After that, both ourselves and you will know if you are suitable.'

'There is one other thing I am for having on me mind, sir: my friend – the woman who was to act as me guardian – I cannot be for abandoning her. She . . . she is in the convent. She isn't bad. Things were after happening to her, and now her family are not for taking her back. She's like a prisoner.'

'Tell me what you had in mind for her.'

'I promised I'd be looking for work for us both, and when I found it, I would go and help her escape. And we'd take a cottage together, though that depended on how much it is I have. She is hard-working, so she is.'

His laughter disconcerted her. Was he thinking she was silly?

'Oh dear, Bridie, never was there such a day as this. Here I was, working hard at a boring task, and in you pop demanding to see me, and before I know it I am offering you a job and listening to tales of kidnap.' He wiped his eyes on a huge hanky that looked as though it would crack with the starch holding its corners from folding. 'I'm beginning to think I've fallen into an adventure-story book.'

Bridie didn't laugh. 'But it is unhappy that she is. Some of the Sisters are kind, but others are for being nasty. And they can't just release her, not without there being someone who will be taking the responsibility for her.'

'Oh, to be young and to see things so simply! You not only think of doing it, but you tell a complete stranger of your intentions. Look, it seems I am in a tangle now, and one my good lady wife will berate me for, but I will try to help. Don't do anything about getting your friend out. I will ask around and see if there is someone needing a maid and approach the convent. I am sure they will be only too happy to release her, once they know she has a position. I expect she has no references, either?'

'No, she was only a young girl when she was put there, and it isn't the way of the Sisters to give references. They think of the girls as sinners.'

'I expect some of them are, though I know that some of them are victims, and it is sad that the sins of the men they come into contact with are put on their shoulders. But as I see it, the Sisters do their best in the circumstances and have no choice but to take all and sundry and try to treat them all the same. We raise a lot of funds to help them in their good work.'

Bridie decided not to argue with him. She didn't really feel she could. The way he put it, she supposed most people would see it. From experience she knew differently, but then it was as if there was only one alternative to it – the workhouse – and Beth had told her the convent was better than that. Anyway, she felt too happy about the fact that a possible solution for them both could come out of her encounter with this kind man, whose name she wasn't yet for knowing.

As if reading her thoughts, he leant forward. 'Well, Bridie O'Hara, I had better formally introduce myself. I am Mr

Proctor. You already know I am the bank manager here. My house is in Birkdale. As I understand it, your aunt and uncle are at present charged with your care?'

'I am staying with them, yes, sir.'

'Then I think it only proper you talk over my proposition with them and you get their approval of it. Once you have done so, and if everything is all right with them, come back here tomorrow evening at 6 p.m. Bring your aunt with you, and I will take you both to meet my wife, and have you delivered home again. After that, if everything is in order, I will arrange for you to start your trial employment in my household. In the meantime, I need your address for the solicitor I will appoint to look into your affairs for you. I will send my clerk back in to take the details. Goodbye, Bridie, and it has been a pleasure to meet you.'

'Sir, I am sorry to the heart of me to trouble you further, but 'tis feared I am as my uncle and aunt's intentions towards me are not good. I have to sleep in the same room as them and when they thought I was asleep I heard a conversation . . .'

'Oh, dear, what have I let myself in for?'

After he'd gone, Bridie sat back, unsure that she could take in all that had happened. Her cheeks blushed once more, as she realized she had told him so much, and how his attitude had changed towards her. He'd remained pleasant, but business-like. He'd given her the name of the solicitor and then taken ages to compose a letter, which he handed to her, saying, 'Take this to the solicitor. His address is on the envelope. It will ensure you are able to keep your dealings with the bank a secret from your relatives. I am doing no wrong in that, as you are our client and our dealings are with you only. The solicitor will make an appointment with you, and you can both take it from there. He will probably get you to sign something giving him permission to receive your mail here. There is also need of a document with your authority to have us communicate through the solicitor about matters concerning you. On the other matter: I am sorry, but I cannot take you into my service without your aunt's permission. I will hold the position, without advertising it, until a week after Christmas, to give you time to work out how to tell your aunt about it. Here is my address. You can come directly there to contact me. You may tell your aunt you saw the job advertised, if you don't want to tell her where you met me. Now, Miss O'Hara, I must leave you, so please don't put anything else on my shoulders. I don't want to regret liking you and offering my help to you.'

Bridie felt a twinge of sadness as she left the bank. Somehow she had offended the nice Mr Proctor, but he was still willing to take her on. That bode well.

Everything went fine with the solicitor, but as she stood on his office step, ready to brave the cold once more and make her way home, she wondered how she would get her aunt to agree to her working and leaving the cottage. She shook her head, knowing the difficulty it would pose. Sure it was a powerful problem, but she would find a way. She had to.

It seemed that Bridie had only just fallen asleep when her aunt tried to wake her. She resisted for as long as she could. She wanted to stay snuggled up in the slumber that had finally come to her after hours of pondering how she would tell her aunt about her plans. With Christmas having passed and the New Year now on them, the vacancy would be advertised by now.

But her aunt persisted. 'Come on, Bridie! Come on, love,

you have to get out of your bed. Your uncle's out the back on the lav, and he'll want to settle near the fire when he comes in. I'm to go out for a while. Mr Bottomley likes a bit of scrag-end on a Sunday, and if I'm not among the first in the butcher's on a Saturday morning, it is all taken, so it is.'

The click of the latch signalled that her aunt had given up trying to rouse her and had left. A fear of being alone with her uncle propelled Bridie from her bed. Grabbing her frock, she had it on over her shift in an instant and started to roll her bedding.

'Where's Jeannie?'

'She's gone to the butcher's.' Suddenly she found she wanted to discuss her intentions. 'Mr Bottomley . . . I mean, Uncle George. I . . . I wanted to say, 'tis grateful I am to you for taking me in. And 'tis as you have no need to be worrying about me being a burden, as I am applying for a place in service.'

A look of shock passed over his face. 'Have you talked to your Aunt Jeannie about this?'

'No, I . . . I thought you would help me. I am not wanting to hurt her feelings, but I can't be staying here. You are for having no room, and I am in the way and . . . and, well . . .'

His body flopped into a high-backed, wooden chair with worn-down arms. He sat a moment without speaking, then said, 'Look, hun, there's no need to go down that road for a while. Besides, your aunt thinks you have the means to help get a bigger place for us all. Is that the truth?'

'I . . . I'm not for knowing. Me pappy wasn't after telling me how much he put by for me.'

'Well, I suggest you find out. I'll get your aunt to take you to wherever it is Michael O'Hara put this stash for you and, if it's enough, you've no problem, have you, hun?' The softening of his voice set a familiar fear running through her. He pushed himself up out of the chair and moved towards her. 'You're a pretty little thing. How about you sort out paying for your keep in other ways, until you get your money?'

'No!' The shove she gave him had no more impact than if she had tried to push over a brick wall.

His nearness crushed her spirit. His hoarse laugh wafted foul breath over her, as he grabbed her hair and pulled her closer to him. So close that the sweat on him rubbed off onto her arm. In a gravelly voice he said, 'You don't have to fight, hun. I'm not going to hurt you. Your uncle's entitled to some of what you gave to your dad, ain't he?'

The feel of his hand cupping her breast and the rancid smell of him clawed at the fear in her. An image of her pappy, and what he did to her, filled her with a horror that ground a path of misery into her memory, but instead of giving into it and cowering at its intensity, she used it to give her strength to fight. It wasn't for happening again! Never, never again!

Lifting her knee, she thrust it into George Bottomley's groin. His pig-like squeal filled the room. His body doubled over. Foul words spat through his pain. A sweet satisfaction at the sound and the knowledge of her victory over him sucked the last of the horror out of her.

Without thinking where she would go, she knew she had to leave. Knew the blame would be hers. She snatched her coat from the peg behind the door and was down the path and by the gate before she managed to get her arms into the sleeves.

At the end of the street, a glance to the right gave her sight of her aunt leaning on a gate in conversation with a woman. This determined her direction. Taking her scarf from her pocket, she covered her hair and hurried as fast as she dared, so as not to draw attention to herself.

The strangeness of her surroundings and the feeling of being lost reignited the fear in her. Tears pricked the back of her eyes, but she gave them no release. She had to stay strong.

'Hey, watch where you're going, lass.'

The bump jolted her body and unsteadied her step. Strong hands gripped her arms.

'Leave me alone.'

'Well, that's a good one. Me, leave you alone? You nearly knocked me reet off me legs.'

Bridie registered that his accent was like Beth's, so different from the throaty Liverpool accent of George Bottomley. Hearing it conjured up Beth and put a longing in Bridie to have her friend here now. Looking up, she saw the man holding her was tall and dark-skinned. He had a tinge on him that she couldn't recognize, but one she likened to the smell of peat burning. His smile lit his face and put a sparkle in his deep-blue eyes as he asked her, 'Are you all reet, lass?'

'I . . . I'll be after being fine. I just need some fresh air in me lungs.'

'Well, you won't get much of that around here. I've never smelt anything as foul as the air in this area. Me name's Will Hadler. I've come across country from Sheffield the day. I just got off the train. I'm visiting me uncle.'

Bridie looked over her shoulder. The young man sounded friendly – and wasn't the good Lord for knowing she had need of a friend right now – but it was also true that she'd to get as far away as she could, for she had to be sorting out what to do . . .

'Is there owt as I can help you with, Miss . . . ?'

'O'Hara. Bridie O'Hara. No, 'tis fine as I am. I just need

to be on me way. I'll be saying goodbye to you, Will. It is sorry I am, but I have to be leaving.'

Turning away from him, she ran as fast as she could. When she reached a narrow ginnel, she dived into it, stopping a moment to catch her breath and to peep around the corner to see if Will Hadler had gone on his way. He had. Something in her felt sorry about this, but she was after having too many worries to give thought to it.

The ginnel opened up to an alley, which led to a rough-ground area strewn with rubbish. She hurried towards a clump of bushes, thinking to hide in the shelter of them, to give her time to come up with what she should do.

A horse brayed. She stood still. The smell of burning wood came to her, sending her senses reeling back to Ireland and the travellers.

'Who is it hiding in the bushes, then? Come out and show yourself! Let me see who it is I'm up against.'

Shock held her rigid. Seamus! It couldn't be him!

'Am I making meself heard, or do I have to take a shot at you?'

''Tis me, Bridie O'Hara. Oh, Seamus, 'tis me.'

'Bridie, Bridie . . . I'm not for believing the ears or the eyes of me!'

Caught in his arms, breathing in the smell of him, dissolved all her problems. Wasn't it as Seamus would look after her? He would be for knowing what she should do.

'Well! 'Tis as fate has intervened for me and brought you to me, which saves me a lot of trouble,' he said as he let her go.

Everything in her rebelled against being released, but she didn't show it. She only asked, 'Trouble? Why?'

'Wasn't it me as was planning to take you away from them two, after I missed me chance at the convent?'

'You have been after looking for me? Why? How?'

'It's a long story, and some of it I cannot tell you of, but I was to meet up with your pappy. When I arrived at the given place, I heard tell of what had happened and where they had taken you. There was money in finding Michael O'Hara, and I was for having some of it. Besides, he owed me a payment, but then didn't he go and take himself to the Devil before he could pay me? But I figured as you would have access to what he has, and can do the right thing by me.'

Shock flared her temper. 'Seamus Finney, 'tis a rat you are! Didn't my parents give you many a slice of bread and meat when you were hungry? Did you plan to repay them by helping those who would have seen me pappy hang?'

'Ha! You have the fire in you the colour of your hair tells of, but you know little of the truth, and if you did know it, I know you wouldn't condemn me. Come and sit down. 'Tis good you have come to me. Those two who had you are not the ones as should be taking care of you. I'm for thinking as they are only out for what they can get.'

It came to her to ask whether he wasn't after wanting to do the same, but shame pricked her. She looked away from Seamus. He knew . . . he knew what her pappy had done to her!

'Aye, well, don't be looking away. 'Tis common knowledge what happened, so I expect you'll be agreeing your pappy was deserving of his fate. He was a bastard, so he was. Your poor mammy . . .'

A beaten feeling took her. Her chest swelled with the deep breath she gasped into it, but the swell folded in on her and the tears she'd fought tumbled down her cheeks, weakening every part of her. Her body sank to the ground.

'Poor little Bridie, protected by a monster, for the use of him. I should have been for kidnapping you years ago, as me heart wanted me to.'

The warmth of his body gave her a safe place. Her sobs shook into him. His kisses felt right. She needed no strength to fight him. She wanted the comfort he gave her. Wanted . . .

'Me Bridie. Me beautiful Bridie. Haven't I dreamed of being in the deep pool of your velvet Irish eyes? Haven't I wanted to stroke this glorious red hair and twirl the curls of it around me fingers and count the freckles on your pretty nose? And now you're all grown and have the body of a goddess . . . Oh, Bridie . . .'

Holding her close, his hands caressed her, his lips planting kisses in her hair, over her face and on the tip of her nose until a peace came to her.

The scent of wood smoke and fresh, unspoilt air on his neckerchief as she wiped her face with it evoked the memories embedded in her of all that he was. And it was for conjuring up the feeling she seemed to have lost of freedom from the cares of the world, and of love. Sure, a childish love it had been, but sweet in the uncomplicated nature of it.

In his comforting of her he hadn't been for doing what the others who were meant to protect her had done. This gave her security, yet a part of her had wanted him to, and she wasn't for knowing how to deal with the trickle of disappointment that shocked the core of her, as this realization hit her.

'Are you feeling better now, me little Bridie?'

'Yes, I am. I feared for me life and didn't know where I could go. Will you be after helping me, Seamus?'

'Aye, if it is in me power. But tell me, what is it you are running from? Have they not been treating you right? Here I was, trying to work out a plan of how to get you from them, and 'tis as if me thoughts conjured you up. 'Tis mystified as I am.'

Bridie told him all that had happened to her, and she didn't shy away from telling him about George Bottomley's treatment of her. She wanted him to understand her urgent need of his help.

''Tis the grown-up world you are in now, Bridie, and without the benefit of your mammy's preparation. The beauty of you is hard for a man to resist, and you have a special quality that will always bring out the urge that drives men wild. Sure, 'tis only men of the likes of your pappy, and the swine you have escaped from, who will use you in that way. You will learn to recognize them and to deal with them. I'll bide me time, but your uncle will pay, so he will.'

Bridie didn't understand all he said, but the knowledge of her own pappy that she couldn't deny pained her. 'Seamus, will you tell me what it was me pappy had done before we left Ireland? I need to understand it all.'

Seamus shook his head.

'But if I know, it will be easier for me. I'm trying to defend him against what everyone hints at. And trying to find a reason for how he came to do what he did to me.'

'Well, some of it will shock and hurt you, but if it is sure you are?'

She nodded and snuggled into him as he placed his arm around her again.

'Your pappy was a bastard. He was for treating your mammy

like she was dirt. He had women doing his bidding in just about every corner of Ireland – women whose husbands were afraid of him and what they knew he stood for.'

'What did he stand for?'

'Before I tell you, remember you had no choice in the man who sired you.'

'I will, Seamus.'

'Your pappy was a freedom-fighter, a Fenian. Now, the wrongs or rights of his leanings were nothing to me. I am what I am: a traveller. I've no Romany blood, I'm just as me family was before me, and I make me living any way I can. 'Tis right I'd not think twice about handing a man of your pappy's character in to the police for the gain as would come to me, but then 'tis what he planned to do to me.' He went on to tell her of how her father had put Seamus's name forward to save his own skin, and then said, 'Bridie, many of the ways I make me living are of a dishonest nature, but still I rank meself higher than him in the morals I follow. The money he has stashed away is blood-money, and some of it he got by going away from his own cause and turning in information. Aye, he was a traitor. I know of it because there was a time I believed in him. I even helped him to gain some of it.'

'How?'

'He was in the drink one evening, sitting by me fire, and he told me of his wealth and how he was going to make sure his little Bridie was going to be all right, no matter what befell him. He convinced me to help him, and I set a fire as killed many who opposed the freedom-fighters. The men of the cause gave money to him to pay someone to do it, but he laughed in me face when it came to the payment and said I needed to do more . . .' He told her then of his last act in killing the wrong man. 'I had the choice to do him in then, or bide me time to get me dues before I brought about his end. I decided on the last course. Why put him to the Devil and lose out meself? No, I was for getting me money, and then turning the bastard in.'

The truth stunned her. None of it tallied with her memory of her pappy and, yet, maybe it did with the man she had seen at the end of his life.

Knowing of his true nature cemented the hate she held in her. Seamus was right: she could not have chosen her father. Memories of her mother weeping in her bedroom, where she thought she'd not be heard, and of the frightening feeling inside herself at these times, cut into her. But then, hadn't the truth of it all surrounded her? The cries in the night, the cut lips, the blackened eyes. But her pappy had only to lift her in the air and call her his 'wee Bridie' to have her heart fill with love for him, and to have her accept that her mother was clumsy and had fallen again.

Thinking of all this, she came to a conclusion: wasn't killing himself the only decent thing her father had ever done? And the redeeming fact of him doing so was because he felt the shame of his final act. Sure, he may never have felt shame at anything he'd done before, but he had at what he had done to her. But what of Seamus? The horror of his part in it all sickened her. At this moment he didn't feel like someone she could trust. But then, wasn't there a strange honesty in Seamus? He had told her he was what he was. He hadn't been for hiding his ways from her. Wasn't he her only hope? She'd have to be finding a way to live with what he'd done.

'Are you not listening to me, Bridie? You have to put it all in the past and carry on with your life. Your pappy isn't worth anything else. He wasn't in life, and isn't in the death of him.'

'I'm all right, Seamus. I'm glad I know what he was like.

I was for thinking everything had been my fault, that there is a sin about me. Even my Aunt Jeannie only took me in because of the money. And then, when her husband tried . . .'

'Don't be upsetting yourself again. Come on, now. You say he tried, but he wasn't for managing to do it, was he?'

'No. I kicked him.'

'Oh, me Bridie, I knew you had a temper in you. You were for showing it many times when you were a wee child. Tell me. How was it your pappy . . . ?'

'I didn't let him. I . . . You can't be thinking I'd let him? I fought. I fought with all me might, but the rolling of the boat and the strength of him. He got all my clothes off. He . . .'

'Aye, I know the way of it. But, Bridie, folk are of the opinion there is no such thing as rape.'

He was right. She knew that. The words of George Bottomley came back to her: 'some of what you gave to your dad . . .' Even though she had managed to stop her pappy, no one would believe her.

'Oh, Seamus, what am I to do?'

'I have been making you think about how it is others see what happened, because I want you to think about getting away. Right away, and to not take against using your pappy's money to help you do so.'

'Where? Where could I go that people don't know the tale of what happened?'

'America.'

'America!'

'Aye, America is what I said. You have memory of Patrick O'Leary, the Belfast tailor? Well, his son Jimmy went to America. Patrick told me he spoke of a land of plenty when he wrote home. He said I would be able to make me way over there, on account of how good I am with healing anything that ails the horses. He says horses are of the utmost import- ance to the Americans. We could go together.'

'How?'

'You have access to the money, do you not?'

'I am hoping to soon.' She told him what had happened at the bank.

'How long is it all to take?'

'I don't know. A few weeks, maybe.'

He fell silent for a moment. ''Tis as I was hoping to go soon. But as it is, with you joining me, there are things I will need to do. You say this bank man won't take you to work for him without your aunt agreeing? Well, Bridie, 'tis little choice you have. You have to go back. Say nothing about your uncle's actions, but talk to them about the money. Tell them how grateful you are to them and how you will be for giving them the lot of it, if only they will agree to you taking this job. Tell them 'tis better all round, and you will meet up with your aunt whenever you can, but you will be from under their feet and can contribute from your wages in the meantime. But, whatever you do, don't ever be alone with this Bottomley again. He could take your silence as you having thought better of refusing him, and be ready to make his move if the chance to do so presents itself.'

'But I don't want to go back.'

'You must, Bridie. 'Tis the only way you will be safe until you can get the money. I will set up camp near to you as soon as you let me know where you are. I will be there for you. You can pretend you need a walk in the evenings once the children are in bed, and come to me.'

This part of his plan softened the rest of it. She knew he was right, but then she remembered Beth. 'There is another problem to your plan, Seamus, and it is one I'll not be swayed from. There is someone I would want to take with us . . .'

Seamus made little comment after hearing all about Beth; he seemed to know he would not be able to turn her mind on it. He only said, 'Well, it will take some planning to get her out of there.'

'Oh, Seamus, you agree to take her with us then?'

''Tis a complication, I cannot deny, but I can see you have your heart set. Do everything you can to get some money soon, Bridie. There are papers we will be needing, and they cost. And there is a passage to book. But tell no one, not even this Beth. Just tell her you are getting her out, and together we will sort out how to do so as we wait for the time of you collecting your money . . .'

'Not my money – 'tis ours, for isn't it that the biggest part of it belongs to you, Seamus?'

'I cannot be at denying that. And the knowing of it helps, as I'd not like to think I'd taken it from you.'

'I know you wouldn't be doing that. And don't be worrying about a plan to get Beth out, as the bank manager said he would be seeing to it. He said he'd ask around for a placement for her, then write to the nuns. Will we be having enough money for us all, do you think?'

'Aye, there should be plenty, with enough left over to get us settled.'

'So you won't be going off on your travels and leave me, once we are there?'

'I'll never be for leaving you again, me little Bridie. If you will have me, I will take you for me bride. For as sure as God is in his Heaven, we were meant for each other. Don't you feel it?'

'I . . . I do, Seamus, and have always done so.'

When he took her in his arms, a yearning came over her. She couldn't understand it, but her resolve never again to have that 'thing' happen to her melted, and more than anything she wanted to give herself to Seamus.

His voice rasped in his throat as he moved her away from him. 'Not yet, me wee love. It is not honourable for a travelling man to take to himself the woman he wants as his wife before the vows have been said.'

'Oh, Seamus, I love you. And I'll be for doing everything I can to speed things along. Everything . . .'

11

Will

Liverpool, 1876
Decisions made

Will sipped the hot rum toddy his uncle had given him and listened to his tales of the sea. The spirit warmed his blood, but not as much as his encounter with Bridie O'Hara had done. He couldn't understand the feelings surging through him. None of them fitted with the fact that he'd only seen her for a split moment, and touched her for even less. But he knew it compounded his problems with Florrie and her persistence in trying to make him help her.

As if reading his mind, his uncle said, 'Now, Will, I can see that's gone down well. Let's hope it loosens your tongue, cos I'm of the mind as you have something troubling you. You know you can talk anything over with me. It often helps to share a worry. And as I see it, you need to start this New Year with a clean slate. God knows you had your troubles in the last one.'

With the relief that comes with unburdening a problem, Will told him about Florrie.

'I see. Well, it looks like you've got yourself into a fix, lad.

You know already you should have denied it the first time you heard your name mixed up with it. But it's too late for "should have done", so what are we going to do now?'

'I don't know, Uncle. I've done nothing but think it over, but I can't come up with a solution. Even denying it at this late stage would put me in a bad light.'

'Aye, as I see it, your silence has given this wench the opportunity to implicate you without even having to tell a lie. She must be a bitch to allow this to continue.'

'No, she isn't. I know that sounds daft, and a contradiction of how she is behaving, but her actions are driven by her desperation. She's been wronged all her life.' He told of how Florrie's life had been and what she'd had to cope with.

'Will, don't you see? Even to me, you're sounding like the likeliest candidate. You have sympathy for her, you won't have owt said against her and you want to protect her. You are in this good and proper, lad.'

'I know, but I have to get out of it. There's . . .' He nearly said there was someone else, but that was ridiculous. But then, as sure as he sat here, he knew it wasn't. For Bridie O'Hara had done something to him in the few moments she'd occupied his life. She'd affected his thinking. Got to him somehow. It was madness, but there it was.

'There's what: someone else? I mean, if there is, there's your answer. You can bring her into the picture and . . .'

'No, it isn't like that. I don't have anyone else. Oh, Uncle, it's such a mess!'

'Look, lad, if marrying this Florrie is out of the question, then you have two choices as I see it. Either you move away – I've told you, you can come and live here with me, and I've said as how I could do with your help – or you find the money and get her to this woman she's on about. And, thinking about it, that's probably why she is keeping this up. She's blackmailing you into helping her get rid of it. Cos surely she can't want to tie you into marriage, with her knowing you don't love her?'

'The first is no good. Like I told you when you offered afore, I can't leave Ma. And the second – well, I ain't saying I have nowt, but what we do have we're going to need. I couldn't ask Ma to let me dip into the pot at such a time, and I couldn't tell her what it were for, either. It just seems hopeless and so unfair.'

'There's a lot about life as is unfair, lad. Look, I've a bit, and I'm not likely to need it, but I ain't for thinking to use it to sort things out in the way as you say. I could do with someone taking care of things here for me. This is a big enough house to take Florrie in. You say as her ma treats her like dirt? Well, she could get out of her clutches by coming here. She can work as me housekeeper.'

'But what about when the babby comes?'

'That won't bother me. She can keep it here – I'd like to see a young 'un about the place. But I have a solution, if she doesn't want it . . .'

Will listened as his uncle told of a midwife he knew. When dealing with a young girl in trouble and unable to keep her babby, she made money for them both by selling the child on to someone who couldn't have children. He didn't ask how his uncle came to know about such a thing, but sat in silence for a moment, digesting everything he'd said. Something lifted in him. If only . . . 'It all sounds good to me, Uncle, but what if Florrie won't agree?'

'Tell her it's the only choice as you are about to offer her. Tell her you'd rather folk thought of you as a rat than marry her. I know – it goes against your nature – but there's a lot at stake here, Will. Your whole life could be ruined by this.'

'You're reet there. Look, I'll do it, but are you sure? What if you get saddled with her and you can't stand her?'

'Well then, I'll get rid of her once the situation is sorted. But you say she is a nice lass, just one as everyone wipes their boots on, so I should jog along with her all right. Besides, I'm not here a great deal. I doubt if owt will change much for me by having her here. She can have the big room upstairs as hers and I'll take the back room. The kitchen is big enough to put an armchair in for her, so she can use that as her living room. Which will mean we don't even have to sit together if we don't want to.'

Suddenly it was as if all his worries had lifted. It all sounded so right. Will didn't even have to feel bad about his uncle making a sacrifice for him, as it sounded like it was just what he needed: a woman to take care of his home. He felt he could jump for joy . . . But, he remembered, he had to convince Florrie first. He had to go against all his instincts and take a hard line with her if she refused.

He didn't need to seek Florrie out. She stood on the corner of the road leading from the station and waylaid him as he tried to pass. He didn't feel ready to deal with it all at the moment, but knew his hand had been forced when a couple of lads from the pit went by and asked, 'When's wedding then, Will?'

Ignoring them, he said, 'Reet, Florrie, I have to talk to you. I have a proposition as will help you out of your predicament . . .'

'Oh, Will, I knew you'd do the right thing by me.'

'There is no right thing for me to have to do! Florrie, how

130

can you put me through this – me as has always been a good friend to you? It beggars belief. I didn't know as you could be so devious.' He stopped as the light from the gas lamp caught a tear running down her face. 'Look, it's alreet. I know as you have no other alternative. At least I have to believe that's why you're doing this, as thinking on other motives makes me hate you.'

'I'm sorry, Will.'

'Stop your crying, now, and listen to me . . .'

At the end of the telling of his plan he looked at her, hoping to see agreement in her, but all he saw was horror. For a moment it nearly undid his resolve, but then he remembered what his uncle had told him: this was his life that he was fighting for – at least the quality of it, and what he wanted to do with it.

'It's all I'm offering, Florrie. I'm not prepared to do owt else for you. I've no obligation to do even this.'

'But me ma . . .'

'What's your ma ever done for you as you have to repay her, eh? She's used you as a slave; she stood by whilst your da beat the life out of yer, and now I hear tell she's desperate to get you out working the streets again. And we all know why, don't we? So she can spend any money as you earn on drink and baccy.'

'Oh, Will, I know. I know what she's like, but she had no life with me da. He beat her just as much as he beat me and—'

'And nothing. She were the adult and should have stopped it, or took you out of it. But she didn't; she didn't even lift her finger to attend to what got your da down. She never put a meal on the table for him; she didn't clean up. The place was like a hovel, and then . . . well, it's well known she put you on the game to bring in more money instead of into service or sommat, so you could make a life of your own.'

Florrie didn't answer him. Her face paled to the colour of the white lilies his ma had put on his da's coffin. The tears brimmed in her eyes, and he pulled her close. Her hair smelt unwashed and she had a musty tang to her. His stomach lurched.

'I'm offering you an escape, Florrie. I've sorted something so you can get away, and you can keep your babby if you want to. But even if you don't want to, his plan is a good one. A safe one. What you propose is dangerous. Me uncle says as he's heard of lasses dying.'

'Alreet, I'll do it. I know I don't have a choice. I'm sorry to the heart of me as to what I've put you through, but I—'

'Forget that. Let's just look to the future. You should go soon. Me uncle has a sailing at the end of next week and says as he'll look out for you coming afore then. I have money for your fare. I'll give you directions to his house. So get what you'll need together, without your ma knowing, and meet me here tomorrow night. Is that possible?'

'It is. I can't get out with a bag, but then I've only one change of clothing anyroad. I'll put them on underneath these. Ma's having a bit of a thing with the bloke as owns butcher's shop, and she's meeting him tomorrow night and going to his house, so the coast will be clear. I'll do it, Will, even though I'm scared and it ain't what I want. You've made me see it is a way out for me. You're reet an' all about me ma. She'll only miss me for what I could bring in.'

'I'm sorry, lass. I'm sorry there was no way I could take you on. You're a bonny lass, but you're just a friend and I couldn't . . . well, you know. I couldn't think on you in the way I should if I were to marry you.'

She turned away, and on a sob she said, 'See you tomorrow night, Will.'

As Will watched her walk away from him it felt like someone had put a pile of bricks in place of his heart. He should feel free – saved even – but all he felt was like he'd committed some crime towards Florrie.

'You're here at last, lad? Train hooted some thirty minutes since. I'd come to think you'd missed it and wouldn't make your shift tomorrow.'

'Oh, I got waylaid.'

'Who by? Not that—'

'Drop it, Ma, I want some peace.'

She huffed at this, and went about her way, getting a hot meal on the table for him. Will hated upsetting her, but no matter what Florrie had done to him, he still couldn't have her bad-mouthed.

He thought to change the subject. 'I had a good couple of days, Ma. I tell you, sea-fishing, even in the rough Irish sea of January, is grand. I reet enjoyed it. Uncle Fred were convinced he'd be swilling me vomit off the deck, but I had sea-legs just like him, as it turned out.'

'Don't even think of taking his offer, Will. I'd not move to Liverpool if it were the last thing I had to do to save me life. I'd sooner exhale me final breath.'

'I'm not going to. I'm just telling you what fun I had. By, I needed some, Ma.'

'Aye, and it looks like you've been after having some, an' all, but that's the end to it.'

For a moment he thought she was referring to Florrie, but she'd not have left it there if she had. His biggest fear was of her getting wind of what folk were saying. Well, once he had

Florrie on that train, he'd tell her himself and there would be nothing she could do about it. To all and sundry it would look as though Florrie had run away. Oh, some might think it his fault, but most knew of Florrie's situation, so would be glad for her.

All he wanted now was to get a good night's sleep and to conjure up the image of the beautiful Bridie O'Hara.

12

Andrew

Breckton, March 1876
Good news turns to bad

'You look tired this morning, dear. Am I making too many demands on you?'

'No, darling, of course not. Though I think those demands are the cause: I have all the symptoms of pregnancy.'

'Dvina, darling, that's wonderful. But are you all right? Have you seen the doctor? When—' Her horsey laugh, the only thing about her he still did not like, stopped Andrew in his tracks.

He hadn't quite taken to her large nose, either, he thought as he waited for her to stop the hideous sound, but it seemed to grow smaller the more he loved every other part of her. Even her well-padded body pleased his eye now, because of the pleasure it gave him. If his friends, who still derided him and showed pity towards him, only knew what delights she gave up, they would envy him. As it was, their disdain had begun to wear thin even to them, and they knew not to upset him by making derogatory comments about her. In fact, Guy had said the other day, 'Don't tell me you are falling in love with her!' And when Andrew hadn't answered, he'd said, 'Good God! Well, she must have something others can't see.' Then he had looked in astonishment at the wry smile on Andrew's face and added, 'Andrew, do tell . . .'

'My wife and I do very nicely, thanks,' he'd said. 'Now, let us leave it there. And you, sir, please have the good manners not to broach the subject of my personal life again.'

In trying to glean further information, Guy had come back with, 'So you are not restarting our Friday-night trips into Leeds any day soon, then? Come on, you know you miss the wiles of the impish Miss Lilly . . .'

'I don't, actually. She is nothing to me. I have all I want at home.'

To this there was another 'Good God!', and that had been the last time he'd had trouble with any of them.

'Don't look so worried, darling.' Dvina brought him out of his thoughts. She was no longer laughing. 'Really, there is nothing to be concerned over. I'm like my mares – I'll take this in my stride. Nothing to it. And nothing for you to concern yourself with. I'm already three months gone and will deliver you a healthy heir in September.'

'Don't compare yourself to your horses, dear. You are not like them. You are a woman – and a lovely one at that.' He still could not say beautiful. He wished he could, because she had an inner beauty and she loved him with every part of her. Inside, he knew he loved her in the same way, so why did he hold something back? What was the something that he knew he was missing? He brushed the thought away. 'And, my dear, you must look after yourself. See the doctor and take his advice. Make sure your maid knows, too. We don't want her forcing you into those corsets, much as they suit you. You have a reason now to—' The look on her face stopped him. 'Darling, I meant . . . I meant to not have to wear them. I . . .'

She stared at him for a moment longer and then her face creased up into a smile. Relief filled him, and he took a step towards her. The movement froze into the dreadful sound of the pit alarm. Its wail took up the space around them. Dvina stared at him with horror.

He couldn't react. His legs wobbled. He found the back of the chair and clung onto it. 'Oh, my God . . . Don't let it be the west seam. I knew I should have closed it until the work we had discussed is done, but it was so rich in—'

'Andrew! You didn't leave it working, not after what you told me about it? Oh God, how many men are down there?'

'I don't know. The early shift is the largest. They will have been down around nine hours now. I have to get over there. Maybe it isn't . . .'

'I'm coming.'

'No, dear. If it's bad, then I don't want you seeing it. I will . . .'

'The women will need me. I am the boss's wife. They will expect me to be there, and I want to be. I can help. I can organize whatever needs doing and reassure them. Keep them from panicking. Please, Andrew.'

'All right. It will comfort me to have you there. Oh, God! That awful droning noise . . . Let's ride over, it will be quicker.'

A crowd of blackened faces met them as they pulled up outside the main entrance. His foreman came forward, saying, 'It's bad, Mr Harvey. An explosion in the south seam caused a fall of huge boulders and earth and water. It's blocked off the south, east and west seams. There's near on fifty men missing, I reckon, including the shift supervisor Mick Harman . . .'

'Oh, no. Oh, no! Isabella's father! What of Denny?'

'The rescue team have evacuated all of those they could reach, and I'm afraid Denny isn't among them.'

Oh God! Isabella and Denny's wedding is only weeks away. Feeling the weight of this and of the other men still trapped, Andrew asked what operations had been put into place so far.

'The screen boys have been put to work with the men, barrowing stuff coming up in the cage, sir, and we posted Aiden Jackson on the gate to stop any of the women getting through. The blankets from the store are already with him to help keep them and any casualties warm. Someone sent for the doc, and we've carts ready to hook to those horses not turning the winding gear, should we need to ferry anyone to the hospital.'

'Good man, good work. Thank God the cage is still in operation.'

'Yes, the shaft is clear and we can lower the cage right to the bottom.'

As he said this a crowd of men came over the hill, followed by just as many women.

'That's good. The other shift workers have got out of their beds and come to help, just as I expected. I'll go down with them to assess what needs doing. Get the clerks working on identifying exactly who has come up and who is still down there. Tell them I want the names, and how many, as soon as possible.'

Dvina leaned over and squeezed his arm, trying to convey some kind of reassurance to him, and in a calm voice he wondered at said, 'I'll ride over and be outside the gates to address the women, Andrew.'

'Thank you, Dvina, but be careful. Don't do too much, dear.' As he watched her go, a heavy fear clogged his chest. From what he'd heard so far, things didn't sound hopeful. Once the tunnels below were blocked off and no air circulated, poisonous gases could kill anyone trapped there. That's if the water deluge didn't drown them, or debris hadn't buried them. How would he cope with such a disaster? How would he face the women and the families, and deal with their grief? It would all lie on his shoulders. And why now? Just when at last he had the money he needed to repair, modernize and put in steam winding gear? Oh, God, those poor buggers trapped in the bowels of the earth beneath his feet. Please let them reach them, please God . . .

Three days had passed. Andrew had hardly slept, or even left the mine to go home to change. The rescue teams were working in rotation trying to get through, but had made little progress. Further falls had occurred. Desperate to make a breakthrough, Andrew had joined the men, working alongside them. Together they had shifted cartload after cartload of coal, slack and rubble, but they had only cleared a few feet into each tunnel, and still a wall of the same material stood in front of them. Every now and then they stopped. They stood in silence and listened, but no sound came from beyond.

They now knew the names of all the missing men. Fifty-one in total. The road outside the gate had become like a gypsy encampment as the women and families set up makeshift shelters to await news of their men. Dvina had a kitchen of sorts working just outside the gate, with a huge open fire from which she and a rotation of groups of women produced hot soup, nourishing stews and copious amounts of tea in tin mugs. Andrew's pride in her actions, and in the courage she showed and gave to the women, deepened his feelings for her, though he worried about her condition and insisted she went home to rest every few hours.

Issy sat on the bank near the fence, where she'd been since Jane had fetched her from Hartington House. Her ma sat with her. Issy's eyes remained fixed on the entrance to the mine. Every time someone came up in the cage, she prayed they would have news of her da and Denny. She tried to keep her mind off what they might be going through, if they were alive. They had to be alive! Her brain wouldn't give her any prayers – she was prayed out – and a dead weight of despair had now replaced the trickle of hope she'd clung onto for the last three days. Her face stung with dried tears. She leaned on her ma's shoulder.

'Ma, I know inside me they—'

'Don't say it, lass. Don't give it sound, as it will make it the truth and I can't bear that, I can't.'

Issy turned. On her other side sat Mrs Leighton, Denny's ma. Her cold, don't-touch-me face was set as if in stone. Issy wanted to comfort her, but knew she couldn't. As she looked back towards the mine the moment of doom resounded in her ears as a bell tolled. A gasp like the wave of a crashing sea swept through the crowd, and she knew the men were lost forever . . . The announcement hit her with a searing pain.

'Ladies and gentlemen, it is with regret that the rescue team, in consultation with Mr Harvey, have decided that it's futile to carry on. No one could have survived. It will take weeks to bring up their remains, but we will not give up. May God rest their souls.'

The bell clanged again. Issy took the full weight of her

ma's body as it slumped onto her. And then another weight hit her other side as Mrs Leighton fainted, too. A terrible moan heaved from every woman, then there was a moment's silence before someone screamed. The scream escalated till it seemed everyone present had joined in with it. Agonizing cries of 'No, no, don't give up! No, please!' blocked out all her thoughts. Her body would not respond to her bidding it to rise; she clung onto her ma, and then knew a moment when the earth shook beneath her as a rush of people surged towards the gates.

A fear stuck the breath in her lungs. 'Oh, God, Miss Dvina . . .' Pushing her ma to one side, Issy rose and ran towards the makeshift kitchen. At the moment she arrived, so did the crowd. Grasping Dvina's arm, she urged her, 'Quick, this way, Ma'am, hurry!' But the crowd were upon them and crushed them against the wire fence. Issy struggled to fill her lungs with air and could see that Miss Dvina's face was turning blue.

The fence gave way. With everything in her, Issy forced her body to the left. When they hit the ground, Miss Dvina lay beneath her.

Feet dug into her back, but with a strength she never knew she possessed she kept it arched over Dvina's body. But then a boot hit the side of her head and her senses left her in a swirling downward twirl, taking her into a black hole of nothingness.

Issy opened her eyes. Confusion, stirred by the hazy world of nuns gliding around her, made her think she had passed on to the next world, but a voice – of this world – called her name. She lifted her head. Ma sat next to the bed, the only dark figure in the room of white: whitewashed walls, white bedding and white-clad nuns.

'Issy. Oh, Issy.'

Memory slapped her. Oh, God! 'Ma, Miss Dvina . . . ?'

'She's going along alreet, lass, thanks to your quick actions. Though the poor soul has lost babby as she were carrying.'

'Oh, no. Oh, Ma . . . and De . . . Denny and . . .'

'Aye, lass.'

'Ma.' Her throat tightened as if something had wrapped itself around it and strangled her words. She wanted to tear what felt like pain-filled tentacles from her, but she couldn't. She couldn't even cry.

'You're going to get well again, love. You've hurt your ribs and have a lot of bruising, but you'll be reet. You just need time. We both do.'

Issy saw the agony of loss in her ma's pale face, felt it reach out and connect with the void inside herself. She knew they both needed more than time. No amount of time would heal them. What had happened almost a week ago had ripped their hearts out. She for one would never get over it. She'd never recover from losing her da – the man who had loved her and taken care of her all her life – or from losing Denny, the man who had brought to her a love she didn't know existed, making her bloom as if the sun had kissed her. And now she would never ever see him again. Oh, Denny, Denny . . .

13

Bridie

Liverpool, March 1876
The betrayal

'Will you get out tonight after tea, Beth?'

Wrapped up against a bitter March wind that she thought would bring snow, Bridie rocked the wooden pram as she spoke to Beth through the railings of the gate. Baby Eliza had fallen asleep at last, and Bridie had walked with her and the two older children to the back of the large house where Beth now worked.

Everything had fallen into place these last three months. Beth was free and had settled in as a maid at a house just down the road from where Bridie herself had a position as trainee nanny to the bank manager's children. Her aunt and uncle had been easy to sway, once she had lured them with the promise of giving her money to them. All that remained now was to await the release of the secure box, and their plans would fall into place. Every time she thought of it – the long boat trip, arriving in a foreign land and, best of all, becoming Seamus's wife – excitement threatened to choke her.

Beth shook her head. 'I don't know. I'll have to see. Problem is, it's dark by the time I have all the dishes finished, and then we're expected to go to our rooms.'

''Tis as if you have no more freedom than you had in the convent.'

'Aw, it ain't that bad, love. I know where I'd rather be. What are you planning for later, then?'

'Seamus is wanting me to bring you to him. He says as there are papers we have to fill out and he needs details of you.'

'Oh, Bridie, I'm not sure on all of this. Why don't you go without me, just you and him? I'd only be a burden to you, lass.'

'Don't talk like that, Beth. 'Tis a wonderful life as awaits us. You are not for carrying on this drudgery, to be sure you are not, for I won't let you. We are so near to having everything ready, and Seamus says we should be sailing away by the end of the month, so we should.'

'You're reet there; the land of plenty sounds a lot better than the land of scrubbing and doing others' bidding. Leave it with me, I'll sneak some paper and an envelope and, after a time in my room, I'll ask if I can slip out to post a letter. That should do it. Meet me at the end of the road at around seven.'

Bridie's heart skipped a beat a few days later when Mr Proctor summoned her to his office in his home. Seamus had everything ready, just waiting for the money to pay for it all. And now, as she stood before Mr Proctor, she hoped he had news. For sure it must be her money he wanted to talk to her about, for he wouldn't be the one to tell her if she had not pleased them as a nanny. That would fall to Mrs Proctor.

'Well, Bridie, I'm having good reports of your work, and

my children love you. You have made a big difference in their lives, bringing them some fun, which they were lacking before. I hope you are happy in your position here and will stay with us, even after you have your hands on what your father left for you.'

Bridie could not look him in the eye. Deceiving him didn't sit well with her, but she couldn't tell him the truth, as Seamus had said she must not confide in anyone. He was fair afraid that if their plan got out and folk started to probe, his safety would be in jeopardy.

'Well, I have news,' Mr Proctor continued. 'Everything is in order for you to come to the bank and access your box.'

'Oh, to be sure that's wonderful, so it is.'

'Oh? I didn't realize it still meant so much to you. After all, you are settled here and your friend is out of the convent. Have you further plans you want to put into operation, Bridie?'

Thinking quickly, she remembered her promise to her aunt. 'Aye, I have, sir. Me aunt is desperate to get out of the hovel she lives in.'

'But . . . well, do they deserve your help? Did you not tell me they were treating you badly and they only had in mind to take what you have? I should think very carefully about this, Bridie. Have they got at you in some way?'

'I . . . I think it was mistaken I was about them. I . . . I was hasty in me judgement.'

'Well, the first thing is to see how much you have. You may have enough to give them something, but your future is what is important and I have given the matter some thought. You and your friend are well set up for now, but in years to come – well, when my children have outgrown the need for a nanny – you may need funds. You may want to set up a little business and a home, or you may meet someone you want to marry and set up home with. There are several long-term accounts that pay very good interest . . .'

Bridie listened to him explaining the prudence of planning for her future. His voice droned on, and each syllable grated into her the difficulty of her situation. This man wasn't for letting her just collect her money. He had in mind to take care of her interests, and she had no argument against him or the good sense he spoke. If only she dared tell him what she really planned to do.

'So, Bridie, I want you to come to the bank on – let me see . . .' His fingers leafed through a few pages of his desk diary.

Sweat dampened Bridie's clothes, and she stood as still as a deer sensing danger.

'Monday, yes. I'll arrange it with Mrs Proctor. The groom will drive you in at eleven. You and I and your box will have a meeting at half-past. Let's hope, once you turn the key, you will find that the contents will give you enough to make a small gift to your aunt but, most of all, will secure your future. Well, is that settled, then? Good. Now, you had better get back to your charges before they cause mayhem.'

It was all she could manage just to say 'Thank you' and give him a smile. He looked quizzically at her, but didn't question her. With luck he might think it had all been too much for her to take in. Too much! Jesus, Mary and Joseph, what was it that she was to do now?

'Can you not go there before Monday, Bridie? Just walk in and ask for your box? 'Tis yours, is it not? Sure, no one can stop you.'

'How? I have an afternoon off on Friday, but when I get to the bank, sure Mr Proctor himself will be there. He'll see me or, if he doesn't, that clerk of his will alert him, so he will. Besides, I haven't the papers. Mr Proctor has them at his bank and—'

'Shush a moment. 'Tis as you have so many barriers I cannot think.'

Bridie had been dreading telling Seamus, and his reaction was what she had expected, as she knew he didn't like things not going his way. She'd worried over it all for the rest of the day, and had had to lie her way out of the house to come and see him to tell him the news. She watched his brow knit together as he stood up and paced up and down, his fist tapping his forehead. Anguish and fear shivered through her body. She pulled her cloak tighter around her shoulders and inched nearer to the fire. Seamus always had a fire on the go. This one was set in a brazier made out of a barrel that she imagined had once had a life as a container on one of the big ships. She had no idea how Seamus had got hold of it, but then his ways and those of his clan had always been a mystery to her.

A delicious smell of potatoes baking came from the brazier, and she could see through the holes on the side that Seamus had poked two large ones into the embers. Although she wasn't hungry, her mouth watered as she remembered the taste of them, but she shook her head against the memories invoked and concentrated on watching the can of water bobbing about as it hung over the fire on a rod. The steam from it blurred her vision of Seamus for a moment, so that when he did speak she jumped. But his words were for giving hope.

'Bridie, you have to use the cunning I know you possess. You have to speak again with your boss and convince him you are powerfully worried concerning the contents of the box. Tell him 'tis as you always imagined being on your own when you opened it in case there is something of a personal nature inside, meant just for you. Tell him you would like to come in on Friday and have a moment in a room where you will not be disturbed.'

'But how will that help? I . . .'

'Listen, Bridie, I have it all worked out. Take with you a bag in which you have put a book. There must be one you can be getting your hands on at the house? Make sure it is as heavy as, say, a jar of the home-made jam your mammy used to make, and no bigger than the Bible as stood next to my grandmother's bed. Cos I am of the mind that your pappy would have put coins in the box – many a sovereign, in fact . . .'

Bridie, still mystified but afraid to interrupt him, listened to his every word. Nothing seemed clear to her yet, or even like a plan that would work.

''Tis quick you will have to be, Bridie, for the next stage to work. You need to replace the contents of the box with the book, and then put into your bag everything you take out. Have something to cover it, and hold it to you; and whatever you do, don't drop it. And don't be showing the nerves you will be feeling. Nothing about you must suggest you are up to something.'

'But on Monday . . .'

'Bridie, will you try to think ahead? You won't be going back to the house. I will wait for you and we will go to the other side of Liverpool until—'

'But Beth . . .'

'Is it an eejit as you are? Have I to work everything out?'

His tone shocked her into silence. Never before had Seamus spoken to her like that.

'Oh, me wee Bridie, I'm sorry. 'Tis fair worried I am, but

I shouldn't take it out on you. 'Tis as you who haven't had the upbringing to make you as cunning in your thoughts as meself and me clan.'

'You put a fear into me, Seamus. And you should know, I'll not be standing for you doing that to me. 'Tis right as I haven't had the schooling you have had in the duping of folk, but then wasn't it me as taught you your letters!'

'Ha! I deserved that, and I can see as I'm not going to get me own way with you. I like that, Bridie lass. I've always liked the spirit of you, and I can see your will is as strong when it comes to taking Beth with us as it has always been. I'll give me mind to the solving of the problem if you will give me a moment.'

Her anger boiled inside her. His saying sorry hadn't settled it. How dare he? She turned her attention from him. The pot bubbled and spat. She would set about making the tea to occupy herself whilst he sat and mulled over the Beth problem. She'd seen Seamus open a hatch on the side of the Vardo and bring out the supplies he needed, so she went to it and opened it up. Inside she found the same tea caddy she'd seen in his grandmother's wagon. The little key still hung from the latch, defying anyone to open it. As she took it out, the feel of it reminded her of the mission Seamus had talked her through. Would she be able to carry it out? Would she get to be alone with the box at the bank? She had to. She willed herself into thinking: *I can do it . . . I can . . .*

By the time she had brewed two steaming mugs of nettle tea, Seamus had begun talking again. 'There is only one solution I can come up with. Beth has to leave the house on Friday. She will have to get away under some pretence and meet up with you when you leave the bank.'

''Tis sure I am as Beth won't be able to do that. It'll have to be next Wednesday, as she has a day off then and we—'

'Is it obstacles you still need to put in me way? So be it, then. Wednesday it is, but she is to play the innocent until then as to your whereabouts. Can she be doing that, do you think?'

'Oh, you have no worries where Beth is concerned. Hasn't she had to come up with many a trick at the convent to get Agnes's letters and . . .'

'And who is Agnes?'

'She is a friend of Beth's, but you have no need to worry about her. Sure she hasn't been in touch for a while.'

Seamus's impatience showed in his sigh. He didn't seem to understand that her tongue ran away with her when her nerves gave her the gyp.

'Well, on Wednesday she is to make her way to the docks. I will meet her there meself and bring her to you. I'll have a lot to do around that area, so I will. I have a man I have to meet who will supply us with our papers, and I have heard there is a ship due in. She sails for America on the following Friday. We have to be on it, Bridie. No matter what happens, we have to be on it.'

An excitement tingled in her, but fear mingled with it as she realized how soon everything was to happen. And what about clothes, and his Vardo and his horse – there was so much they hadn't discussed, and she didn't think she could get out again on a pretext of needing some air. Mrs Proctor already showed signs of suspecting there was more to her little walks.

'Don't be firing off at me again, Seamus. It may be as I sound like an eejit, but a lot is on me mind.' She outlined her worries.

'There'll be money enough for you to buy essentials, and I have thought of the clothing you will need. There's a shop. It is for taking in frocks and coats and stuff from those who still like to think of themselves as ladies of means. They sell their stuff on to this shop, and the money they're due comes off the making of new outfits. 'Tis run by the wife of the man I told you of, who is to get our papers. It seems the pair of them get up to many tricks, but are after making a fair living, so they are. You and Beth can go there on the morning of the sailing. I've already spoken of it to the owner, and she will close to all other customers so as not to delay you. And for the money I am to give them they will have a trunk ready to pack with whatever you choose to buy.'

As she listened, her nerves calmed. Seamus went on to tell her about a clan of Romany gypsies in the area who would take his Vardo and horse and all the belongings he would no longer need. He really had thought of everything. She had nothing to worry about.

Seamus had paced up and down for an hour now. He'd even walked up the gangplank once, but had turned back just as the steward had started to welcome him aboard. Where were they? Hadn't he hired a hansom cab to take them to the shop and to wait for them until they were ready? Sure, they should have been here an hour since. His own trunk had gone on, and the steward loading it had asked him if it should go in the hold or into his cabin. He'd been for choosing to have it with him, as it contained the rest of his and Bridie's money. Now upwards of a hundred people had boarded. Most seemed to have crowded onto the decks and were hanging over the rails, waving at friends and family milling around the dock.

The boat had been in Liverpool for a week, and every day

he'd come down to gaze at her and watch her crew prepare her for her journey – his journey, the one that would change his life and put him into safety forever. He looked around once more. The girls were nowhere in sight. As he turned back, Seamus caught a glimpse of one of the dockhands and his heart stopped. Joseph Kilroy! If he was to look up and see Seamus, he'd be lost, for wasn't Joseph in the pay of the Fenians, and wouldn't he know of the price on his head?

The choices that he'd had now left him. There was no longer the option of waiting for Bridie, and maybe travelling on the next boat if she didn't make it. His pace as he sprinted up the gangplank would have earned him a first in any race. He shook the hand offered to him, accepted the 'Welcome aboard, sir' and hurried inside the ship.

Sweat rolled off his face, and he loosened his cravat. Bloody silly piece of attire, if ever he'd seen one! Why wear a scarf in such a way? Wasn't it good enough just to tie it around your neck and have done with it?

Finding an empty couch in what seemed to him like the inside of a palace, he sat down to try to think what to do next. In his hand he held the papers that would give passage to Bridie and Beth, and he'd only given them enough money to purchase a few outfits.

Could he take their papers to the steward at the top of the gangplank? But then, weren't they after being forgeries? And wasn't it possible the man would notice that, if he held them long enough?

Fear held Seamus back from going out onto the deck to look out for the girls, in case Joseph happened to look up and see him. There was nothing he could do other than leave without them. The heart of him felt heavy at the decision, but he had to accept it. Wouldn't he come back and fetch

Bridie in a few years anyway? Once all the fuss had died down, there would be nothing to stop him. Bridie was very young and would fare well. That bank manager fellow seemed to have taken to her, and didn't she say she'd left him a note in her box telling him how sorry she was, and explaining that she had plans she knew everyone would stop her from following? And in it she asked him to forgive her, and not to worry about her as she would be safe. Sure enough he'd be after looking out for her. He'd take her back. Bridie would be all right . . .

'Please, please find a way around this. To be sure, there must be another route you can take. We have a boat to catch.'

'Miss, if I could turn around I would, but there's not enough room to do so.'

'But you could back the horse up! It is stubborn you are. Can you not understand we have to make the dock before noon?'

'Don't take what she says as her being rude, driver. She's just anxious.' Beth took Bridie's hand and squeezed it. The look, and the shake of her head that went with it, conveyed that Bridie should not make things worse, but the action only fuelled her temper. The driver could get them out of this mess if he tried, but he just sat there!

'I'm telling you, if I could do sommat, I would. I have to earn me living, and being stuck here and not picking up fares ain't doing anything towards that. I've checked out the possibilities and there's nothing as I can do. There's a dray stacked with barrels behind us and a horse and cart behind that, and then two or three cabs. And even if they did all agree to back up for us, the roads coming onto this one are blocked an' all. So we have no choice but to wait.'

Bridie looked from the driver to the carnage in front of them and then to Beth. 'Oh, Beth, can you think of something? We'll not make it unless we can get going now.'

'I can't, love, but Seamus will wait for us, even if he has to miss the boat and book us on the next one sailing in a few weeks.'

Bridie felt sure Beth was right. Seamus would be annoyed beyond anything, but he wouldn't take all the money and sail to America without her, sure he wouldn't . . . She leaned out of the side of the hansom cab. Nothing moved. From what their driver had found out, it seemed a horse had reared and thrown its rider, spooking the horses pulling a dray. They had bolted, and the dray had capsized and landed on top of the fallen rider. The driver of the dray had sustained injuries, but the horseman had been killed. Although the rescuers had dispatched the casualties to hospital, the dray still lay upturned across the road. Its contents – boxes of fruit and vegetables – were strewn everywhere. It was sorry to the heart of her she was for those poor men, but why had it to happen now, and here, on her route to meet up with Seamus?

At last a gang of men arrived and set about righting the dray and pulling it to one side of the road. And from nowhere, it seemed, women and children appeared with bags and began scooping up the spoils. Their laughter and cries of joy did nothing to lift Bridie's spirits as another noise drowned them out. The nearby church clock was striking twelve! Each boom clanged the hopelessness of her situation deeper into her. She called out again to the driver, 'How long will it take to get to the dock from here?'

'Twenty minutes or so, if we're lucky, Miss.'

The cab began to move and once more shake their bones, as the horse trotted over the cobbled streets. Willing it to go faster, Bridie sat forward in her seat. Soon the buildings began to look familiar and a hope entered her. Never did she think she would welcome the smell of fish in the air, but as the first whiff of it stung her nostrils she knew they were close, and she could have jumped for joy.

That joy turned to despair. The sea, grey and churning, mocked her as it crashed onto the quayside unrestricted, where once the ship had stood majestic. On the horizon, picked out by the sun, all her hopes and dreams sailed away from her. Steam and smoke belched out of the two black funnels, as if making an effort to put as much distance between them as they could. Dismay thumped in every beat of her heart. Looking through the cab window, she searched among the people milling around and gazing out to sea, watching their relatives and friends disappear from view. Some cried; others stood in silence. Children still waved flags and played around in excitement, oblivious to the sad side of a farewell. Dockworkers went about their chores, winding in chains and clearing debris. Nowhere could she see Seamus.

'I'm sorry, Miss. Look, I have another fare to go to – one of me regulars – but I'll call by here in about an hour. And if you're in need of a lift somewhere, I'll take you for nothing.' Taking the arm he offered, Bridie didn't answer him. He'd already put her trunk on the ground, and she went to it and sank down onto it.

Through the mist of tears stinging her eyes she saw Beth give the driver some coins and heard him gee up his horse. The wheels grinding over the stones had a finality about them. 'Tis as it had happened again. Hadn't she been cast aside once more by someone who should have been keeping her safe?

14

Bridie

Liverpool, April 1876
A path is set

'Well, lass.' Beth sat down next to her on the huge case. 'It looks like it's me and thee. Hey, don't take on so. We've come through worse.'

Yes, she had been for coming through worse and hardly a tear had left her eyes, but they were for coming in a deluge now and she couldn't stop them. The very core of her wept. For her mammy, her sweet mammy; for the pappy who'd turned from a loving father to a monster; for the loss of Seamus, the love of her life, and his betrayal of her. And for her desperate situation. Sure it was she had no money, no home, and was alone in the world.

'Cry it out, Bridie, love. Happen as it is the best thing for you. You've not done your grieving yet and have had a lot to contend with these last few months.'

'What is it we are going to do, Beth? I . . . I love him. He couldn't have left me. How am I to live without him?'

Beth's arms came around her. Bridie snuggled into her like a child would to her mother, and that was how Beth spoke

156

to her now. 'I know as it seems like the world has come to an end, love. For a young 'un, you've been through mill and back. But you've your whole life in front of you, lass – and you have me. I'll not abandon you. We'll work sommat out.'

Young? She didn't feel young. Hadn't a million years gone by since she'd sat with her mammy a few short months ago? A tremble passed through her and she thought the time since then was like that shudder, for its heartbreak had rocked her world.

The faint smell of someone else's perfume on the dress Beth wore brought her back to the reality of their situation. It reminded her of the second-hand clothes. They had been for buying a whole trunk full of them. An idea came to her. She sat up and dried her tears. ''Tis as we could sell the clothes. What do you think, Beth?'

'That's the spirit, love. Aye, I was thinking along those lines. Happen as the woman'll take them back. Oh, I don't suppose she'll give us what you paid, but anything will help. P'raps we could get cab driver to take us back there.'

'Yes, but then what? We can't be going back to our place-ments. Even if I could be making Mr Proctor understand, you'll not be for standing a chance. I mean, we just upped and left. Oh, Beth . . .'

'We could go to Agnes, but – well . . . you see, Agnes works as a prostitute and . . .'

'A prostitute! But . . .'

'Aye, I know. It ain't what she wanted to do, not at first, but when she escaped from the convent she had no references and no skills other than housework and gardening. She had to survive, as we will have to.'

'Are you thinking we should do that? Sell ourselves? No,

never. I'd denounce St Patrick first, so I would, and that's something I'd never do.'

'No, well, I hope we don't have to, but I have thought on it meself this good while. Don't look so shocked. At times it seemed like the only alternative to me life in the convent, and it's one I'd take now, rather than go back there. You were only there a short while, Bridie. You have no idea.'

'But to sleep with men . . .'

'Look, neither of us are virgins – we had that took from us. And the taking rendered us soiled goods. There's not many men as would have us as their wives, but they'd pay for what we have to offer. Anyroad, I'd do anything not to have you go down that path, but I'd go down it meself to take care of us.'

'Oh, Beth, you're the best friend a girl could have, and I have dragged you into this. It is sorry I am.'

'You've done more for me than you can know, lass. If it hadn't been for the accident back there, we'd be on that ship.'

'Yes, but Seamus – the bastard that he is – played his part. Oh, why did he not wait for us? He said he loved me.'

'Don't start again, love. Seamus is a traveller. He's not like us. He has no loyalty.'

'That's not true. The travellers are for having a name they don't deserve. They have many qualities their way of life has given them, and they are always fighting against what folk put on them. I know things, Beth. And now I come to give them thought, they are probably the reason he couldn't wait. Though in the saying of that, I'm for knowing he has taken many chances in the past, and he could have been for taking one last chance to keep his promise to me.'

'Aye, that's my thinking too, but it'll do us no good dwelling on the fact. I think our best chance is to go to Agnes. She's been out in the world for a lot longer than us, so she might be able to help us. I have her address. She left me another note after you'd gone, but I didn't say owt about it to you. It didn't seem to matter . . . Anyroad, now I know why I didn't hear much from her, like she promised. She's living in Sheffield, and it's a fair trek from here.'

'Sheffield?'

'Aye, have you heard of it? It's an industrial town up north, the other side of Leeds where I come from, and . . .'

'I have, and 'tis right for us to go there. 'Tis as Seamus's grandmother's saying is coming true. She was always after telling me: "If something is meant for you, me wee Bridie, you will hear of it in many ways, before it is presented to you . . ." And here it is as I am hearing of this place for the third time.'

'Where have you heard of Sheffield before, then?'

'Seamus told me tales of it, and of Leeds and the surrounding countryside. He fought in bare-fist fights in both of them. And then there was this man as I bumped into. I only met him for a second, so I did, but in that time he told me he was for coming across country from Sheffield on a train to stay with his uncle in Liverpool.'

'Well, there you go. The signs are all there. Eeh, Bridie, you're a daft ha'porth.' Beth burst out laughing. 'And best is, you've no idea how funny you are at times.'

Going so quickly from crying with every fibre of her being, to giggling fit to burst, burned exhaustion into her, but somehow Bridie now felt able to cope. Prayers hadn't been the companion to her they used to be, not since . . . But what the feck, she'd send up one now and He'd better be for listening . . . Thank you, God, for sending me Beth. And Jesus, Mary and Joseph, can you please see your way clear to intervene

159

for us and be helping us? Don't be for making it as we have to be doing the sinful thing Agnes has to do . . .

Beth broke into her thoughts. 'Reet, that feels better. There's nowt like a good laugh to heal you. Now let's pull ourselves together and get busy sorting out what we can keep and what has to go. Cos we'll need to keep some of the things, the less fancy ones, as we've nowt else.'

Seeing some of the clothes they had bought for the second time, Bridie wondered what had possessed them to choose them. She pulled out an emerald-green gown. Beautiful as it was, she couldn't really see herself in something so fine. And the velvet cloak with the heavy embroidery . . . She flung it around her, and a musty smell was released into the air. The hem swept the floor. How could she have thought it looked good on her? Wasn't getting rid of the stuff the best thing? Sure, they had seemed like the most wonderful and exciting purchases, but it wouldn't be a hardship to part with them, as now they had nowhere to wear them anyway.

As the train slowed, wisps of smoke trailed by the window, some of it finding gaps and filling the carriage with a smell like the one Bridie remembered catching on Will Hadler. As they alighted and left the station, it seemed the smoke had touched everything in Sheffield and blackened it. The air was thick with it. It poured from the factories and from the huge chimneys rising up from the ground. It clogged her throat and stung her eyes.

'Agnes said as it were an industrial town, but I didn't expect owt like this!' Beth said as they stood outside the station. 'Oh, well, where there's muck there's money, so they say.'

Bridie didn't answer. Didn't she have a bad feeling about this place in the pit of her stomach, and didn't it take from her all the hope she'd had the moment she'd set foot on its pavements. If she was for having anywhere to turn back to, she would do so in a moment, so she would, but it was as if there was nothing left for her on the road she'd travelled since her mammy had died.

'Come on, love, let's make a move. It's been a reet April shower day today and it looks like another is on the horizon. You carry the smaller bag. Let's go over to that tea room and get ourselves some tea and cake. Eeh, I'm fair parched, and I can't sort nowt out on an empty stomach.'

Beth sounded like she did this sort of thing every day. It made Bridie feel better, and as they crossed the road she asked, 'Beth, are you for thinking they'll maybe know how we can get to Agnes's place?'

'Aye, happen they will.'

The man behind the counter reminded Bridie of her Uncle George. His cigarette hung from his lips as he poured steaming tea into two grubby-looking cups. To call the place a tea room was a gross exaggeration; she'd never seen its like before. It smelt of fat and stale bodies. The customers in there, mostly men, looked like they'd just come from a house fire. Their blackened skins told of their labour, but gave no clue as to whether that had been in the steel works, the foundries or the coal mines – all industries that were in abundance in the area.

The stir as they'd walked in became a hubble of catcalls when they asked for directions to Grimble Street. 'I've got tuppence. Will that get me a shag or a hand-job, love?' And 'What's your name, redhead? I'll ask for yer next time I come calling at Bruiser Armitage's place.'

'I wouldn't be for having the likes of you near me, you

fecking scum! Not even if you had a guinea to pay me. So you can shut your mouth.'

'Eeh, she's got spirit, and an Irish t'boot. Bet I could tame her, though.'

'Don't be so sure, Cain. She looks as though she could chew you up and spit you out.'

'Ignore them, Bridie. The more you banter with them, the worse you'll come off. Let's sit over there.'

'Are you sure about going to Agnes, Beth? I'm thinking 'tis a known area for what she does.'

'We have no other choice, love. It's nigh on five o'clock now and it'll be dark in another hour or so. Then what can we do? We know no one else, or how to get about this place.'

''Tis right as you are. We have to go there, I can see that.'

'Come on then, best do it whilst you're for it, as you've changed your mind as often as a prostitute's knickers go up and down as it is!'

Bridie laughed at this and felt better for it. Chiding herself, she thought: *Haven't I no choice other than to go with Beth? And wouldn't Beth choose not to go there if she could?* So she'd to stop her moaning and try to go with a light heart.

The red door opened almost as soon as Beth knocked on it. A big man stood in front of them – not big like George Bottomley, or anywhere near his age, as this man looked in his mid-twenties. The vest he wore exposed most of the top half of his muscular body. He had a handsome face, rugged with hard-cut features, similar to Seamus. His head sat on a tree trunk of a neck, and his hair – dark and shining with the oil that sleeked it down – hung longer than most men wore it. His hazel eyes stared at Bridie. In them she read admiration and something she couldn't put a name to, but whatever it was it stirred a muscle in the bottom of her stomach. She stared back at him.

'We're looking for Agnes Pickles. Does she live here?' Beth asked.

'Yes, she does. Come on in, she's . . . um, busy at the moment. Come through.'

They walked into a room twice as big as her aunt's living room, and yet the house had looked similar from the front. The other odd thing was the furniture. Dotted around the room, but not overcrowding it, were sofas that you would expect to see in a much grander place, with an occasional table by each one. These again looked more used to standing among riches. The threadbare carpet let the room down, as did the fireplace. The cooking range, blackened until it shone and glowing with a huge pile of burning coal, just didn't fit with its surroundings and would have been more at home in a working man's kitchen. This room aspired to be much more.

'I see you like our home, redhead. You can make it yours if you want, yer know. We have a room going spare.'

His smile spoke of more than just a welcome. She wasn't for understanding why, but the message it sent tingled through her. Confusion filled her. Sure, this man had a strange effect on her.

'Me name's Albert Armitage, though folk call me Bruiser, on account of me quick temper and me fist-fighting ability.'

Bridie didn't know how to handle him. The nerves of her dried her throat. A feeling inside of her seemed to be linking her to him, as if he had something she wanted . . . needed even. *By all that is holy, what has got into me?*

Beth spoke for them. 'We are looking for a room, and we intend to get jobs, but we're not sure . . .'

'You won't need jobs if you move in here, not two

good-lookers like you. I could put work your way. Agnes'll tell you. She does reet well, does Agnes.'

'I'm not for doing the work Agnes does. I – we – came here to get her help, as we haven't anywhere. We . . . we were after losing our jobs and the rooms as went with them.'

'If you're from that convent Agnes came from, I don't give much for your chances. Folk as take girls on round here want to know where they come from, and want references. There's nowt so snobby as those who've made money. They're nothing like them as were born to it. Have you any skills? Dressmaking or owt like that?'

'No, but to be sure we are quick learners, and as true as it is we have no background, we're not scum, either.'

Before Bruiser could answer, a door latch clicked behind her. A voice, not dissimilar to Beth's, made her jump, 'Eeh, 'ark at her! You've brought a reet one with you in that one, Beth, love. Eeh, come here. Where did you come from? I've never been so surprised!'

Bridie watched the person she assumed was Agnes put her arms out to Beth. There was nothing about her that fitted the mental picture she'd built up. The man who'd followed her down called out just before he closed the front door, 'See you next week, Aggie, love.'

Smoke billowed from Agnes's thin, painted red lips. It curled up in front of her pretty face with its tiny features and huge brown eyes. Bridie took in her slim body, with its ample bosom swelling out over the top of the tight-fitting basque she wore.

With Beth enclosed in her arms, Agnes spoke to Albert Armitage: 'Eeh, useless bugger, that one. It took him bloody ages. I were reet fed up.'

Albert laughed. 'He pays well, so you put up with it. There's not many like him.'

Agnes snorted and eased herself back from Beth. 'Well, love, it's good to see yer. Eeh, give us another cuddle. You got out, then?' Turning Beth to face Bruiser, she said, 'Bruiser, this is Beth, as I told you of. She knows the score, and I reckon as she'll be a good asset to yer, but I don't know who this is standing there trying to give the flies a home, but she looks like trouble to me.'

'I'm not for being trouble.'

'Eeh, I'm only funning, lass.'

'This is, Bridie, Agnes. We met in the convent. She helped me. She's a good mate.'

'Pleased to meet you, Bridie. Any mate of Beth's is a mate of mine an' all.'

The smile on her touched Bridie's heart, and she was sure it was sincere. She knew she would be for liking Agnes. Before she could speak, Bruiser gave a nod of his head and Agnes, in response, took hold of Beth's hand and led her through the door. As the door closed, Bridie knew an excitement rise in her. Once more the feeling confused her, for shouldn't she have been experiencing fear?

Bruiser stood up and came over to her. 'I don't think you are going to be trouble, now, are you? I'm going to look after you. No one will touch you. You are mine.' His warm breath on her face and the look in his eyes rekindled the trembling of the nerves in her stomach. When she looked away he laughed. 'Come on, sit next to me. Let's get to know one another better. You'll be reet with me. No one messes with Bruiser Armitage, and no one touches owt as belongs to me, without my say-so.'

'And who was for saying as I belonged to you? 'Tis arrogant as you are to presume.'

'Ha, I like the spirit in you. It lights up your eyes. Stop fighting it. You felt it, as I did. I've a fancy for you, and I reckon as you have one for me. Here, have a drink; I've a good bottle of gin. It'll warm yer and make you relax.'

Why was she for ignoring the voice inside telling her she shouldn't? Instead she took the glass.

'Now swallow it down in one; it's the only way for your first one. That's reet, lass.'

The liquid burned her throat and spasms of coughing took her. He laughed as she mopped her streaming eyes. The fire of it hit her stomach, filling her with a wonderful feeling, for didn't a welcome heat spread through her body and a glow of happiness fill the empty spaces in her, giving her a powerful urge to giggle.

'I knew as you'd like it. Have another, but take it slower – get used to the taste. Here, let me have your cloak, you don't need it any more. Your cheeks are reet rosy.'

Taking her cloak first, he then gently pulled the ribbon of her bonnet and removed it, releasing her hair. The strands of it brushed her skin as he lifted it and let it run through his fingers. Throwing her outdoor clothes onto one of the couches, he took hold of her. No resistance came into her as he guided her to the sofa. Inside she had a feeling that she didn't care any more. Why was it that she should? Beth was speaking the truth when she said as they were spoiled goods. Another sip of the gin and she was for having an eagerness in her, and knowing she would not be at the fighting of it.

Putting her hands down to steady herself, her fingers glided over the velvet cushions. The touch of them heightened feelings within her that she tried to deny. Bruiser sat beside her and brushed a ringlet from her forehead. 'By, I've never seen anyone lovelier.'

She tried to dispel the shyness that crept into her. Sipping the gin helped. Bruiser leaned over her, his face so near that his breath fanned her. She leaned back, the soft cushion accepting her like comforting arms. The glass clinked as he rested it on the table beside her, stretching over her body to do so. As he came back over her, he stopped and once more put his face close to hers. Deep in his eyes she saw a need in him. It matched the one in her, and she knew she wouldn't be for denying it.

She closed her eyes. His lips brushed hers, and his tongue probed its way into her mouth. The sensation curled everything within her into a tight knot of expectation. It splintered her emotions, sending urges through her that she wasn't for understanding, but that made her want to beg him to release her from their grip – so sweet and so violent was the force sizzling through her at his caress of her breasts.

The taking-off of her garments was hurried. Desperate to be out of them, she helped: she peeled off her underskirts, untied her bustle and slipped off her pantaloons, but he stayed her hand when it came to her bodice. Taking the cord, he threaded it out through the eyelets, then opened it with care, setting each breast free in a slow, controlled movement. Standing back, he looked at her, his eyes making slow progress over her body, burning a desire into every part of her. Nothing in her conflicted or resisted. The need in her flamed in its intensity. His words, telling her how beautiful she was and how her skin had the texture of silk, sang in her ears.

The dampness of his lips moistened her cheek. They reached

her lips and sucked them in, nibbling them until, without her bidding it to, she thrust her body towards his. The gesture felt natural and was for telling her that this was what she was made for – wasn't that what Mrs Finney had said? *'You will find a burning need in you for what men have to offer.'* Now she understood. This all-consuming need that this man had awoken in her *was* her: the very core of her. When at last he entered her, her whole body let go. It took her over. She screamed her joy. His every move sent shivers of thrills racing through her. He didn't stop. He pounded his pleasure from her, filling her with ecstasy that built and built until the whole world burst around her and delicious, violent spasms took her. Then she begged him to hold still, let her keep the fragile pulsating of her very being, which threatened to slip away from her if he carried on. He did as she bid and she clenched her muscles hard onto him, and then she was drowning . . . drowning . . .

When at last a calm feeling came to her, she relaxed back. Tears, the cause of which she did not know, wet her face, and total peace warmed its way through her. Not even his deep thrusting in and out of her disturbed her; she had ridden her crest. Her body had given its all. At last she felt his movements take on a new urgency. His groan became deeper, then he suddenly left her and rolled off her. His cry told her this was his moment.

The silence didn't give her questions. She lay content in his arms, thinking. Inside her she knew she was for wanting to do what they'd just done as often as possible – now, even. For didn't the fire still burn inside her? And wouldn't she be longing to do it with Seamus, as cross as she was with him? Imagine taking Seamus to her in that way; or Will Hadler . . . *Would you listen to me! What was it that had made me think of him? A stranger I've only ever met the once, and for such a short time?* But then, whatever had brought Will to her mind, she was for knowing that he did figure on her list of men she could lie with and take pleasure with. Was it sinful that she was?

Bruiser stirred. He took his arm from around her and sat up, wiping his hands on a handkerchief he'd pulled from the pocket of his trousers, before turning to her. 'So, you've had it afore, then? You're good. I've had plenty – I live for it at times – but what you gave me were best ever. Now, what to do with you, lass, that's the thing. I could sell you for a good price. I know a few pimps . . .'

'Sell me? Wasn't I just telling you, you are not for owning me, and I'm not something to be sold, either! Jesus, Mary and Joseph, you fecking talk as though I'm a sack of potatoes.'

'Oh, you're not – you're anything but that. You're beautiful in every way, and with the core of a real woman. Here, put your things on. We have to talk.'

The wonderful feeling that had settled in her had gone, and there was a pit of rage in its place. Just who was he thinking he was? As she dressed she asked, 'And what is a pimp anyway?'

'Oh, you didn't learn what you know from being on the game, then? Have you a man in your life, someone who learned you your skills?'

'What skills is it you are speaking of? How is it you can do what you did just now, and then talk as if it was a business thing, or something? Didn't you be for . . . ?'

'It was business. Nice – in fact very special – but business all the same. Though, having tasted what you have, I am

169

tempted to keep it all to meself. But then you could be worth a packet to me.' He explained what a pimp did.

Bridie sat down. She swallowed hard to keep her temper locked inside. Something told her this was a dangerous man. The need of her was gone from his eyes; they now glinted with a cruel light. A warning conveyed itself to her. Oh, holy Mary, Mother of God, what had she done? But then she was for not being able to help herself, and she knew the truth of it – she would be for doing it again, if he asked . . .

PART TWO

Warts and All

1880–93

15

Andrew

Breckton, 1880
A change in fortune

Andrew's eyes prickled with unshed tears. How much more could they bear? He smoothed the stray strands of Dvina's hair, trying to soothe her with the gesture, but knowing it was futile. Her sobbing continued and he thought it best not to stop her, and just held her until she could come to a place of calmness. He felt her agony. God knows they had plenty to cry about, but this latest news, coming as it did after her losing yet another baby – their third in the five years since they were married, was too much for her. As it was for him, but as ever he had to keep strong. He'd liked his father-in-law very much and would miss him. His passing had been a blow to them both.

'My poor darling, you have so much on your shoulders. You have been very brave and have shown a remarkable strength.'

'Oh, Andrew, what would I do without you?' Dvina lifted her face to his, her misery clutching at him.

He brushed her wet cheek with his hand. 'Come, dear, let

me help you to your bed. You need to rest. I will get Jane to help you.'

She didn't resist. Once in her room, she asked, 'Will you come to see me in about an hour or so? I will feel better then, but I'm just so tired. Maybe we could ride out later – that always makes me feel better.'

'Yes, of course, darling. I will bring you up some of the lovely chocolate drink the new girl in the kitchen makes. You love that.' He kissed her tenderly and went in search of Jane, her maid.

Once back in his study, he thought over the implications of his father-in-law's sudden death. It wasn't a huge mine, but Tacker's Mine would now belong to him, along with all of its assets. It was his nearest rival, though he had lately been in talks with his father-in-law about joining up the two. The engineers had done a survey and had found that it was a viable proposition. The seams of Tacker's Mine were rich, and not mined to their full capacity. If he went ahead with the plans to amalgamate – or even if he didn't – he would need more of a workforce to make sure the mine reached its potential. He pondered this. Where would he get the men he would need?

With this question came the awful memory of the tragic disaster of nearly four and a half years ago, which had taken almost his entire workforce and left a gulf filled with an agony of grief that was still felt to this day. He recalled how replacing those skilled men hadn't been easy, and how he'd had to go as far as Ireland to make up the shortfall. Even if he did manage to get over the recruitment problem this time, he would need more housing. That wouldn't be too difficult, as there was land available. The fields he leased out for grazing at the top of the lane would be ideal, and he had the funds to finance such a plan.

He'd have to talk it all over with Dvina. Thinking about it, maybe it was time to sort out the Irish a bit better. Their accommodation wasn't really suitable and hadn't been intended as permanent homes. It might be an idea to build enough cottages to move workers who had been with him a long time from the Miners' Row into the new, bigger houses. He could then move the Irish into the present cottages. Yes, he thought Dvina would go along with that – she'd taken him to task in the past about the conditions in which the Irish community lived.

He sat back and thought of how Dvina had made a difference to every aspect of his life. They shared everything and he discussed everything with her, including his business worries, and her advice was often invaluable. And then there was the other side to her: as a wife and lover, she had all he could wish for – except, well, he still found it difficult on social occasions, and more often than not he turned down invitations. *God, what has put this stupid pride – this fear of humiliation – into me, where my peers are concerned?* And was it the same bravado that kept him seeking the excitements that Lilly offered him? Because, to his shame, he'd long since resumed his visits to her, and they had become more frequent with time. *But why? Why?*

He struggled to explain it to himself, because Dvina more than satisfied him. Even thinking about the pleasure she gave provoked a twitch in his groin. His hand sank deep into his pocket and he felt the throb of an erection pending.

Standing and walking over to the window, he tried to decipher what it was that he needed from Lilly. He could only think it was the stimulation of the illicit nature of having sex with her, and her raw approach to it. No loving feelings, just animal-like coupling, with nothing barred. He flushed, thinking of some of the more bizarre sexual practices she enjoyed and the pleasure they gave him.

A walk would be the thing. To calm himself. He was behaving like a young whippersnapper, with nothing other than sex to think about. Good God, with everything that was happening, he felt ashamed of himself.

The garden looked lovely. The hazy, early July sun drenched it in light, and made the colours of the many flowers more vivid: reds, golds, pinks and whites danced before him. He'd remembered to pick Jeremy's letter up off his desk and had it in his pocket. He hadn't had time to read it yet, though he'd had it a couple of days now. Of course the news in it would be out of date, as it took weeks or months for Jeremy's mail to arrive from Africa. Andrew knew the reports from that quarter were not good, so in some ways he had been putting off reading it.

Sitting on his favourite bench under the ancient oak tree, he tore open what had started life as a crisp brown envelope, but – after much handling on its journey of thousands of miles – was now crumpled and a little grubby:

My dear stepbrother – Jeremy had called him that from the moment his mother had married Jeremy's father, even before the official adoption – *I haven't anything promising to tell you. Things here are escalating and we are suffering many losses against the fiercely independent Boers, even though they have no regular army. The farmers form military units and call themselves commandos. They elect officers as they need them. Their uniform is non-existent, but their dress is effective, as they don everyday dark-grey or earth-toned farming clothes, whereas we stick out against the African landscape in our red jackets and black trousers with a red stripe down each side. They are not very well equipped, but lethal with their single-shot Westley Richards rifles. As natural hunting men, they have learned over the years to fire from cover and make the first shot count, knowing that, if they missed, the game would be long gone.*

We are no match for them. They can draw on years of experience of fighting frontier skirmishes with numerous and indigenous African tribes. They rely more on mobility, stealth, marksmanship and initiative, while we British emphasize the traditional military values of command, discipline, formation and synchronized firepower. We fire volleys on command, which is useless against an unseen enemy, but we haven't had training in the art of marksmanship. They are just picking us off.

The Irish have suffered heavy losses, and their leader – a friend of mine, Lieutenant-Colonel Anstruther – lost his life. This devastating event has prompted me to write in such detail to you about what is going on, because: one, writing it all down helps me come to terms with it; and two, I fear I will not make it home.

I want you to know, my dear stepbrother, that if that happens you are to take the inheritance my father spoke to you about, without any compunction. I know you will be a worthy owner and keeper of Hensal Grange. Look on it that in some ways fate has taken a hand and brought you back to your destiny, because but for mistakes made in the past, it would all belong to you anyway. Besides, I chose to do what I do: my life is the Army, and fighting for my country is an honour. Should I lose my life doing so, then I would have given my all for my beliefs and my principles.

Just in case: goodbye, my brother. Live a happy life and prosper.

By the way, I received your letter. I am so sorry you still have no heir and I feel the pain of your losses, but it will happen, I am sure.

Give my fondest love to my dearest cousin Dvina, and God bless you both. Take care of my father, if what I fear happens, and of course your beautiful mother. I am so happy to have seen them find such a deep love together, as it seems you and Dvina have.

My love and very best wishes, Jeremy.

Once more the tears threatened. Something told him Jeremy was gone. How could he survive? As an officer, he would lead from the front, and if the Boers were that accurate, what chance did he stand? *My God, he didn't realize how much he thought of Jeremy.* But then they had always found a common ground, and the marriage and the adoption had cemented their friendship. Andrew had been saddened when Jeremy did go into the Army. He'd hoped it had been a whim, but was glad Jeremy was doing something he'd wanted to do. Such a pity this bloody war with the Boers had happened.

An overwhelming urge took him to be with Dvina. He called into his dressing room on the way to her bedroom and refreshed his face. Going through the connecting door, he saw that she was still asleep. Taking great care not to make a sound, he tiptoed over to the door, turned the key, then slipped off his clothes and climbed in next to her. It seemed as if, even in sleep, she knew he needed the comfort of her soft body as she snuggled up to him. The feel of her re-awakened his earlier ardour. He pressed close to her, enjoying the feeling of his need taking hold of him. Dvina stirred, and in a sleepy voice said, 'My naughty man, this is not what I meant when I asked you to come to me. And it's not chocolate you have brought to me, is it?'

'Sorry, darling, but now you will have to punish me, won't you?'

She laughed, and it bordered on the horsey sound that still irritated him, but he didn't mind. Better that than her tears. He couldn't bear her to be unhappy. He knew, of course, that she would be, very much so, over the next weeks and months, but they would still have these moments – when he could do something about her misery, when he could love her so intensely that she forgot everything, for a short time at least.

A huge, satisfied sigh told him Dvina had enjoyed, needed and wanted the marathon love-making session they had just indulged in. 'I take it you can cope better now, darling?'

'Yes, just a little. That was wonderful. The best yet.'

'Ha, you always say that, but I'm glad it helped. It certainly helped me.'

'Oh, Andrew, I'm sorry. Those were wonderful feelings you just gave me – and I did forget during it – but it is back with me now. I am so going to miss Daddy.'

'I know, and you must cry whenever you need to, and come to me for comfort. I'll always be there for you.'

'And will your means of comfort be like you have just demonstrated? If so, I may come to you more often than you would like.'

Her giggle warmed him, and he wondered if she could manage to talk about the all-important things on his mind. 'Have you given thought to the future, darling? The mine and Hartington House?'

'I haven't, but I suppose I must. I am the sole heir, so we

have a lot more responsibility. Of course, the mine and its future will be down to you, my love.'

'And the house and land? They are much bigger than we have here. Would you want to move into it? Only . . . well, I'm worried about the distance from Hensal Grange Mine.'

'No, no, I couldn't go back. Too many memories. Mummy dying so slowly, and now Daddy taken from me without goodbyes . . .' She swallowed hard. 'And, you know, I didn't have a happy childhood there: no friends or family of my own age. I only really had the animals – the horses in particular – and the servants for company.'

'Oh dear, that makes me feel sad. But you are happy now?'

'Very, you know that. Anyway, I think we should sell Hartington. It would give us an amazing amount of capital, and I guess you will want to go ahead with the plans to merge the mines?'

'Yes.' He told her the problems he envisaged and, as he expected, she put forward solutions.

'There are a few mines struggling and laying off men, don't forget, so we could pick up the skilled labour from those now unemployed, or facing that prospect. We'd need to advertise in the local papers in Sheffield, Leeds and the Midlands for that. Then there is always Ireland again: the Irish have a little community of their own in Breckton, so they would know of family and friends who would jump at coming over for a job. That would solve the problem of the unskilled labour you might need.'

'Nothing seems much of a problem when I discuss it with you, my darling. You are such a support, but . . . well, there is something else. Do you feel strong enough to take in what might be more bad news?'

'Oh, Andrew, what is it? Please don't say Jeremy . . .'

'I'm sorry, darling. It isn't as if there's been any definite news, but . . .' He told her about the letter.

'Oh no, poor Jeremy. And poor Uncle Edgar. How will he cope?'

'I don't think he will. He has looked very frail lately.'

'Well, nothing is certain; not like my darling daddy. Can we talk about that for a while? There are a lot of arrangements to make – an announcement, a funeral – and it won't let up as we get into sorting out the house and the business.'

'You're right, of course. I am planning on meeting up with Guy tomorrow.' Guilt wormed into him, as he knew how his meetings with Guy always ended. And after what he'd just had with Dvina, he felt surprised that the prospect still excited him.

'Couldn't Guy come here? I . . . I mean . . . well, I don't want to be alone . . . not to dine alone.'

Good God, did she know? No, of course not. Dvina had no side to her: she said what she meant, and it was natural that she wouldn't want to be alone, but . . .

'That wouldn't solve a lot of the things I have to do, darling. I have to go to the solicitor and the bank. Then I need to meet with the undertaker and the vicar, besides arranging the opening and cleaning of your family vault, and I need to see to the announcement in the paper. I thought to do all that before I met Guy. He will be very useful in the selling of Hartington.' *I'm going on too much, if she suspected anything* . . . 'Look, why don't we ride over to Agatha's and get her to come over to be with you. I shall never know why you two get on so well. You are the first person I have ever met to actually *like* my sister.'

'No! I mean – I'll be all right. Agatha says things. She makes me think that you . . .'

181

Damn and blast that bitch of a sister of mine!

Andrew's shock at what she'd said must have registered on his face, because Dvina, seeming to misread the reason for it, stammered out an apology. 'I . . . I'm sorry, my darling, please don't think I ever doubted you. It's . . . it's just – well, at this time when I am so vulnerable, I can't take listening to her innuendos. Usually I can brush them off, but . . .'

Her arm had come around him and the remorse in her voice, though it soothed his fear, only served to compound his guilt. 'I never thought that for a moment, my dear, but I am so angry. That blasted sister of mine – how dare she? She is so riddled with jealousy over our happiness, because she thought I would wallow in misery. She hates it that I do not.'

'Did you think you would wallow in misery being married to me?'

'I was very apprehensive, as you must have been.'

'Yes, but you were a catch and I had always had secret feelings for you. I was, and am, a plain-Jane, frumpy, horsey . . . Oh, I know what everyone says about me, and the pitying looks they give you. After all, I cannot even give you an heir. And they must think, poor you, for having to do your duty with me, to try to produce one.'

'Dvina! My darling, how can you think that?'

His heart sank into a miserable pit of guilt. He knew what she said was true. He'd had to defend her against snide remarks on many an occasion, but he hadn't helped things with his visits to Lilly . . . *Oh, God! I feel so wretched. Why can't others see her inner beauty and my happiness with her? And why do I still need to visit Lilly, which only fuels their assumptions?*

'Dvina, my darling, I love you beyond anything. You are my soulmate, my life, but . . . well, maybe I have kept that to myself too much, instead of celebrating it openly. I don't know why. It was just something we knew we had, but from now on others will know, too. I will no longer allow them to speculate about whether I want to be with you. I will shout it from the rooftops. Once our mourning period is over, we will entertain more, socialize more. People will see our happiness at the dinner parties we will throw, and we will attend their functions. They will see the beauty in you that I see.'

'Really, you mean it? Oh, darling!'

The relief he felt in her hug jarred him even more. He'd insulted her by keeping their relationship so private. My God, he had a lot to answer for – and after all she had given him. But then she had never once complained about their lack of a social life; she had seemed happy to just have him.

Of all the pig-headed thoughts! For almost five years I've kept her hidden away, enjoying all she had to offer, but afraid of what others would think of me for doing so. And the Lilly thing – that was part of it, I know that now. All part of me trying to show my friends I am still the man they thought I was. Well, they would bloody well learn that a man needed no more than what Dvina could offer. There was no more – nothing that could compare. And to think I've put myself in danger of losing it!

He held her tightly. The stinging tears that had threatened him so often of late brimmed over. Sobs racked him. If Dvina guessed why, she didn't say; she just held him and spoke soothing words.

'It's all right, darling. I know how you feel about me, but I do want the world to know. I don't want to feel you are ashamed of me, but because of the happiness you have brought to me, I haven't minded, really. If this means, though, that we can go out together to other than family functions and let others see our happiness, then you have just completed my world.'

'What can I say? I feel so ashamed. So ashamed . . .'

'You don't have to say anything. It is over. We can go forward, like you say, after the mourning period. Not that my mourning of Daddy will cease when the official mourning period does. It will always be with me. He was very special.'

'He was. I was very fond of him.'

'You know, he knew where my heart lay, and when he saw a chance – with Uncle Edgar marrying your mother – he moved Heaven and Earth to get you for me. He did that with everything I ever wanted. It was his way of trying to make it up to me for not having given me any good features, to enhance my chances as a woman. Or so my aunt – his sister – told me. She was very like Agatha.'

'But, he did, darling. He gave you your kindness, your understanding and the inner beauty that shines through your lovely grinning smile, which lights up the world.'

'Oh, yes, and what about my horsey laugh?' She bellowed it out at that moment, and he couldn't help but laugh with her. He knew it to be a healing laughter, giving closure to the selfish way he had run his marriage. At least at this moment he thought it had. *But can I really live without my visits to Lilly . . . ?*

16

Bridie and Will

Sheffield, 1880
Love cannot be denied

'Well, young Will Hadler! We've never had the pleasure of your company in the bar afore, lad. What's brought you in of a sudden?'

'He's having his first jug of ale and looking for his first dip, if you ask me owt, Alec,' Brian Higgins said. The men in the pub, most of them pit workers, laughed.

They'd not be for taking into account the blushes of Will, Bridie thought as she handed the jug of ale she'd drawn to Brian Higgins. Her stomach turned over as he brushed her hand with his. She looked around. Hadn't she the measure of every one of them, and not one of them worth the tuppence they paid her to lie with them. Not that Bruiser had been for asking her to prostitute herself so often, since she'd been after bringing in extra from this job.

It had been for starting out well in the beginning, so it had. Bruiser had not been able to stand the thought of others having her, and she'd found some happiness with him. Beth had moved into the vacant room and had taken to the life

Agnes led as if she were born to it. Bridie had never understood why at the time, and was for understanding even less since she'd been forced into prostitution herself.

It was the gambling that had been for taking Bruiser over, and as he'd needed more and more money to fund his habit, and other pimps had moved in on his 'girls', he'd put Bridie out to earn. She'd stood up to him at first, but as his desperation set in, he began to knock her about until she gave in and did his bidding.

In the end she was lying with others he knew nothing of, for wasn't she needing more than a drop of gin to get her through the day?

The saving of her had come when Bruiser's debt took his house, as she'd taken her chance and moved into a room in the same house Agnes and Beth now lived in. And they were for giving her some protection. Not that she'd escaped Bruiser, for he visited most days and had a control over her that no one dared interfere with.

'Haven't you dipped it yet, then?' Alec Green, 'the fumbler', asked of Will.

Bridie had a name in her mind for each of them. To listen to the accounts of Alec, folk thought of him as a good fellow – a church-going man who exercised moderation in all things – but Bridie knew a different truth. Alec had never lain with her, but hadn't he been after letting his fingers have the feel of her whenever he thought he'd get away with it? And his eyes told of his sinful thoughts.

'How old are you now, Will? You must be well over supping age, and this your first visit! Now, that's no way for me to get rich, lad.' This from Bob, the landlord of the pub, caused another burst of laughter.

'I'm going on twenty-four, and by my reckoning that's old enough for everything as is said I'm in here looking for.'

'Aye, and he ain't no innocent, either. You're all forgetting Florrie Makepiece and her mysterious disappearance.'

The bar fell silent, and the atmosphere thickened. Bridie had heard of Florrie. Her mother had died not long since, and it was said as she never knew where it was her daughter had gone. Not that she seemed to care, for wasn't she always calling the girl every name she could think of? Bridie had often thought Florrie was better away out of it.

Will turned to face what now looked to Bridie like a lynch mob. He stood tall, but she could see he struggled to hold onto his pride. 'It's time for an end to that tale. You've always thought – all of you – as I fathered Florrie's child. Well, I didn't, but just as you sit now as me judge and jury, so you did then, when me life were turned upside down with the losing of me da. I couldn't speak out for meself then, as you'd have turned that on me an' all. Well, I can tell you, now that Florrie's ma has gone and there's no need for me to fear for Florrie any more . . .'

Bridie couldn't believe her ears, as Will went on to tell how he'd helped Florrie escape to become housekeeper, and now wife, to his uncle. 'She's very happy. They have a large family and are well off, and best thing is, none of you has been able to take advantage of her.' Bridie watched him look around at the silent, staring faces, before continuing, 'Cos I'll tell you all sommat for nowt: she stood no chance amongst you; nor did she with that mother of hers. So let that be an end to your speculation and tales about me and her.'

Derek Hardacre, the man who had brought up the subject, stood up. 'Well then, I reckon as the truth's out at last, though it might never be known who put her in the family way. But,

187

lad, as I've been one of them as condemned you, you should let me stand you a drink. Give me a chance to make amends.'

'I'll not say no, though I can't say as your gossip has bothered me this good while. I've always been a man with a clear conscience, and that is something few of you can say.'

'You're reet there, lad. Here, fill a jug for him, Bridie, and stop catching flies.'

Bridie laughed with everyone else at this. She didn't like to be the brunt of their jokes, but was glad to see the moment pass and the atmosphere lift. Will had done well to stand up for himself.

She caught his eye. He had a lovely smile on his face; the same one she had etched into her memory. Then, and now, it held an extra feeling, which was smouldering his eyes when he looked at her. She didn't like to think of the first time she'd seen it, locked as it was into everything she wanted to forget about the happenings of nearly five years ago, but hadn't she bumped into him this morning after all these years of living in the same area? And didn't his smile start up the same feeling inside her?

He'd knocked her and her shopping flying almost to kingdom come in the market place earlier in the day. She'd bought some onions and had just ordered some black-eyed peas for Maureen, the landlady of the pub, when Will had come round the corner. The collision had caused her to drop the onions, and she'd found herself saved from falling by his strong hands and mesmerized by his eyes. Memory had stung her. And the time she had wanted to forget – her pappy's and Seamus's betrayal of her – had catapulted into her heart, igniting her temper. She'd been about to bring the wrath of God himself down on Will, but he hadn't given her time to.

'I'm sorry, lass, I didn't see you. Me head's all over the

place. I were looking for something for me ma's birthday, and I'm undecided. I'm at odds with shopping as it is. Here, let me help you,' he'd said.

'To be sure you were after giving me a right shove.'

This had prompted the smile. And with it a kindling of something inside of her that she had never thought she would feel for any man again.

'You're a colleen! Even if you hadn't have spoken, I'd have known. You have lovely eyes, and your hair . . . it's like – well, thou knows: burning embers or sommat.' He'd blushed at his own words, and in his attempt to hide his discomfort had bent down to retrieve her purchases. She'd known he wasn't for giving her a touch of the blarney.

She'd marked him as a pit worker. The tinge of him that she hadn't been able to recognize when they had first met five years ago she now knew came from coal dust. How often that smell had repulsed the insides of her since! But that repulsion hadn't entered her when she had first met Will, and didn't now as she caught the faint whiff of it on him, this second time of their meeting.

The same things she had noticed before struck her again. His sun-kissed skin, taken with his dark, oval-shaped eyes and handsome looks, could have meant he had foreign blood in him, though his voice gave her knowledge of his Yorkshire roots. But then, likely someone from across the water had a hand in the making of him.

'Me name's Bridie – Bridie O'Hara. We've been after meeting before, a long time ago. You nearly knocked me off me pins then, too, so you did!'

Still on his haunches gathering up her onions, he'd lifted his head. His look had held a question. 'Oh, aye, I remember. You were lass as was running like a scared rabbit, the day as

189

I went into Liverpool. By, that were back in January '76. Aw, but if I remember reet, that time it was your own fault. You weren't looking where you were going, so that makes us quits! How come you're in Sheffield now?'

'It's a long story, and one that has seen me become a lesser person than I was. I've no time to talk of it, though. I work in the bar at the Red Bull, and I'd be giving you a hand with your choosing of your mammy's present, but Maureen needs this lot, so I'm to be on me way.'

'I'm Will – Will Hadler.'

'I'm not after forgetting your name, as it seems you have done mine.'

'No, I've never forgotten you. Well, how you . . .'

She thought he was about to say, 'how you looked then', but before she could think on this he surprised her by taking her hand and shaking it. 'It's nice to meet up with you again. And, thanks, but I'll be reet. I won't need your help. I'll probably settle for some of them lavender bags I saw on a stall back there. Ma likes to keep her clothes smelling fresh. Aye, I think they'll be the very thing.' He'd looked like he would leave then, but instead he'd stopped and said, 'I'm no drinking man, but I might find a thirst. If so, I'll come into the Red Bull and sample your ale.'

He'd laughed as he'd gone on his way, but she'd not been able to get him out of her mind since. It seemed he'd been thinking the same way, seeing as he had sought her out so soon.

She scraped some of the froth off the top of the jug of ale she'd pulled for him. As she passed it to him and took the money for it from Derek, Bob said to him, 'Mind you, drink it slowly now, Will. You're not used to beer. It'll take time to get accustomed to it. At first off, one jug can have the effect of ten.'

'Give over, Bob! Size of him, he can take a few, thou knows. Here, put another up for him.'

Brian Higgins threw a halfpenny onto the bar. Bridie took it and drew a second jug of ale for Will, giving her another chance to catch his eye and give him a smile.

'Well now, Will.' Bridie saw Will's shoulder jolt as Brian slapped it. 'That's your drinks seen to. Now what's to be done about your other pressing need, eh?' He cocked a wink at Will and lowered his tone, but not enough, for what he said could be heard by everyone. 'I'll tell you something for nothing, Will: if it's a dip you're after, you'll get it easy with Bridie here. She'll open up for anyone as buys her a gin.'

Will's body straightened. His face drained of colour. Bridie held her breath. Brian was a bare-fist fighter and a prize-winner at that. Some said as there was only Bruiser as could beat him in his day . . .

Please don't let Will be after trying to fight him!

'You've a dirty mind, Brian Higgins, and a foul mouth. Just because lass serves behind bar don't give you the right to soil her name. Here, you can have your jug back. I'll not sup ale as you've bought. It'd choke me.'

Brian reeled backwards under the force of the shove, his gasp audible as the ale he'd just paid for soaked his hair and ran down his face. His eyes blinked away droplets of it.

Before anyone could react, Will's body hit the ground hard. The snake-like jab caught him square on his chin.

'Come on, Brian, leave lad alone. That's enough. It'll happen be the effect of his first sup of ale. Give over now. We all riled him, having a poke of fun at his expense.'

'Aye, happen you're right, Alec, but he had it coming. I'm wet through, and it were a waste of good ale at that.'

'Any ale as touches you is wasted, so it is, Brian Higgins. You're a bastard, so you are. Dilly May herself wouldn't be letting you have a dip, even if you topped what everyone else has ever paid her!' This Bridie knew would insult him, as Dilly May was the last resort: only those who couldn't afford to pay anyone else had it with her. She carried a disease that left men sick for weeks, and the smell of her tainted any room she was in.

Brian turned towards her, his face white with anger and his mouth open ready to retort, but her own temper knew no bounds. She got in first, saying, 'Is it a woman as you'll have a go at next, then? 'Tis brave you are, for someone who has trouble getting it up! Aye, and that's why you've no wee ones. Be Jesus! I'd knock you over meself if I was a man.'

'Now, now, Bridie, let's have no more of it. Maureen, take lad in back and see to his face. He's right bloodied. And, Brian, get yourself off home. I'll stand you a jug next time, for one as was tipped over you, but I want you out of here now! Go on.'

Brian made no protest at this from Bob, and Will was glad of it – he was sure Bridie would have pitched in again. Shaking his head, he tried to clear the fuzziness in it. Bridie's red and angry face swam into his vision. By, she were a wild one! Hadn't she been about to go for him this morning, just cos he'd bumped into her? And the way as she'd spoken just then! He were beginning to think as she wasn't the girl he'd first met. In those few seconds that he'd held her, all those years ago, he remembered that she'd appeared vulnerable. But then, if he were truthful, he'd heard tell of a lass who worked behind the bar here, without realizing who she was, and what he'd heard hadn't been good.

The haze fogged his brain again as he tried to lift himself up. He lay back down and closed his eyes. Bridie wouldn't leave his thoughts. She filled what clear space his brain had. There was something about her; she had got to him. He tried to make light of what he'd heard about her, thinking: *Happen as it were just talk. After all, her job would give her a reputation, without her trying for one.*

Bob came into his view, his voice kindly. 'Come on, Will, you're all right. Here, Alec, give us a hand. Lad's a bit groggy.'

The two men put an arm under each of his and lifted him.

'Happen you'll remember your first sup, eh? Come on, and don't be worrying. Brian only hit you to save face. He'll forget about it, come morning.'

Will didn't answer Alec, but hoped he was right.

Alec and Bob helped him through to the back parlour and sat him on a chair. He'd no sooner sat down than the landlady started to fuss over him. 'Will, Will . . . what's to do with you? I didn't have you down as a fighting man. What your ma's going to be thinking, I don't know.'

Bridie came in and took over before he had time to answer, though he knew what lay behind the agitation in Maureen's voice. Folk had a lot of reverence for his ma; her straight talking had earned her that. She'd kept a tight rein on him, when others around had allowed their young 'uns to do as they pleased. Some of the respect she commanded held fear, he knew that. She wasn't one to be crossed, though he'd stood up to her of late.

'I'll be seeing to him, Maureen. To be sure it's my fault as he finds himself in the mess he's in.'

'All right, Bridie, I'll leave you to it, but . . . well, Bob's not going to be right pleased after this.'

'I'm sorry, Maureen. I try not to be giving me tongue its own way, but it wags on its own when the likes of Brian Higgins start, so it does.'

'Well, we'll see. I'll talk to Bob after. You get on with bathing that cut on Will's face, then get yourself back behind bar. We've the steel-works lot coming off shift just on last orders, so we'll need you.'

'I'll not take long.'

Will watched Bridie fill a bowl with cold water from the jug on the side of the sink. Her actions were calm. She must have cooled her temper. Her words as she started to bathe his eye made him smile. 'Holy Mary, Mother of God, I'll be losing everything on your account, Will Hadler! First me onions, then me job. You've brought nothing but trouble to me door. There! It's not too bad. You'll probably be having a shiner, but it'll not be for spoiling your looks. So don't be worrying.'

'That's all right then, cos if I keep me looks, happen as you'll say yes if I ask you out?'

'Are you not for thinking as I might be spoken for?'

'Are you, then? Is there someone?'

'Aye. Bruiser Armitage.'

This shocked him. Bruiser Armitage! Tackling Brian had been more than he could handle, but Albert Armitage! 'In that case we'd better forget I asked you.'

'I'm only taking you on. Would you be seeing the likes of little me with Bruiser? What do you take me for?'

'Well, I'll do me asking, then. How do you fancy taking a walk with me on your night off?'

She tossed her hair back from where it had fallen over her

face. A ray of sunlight beaming through the window licked the auburn curls, like a flame bursting into life. A muscle clenched his stomach. Her eyes held his for a moment, and then she turned to leave the room, looking back as she reached the door. 'Well, 'tis as me shift ends in half an hour, and I'm not for fancying walking home on me own after all the goings-on. I'd be glad if you would walk with me, Will.' Before he could answer she added, 'After the trouble you've brought down on me today, it's the least you can be doing for me.'

He laughed at this. 'Aye, all right. I'll do that.'

Bridie felt a pang of guilt. What had possessed her to suggest such a thing, and why had she said she wasn't Bruiser's girl? Bruiser did still consider her to be his, although they no longer lived together. His visits were full of the passion they'd kindled since their first meeting, but it was fear that held her to him now. Fear of his brutality, and of his threats to hurt Beth if she didn't do his bidding.

Trepidation fluttered in her heart. What if Bruiser was for turning up while she was with Will – because she didn't have it in her plans to leave him at her door? Will Hadler had touched something in her – something she'd not been for feeling for a long time. And she was for knowing as she needed more of him. This thought made her mind up. 'After me shift it is, then.' She gave him a smile just before closing the door.

Will couldn't help wondering what it would be like. Like all lads he'd relieved himself, so he knew the feeling that gave – but to actually enter a woman! By, he needed to do that! Maybe when he had, he could move on. Maybe that's all Bridie was to him: a means of becoming a man. Maybe, but he didn't think so. Somehow he'd always known that the first time he went with a woman proper, it'd be with the one as was meant for him.

As they walked past the pit gates and round by the steel works, they talked of nothing in particular. It wasn't until they turned into Canal Street that the subject on his mind came up. Bridie said, 'When we get under the bridge you can kiss me, if you be wanting to, Will.'

'Aye, I want to, lass. You won't mind, then?'

Taking his hand and using her other one to gather up her skirt, she pulled him the last few yards to the bridge. Once there, she turned to him. He let her take charge – he didn't want her to think of him as being the same as the others.

Standing looking up at him, her expression was quizzical. As he held her gaze and knew it to intensify, he had a feeling that his whole self would be sucked into the beauty of her eyes.

The movement wasn't a conscious one, and he had no knowledge of whether he'd leaned forward or she had, or if they had swayed together in unison, but now their faces were inches apart and a feeling had taken him like none he'd ever experienced. When her lips brushed his, a shock vibrated through him. The kiss started as a tender pressing together of lips, then deepened, touching all of his senses, bringing them alive as if the inside of him were a ready-laid fire and someone had ignited the kindling.

Bridie felt the shock of it, and the tenderness of the moment was for overwhelming her. It was an innocent giving, like she'd never been after knowing before. Something special happened to the inside of her. The usual animal-like hunger wasn't there, but in its place other feelings were awakened. Feelings that were for making her know what it felt like to be cherished, feminine even, and treated as if she was after being the vulnerable one who needed gentle nurturing. But then the heart of her screamed as though it would splinter into shards of agony, each one holding the vile things she had done. She was wishing nothing had gone before this moment. She wanted to transport herself back to the green fields of Ireland, running barefoot and pure in mind and body, to meet this man then, so that the soul of her could match his.

The arousal of him that she could feel happening she knew wasn't for being something driven by the need of just any woman. She sensed that it went deeper than that: it was an expression of his feeling for her, and she didn't feel worthy.

'You're crying. Eeh, lass, have I taken liberties? I thought . . .'

'No, you haven't been for taking anything, Will. It was the giving of – I don't know, I'm not sure I can find the words to express it. It was like . . . like respect. Is that for sounding silly?'

'Naw, lass. I do respect you, and allus will. And I have a feeling for you, Bridie. I think I'm falling in love with you. No, I *know* I am. Now I'm the one sounding silly, with us only just having met up again. Though sommat hit me that first time, and it weren't just you barging into me full tilt, either.'

The smile of her came up from deep within her. 'Maybe love is what I felt touch me, but I wasn't for recognizing it. It's not been in me life for a long time.'

His arms enclosed her. Pressed against his body, she felt as safe as she had once known herself to be, a long, long time ago. Resting there, she didn't want ever to move away.

'Is there somewhere private we can go, Bridie? I have a fear as someone will come round the corner any minute and catch us, and I wouldn't want that.'

'I have a place of me own, and it's after not being far from here. Come on, me wee love.' The endearment had come as if she was born saying it, but she hadn't ever before used it to a man.

As they ran the last few yards to her room above the corner shop in Canley Street there was joy inside her. But the joy had a bedfellow, because she also held fear – a fear of spoiling something beautiful and delicate, for wasn't that how it was, this newfound love? Fragile? And she was afraid to the heart of her that she might break it.

Once they were in her room, a shyness descended. Will helped by saying, 'I know you're not for knowing me, Bridie, or anything about me, but I want you to know I'd never hurt you. And neither would I force meself on you, so if you don't want owt to happen, then it won't.'

Oh, God, why were You for keeping this man from me? Isn't he just what I am needing, and have needed, all of me life?

'I'm for wanting the same as what you want, Will.' Going once more into his arms and seeking his lips, she allowed herself for once just to let things happen. Although she'd been taken many times to heights she didn't think could be bettered, she found a place her body had never visited before, and it wasn't just her physical being that went there: it was the very soul of her.

Lying in his arms afterwards, with her emotions fragmented into a million pieces, trying to hold onto the remotest parts of her, she sobbed.

'Tell me about it all, Bridie, love. I have a feeling you have a lot to tell. I know as I won't like a lot of it, but it's better out of you and laid bare for us both to deal with. What you just gave me . . . I have to hold onto. You have to be a part of me life, as you're embedded in me. For me not to have you would be like not having me heart. But we have to start on sure ground.'

'Is it safe as I will be? When you are hearing all I have done, and the vile things done to me, will it not kill what you feel? I am not for bearing that, Will.'

'I promise. I'm not all green. I have heard stuff, but I want the truth of it from the only person who can give it me. I don't want to set store by tales I might hear. And I meant what I said: I love you, and at this moment I know I want to be with you and take you as me own lass, warts an' all.'

'I'm not sure if I can tell you all of me doings, Will, cos for the first time since I was a girl I have a shame on me.'

'I reckoned as it wouldn't be easy for you. And maybe now ain't the time. How about we do sommat ordinary first, like you making me a sup of tea? I'm reet parched.'

This made them giggle, as it was so out of context and unexpected. Bridie sought to keep the mood light, saying, 'That'll be the ale, so it will. It quenches your thirst, but then leaves you with a bigger one. I'll not be a mo. I'll get me clothes on, and then I'll be after making us a pot.'

Will looked around the room. Small and holding nearly as much as it could in the way of furniture, it had a screen taking off one corner of it. He could see no stove, or a door that might lead to a kitchen or parlour. 'Where's your kitchen, Bridie? And, more importantly, where's the lav, cos I have another pressing need on me that can't wait.'

'We share a scullery at the back of the shop. It—'

'We?'

'Aye, there's four rooms in all and they house seven lasses. 'Tis as I'm the only one who has a room to meself, and that's because I am for paying me own rent. The others are controlled by their – well, anyway, they are after having their lodgings paid. We all tip up a bit more on top to Joseph, the fellow who owns the flats and the shop below. That covers us for some provisions, and he is after keeping the grate burning in the scullery for us.' She picked up Will's trousers and chucked them at him. 'Come on, if it's the lav you need, 'tis out the back. Or if it is for being more urgent, sure I have me pot behind the screen. But 'tis as you'll be after emptying it yourself; that's one job I'll not be doing for any man.'

Will's heart sank. *'Any man' – there had been a few then, and in here an' all* . . . The realization that what folk said about Bridie might all be true trickled a doubt into him. Part of him didn't want to hear her tale. This place where she lived was no more than a whorehouse, and it seemed that she was one of them. But despite it all he had a feeling in him for her, and it wasn't one as he could easily turn from. No, he'd listen to what she had to tell him, give her a chance to do that at least, and then make his mind up. But a voice inside him told him he'd not a lot of choice in the matter.

As he took a sip of the tea she'd brought up to him, she said, 'I'll be after understanding if you want nothing more to do with me, Will, when 'tis as you have heard me tale. Though I'll be swearing on the Baby Jesus, me life's going to be different, if you do. No more – not even Bruiser himself – will be having me from now on.'

'Bruiser?'

The way he leaned his body away from her held anger, and his face showed his disbelief. The tension in her had her clutching her hands together under her breasts. 'Aye. I'm sorry to the heart of me, Will, but I've not been honest where Bruiser is concerned. 'Tis as I've been like a mistress to him, since not long after I first met you that day in Liverpool.'

Unable to face the look in his eyes, she kept her head down

and told him how she and Beth came to be in Sheffield and how, at her most vulnerable – having just lost her mammy, having suffered at the hands of her pappy, having been betrayed by the man she thought she loved and left with nothing – she had fallen for the charms of Bruiser. How he'd seemed like her saviour, and wasn't for putting her to work like he did Beth. How he'd kept her as his own special girl, so he had. And how it was not for being a long time before she had to prostitute herself, but Bruiser gambled away his home and had to take a room and go back to the steel works. Then wasn't he for forcing her, with the brutality of his ways, to earn money for him.

'I was for getting out of it when I could, though, Will. 'Twas me getting me job at the pub, so I could give Bruiser extra, as keeps me from not having to do it. I hated it with me heart and soul, Will, but Bruiser would've been for killing me if I hadn't.'

Will's silence brought her eyes to his. He glared at her. The battle raging in him was as visible as if he were ranting and beating his chest. It was a relief to her when he finally spoke. 'Does you care for him?'

'No! I . . . it was nothing but an attraction, like an animal thing, and – well, it was about survival, so it was. Mine and Beth's. If I let him have me, then he would take care of her. Not in the way I wanted for her, but then Beth had already made her mind up what she was going to do. She had no self-worth, and that is still true today, so it is. I couldn't stop her doing what she wanted, but I could make sure she was safe, by doing as Bruiser said.' She waited a moment, trying to read his silence. Desperation flooded her. She had to make him understand. 'I didn't think until this day I had the ability to love. I was after thinking as I weren't like others, and me heart was so sore I couldn't give it to another, but you've taken it from me, Will. And whilst you're drawing your breath, no other man will be taking his pleasure on me. And I can't see a time coming when I'll ever look at another man.'

'Oh, Bridie, it's a mess. I can't get me head round it all, and it hurts. It's ground a pain into me chest. I feel me body weighted down under the burden of it all . . . aye, and the disgust of it. I have feelings for you and, aye, they're strong an' all, but at this moment it feels as though you have ripped me heart out, and I'm not sure if I can cope. I don't know what to do! Me heart won't let me walk through the door and away from you, but me head says as I should. I know one thing, though: I'd like to meet up with your da. I'm not a fighting man, but me blood is boiling with rage on account of what he did to you. If it were possible, I'd beat him to a pulp. Aye, and Bruiser an' all.'

'I'm for knowing how you're feeling. Haven't I meself wanted to do that very same thing when it settled in me, as me pappy wasn't worthy of the love me and me mammy gave him? That took a while. It was hard to separate the two men that he was. And the image of his death will live inside me forever, haunting me, waking me in the night with the sweat running from me. Aye, and the bastard that he was, his leaving me with that legacy has meant I took to the gin. I have to be telling you, Will, while it is I am exposing me soul: I am for supping more of it than I should. It is a need in me. And that is why they say I open for the price of it. It's me only defence, me only way of blotting it all out, and I'm for thinking that one day I'll be for taking just one too many gins and . . . and that'll be me peace – the death of me . . . an end.'

'No! Come on, lass. Come on, me little love. That'll not happen whilst I'm around. I have to think on what has gone afore me as over, and nothing to do with me. Me mind's made up: you're me lass now, Bridie, and I'll stick by you.'

She moved closer to him. 'Oh, Will. 'Tis sure that you are as you can take me "warts an' all", as you were after saying?'

'Aye, lass, I'm sure. We'll face them all together. They'll not break us, if we stand together.'

'We can't, Will. Oh, I am for knowing we could face the talk, but Bruiser? He'd be for killing us both, and glad to hang for it. If you are for having me, Will, we'll have to go right away from here. And we'd have to do it without anyone knowing of us, or knowing where we've gone. Except Beth, of course; I couldn't ever lose touch with Beth.'

'Move? But I can't.' His face took on many expressions in no more than a few moments as he fell into silence, then he spoke again, telling her of his own burdens. 'I said as I'd take you, warts an' all, Bridie. But I am not shackle-free, either . . .' He told her about his ma and how he couldn't leave her. 'If we were just getting married and living in me cottage, then she'd take a couple of rooms above the shop where she works and I could still look out for her. But to go away and not be able to come and see her, and see as she's alreet – that's not an option.'

'Could we not take her with us?'

'She's not an easy person. I don't reckon as she'll take to the idea of moving. Look, we could talk until the cows come home of all the possibilities and not come to a conclusion. We have to sleep on it. See if we both think the same tomorrow. I'm on late shift, but I could meet you before, or come round here after. But that would be gone midnight.'

'That's best, so it is. Bruiser is working the night shift this week and won't be for catching us out if you come after midnight. Just be taking care when you leave, now, as he could take it into his head to visit me on his way to work. If you see him, look pleased with yourself and say something to him.'

'What can I say? Bridie, how's it all going to work? What'll he do if you even tell him he can't visit any more?'

'I can't be doing that, Will. When I said I'd not have any more to do with him, I was thinking you would take me away right now. It was a silly promise that I'm not able to keep. Not until as we can get away from here.'

'Oh, Bridie, love.'

'Are you thinking we can't get through this, Will?'

'We'll try. As painful as it's going to be, we'll try. So what do I say to Bruiser if I meet him?'

'Tell him if he's looking for a woman, you can recommend Beth. Then he will be thinking 'tis her you have been visiting.' She could see by Will's face that what she'd said about the danger they were in had finally dawned on him. She was glad of that, because the danger *was* real. 'It'll be all right. Don't be worrying. He'll believe you. He has no reason not to. And it'll be better he does come to see me, as then he will hear my side of things before he hears it from anyone else. I'll put it so that he'll be for thinking you did the right thing to stand up for me, and I did the best thing for you in return, by seeing you got from Beth that as makes you a man.'

They both laughed at this and it lightened the moment.

Will didn't bump into Bruiser when he left, and he hoped with everything that was in him that Bruiser didn't visit her. Oh, he knew what Bridie said was true – that it would be better if Bruiser heard the tale from her – but he couldn't bear thinking on what might happen between them, as he knew that would kill him.

By, I've got it bad, and it isn't just because of what has happened between us today, either. 'Cause truth is, I've thought about Bridie a lot over the years.

Aye, she'd changed, but then she'd only been a young 'un when he'd first seen her. Now she had a raw beauty, tainted by her way of life, but a beauty that tore at him all the same. And if things went well and he took her away from all of this, she might blossom again. Not that it would matter. She was under his skin, and that's where she would stay . . .

17

Andrew

Breckton, September 1880
Be faithful unto one

The last couple of days had held a peace. The funeral three months ago had gone well, and with all the aftermath of solicitors and bank visits behind him, Andrew felt secure in his wealth and in his ability to keep his promise to himself not to visit Lilly. The urge to do so had nearly undone him, but he'd stayed strong and felt proud of himself for resisting. The reward for him lay in not having to avoid Dvina's gaze when he came home from his many necessary visits to Leeds. He liked, too, how he could visit her bed and enjoy her pleasures whenever he wanted – something he'd been unable to do for a week or so after he'd been with Lilly. Some part of him had been disgusted at the thought of going from between a whore's legs to between the wonderful fleshy ones of his loving wife, without letting a decent amount of time pass. If Dvina noticed this difference she didn't say; she just swallowed him into her and bathed him in pleasurable love.

She had busied herself sorting out her house and estate, preparing it for sale. In doing so she had coped well with her grief and seemed to have come to terms with her father's loss. Now they could both relax.

Three weeks into September, the weather continued to bless them with warm, balmy days. Andrew looked over at Dvina as she lay back in her garden chair, her eyes half-closed. But then, as if sensing his stare, she turned. 'Are you all right, my love?'

'I am,' he told her, but wished he could broach the subject that was worrying him. He wasn't sure if she was eating so much to find comfort, but he'd seen an increase in her portions and it showed in her ever-rounding figure.

'I can see there is something on your mind, dear. What is it?'

'I – well, I am concerned for you. You . . . seem tired.'

'Don't worry, it's natural. It's happened again, my darling. I'm pregnant.'

'What! How?'

'Well, I didn't expect that question, you goose! I think it happened as soon as I was well from losing the last one. Probably that afternoon: the day we'd had the news about poor Daddy and you came to comfort me.'

'But you had only just stopped your bleed then. Are you sure?'

'Yes. I have consulted Dr Payne, and he is certain. He said it often happens this way. They have noticed that women seem more fertile immediately after a miscarriage. Anyway, he thinks I am almost three months.'

'But that's wonderful, darling! How do you feel?'

'Very well and very happy. I have a good feeling about this one. I think he is here to stay the course.'

Reaching over, he clasped her hand. 'I do hope so, darling. I can't bear for us to go through another loss, and all the pain it puts you through.'

'It won't happen, I promise. Let's just enjoy it day by day, with no worrying. I think I am a lot more relaxed in your love now, so that may help . . . I mean, I have always known you love me, but – well, I didn't always feel . . . Oh, I don't know what I want to say. Anyway, it's not relevant. The thing is, we can start to look forward again, darling, and soon the Season will be on us and I have all those wonderful invitations to look forward to. And maybe we could throw a dinner party ourselves.'

A silence fell between them. He couldn't see any sign of anguish in Dvina's smile, yet he felt certain she referred to more than just the fact that he'd kept her away from his circle of friends. If she had known or suspected that he visited a whore during her previous pregnancies, had that contributed to them coming to an end?

'Darling, don't look so worried. Everything is going to go well – *is* going well. And I know nothing will mar our excitement over the coming months.'

Standing up, he took both of her hands. He helped her up, then pulled her to him and held her close. 'My clever darling, but please take care of yourself.' He didn't know how to suggest that she be careful not to overeat, but he wished he could. It seemed that when anything changed in her life she turned to food, whether it was a sad happening or a joyful one. Perhaps a word with their doctor might help. He'd try and see if there was a solution.

She stirred in his arms. 'I will, I promise, but now you are to stop worrying. That won't help. Dr Payne said I must stay relaxed, take plenty of rest and hope not to have any stress in the coming months. Then all should be fine. And . . . and, well, I want us to carry on as normal, Andrew. I don't want you to – well, to stop coming to my bed. I am here for you, and I need you as much as you need me.'

'I won't, not this time. I can't, anyway. You are such a temptress . . .' Something in her let go, making her softer in his arms. Stroking her hair, he allowed the thoughts in: there was no denying that she had known of his indiscretions, and the knowing must have given her so much pain. As always, his guilt sat inside him like a heavy meal that he couldn't digest. He kissed her hair, murmuring, 'I'm sorry, I'm so sorry.'

She didn't ask what for; she just held him closer.

After a moment he helped her back to her seat and sought to change the subject, saying, 'I'm going over to Hensal Grange later. Do you want to come? You can announce our news, and I want to see how things are with Edgar; he isn't at all well. I feel he is fretting for Jeremy. It is the not knowing that is the worst thing. I mean, we wouldn't expect to hear from Jeremy for a few months anyway, but it has been a long time since his last letter and there has been no news, except bad news from the War Office about the worsening situation out there.'

'I always think that the longer it is we don't hear, the better. Surely if anything happens to Jeremy they will inform us as soon as they can? So hold onto that hope, darling; and yes, I will come. It will make a nice change. I won't ride over, though. I have been warned that straddling the horse as I do may not be good for me, and I would rather give up the pleasure of a mount than ride side-saddle!'

Her laugh at this helped release some of the tension in him. When he joined in, his laughter was even more enthusiastic than hers, as the image of her bulk sitting side-saddle really tickled him.

'It's not that funny!' She hit out at him with her shawl, and then laughed even harder as his step back made him lose his footing and fall onto his rear in a most undignified way.

He supposed he deserved her reaction, and acknowledged it as a touché.

Although Dvina couldn't ride with him, Andrew had decided he would do so and meet her there, rather than go with her in the carriage. Riding over the hills gave him the stimulation of the wind rushing into his face and the challenge of negotiating the rough terrain.

As he came to the road where the stream washed a small river of water across it, he saw Isabella walking with her head down. Her whole demeanour told of the sadness that seemed to be her constant companion whenever he came across her. He pulled his horse to a standstill, calling, 'Good afternoon, Isabella. How are you?'

'I'm as reet as can be expected, given the circumstances, sir.'

'And what are these "circumstances" that are putting you in low spirits?'

'The selling of Hartington House, sir. We none of us know if our positions are safe, and with no family to look after at the moment, and the sadness we all feel over our master's passing, it seems like a cloud has settled over us all. Then there's me ma . . . and, well, the master's funeral didn't help. It sort of brought it back, how we never had a proper one for our loved ones . . . Oh, I ain't saying as it were anyone's fault.'

'No, I know what you mean.' Andrew had been deeply saddened that by the time the men were brought up it was impossible to tell who was who. They had no choice but to allocate a body to each grieving family to bury. 'But you were all united in your loss. You all felt for each other, as well as for your loved one.'

'I know. It couldn't be helped, but every time I tend me da's or Denny's grave, I wonder if it really is them lying there.' Her anguish showed in the tear Issy wiped away, but she recovered quickly, adding, 'Still, no use harkening on about it. There's other challenges to face, and I must be on me way so I can spend as much time as I can with me ma.'

'I'm sorry for your troubles, Isabella, and if I can lighten them, I will. I will speak to my wife about the unrest amongst the staff at Hartington. Now, your worry over your mother I can understand – we too have our concerns, and have taken on extra help for her, but she insists she wants to carry on working.'

'I know, sir, but I am reet fretting over her and can't get her out of me mind in the weeks between me visits. Her legs are swollen fit to burst and . . .'

'Look, what if you transferred to us at Tarrington House? You could take your mother's position and we could retire her. Would that help?'

'It would, sir. Oh, it would! I'm not needed up at Hartington. The second cook can cope well, as there's only the staff meal to see to at the moment. I know Ma won't like it, but I'll persuade her it's for the best. Anyway, she'll still have her deliveries, and they keep her busy.'

'Her deliveries?'

'Aye, she brings all the Breckton young 'uns into the world – has done since as long as I can remember. And as most of them come during the night, she often loses her sleep. Anyroad, the point is most of them drop more young 'uns than rabbits do, so she's always busy trying to keep up with them all.'

'Ha, Isabella! You're a tonic, even when you don't know you are. Well . . .' Andrew couldn't finish his sentence for laughing, but then a more serious thought hit him: how come these women could 'drop more young 'uns than rabbits do' and not have problems like Dvina had? Oh, he knew infant mortality was high amongst them, which was down to many things and saddened him, but they did carry their babies full-term. What was the secret to that? Not that he had the time or inclination to discuss the matter with this servant girl. 'Well, I'll not keep you, and I have to get over to Hensal Grange. How long are you at home for?'

'I have three days, sir, as I missed having my day off last month and the month before, with all that was going on.'

'I'll be in touch. Just give me time to speak to my wife about the situation, as I think there might be a solution to your mother wanting to stay on with us . . . Look, it isn't common knowledge yet – nor do I want it to be, as it's early days – but Mrs Harvey is expecting a baby. The thought has occurred to me that maybe your mother could assist her over the next few months. She must have a good knowledge of these things, and perhaps her advice would help prevent another loss.'

'Eeh, I'm reet pleased for you, sir. It's nice to hear some good news at last. And I know me ma could help; she's known for coaxing along any as has trouble getting to full-term. She's like a sponge – like knowledge has just soaked into her from nowhere. Even Dr Payne consults her on occasions, which gives her a real kick into boastful land. You should see her strut around, like she's a doctor herself or sommat.'

Isabella never failed to make him laugh. *Boastful land, indeed! Where did she get her sayings from?* Her mother had always made Andrew laugh in the past, too, but of late she had been very weary and had lost some of her zest. If Dvina agreed, and Mrs Harman gave up the drudgery of kitchen work and took on the care of Dvina in a nursing capacity, maybe she'd get back her jovial way of looking at life. If she did, she'd be good for Dvina, keep her spirits up. And who knows, maybe she could help this child make it into the world.

'Well, goodbye, Isabella. Take care and enjoy your break. I'll speak to you soon. In fact, come up to the house at two tomorrow afternoon. I think I may have some news for you by then.'

He waved to her as he rode off. Issy felt her mood lift. She'd many a time longed to work nearer to home, and had wanted of late to have her ma give up the long hours of standing on her feet. It seemed both things could come true at last, and she knew her ma could help Miss Dvina. Funny how she still thought of Mrs Harvey as Miss Dvina, though she'd have to be careful not to use that term to her face, if things did work out how Mr Harvey had said.

It's strange, she thought, but the last couple of times Miss Dvina had been pregnant, her ma had said she could have prevented the losses. She'd said as much to Dr Payne, but he'd not wanted her to interfere with the gentry. He was glad of her help with the working class, though, as she saved him money and time.

Issy wasn't sure what it was her ma did, though she knew it must be something to do with her herbal potions, her good advice and the general reassurance she gave. Maybe if she lived at home, her ma would teach her. This thought warmed her as she realized it was work she'd love to do.

After she'd walked another couple of miles, Issy remembered her other worry and wished she'd broached it with Mr Harvey. In her last letter her ma had told her how worried she was about keeping on her cottage. It seemed there were plans to bring in more men, now that Tacker's Mine was joining Hensal Grange Mine. She'd heard how all the widows might have to leave, at least those with no young 'uns still dependent on them. Not that there was many of them left now: most women had remarried or left the area. But her ma still lived in the cottage she had shared with Da, and in which she herself had been born. How would she cope with having to leave it?

A movement in the bushes made her jump. The smell of wood burning and the sounds of a fire crackling heightened her sense that someone was in the thicket. She looked around her, and the vastness of the wide-open space increased her fear. No cottage or building was in sight. The hills to the left stood looking back at her, barren and rugged. Sheep dotted the field to her right. Something had spooked them and they had set off running, their bleats blotting out all other sound as Issy stood still listening. Her breath laboured in her lungs and sweat stood out on her forehead. How many times had she walked this route and never had a care? Now it seemed like a frightening place.

A twig snapped, and Issy's body stiffened. Maybe it was a poacher. The thicket was a good place to set snares: its dense foliage attracted the rabbits, and she'd heard of wild boar in the area. If it wasn't for the tinge of smoke, she'd have thought an animal was responsible for the noises. The painful thumping of her heart against her ribs warned her of danger. Pollyanna Smith had been attacked on her way home a few weeks ago, and said she thought her attacker was a gypsy. Issy shuddered as she remembered what had happened to Polly. She had lost more than her wages . . .

A voice came from the thicket and the accent told her he was one of the Irish: 'Aren't you a bonny looker? Will you throw me your purse, or have I to take it from you?'

Though fearing for her life, she stood firm. 'You leave me

214

alone. Mr Harvey has just ridden past. If I scream he will come back, and then you will catch it.'

'I was for seeing Mr Harvey meself, so I was, and I watched him talking to you. He has long gone and won't be for helping you. Now throw me your purse and I might let you go unharmed.'

Issy peered in the direction of the voice, but she couldn't make out who he was or how big he was. Her purse held three months' wages. This was money she and Ma needed to survive, especially if they'd to look for somewhere to rent in the near future. She decided to try to bluff her way out of giving it up. 'I haven't any money on me. I'm just out for a walk.'

'Don't be giving me that. Sure I know who you are and where you work. You have a good position, so you do, and you haven't been home for a while. So it's heavy that your purse is, if I am guessing right.'

The bushes parted. A large man stood in front of her, a scarf covering his face, like the highwaymen whose pictures she'd seen in the books she used to read as a child.

'In fact, I've a mind to take more than your money. I have it on good word you haven't been taken down before, Isabella Harman, and I think I am the man to be putting that right.'

'No, no! You can have me money. Here.' She threw her purse at him and turned away ready to run, but his hands grasped her from behind. She kicked her legs back, trying to aim for his crotch. She knew that would disable him, but he was nimble and moved his body out of her way.

'You vixen! Is it that you are trying to damage me manhood? Well, the only damage it's going to have is in breaking you in, you old spinster. What is it you are now? Mid-twenties at least, and you still a virgin. Yet you've been ripe for the pleasure of a man this good while.'

As he spoke he wrestled her to the ground. Before Issy could right herself enough to stop him, he had both her hands trapped under his knees. He sat back on his haunches, and his hands went to his buttons.

'No, please don't! Don't . . .' She twisted her body, trying to dislodge him, but she couldn't. 'No . . . No!'

Her screams assaulted her own ears, but did nothing to help her. His hand lashed her face. A stinging pain from her eye to her chin made her catch her breath in her lungs. Blood trickled into her mouth. His weight crushed her arms. She tried not to watch, but as she turned her head she saw what he'd released from his trousers. Her heart beat despair through her body, but she couldn't take her eyes from it. His laugh brought her eyes to his face, and there she read the depths of his lust. His voice thick and husky, he said, 'Is it to your liking, then?'

She turned her head away, but then a searing pain ripped her as he yanked her by her hair, forcing her to look at him.

'You're going to have this, as sure as there is a sun in the sky, spinster.' He moved his knee off her left arm and started to tug her skirts up above her knee. She writhed about as much as she could, flailing at him with her free arm, but she could not free herself. His knee prised open her legs, and his hand pushed up her bloomers.

'No, don't . . . No . . .' Her voice hung in the depths of nowhere as she took the weight of his body. She could do nothing.

It didn't hurt when he entered her. She supposed the fumbling she and Denny had engaged in, and enjoyed so much as a forerunner to being husband and wife, had paved the way for a man to do such a thing to her. But though she felt no physical pain, the hurt to the very core of her was immense. How could this vile man do this to her? Oh, God . . .

His body thrust into hers. The stones of the rough ground beneath her dug into her back. She pushed him, hit out at him, begged him to stop, but none of it made a difference. His pleasure hollered from him. His sweat dripped onto her, and with his hands he ripped open her bodice. The breeze chilled her exposed breasts. He stopped his pounding and grabbed her upper arms, holding them so that she could no longer hit him, then he lowered his head, manoeuvred his scarf up so that she still couldn't see his face and began to lick and suck her breasts. This shocked her. He'd stopped being rough and caressed her with his tongue whilst he moved gently in and out of her. To her intense shame, something in her responded to this treatment. Feelings she couldn't understand, but didn't want to stop, took her over. She willed them to increase, knowing they would intensify – she wanted them to. Oh, God, what was happening to her? Why did she want this? It was wrong . . . wrong . . .

Her body started to writhe with him, instead of against him, as it took the onslaught of the thrills sizzling through her, fragmenting her resolve to fight. When he released her nipple and looked up, he said, 'Good girl, that's right. It is for you to enjoy, my lovely. That's right, so it is – take it, take it . . .'

The feeling that took her as he thrust ever deeper into her forced a cry from her. The shame of her mixed with the heightening of the pleasure he gave her. Her inner self fought with the part of her that knew she should resist; she begged him to stop, even while wanting him not to, as the feeling built in violent waves of pleasure that she could hardly bear.

His moans joined hers as he held himself stiff. She felt him pulsate inside her and she was lost . . .

After a moment it passed and he slumped down onto her. Tears flowed down her cheeks. Drained of energy, she lay still under him until he rolled off. Something about his silence disturbed her. Moving away from him, she went to rise, but he pulled her back down. ''Tis sorry I am for taking you in such a way. But 'tis as I am glad for knowing you enjoyed it, too.'

'I didn't, you filthy scum. You bastard! Leave me alone. Let me go!'

'Is it a teasing bitch as you are? Didn't I feel the pleasure I gave you rock your very being? Are you to deny that, Isabella?'

'Who are you? How do you know me?' Her voice shook with the emotion still vibrating through her. She went to grab his scarf, wanting confirmation of who she knew him to be. He stayed her hand, and she said, 'If you were a man, you'd take off that scarf and show your face to me.' She straightened her skirt down and did up her bodice. 'I hope the law catch you. You think you can waylay women and steal their money and rape them at will, but they'll catch you, and then you'll hang. And I'll be outside the gate cheering when you do. Now let me go.'

'Ha, 'tis funny you are. Off you go, I've no more use for you. But if you be wanting some of the same, just come down to the Irish quarter and ask for the traveller . . .' His laughter echoed around the silent valley as he stood up, pulled up his trousers and did up the buttons, before picking up her purse and disappearing back into the thicket.

Issy tried to stand. Her legs shook. Sobs racked her body. Disgust with herself shuddered through her. Pulling her shawl around her, she bent her head and started to run. But then she stopped; she needed to see him, get a description of him. No other lass should have to face an attack by him, and this resolve gave her courage. She stood for a moment and thought it through. If she turned into the thicket, she could approach his camp from the clearing just beyond. She'd be able to see the smoke from there and follow the trail to it. As long as she kept in the shadow of the trees he wouldn't see her, and he wouldn't be looking out anyway, as her seeking him out would be the last thing he'd expect.

She had him in her view, watching the water that he splashed himself with run off his naked, bronzed body. If only he would turn around. Not that she needed him to, in order to know his identity: seeing his painted Vardo had given her an inkling of who he was. It had been many years since he had been in the area, but it could be the travelling lad who used to visit every season and help on the land. She couldn't remember his name, but Mr Harvey would, as he used to welcome him and give him work.

A sick disgust settled in her when he did face her. It *was* him! He stopped rubbing himself down and looked over to where she stood. Every nerve, every sinew of her body froze. He cocked his head and peered harder, then laughed and shouted over, 'Is it that you have come for more?' She shrank back. When he spoke again his voice had lost its humour. 'Just let me put me clothes on and it'll be your last breath you are for taking.'

Branches clawed at her hair as she stumbled through the thicket. Daring to look back, she could no longer see him or his camp. Gasping in air, it took all her effort to keep up the pace she had set. But she had to get away . . .

A crack split the space around her, setting up a mayhem of birds taking to the air. Their cries and squawks deafened her, and a rabbit scuttled past. Issy stood still, unable to move for fear. He had a gun! Sweat trickled down her cold body. Her throat ached. Everything around her settled back to normal, leaving her stranded in a silent cocoon. Footsteps snapped twigs and crunched through the natural debris of the woodland. They stopped. A gun cocked. Her legs shook. She waited.

A mocking laugh snapped her nerves. 'Not this time, spinster, but you're marked, if it's the law you think to put on me. I will be after doing you a favour in return. Haven't I heard you have a sick mother? If you're not for wanting her dispatched to her maker before her time, then be after keeping your mouth shut.'

The footsteps retreated, and with the relief of this Issy found she could move again. She made it to the nearest tree, slumped against it and wept. After a moment, trying to piece together the fragments of herself, she set off for home. When she came to the road, she started to run and didn't stop until she came to the Miners' Row. Slowing her pace, she tried to look as if nothing had happened, keeping her head down and praying no one would come out and stop her. It wasn't to be. Gertie – the one to pass on any gossip to, if you wanted it spreading – stepped out of her door just as she came up to it, saying, 'Issy, love, what's happened? Oh God, your face!'

Her mind instantly gave her a lie as she pulled her shawl tight around her. 'I went into the thicket to have a pee. Oh, Gertie, love, I lost me purse. I didn't notice till I'd walked a mile or so. I had to go back to look for it. I tripped and fell and hit me head. I . . . I've lost all me wages.'

A sob wrenched from Issy, hurting her breastbone and making her want to give into Gertie's suggestion as she said,

'Aw, lass. Come on inside. Me ma'll help you. She'll clean you up. And don't worry about your purse. It'll still be there; no one goes in them woods. We'll get a few of us together tomorrow and go and look, eh?'

If her lie had been the truth, Gertie's words would have soothed her, but instead the thought of the deceit she'd have to keep up made Issy sick to the stomach. And what would she say if that bastard had planted a babby inside her? Oh, God, she couldn't think on that. She just needed to get home to bathe the filth from her and shut the nightmare out of her life.

'I won't, Gertie, if you don't mind. Me ma'll be in soon, and she'll see to me. Ta, though, for your thoughts, and don't go looking for me purse. I have a mind you won't find it. We'll have to stand the loss.' The thought of the gypsy seeing them and thinking they were looking for him terrified her.

Gertie hugged her to her. 'All right, love, if that's what you want. I'll look in on you later. And don't worry: when that thing happened to Pollyanna, them at the social club all chipped in for her. When they hear of this, I'm sure as they'll be doing the same.'

'Don't, Gertie. Please don't be telling anyone. Leave it be, eh?'

Gertie looked at her. A shadow of shock passed over her face as she said, 'Issy, no, lass . . .'

'Look, love, I lost me purse. That's all. If you never do owt else for me, just accept that and keep your mouth shut. Promise me.'

'Aye, alreet. Keep your hair under its pins. I were only trying to help.'

Using the last of her strength, Issy took hold of Gertie's

hand. 'I know, love. You have a kind heart, but in this case least said, the safer I'll be.'

'Oh, Issy . . . alreet, love, but you know I'm here for you.'

She hated deceiving Gertie, but she had no choice, and she wasn't at all sure she'd managed it. Gertie could be canny about things, but although she liked to spread a snippet if she got hold of one, she had no harm in the bones of her and Issy felt she could trust her on this.

When she reached home, she let herself in and sank to the floor. Her body wept with every part of itself, but her mind held onto a small pocket of the feelings that had assaulted her very being and turned the vileness of it against her: accusing her, telling her that in the end she herself was to blame and that she'd given in to her own awakening. Realizing this made her look at her barren life and want more than the existence she had now. But not more in the form of a babby, though. Not that, please God, not that . . .

Andrew rode up the sweeping drive of Hensal Grange. His eyes wandered over the magnificent house, with its many windows glistening in the sun and the majestic pillars at the entrance to one of the grandest front doors he had ever seen. The lawns surrounding the house – flat and stunningly green, despite the hot, dry summer – looked more like a carpet than grass. In front of the house stood his sister's small carriage, and just disappearing around the corner of the building was his own carriage. His driver, having dropped Dvina off, would park it at the back until they called for it.

Agatha alighted, looked back at him and then walked up the first set of steps of the entrance. The steps swept around the grand pillars in a half-moon and were in stages: three, then a patio, then three more, another patio, and finally one step into the house. She turned again before proceeding to the second climb and half-waved. He had no inclination to wave back; his anger at her had not dissipated. It had been all he could do not to go over to her home and bawl her out before now. He'd worked at trying to calm down, so that he could act politely with her when they met, but just looking at Agatha, he knew he hadn't managed it. He wished she hadn't chosen to visit on the same after-noon they had.

The door opened and Jameson, the butler, welcomed Agatha in; then, as if by magic, a groom appeared from around the west wing of the house and took Andrew's mount to the stable. Andrew followed his sister into the hall and waited whilst the butler took her cloak. Swallowing hard, he made a desperate effort to greet her amiably, but to his chagrin he heard himself say in stilted tones, 'Agatha, before we go in, I feel I must say that I am very angry with you. You had no right to hint to Dvina about my private life, and you upset her greatly.'

'Oh, my dear brother, stop being such a pompous hypocrite. You marry a frump for nothing more than her money, you take your pleasure with a trollop, and then you have the gall to act in front of Mama like you are the perfect husband. Well, I for one did not think it right Dvina should remain innocent of your disgusting ways.'

'It is none of your business how I conduct my affairs, and you have it all wrong anyway.'

'Oh, come off it, Andrew – everyone knows. They pity you, and you know it. "Poor Andrew," they say, "lumbered with that lump and having to try to get an heir out of her. No wonder he needs to visit his whore on a regular basis!"'

Neither of them noticed a shadow draw back into the withdrawing room, or heard the faint sob.

'That is not the truth of it . . .'

'Yes, it is. Anyway, I am glad Dvina understood my innuendos, as it seems she did, and has taken you to task. You deserved it.'

As she said this, she swept away from him and walked up to the door leading to the withdrawing room. It stood open. In an over-elaborate way she said, 'Ah, my dear Dvina, how lovely to see you. Oh dear, are you all right? You look very pale, dear.'

Andrew's heart dropped like a stone in his chest. *Dvina couldn't have heard, surely? Please God she hadn't – not the bit about everyone pitying me. Oh God, how much that would hurt her! It would resonate with the way I have kept her away from society! How could I ever make it up to her?*

'I'm perfectly well, thank you, Agatha. The nurse came down a little while ago and called your mother to Edgar's chamber. Your mother asked that we should go up as soon as you both arrived.'

'Darling . . .'

'We will talk later, Andrew. But to put you out of your misery, I heard every word. I . . . I am very upset, but my feelings are of no importance at the moment. It seems Edgar has taken a turn for the worse, and it is he and your mother we must think of at this time.'

She turned from him. Never had he seen such devastation in anyone, or such coldness in his wife. At that moment he knew he loved her above everything – he'd been a damn fool! Fool enough to lose her, for he'd never felt surer of anything. He had lost his gentle, kind, loving Dvina . . .

18

Will

Sheffield, September 1880
Finding a way

Will played around with his jug of ale. He hadn't a taste for it, but his taste for the one who had served it to him consumed him. So much so that he had taken to frequenting the bar more and more since he'd first entered it three months ago, just to be near Bridie and to take the odd chance of walking her home and making love to her – a need he couldn't deny himself.

He looked around the pub. His first visit here and the fight seemed so long ago, and the men had long since accepted him as part of the scenery. A haze of smoke from the fire and from their cigarettes hovered over the heads of the men. Some sat in gangs playing cards, others dominoes and others shove-halfpenny – these last were the ones responsible for the shouting and bouts of excitement that filled the room every now and then. A few just stood around on the freshly laid straw and talked. The main topic was the fliers stuck up all over the place asking for skilled workers for a mine over in Breckton. Most didn't know where Breckton was, and he was able to tell them it was a small town halfway between Leeds and York. He'd been that way fishing sometimes, as it was awash with lakes hidden in the valleys of the hills.

None of them seemed interested in taking up the offer, even though the advert promised good wages and conditions which they didn't have at the moment.

To him the opportunity offered a way out, and he intended to travel there to try his luck the next time he had two days off, which wouldn't be for a while.

Talking to Bridie about it as they stood under the bridge an hour later, she surprised him by urging him to go sooner. 'Will, 'tis as things are getting difficult. I dare not even ask you back to my place today, for the fear Bruiser might catch us. He said as he was for hearing rumours about me and some virgin, and he didn't like what he heard.'

'But he's on late shift, Bridie. He won't be home till on eleven, and I'll be long gone by then.'

'No, Will, I know him. He'd be for catching me out if he can, and it is for sure he'd be for killing me – and you too, me wee love. Please, Will. Take yourself along to this Breckton and be seeing if they would set you on. There's talk as houses will be found for all of the new workers in due course. Just think, it will be after being a new start for us, so it will. You could go and live in lodgings until you are allocated a cottage, then me and your mammy could be after joining you.'

'Aye, it all sounds good, but what if I don't get set on, but lose me job here for being absent? Everything would be much worse for us then. I can't take the risk, me little love, I can't. Me ma's getting on in her age. She had me when she were in her forties.' He smiled, adding, 'I were her "little shock", so she's always telling me. After years of nowt happening, I popped out with no warning and turned her and me da's lives upside down.'

'I'm for thinking you make a habit of that, Will Hadler, cos you're after doing that to mine too!' This made them laugh, and he felt glad because all seemed hopeless at times, and having a joke together helped them get through.

'Look, I'll make a start by talking to Ma. See how land lies with her.'

Though I've a good idea as she'll blow her top. Even more so at me wanting to go, before I've any official time off.

'Anyroad, if I'm willing to take the chance of Ma's wrath for you, Bridie O'Hara, the least you can do is repay me.' He kissed her neck, moving his lips up over her lovely soft skin until he reached her mouth. 'Eeh, Bridie, don't be telling me I can't have you, lass. I have a need on me as is too much for me to calm on me own.'

'I know. I'm for feeling the same, me wee love. If only we could go somewhere else.'

The need in her fired his longing to a pitch that he could hardly bear. His kissing of her wasn't enough. Their hands explored each other, finding and giving what pleasure they could, until a mocking voice crashed into the private world they'd thought themselves in. 'Ha, Will, give it to her, mate.'

Then another joined in. 'Hope it's worth it, though, as Bruiser's already got whiff of yer antics with his woman.'

The fear in Bridie singed through him. 'Don't worry, love. If they had malice in them, they'd have not sounded like they were taking us on.'

'Were you for seeing who they were? Is it as you know them, Will?'

'Aye, one of them works in the steel, but his brother and da are down the mine, so he lives in our road. Happen he's heard sommat when he's at work and he thought he'd have a laugh. He ain't a bad bloke. I can't see him making anything of it. Anyroad, I'd better be off.' He held her close. 'Eeh, lass, you're shaking. I'll make it reet, I promise. I can't have you afraid like this. What time are you expecting Bruiser to come by?'

''Tis as he could come round any time, and is why that lad knew of me. For hasn't Bruiser taken to coming out of work, to make sure as I'm not cheating on him?'

'By, lass, he's sommat else. Look, I'll take me chance and come round later.'

'No . . . ! Will, 'tis heart-sore I am to refuse you, but . . .'

'Look, I'll tell you what I'll do. I'll give Beth a knock first and see if she knows if he's with you. And if he is, I'll make meself scarce – how's that?'

This settled her.

'Reet, then, lass, I'm loath to leave you, but I have to.' Not trusting himself to kiss her properly, he pecked her cheek.

Walking home, his mind dwelt on how he'd get his ma to accept his going, because he knew now he was going, no matter what she decided and whether she liked it or not.

The saying *having a ramrod for a back* applied to his ma at this very moment. Standing looking out of the window, she hadn't spoken. When she did turn to Will, her face looked ugly with distaste. 'Not Bridie O'Hara . . . not that whore!'

'Don't call her that, Ma – you know nothing about her. Yes, her life ain't been what I'd like, but there were reasons. She were put on the path she's followed by men as did her wrong, not least her own da!'

'You won't convince me, son. Think on. Think of all those who've been there afore you. That's what will eat at you as the years pass. She ain't the kind for any man to marry. She can only bring heartache to you.'

'I know you are concerned for me, but I am a man and can make me own decisions. And I'll tell you this for nothing, Ma: I'm going with her whether you come or not, but it won't be how me heart wants it. Just give her a chance. You know what you always say: don't meet trouble halfway, when it might not be travelling your road in the first place. We'll be reet, Ma, I know we will, but we have to move. We can't risk Bruiser Armitage's wrath . . .'

'Bruiser Armitage! What's he to do with owt? She's not tied up with him, is she?'

'Aye, he thinks she's his girl, but she's not, never has been. Oh aye, he's been with her a long time and he got customers for her, but . . .'

'Customers! God in heaven, listen to yourself, Will! What're you thinking? How're you going to live with it all? It'll fester in you, son, it's bound to. All those other men that have had her! Taken her down for . . . for money! Will, please, I beg of you, think again. Give yourself some time. Have your fun, but keep yourself for a decent lass.'

'Bridie is decent! Look, Ma, her own da raped her when she were no more than sixteen years old. Then a gypsy lad tricked her out of everything she had in the world. She had no choice; she only had a girl from the correction convent to look after her and that's how she came to land up here, doing what she does.'

Watching his ma slump down into the chair opposite him and lower her head into her hands, he felt heart-sore to bring this trouble to her door. But he couldn't help himself, he couldn't. He loved Bridie with everything he was, and he had to be with her for the rest of his days or there was no point to living.

'Time's not going to make any difference, is it, Will?' Her voice shook. 'I'll say sommat, though: in some ways me and your da gave you your impulsiveness. I haven't told you afore, but I only set eyes on your da the once, and from that moment I knew he were my man. We shocked everyone by marrying within two months of meeting. And, though I'm embarrassed to say it, I was already his – completely his – cos I gave meself to him just one day after meeting him. It seems same has happened to you, Will. And just as I needed folk to accept me situation, you do too. Yet here's me, your own ma, denying you that acceptance.'

She looked at him. Her eyes held love, but he saw the pain in her face. Was she going to make him choose between her and Bridie? Her face changed, and he couldn't read her expression. It was a relief when she said, 'I'm sorry about what I said. It was the shock of it all. I'll do me best to take to her. I'll look for good as is in her, and forget the bad that's gone afore. After all, wasn't Mary Magdalene herself a prostitute? And look at her; she turned out to be a saint!'

Will laughed at this and the tension broke. 'Thanks, Ma. Thanks. I doubt as Bridie'll turn out to be a saint, though! But I couldn't have been happy without your blessing – not truly happy. And I'm sorry about all the upheaval it'll cause, with us moving and everything. But I don't see another road as would work.'

'You'd better see if you get the job first, Will. There's that hurdle, thou knows, and it'll probably be first of many an' all, with what you're going in for. But we'll take each one as it comes. Now let's get tea on table. It were ready two hours since and'll be spoiling by now.'

He couldn't put his relief into words, though he knew his ma could still be difficult. Something had clicked with her, to go along with him, and he didn't think it was the tale of her and Da that she'd told him, though that had shocked him. He'd always thought they'd had a long and proper court-ship, not – well, not at it after they had only just met!

Pondering over it all while he ate, he found he'd a good appetite on him. He took seconds and thirds, but made no conversation whilst he did so, and his ma didn't question him on his silence. Plans formed in his head. Putting his knife and fork down, he sipped at his tea, announcing, 'Ma, I've made me decision. I'm going to Breckton tonight, if there's a train, but I'll get to the station anyroad and stay there till there is one.'

'Tonight! As soon as that?'

'It has to be soon, Ma. Bridie's thinking as Bruiser knows sommat is going on. If he finds out, he'll cut up rough about it. Besides, I'm not at work till ten tomorrow night, and I can make it back for that, and no one will be the wiser. That way, if I'm not successful I won't lose me job here.'

'Oh, Will, it's a lot to take in. Where shall I say as you've gone, if folk ask?'

'Just say as I've gone fishing or walking, like I do on occa-sion. In fact, I'll take me fishing basket with me, then if I'm seen on station no suspicions will be raised. I'll call in on Bridie on me way and let her know me plans and tell her as you'll be coming with us.'

As he took another sip he noted her distress, and knew she hadn't really won the battle going on inside her. She'd only voiced what she'd known he wanted to hear, but he wouldn't press the point. He couldn't. He had to take her acceptance of the situation as it stood. The moment held an awkward silence, until his ma broke it.

'I can't say as I'm not vexed about it all, nor as I'm not upset about having to up sticks. But me mind's made up to give me best to it all. I can do no more than that.'

'Well, that'll do me, cos your best is twice that of others. It'll pan out, you'll see.' He rose and kissed her cheek. 'I'll make it work, Ma. It'll be reet, I promise, and I know as you'll grow to love Bridie.'

The corner of the wardrobe sliced Bridie's face as her body hurtled into it. 'No! Bruiser! For all that is holy, will you listen to me . . .'

The last shred of her bodice ripped from her as he clawed her and pulled her towards him. Evil bled from the black coals of his eyes. His spittle sprayed onto her cheeks as he hissed, 'Tell me the fucking truth! Who is the fucking virgin you've been seeing?'

''Tis the truth I've been telling you . . .' The force of the blow sent her reeling again, and she landed on her knees. Red spots dripped onto the floor beneath her, merging with the small puddles of blood already making patterns around her. Every ounce of her strength ebbed away into a pool of tears. 'Stop it, Bruiser, for the love of God, stop!'

A sickening cracking sound brought with it immense pain and the knowledge that his foot had broken her ribs. She rolled over onto her side, moaning like an animal.

Trying to put space between them, she stretched out her hands, hoping to edge forward. Through the mist crowding her brain, she saw his boot a second before it came down to crush her fingers. *Oh, sweet Jesus, be at the helping of me*, she beseeched Him. But as her body lifted like a rag doll, she knew no one would be answering her prayer.

The edge of the bed dug into her stomach. Bruiser had placed himself at the back of her, between her legs. Fear gripped her as she realized his intention, felt him near to where she'd always refused him entry. Not able to fight him off, she tried to beg him once more. 'No, please, I'll be at doing anything, but not that, not that . . . Please . . .'

By the time Will left home and headed for Bridie's, the good feelings he'd had inside him earlier had come back to him, though they still had a taint of the emotional blackmail he knew he'd used on his ma.

When he arrived, he took the stairs leading to Bridie's room two at a time. Eager to see her and to tell her how he'd sorted everything, he'd forgotten all about their arrangement.

The moment he reached Bridie's door, his smile and excitement left him. Instead, a frozen shock and a deep fear held him as he heard Bridie's pitiful voice whimpering, 'No, Bruiser . . . No! Please don't . . . Stop! Stop! Will you stop . . . Oh, God! Oh God, help me . . .'

'It's more than fucking help you'll need afore I'm done. You bitch! What did I tell you, eh? You're my woman. Mine! And when I'm finished with you, you'll know who your man is. Me! Not some snivelling virgin. Stop fucking kicking! I'm telling you – you bastard whore! You . . . What the—?'

The door had shot open in response to Will putting his shoulder to it. Bruiser's red-streaked, shocked eyes stared at him. The scene before Will froze in a split second of time. Bridie turned her head towards him, her eyes wide with terror. Rage filled his veins; his blood pumped it around his body. It came from him in a scream that pierced his own ears with the sound of his anger and hurt. 'Noooooo! You leave her!'

'The fucking virgin! And screaming like a stuck pig. Fancy your chances, then? I'll fucking kill you. You little squirt! You had her in broad daylight . . . you fucking humiliated me, the pair of yer.' As Bruiser moved towards him, Bridie's cries held anguish and fear. 'No! No – don't. Bruiser, no . . .'

Will had no conscious knowledge of crossing the room or of what had lifted his foot so swiftly and with such force, but he knew the vicious kick had found its mark as his foot sank into Bruiser's groin. The ensuing cry of agony filled the space around them. Bruiser's body slumped and then heaved. The sound and smell of his vomit sickened Will's stomach, but didn't stop him. He took Bridie in his arms, saying, 'It's all right, me little lass. Come on now, come on.'

As if she were a baby, he lifted her up and carried her down the stairs, the sound of her weeping tearing at his heart. When he reached the bottom step, he sat down, holding her on his knee.

'Bridie, you'll be reet, me little love. Come on now. That's reet. Here, wipe your eyes with me hanky. It's clean, thou knows.'

She looked up at him and smiled through her tears. 'Aye, well, isn't it the way of it? And to be sure it has to be, cos I'd not be for taking on a fella as doesn't carry a clean hanky!' They giggled at this and felt a lightening of the horror and a deepening of the bond between them.

'Hark at him, Will! I'm thinking it'll be a while before he can use any girl again. He were going to . . . Oh, Will, it must have been God in Heaven answering me prayers and bringing you to me.'

'More like me love and me plans. I'm a bit worried, though,

as I might have done him an injury. Me foot sank in really deep. Do you think we should call in the doctor?'

'No, Will, you'll only be bringing trouble down on yourself if you do that. The doctor would be after bringing in the law. Leave Bruiser be – let him be suffering. It'll serve him his just rights. And, if I know him, he'll not be for telling anybody as you brought him down.'

'Aye, happen you're right. Anyroad, noise as he's making will alert someone eventually, if he don't recover himself soon.'

'Forget him, Will. Beth will see to him when it is as she thinks we've had enough time to get away. She doesn't miss anything, Beth.'

The door at the top of the stairs opened just as she finished saying this, and Beth stood there. 'Eeh, Bridie, what's going on, lass?' She nodded at Will. 'What have you done? I heard you having a barney, but it sounds like you've near-killed Bruiser, by the way he's hollering!' She descended the stairs as she spoke. 'Oh, Bridie, look at you. Oh, love, come on, come to me room. Let's get you cleaned up and dressed.'

'I can't. I have to get away, in case it is he recovers enough to come after us. Just hand me something to wear, Beth.'

'But where will you go, love?'

'I'll take her to me ma. She'll take care of her.'

'Your ma? Will, is it that she's all right with you taking me on, then?'

'Aye, after a fashion, but she'll do her best. I know me ma: if she makes her mind up, she'll stick to it. And she promised me she'd try to accept the situation.'

'You mean you're really going, Bridie, to this Breckton place as you mentioned? Eeh, love, what am I going to do without you?'

'You can come if you want, Beth. Yes, why don't you? To

be sure it would make me happy to have you along and to get you out of this lot.'

'I can't, Bridie, but thanks for asking. I've plans, you know that, but I'm going to miss you, lass. Write to me, and let me have your address once you get settled. Promise me.'

'I will, Beth. I couldn't be for doing any other.'

Beth ran upstairs and emerged from her room carrying some clothes. She helped Bridie into them, tears streaming down her cheeks as she did so. 'Eeh, love, you'll be reet. Will'll take care of you.' Bridie winced with pain as Beth tried to hold her. 'That sod! You'll be well out of it, love, and that's the only thing as is helping me with parting from you. Look after her, Will.'

'I'll die trying, Beth, I promise you that. But first I've to get her over the shock of meeting me ma.'

They both grinned at this. Beth's face had a sign in it that said he was doing the right thing; Bridie's held pain, and the creasing of her face dripped more tears from her eyes.

'Stay with her a mo whilst I fetch a cab, Beth. It's not far, but she'd not make it, with pain as she's in.'

Luck was on his side. Outside the theatre, about a hundred yards from the corner, stood several cabs. The drivers had tethered the horses to the railings while they busied themselves feeding them and getting them ready for the theatre-goers who would soon emerge. Haggling with them took a moment; they all wanted to be sure they would make enough out of the trip to warrant missing a fare from the theatre, and to know Will had the money to pay them with.

At last one of them agreed and Will climbed up the steps. He'd never been in a cab before, and in better circumstances would have enjoyed the experience as the carriage swayed from side to side to the rhythm of the clip-clop of the horse's hooves on the cobbles.

When he arrived back, Bridie posed him a problem. 'Will, it is that I cannot go without some of me things. Me papers and clothes and shoes. I must have them, for sure Bruiser won't be for letting me get them later.'

He could see her anguish and understood it. It was a lot to ask of her to leave with only Beth's dress and shawl to her name.

Beth gave him the solution: 'I've listened at the door and Bruiser is still moaning, Will,' she said, 'so I think we'd get away with going in and taking what she needs.'

Before he could answer her, the cab driver shouted, 'Are you coming or not? I'm not waiting for Christmas, thou knows.'

Torn for a moment, Will stood there, but his indecision left him and he told her, 'I'll go, Beth. It'll be better for you if Bruiser doesn't know you are involved, or know anything about where she's gone. You get Bridie into the cab and keep the driver happy for a mo for me.'

Back in Bridie's room, Bruiser, curled up in a ball of agony, turned his head almost in slow motion as if the very act caused him more pain. His eyes, bloodshot and wet with tears, bulged out of their sockets. His swollen face had a purple tinge to it. Will felt a fear enter him. Was Bruiser about to die? Could a hard kick to a man's bollocks kill him? He didn't think so, and Bruiser was breathing all right – had to be, to cry like he was doing. It came to Will's mind to ask him, 'Who sounds like a stuck pig now?' But he didn't. He just walked past him, crossed the room, grabbed the clothes from the cupboard and threw them onto the bed. Opening the drawers of the chest one by one, he scooped out their contents. One held Bridie's undergarments; another, sweet-smelling bottles and pots. A third drawer held some papers and a large half-full bottle of gin. He took the papers, leaving the gin, then thought better of it and took that, too. Bridie might need the comfort of it later. Lastly he picked up three pairs of shoes and one pair of ankle boots, and took down her coat from a hook behind the door. He wrapped the whole lot into a tight bundle with the bed sheet. At the bottom of the stairs he grabbed his fishing basket and rod and somehow managed to get everything out to the cab.

Bridie snuggled up to him on the journey. He wasn't sure if her weeping was at having to say goodbye to Beth or because she was in pain, but he just held her and let her cry it out. He had so many fears in him, not least what his ma would do when they arrived there.

There had been no need for him to worry. When he reached home he felt sure that no one had seen them. It was getting dark and the weather wasn't good, so none of the womenfolk had been standing on their doorsteps having a chinwag, and he knew the men who weren't on shifts would be in the pub.

Shock registered on his ma's face. He saw her trying to mask her disapproval, but when he told her what had happened and she saw the state of Bridie, she took charge. 'You get yourself off. Go on, she'll be reet. Get off like you intended, and let's get on with our lives as they're going to pan out. And don't worry on anybody finding out she's here, or about our intentions, cos you're right to do it all in secret after this. I wouldn't trust Bruiser. He'd find us, and then God knows what he'd do.'

Will leaned over and kissed her cheek. Like Bridie, his ma was a little woman, and despite her sixty-odd years, still a pretty one. Going by appearances, you'd think she needed looking after or someone to lean on, but in this too she was like Bridie: a survivor, independent in her ways and in how she thought. Not many mothers would take what he'd dished out today in the way she had.

His goodbyes to Bridie were full of anguish. Leaving her in such a state and with the fear of Bruiser hanging over her wasn't easy. They held each other as best they could for a short while, and whispered words of deeply felt love, before Will tried to reassure her. 'Don't worry, he won't come looking for you here. Everyone'll tell him as me ma wouldn't put up with it. They all see her as a little tyrant, cos she has standards far above what they have, but they don't know the centre of her like I do.' But as he spoke these words, he still couldn't believe how his ma had given in and accepted what he'd brought down on her. And something in him told him that he'd probably pay for it one way or the other, because she was no saint and, if crossed, she could be more akin to the Devil . . .

19

Will

Breckton, October 1880
A meeting of like minds

It was noon of the following day when Will finally stood outside Hensal Grange Mine in Breckton, some ten miles east of Leeds. He'd travelled by rail and on foot. A couple of times a sparkling lake had tempted him to sit awhile and set up his fishing rod, but he'd stayed focused on his mission and had mostly rued the subterfuge that had necessitated bringing the heavy equipment along with him.

He felt a relief in him when he saw the list of vacancies he'd heard tell of still posted up on the gates. He went in, walked over to the lads doing the screening and asked the whereabouts of the foreman. On their direction, he headed towards the small shed opposite the yard gates.

The foreman, a thickset man who looked to be in his late fifties, looked up from the forms he was busy filling in and greeted him. 'Morning, young man. And a grand one it is, too. What business are you on? And what's your name?'

Will answered him, glad to find him an amiable fellow.

'Well, now, I'm pleased to meet you, Will Hadler. I'm Dave

Grindle and I'm foreman, as you've probably gathered. Now you're right in that we're taking on, but I'm not the one as does the hiring and firing. Mr Harvey, owner of the mine, does all that. Well, hiring anyways, cos it's a grand place to work and there's never any firing needed. The jobs as we have going now are through expansion, as there's another seam for opening up. But he's choosy, lad. Have you references as to your skills and reliability?'

Will ignored the question, in case his answer didn't get him to see the owner, saying instead, 'How do I get to see this Mr Harvey, then?'

'He's over in the office. Go back towards the gate and then carry on. You'll see offices. Mind, you'll want an appointment. He'll not see you without. Have a word with the clerk who sits just inside. He'll fix you up, and good luck to you.'

'Ta very much. I hope as I'll be seeing you again.'

A few minutes later Will sat on the verge outside the gates. Getting the clerk to fix an appointment had proved difficult, and he'd been hard pushed to keep his temper. The man had been rude and offensive, looking down his nose at Will as if he were no more than a piece of dirt. Eventually he'd made the appointment for three o'clock that afternoon. The large clock on the office wall had marked the time as just on twenty past noon, so he'd sat awhile, eaten the last of the sandwiches his ma had put up for him, and thought on the new life he was hoping to make for them all.

He'd liked what he'd seen of Breckton so far. As he'd walked down through it, he'd passed by rows of back-to-backs, which he thought were probably the miners' cottages. Opposite them he'd seen a lane with a few cottages down it, which he thought might be for the men who worked the land. He'd noticed farming going on all around.

He'd found a peace in him when looking over the fields. This being the beginning of October, plenty was going on in the fields: men and horses at the harvesting and ploughing for next year. He liked the countryside. Mind, he didn't have Breckton down as a hamlet or a village, because he'd seen a good few shops on one of the streets he'd looked down. It was more of a small town, as far as he could see, and he was glad of that. It gave the best of both worlds: places to get provisions and such, as well as plenty of open space. And then there was the lovely backdrop: the hills, large and small, that he'd seen on his travels here. He was looking forward to walking them, and to fishing in the lakes or becks in their midst. And folk seemed friendly enough. He'd passed one or two womenfolk hanging over their gates having a natter, and they'd looked at him in a way as he could see they were wondering who he was and what was his business, but they'd all greeted him. He hadn't heard the comment one of them had made, but he'd heard their laughter about it. They sounded a jolly crowd; his ma and Bridie should fit in well with them. And he'd found the screen lads and foreman welcoming, though the clerk were sommat else. But then those jumped-up types always were, wherever you went.

It was odd, him having to see the owner, because back in Sheffield it was always the foreman or manager. And what did the foreman say? 'It's a grand place to work.' Well, he'd never heard that said of a pit he'd worked at before. All in all, this could be a good move all round.

The church bell woke him. He sat up in surprise, wondering for a moment where he was, then panic struck him as memory flooded back. He'd dropped into a deep sleep. Had he missed his appointment? It was too late to count the church bells;

they'd struck several times already. Listening again, he realized it wasn't the time they were marking, but the slow, dull chime of the death-knell. *Must be a funeral*. Dusting himself down, he made his way to the foreman's shed, hoping against hope he'd not overrun his time.

Luckily he found he hadn't, and had a few minutes to spare. Dave Grindle gave him a drink of water, some of which he used to splash his face.

'Don't worry that you look presentable enough, lad. Happen you needed that sleep. Mind, it'd been better if you'd asked me to give you the nod when it were nearing time, then you wouldn't have this panic. Get yourself over there now afore it's too late.'

Crossing the yard in a few quick paces, he once again faced the sour clerk. There was no time for any aggravating banter this time, as he was shown almost immediately into the main office.

'Sit down, Mr Hadler.'

The office didn't have anything posh about it. Far from it: it was shabby in fact. This surprised him, and the man in front of Will surprised him, too. He was only thirty to forty in years, but far from looking like the owner of a mine, he looked more like one of the workers, dressed as he was like a hands-on man. He did have a good suit hanging on a coatstand in one corner of his office, though, and his top-drawer voice was at odds with his appearance. Will felt unsure what he was dealing with. He knew how to act with moneyed folk, but this one wasn't clear-cut. And the man asking him to sit and calling him 'Mister', that wasn't usual either. But sit Will did.

'So you've come about the vacancies. What experience have you had?'

'I've been down since I was a young 'un, some fourteen

years now, sir. I've worked up from being a hurrier to being a face-worker. Me da afore me was a miner, as was me grandda – me ma's father, that is . . . I'd come with a good reference, only I need to move quicker than the notice I should be giving. But I could get foreman to speak for me, if you needs me to.'

'Are you in trouble with the law, Mr Hadler?'

'No, sir. Look, I'll be honest with you. Me and me lass, well . . . we needs a fresh start. I mean, well . . . she has a reputation, and there's someone who would make things bad for us. And not just him, either, cos a few tongues would wag and make it difficult for us. She's not had it good, me lass, and she fell into a bad way of life, but I love her and, with a chance being given to her, she can change. I knows that.'

Drawing in his breath, Will stopped and his colour rose, making his face burn. What had possessed him to tell this man all that? Well, he might as well put his cap on and leave, because he'd surely cocked it up. Mind, the fellow had a smile on his face – was he amused at his tale? Or laughing at the cheek of the likes of Will asking for a job?

'Well! It strikes me you're an honest man, William Hadler, and I like an honest man. If I give you a job, what are the chances of this "someone" finding you and causing trouble here?'

'He'll not know where to look, sir. And it'll be a shock to all when me ma goes, cos she were born in the cottage as we have. Me da took on tenancy when her father died, and I did same when he passed on. As well as that, we intend coming afore anyone can ask any questions. Of course, me ma's going to find it a wrench, but she's willing to give it a go, cos she can see me mind's made up and she respects me as head of house now.'

'And what about the expense? It won't be cheap to move over here from Sheffield.'

'I'm not worried over money and won't have a problem with funding the move, nor me wedding, as will take place as soon as we get here. Cos with me not being a drinking nor gambling man, I have a bit put by.'

'Umm, it sounds as though you have thought it all through, but there is one problem. The men I take on won't have a cottage allocated immediately. I have some lodgings sorted out with some of my present workers whose families have grown up and left home. It could be up to six months before the building of the cottages is complete and they're ready for occupation. So I think you will have problems regarding the accommodation of your family.'

'Does you think as I'd find something to rent in the town, sir?'

'You could try. You may get rooms above one of the shops, perhaps. Look, let's put it like this: I'll employ you from next Monday, and that gives you two days to sort out where you're going to live. If you don't find somewhere by the end of that time, then you must let me know immediately, so I can continue to find someone for the position I'm going to offer you. I've also decided to take you at face value, William Hadler. That is, I won't be asking for references. This is a very unusual step for me to take, but I don't want to complicate your position. This means I have to take you on trust, so please don't let me down.'

'I'll not, sir, I promise you.'

'Right. Now then, the terms and conditions: the pay rate is one and tuppence per ton of unriddled Wheatley Lime Coal, rising on a scale to two shillings per ton for New Hards or Silkstone Coal. You will receive a full list of all the rates, and you can expect to get a fair share of doing the cutting. The pay for this is a shilling per yard. On top of this, we add thirty-seven and a half per cent, though this is subject to any deductions, such as tools, candles, oils and rent, et cetera. You will start on the day shift, descending at 5.30 a.m. and ascending at 2 p.m. On Saturdays it will be 1 p.m. On the afternoon shift you will descend at two and ascend at ten, and on the night shift descend at nine forty-five and ascend at five forty-five in the morning. This shift begins on Sunday nights, when you will descend an hour later than normal. The shifts rotate on a three-weekly basis. We will shortly be introducing a crossover shift of 6 a.m. to 6 p.m., but that won't be in force until the new seam is well under way and we are up to full strength. Do you have any questions?'

'No, sir – them's fair prices and I'll be giving a fair day's work for them. Thank you, sir.'

'That'll be all then, Mr Hadler. I will expect you to let me know as soon as possible if you will be starting on Monday or not.'

With this, Will got up and left. Donning his cap, he almost skipped across the yard. *By, I've never known the like. Never before has anyone treated me to such courtesy, and the rates are good an' all. It's as if I've met a man of a like mind to me: an honest man. If I could just sort everything, we'll land on our feet all right. But where to start?*

He decided to walk down the high street to look in the shop windows and make a few enquiries with the owners about accommodation. There must be something! And he'd not worry about getting back, as he no longer needed his job. He just had to hope him not turning up would give Bridie hope instead of worry, and she'd know he must have struck it lucky.

*

'Well, lass, how're you feeling? Did you have a good night?'

'Aye, I did that, Mrs Hadler. And it'll be down to you that I did, so it will. You've taken such good care of me that I'm for thinking the Holy Mother herself would not be after doing a better job.'

'Me name's Janet, and I'll warn you right away that the blarney won't wash with me, so you can cut the flowery talk. Here, I've brought you a sup of tea and a bowl of oats. Best get something down you. It'll build up your strength.'

'Ta, it'll be welcome. It's fair starving I am. And you can take me words as truth. I'm not for giving you the flannel.'

'No, well, I'd say your good night was more down to that empty bottle of gin than anything I did for you. We're not a drinking family, thou knows, so I hope as it were for medicinal purposes.'

Oh, God, why did I not hide the bottle? Didn't I know as Will's ma isn't approving of the drink?

'Reet, I've me copper on boiling out in the back scullery, so I can't stop. I'm trying to keep up with me washing and everything. With Will not coming back, it looks like he has a move all lined up for us, as he wouldn't miss his shift if he hadn't. And all I can say on that score is, I hope you're worth it.'

Watching Janet disappear down the ladder that led to the kitchen below, Bridie wished she could start all over and have things like they used to be: for her to be as she was, back when she didn't have to use her tongue or her bodily attractions to try to wile her way into folks' affection. She'd done it for so long now that she'd lost her real self and seemed no longer able to recognize honesty of the kind Will's mammy liked to live by. And now she'd put the woman's back up, which wasn't for making a good start. She'd have to try harder.

The effort it took for her to get out of bed surprised her. Her body cried out in protest at every movement. She'd taken a few beatings in her time from men, but not like Bruiser had given her this time. The hurt extended to her heart, as she had done Bruiser's bidding since the first day she'd met him, except what it was he'd wanted to do to her yesterday. He'd asked her before, but had respected her refusal. But hadn't he been about to take her that way despite her protests? She shuddered at the thought.

'Oh, you've managed to dress and get down, then. Did that strapping I put around your ribs help?'

'It did, Janet, ta.'

'By, you look like you've been through mill, lass. You should've stayed in a while.'

'I was after thinking you might need some help.'

'Eeh, look at you, you're shaking. Go into the front room; there's a fire lit and you can sit down and get warm. I'm nearly done, anyroad. I'll be in with you in a minute . . . Look, happen as I were a bit sharp with you. I'm not approving of the life you've led, but Will explained circumstances as put you that way, and I'm sorry for you, lass. I'll do me best to accept the situation, but it ain't easy for me.'

'I know, and I'm not deserving of your son or his love for me, but with the chance he is giving me, I can change. I don't know how it was I came to be so low. It just seemed the only way, but then I had me spirit knocked out of me before I had a chance.'

'Don't cry, love, it doesn't help owt. What's happened has happened; it's what's in the future that matters. No one will know us where we're going, so we can make a fresh start. And don't think as I'm not ready for a change, because I am. Folk round here have sickened me for a good while. Let's hope we meet some decent neighbours over at this Breckton place.'

'Well, I'm glad about that, as I was for thinking I was uprooting you against your will. Is it sure you are I can't be for lending a hand?'

'It is. I have me routine. You just go and rest yourself. And don't worry on folk coming in, as I've locked me door. They know when the latch is on I'm not wanting visitors, so they'll just take it as that.'

Bridie welcomed the warmth of the fire, although it didn't stop her shakes. But she knew those weren't all down to her injuries and the cold, but the lack of a sup of gin to steady her. Inside she felt easier, though. That little talk with Janet had gone well, so it had. If she trod carefully, maybe they would get along together. And somehow she was to try to do without the drink. But that was a step she didn't know if she could take or not, for she had a powerful longing on her, so she did . . .

Getting the job had been the easy part for Will. Finding somewhere for them all to live, though, was proving to be nigh on impossible. He looked again around the three rooms above the hardware shop on Main Street, but no, he couldn't. Bridie'd be all right, he knew that – she'd put up with worse than this – and he'd be for making do, but his ma? No, he couldn't bring her to such a place. The move would be hard enough for her as it was. But then, what was he going to do?

He'd trudged the streets for what was left of yesterday afternoon, and he hadn't stopped since he'd risen early this morning. Now here it was on midday and all he'd found had been an old croft house with no windows, which the black-smith had offered, telling him he could have it rent-free for six months if he did the place up. Its damp, smelly rooms provoked a despair in him. He needed to be telling Mr Harvey one way or the other later today, and get on his way home.

The move was all planned in his head. He'd decided he'd hire a hauler from across the other side of Sheffield; someone who didn't know anyone who lived around their area. He'd planned on getting him to come around midnight on Saturday night. If he paid the right money they'd not question him; they were well used to midnight flitters. He'd have to have one who could take all three of them on board as well, because they'd not get away with coming here on the train. Someone would see them. If things went well, they would have settled in by Sunday night and he'd be ready to start on the Monday-morning shift. But first he needed a place to live!

'Are you taking them then, Mister? Only me da wants to close shop for dinner.'

'No ta, but does you know of owt else going? It wouldn't matter if it were five miles or so out of town even, but it needs to be half-decent and big enough to accommodate three of us.'

'Ain't these good enough for you then, Mister? I thought as you were a pit worker and'd be glad of them.'

It came to him to say, *No, they bloody well ain't*, and clip the lad round his clouts, but he didn't. Instead he said, 'It's just as they're not big enough, lad.'

'Well, I don't know of owt else, but you could try at the Farmers' Market on the morrow. Though like as not they'll want one of you to help on the land. They set up in the square down yonder, from about nine every Saturday.'

Thanking the lad, Will left.

Outside he took his cap off for a moment and smoothed his hair back. His mind wouldn't give him a solution. The only part of him knowing what it needed to do was his belly. He tapped it, saying, 'Stop your griping. I'm going to see about getting some grub into you right this minute. Aye, and a full belly might help me to decide what to do.' Across the road from him he saw a pub. As he placed his order for a cheese-and-onion butty and half-jug of beer, it came to his mind how all this had started. *By, what can happen in a few months!* Life had changed beyond recognition for him since he'd met Bridie. *Eeh, Bridie. Bridie, me own little lass. I can't wait to make you me wife.* He pulled himself up. If he let his mind travel the road as to what that meant for him, he'd not be able to concentrate on the matters he had in hand. He just hoped she was all right with his ma – or, rather, his ma was all right with her . . .

The bartender bringing over his butty broke his chain of thought, and he was glad of it. Dwelling on what might be happening at home would not get him anywhere.

'You're not from these parts, are you, lad? Have you come looking for work?'

'Aye, I have, and that bit's been easy. I can get set on at the pit, but finding a place for me family until pit cottages are ready is proving to better me. There's nowt around.'

'No, and cottages ain't much, either, but I think new ones as they are building are going to be two-up, two-down, or so I've heard tell. Mind, it could be as you end up in old 'uns, cos a few pit workers have put in for a move to the new row. And I'm thinking as Mr Harvey might listen to them, so I wouldn't be getting your hopes up.'

For all his big, jolly appearance, the bartender had a sulky kind of disposition and seemed to enjoy dampening folks' spirits rather than lifting them. Will had heard him prophesying doom and gloom for the weather and harvest with a middle-aged man who stood in the corner of the bar.

This same fellow turned now and put in his penny's worth, though he was a sight more optimistic. 'Give over, Dick, thou's giving the fellow a reet gloomy picture, and him up looking to better himself. Me name's Henry – Henry Fairweather. I work up at big house, Hensal Grange. It's home to Mr Harvey's mother and her husband. They have an empty cottage – it's usually allocated to the groom, only they haven't got one at the moment, nor are thinking of setting one on. They've got rid of all the hunters and mounts. They just keep the shires for working on the farm, and I look after them. Happen if you ask Mr Harvey about it, he could put a word in for you.'

'Well, he ain't never done owt like that afore, so what's with you thinking as he will now then?' the bartender asked Henry.

'Cos I happen to know he's desperate for pit workers. None's been coming through, and folk reckon as it's cos of there being no accommodation ready yet.' He turned back to Will and gestured with his hand, as if pointing to someone. 'Mr Harvey wants new seam up and running afore winter sets in. When did you say you were given job?'

'Yesterday afternoon. Mr Harvey said nothing about a cottage then. In fact he gave me a couple of days to find sommat or let him know, so he could find someone else for the job.'

'Well, happen he'd not thought on how difficult it was, or even given his ma's empty cottage a thought. You mark my words, he ain't gonna find anyone else, so you've a good chance. Have you a family, then?'

'Aye, me mother and me future wife. I'm for posting banns within three weeks of us registering here.'

'Well, if I were you, I'd get back up to pit and try your luck.'

'Ta, I will. Thanks, Henry. It's good of you. And with a bit of luck I'll be seeing you again. Me name's Will – William Hadler.'

'Aye, all right. Good luck to you, Will.'

'Good luck to you' seemed to be a saying round these parts, as he'd had it said to him a time or two in the few hours he'd been here. And it'd worked, too: here he was, not two hours since he'd last heard the phrase, and he had a cottage. And what a cottage! It was lovely. Pity it was only for a short lease until the new row was finished, because he could imagine being very happy here. It was a two-up, two-down, with an added porch on the back leading to the coalhouse and a back scullery with the copper in. His ma'd love that.

He could have hugged Mr Harvey when he'd returned to the office to see him earlier and told him what he'd heard from that Henry fellow. Mr Harvey said, 'That sounds like a possibility. Now why didn't I think of it? Right, as luck would have it, I'm just about to go up to see my mother. I'll put it to her husband. I'm sure he will lease it to me for a short while. You wait here, Will. There's a canteen across the yard. I'll be about an hour.'

And now here he was, standing in the garden of the place he'd soon be calling home.

Something Bridie had told him came to his mind. She'd lain back in his arms after their love-making and given a little giggle. When he'd asked what had amused her she'd said, 'I was for thinking about something me mammy used to say to me might just have come true,' and then had told him the saying about having a dream and being ready to catch it. 'And you know, Will?' she'd continued. 'Though I've not been a good girl, I have always said me prayers, and I always did have a dream. Me dream was of having a good man to love me and, now it's happening, I am ready, and I am going to catch me dream, Will.'

He'd said nothing, for his heart had been too full, but as he recalled it now, he knew they would both do as her mammy had said. They'd both catch the dream.

20

Andrew

Breckton, December 1880
A day never to forget

As he held his mother in his arms, Andrew knew he would never forget today: 1st December 1880.

The two officers stood to attention in front of them, both visibly moved by the dreadful news that one of them, a captain, had just read out to them. After a moment the colonel took the scroll from the captain and handed it to Andrew. 'Sir, Captain Eastland was a good officer and a very brave man, and the regiment will miss him. But for such news to come just hours after his own father died – I cannot tell you how sorry I am.'

'Thank you.' Andrew reached out and picked up the bell on the small table next to him and rang it. 'You will have some refreshments, Colonel? Captain?'

The butler appeared just as the colonel answered, 'We wouldn't want to intrude. I noticed an inn in the village. We will go there.'

'No, no, we won't hear of it. Jameson, show these gentlemen into the front drawing room, and please inform the kitchen to provide lunch in half an hour. Others may arrive: my sister and her husband, and my wife is on her way. I'll join you in a moment, Colonel. There are questions I need to ask.'

'Of course, sir.'

'Andrew. Sorry, I should have introduced myself. Andrew Harvey. I am – was – Captain Eastland's adoptive brother. I'll just see to my mother.'

He nodded at Jameson, who took over the situation and led the two officers out of the room.

'Oh, God, Mother. I don't know what to say. It has all been such a shock. How are you going to cope?'

She stood away from him, her composure regained. 'I will, darling. Somehow I will. We have been expecting this bad news for some time, but I never dreamed it would all come on the same day.' The door opened and she added, 'Ah, here is Agatha now.'

As Andrew looked at his sister, his heart felt like stone. Nothing touched it, not even his anger at her, which still festered inside of him. 'Agatha, we have further bad news, I'm afraid.' As he told her about Jeremy's passing, she showed no sign of it affecting her.

'I would say that *for you*, dear brother, this is all good news. Very good news, in fact . . .'

'Agatha!'

'I'm sorry, Mother. I didn't mean to upset you, but my pompous brother here doesn't seem able to put a foot wrong. Everyone's bad news is his good news.'

Andrew gave her a withering look, but decided to treat what she had said with the contempt it deserved. 'Please stay with Mother and help her, Agatha. We have guests – the officers who brought the terrible news about Jeremy. They are staying to lunch, but I need to ask them some delicate questions in private.'

He found out as much detail as he could about Jeremy's death: it was as he had thought, Jeremy had led his platoon from the front and had been shot by a sniper. He ascertained that Jeremy's body would not be brought home; due to the heat, they'd had to bury the dead very quickly. He rejoined the gathering in the withdrawing room to find that Dvina had arrived. She sat on a chair by the fireplace – filling it to capacity, he noted – holding his mother's hand. Floods of tears rolled down her cheeks. But then it wasn't that long since her father's death, and now she had to face losing her uncle and cousin.

Pity for her softened the hardness of his heart. Their relationship had been very strained since Agatha's outburst a couple of months ago, but now was not the time to perpetuate that. He went to her side and placed his arm around her shoulder. 'My dear, I am very sorry. It has all come as a shock to you, I know. You had such faith your uncle would recover, and that Jeremy would come home. And all so soon after your own father's passing.'

She remained with her head bent, but took the handkerchief he offered her. Did he feel a slight squeeze of his hand as she did so? God, he hoped so. These last months had been agony.

Issy used her pinny to rub the flour off her hands. It seemed she'd only just settled into her job in Tarrington House, sorted her ma and got used to the likes and dislikes of Mrs Beale, the housekeeper, when it was all set to change again!

A few days after Mr Eastland's funeral they had learned that, due to his death and that of his son, Mr Harvey had inherited Hensal Grange. He and Miss Dvina were going to move into it, and Mr Harvey's mother would be moving back to this house.

'What a carry-on, and all in the space of a few weeks. I don't know . . .' Mrs Beale grumbled for the umpteenth time. 'And poor Mrs Harvey. She's now six months with this one, and they say as he hardly speaks to her.'

'Well, I wouldn't listen to such gossip if I was you. There's none of us knows what goes on for sure upstairs, and them as works up there only thinks they do. So I wouldn't spread anything you hear. Now, if you don't mind, I am up to me elbows in baking.'

'Well! You never have learned your place, Isabella. If it wasn't for the fact of Mrs Harvey bringing you here herself, you'd have been up the road by now.'

Issy ignored this. Mrs Beale had a bitter tongue, and arguing with her only made things worse. Besides, she had no time to do so. Mr Harvey's mother was coming to dinner, and so were several guests of the legal persuasion, with their wives, and she had been asked to make it all very special. 'I want Mrs Eastwood to see I am more than capable of being hostess of the grand Hensal Grange, Isabella,' Miss Dvina had said. She often spoke directly with her, on the rare occasions she and Mr Harvey entertained, but then they went a long way back together. Issy had started in Hartington House when Miss Dvina had been just a lass and, always hungry, Miss Dvina had often visited the kitchen. They'd all had a laugh with her, and they'd all loved her. It hurt to hear from Jane that things weren't as good for her as they had been.

When they met as they went about their duties, she and Jane tried to speculate about why this was. It all seemed at odds with how things had started out. Oh, they knew Mr Harvey wouldn't visit her chamber as often now Miss Dvina was pregnant, but the pregnancy should have kept them close. Surely it wasn't all about what happened in the bedroom, was it? A pang of irritation with herself entered her at this thought, because she now knew how important that part of a marriage must be. Her face, already red from the heat, blushed even redder as thoughts she tried to suppress came into her. *Eeh, Issy, give over. Just be thankful nothing came of it, and stop getting these longings for it to happen again! You're no better than a whore!*

Not that she ever wanted it to happen again as it had done, of course, but finding someone of her own would complete her world.

It had been three months now, and the gypsy hadn't been back around these parts. She'd never told anyone. She couldn't. They'd have painted her with a tarred brush, and would have put some of the blame onto her, saying she must have egged him on. And then the threats he'd made . . . She shuddered even now at the thought of them.

Not for the first time she wondered what had happened to the gypsy to make him change. He'd never given any trouble when he used to visit each autumn a few years ago: he never stole, he worked hard and he was generally welcomed. His visits were even looked forward to. But since his raping of her, she'd heard tell of a few tales as to his ways, especially amongst the Irish. Helping her ma deliver babbies up in that quarter had made her privy to some of the things folk said about him, and it all horrified her. It seemed he loaned them money and then punished them if they couldn't pay back. One had even said he'd taken little children as payment, and they had disappeared for good. She couldn't take this in, or believe it as a truth. Everyone knew the Irish lot could tell a tale and make it grow ears, but she had to admit they did all seem very afraid of him. They had begged her not to say anything, for fear of him. Well, she knew what that felt like, for hadn't she kept everything to herself, not even telling her ma? And she'd never stopped thanking God it hadn't resulted in a pregnancy.

Putting her mind to attacking the dough on the board in front of her, Issy determined to banish it from her mind. She wanted to lock it away for good, but she knew she couldn't do that. Not in the small hours of the night, she couldn't, for then the feelings he'd given her visited her and she shamed herself by giving them a release.

The door to Andrew's office opened without anyone knocking, and he looked up from his desk in surprise. This was replaced by discomfort when he saw Dvina standing there. His concern made him stutter, 'What . . . are you all right, my dear?'

'Yes. I'm tired, but I wanted to talk.'

'Oh, not about anything serious, I hope. I have such a lot of stuff to read. I have to make sure I know the exact questions that I need answers to tonight, and the implications of everything.'

'I won't be fobbed off again, Andrew. We have to clear the air.' She closed the door behind her. 'You will have to forgive me for intruding, but this is the only place where we are not likely to be disturbed by the servants wandering around. I swear some of them have ears that can bend around corners.'

He laughed at this. She always amused him. Even over these tiresome months when relations between them had been strained, she'd often found some way of lightening the really awkward moments. But still, in many ways, she was to blame for it all. She had said in the beginning that as long as he was discreet she'd understand if he had the odd liaison, so how come – when she found that he had done so – she played up in such a dramatic way? She'd banned him from her bed, and only talked to him when necessary. It had been hell, pure bloody hell! So much so that, despite a melting of hostilities since the day Edgar had died, he still felt inclined to make her do the running. 'So, you have my attention. What are you proposing we do about our situation?'

'I want you to stop – well . . . extramarital activities.'

'What?' *Bloody woman! She knew no boundaries of propriety at times. How dare she speak to him – her husband – in that way?* His only defence seemed to be a counter-attack. 'Well, there aren't any marital activities, as you call them, so how can I indulge in extra ones?'

'Trying to be clever won't help matters, Andrew, nor will it ease your guilt – which you seem to have wrapped up and put onto me.'

God, she had a way with words. It seemed like she could see inside him, and it gave her an advantage. He'd very nicely blamed her for a long time now and did not want to go back to shouldering it all himself. It was at odds with him to do so. 'So, knowing all of what Agatha said that day, and both of us having made a plan together to deal with it, meant nothing to you?'

'I . . . I did know, but having it spelled out, and you not denying it, hurt me so much. It meant me realizing how aware of it everyone was.'

'But you knew that, too. We'd spoken about it. We had made plans to put it right. I honoured my part of that bargain, Dvina. I honoured it because of my love for you. But from that day, when that bitch of a sister of mine took great pleasure in spouting it all out for you to hear, you chose to ignore that fact.'

Dvina's face paled. Andrew watched her grope for a chair, her bulk too much for her to carry in a standing position for very long. He felt disgust as he looked at her bloated body and rounded face, with its chins hanging in folds, almost hiding her neck. Yet inside her body she carried something so precious to him, and he didn't want anything to happen to it. He moved towards her. As she looked up into his face he saw in her eyes the beautiful woman still encased inside her, and his love of that woman touched a fragment of his heart. 'My dear, you must take care. You mustn't overdo it. You have done so well to carry our child this far.'

'But it would all be so futile if I was to lose you.' A tear rolled down her cheek. 'I . . . I came in to say I'm sorry. You are right. We had discussed it, in a way, but without actually naming things. We had understood each other, and you had promised to change things. And I know you did stop . . . stop going to town in the evenings; and I know that, because of my condition, we couldn't put the other part – the enter- taining and socializing – into practice straight away. I just don't know why I couldn't cope with it all when I actually heard it said, in no uncertain terms. Can you forgive me, Andrew? Can you love me again like you once did?'

At this moment he couldn't be sure whether he could. He hadn't stopped loving her in a way, but some of the edge had gone from it. There had been no intimacy, and he had resumed his visits to Lilly without guilt. What she gave him had become his satisfaction, and though he had tried, he couldn't really recall the depth of feeling he'd had when he coupled with Dvina. As he looked at her now, he wondered if it had all been a figment of his imagination, or even how she could have aroused in him any passion at all, let alone the deep passion he thought he remembered.

When he didn't answer, she said, 'If you cannot, then I want us to separate. I will move back to Hartington House, as it has not yet sold. You are very wealthy now, so I would expect you to support me and our child.'

'No! No, not that, Dvina. I won't allow that to happen.' The shock this gave him tugged him out of the world he'd drifted into since that awful day when she'd heard the truth of everything. *My God, how had he allowed things to slip to this depth?* 'Dvina, I couldn't live without you. I know that now.'

He watched as more tears tumbled down her cheeks. She tried to rise, but couldn't. His heart twisted with the thought of having done this to her.

'Oh, my dear . . .'

'Don't, Andrew. It's not your fault. It's mine. And now . . . look at me, I have buried myself in food again. I know I do it, so why do I do it? Oh, God!'

He knew then that she had seen the disgust in his face. 'If we were happy again, would you try to control how much you eat? Oh, I don't mean that would be a condition – I just want us to be happy, no matter what – but would it help? I am so fearful for your health and for our child, my dear.'

'I seem to have made things so much worse. I have wallowed in my hurt, and used it as an excuse to give in to my greed. But yes, Andrew, if I thought I had regained your love, I could cope again. I could find a way. Mrs Harman is always advising me on what I should be eating and says she has some potion or other.'

'Well, take her advice, but not her potions. We don't know what is in them.'

'She says they are all made of herbs, and she has a deep knowledge of what they purport to do. Some may help with the variation of my body temperature – how I feel cold a lot of the time – but the one she wants me to have cleanses the body of impurities. She says once that is accomplished, I won't crave food like I do. She says I am eating all the wrong things, that I have a sweet tooth; she has a potion – well, a tea – that will diminish those cravings.'

'It is true that she does have a good knowledge and has come up with cures for ailments. Even diseases that spread like wildfire have been stopped by her intervention, but I am afraid. Supposing they harm the baby?'

'Well, I will talk to her again, but I cannot see as herbs could do any harm. The important thing is that you still want me as your wife and in your home. That has lifted my spirits so much. I feel better already.'

Kneeling down, he took her chubby hand. He knew he could not make her any promises, but he also knew he couldn't bear her taking the drastic step of leaving him. Somehow they had to resolve their problems. 'Dvina, I can only say that when you said you would leave, it was so far from what I wanted, it shook me to my core. We will need time to get ourselves back to—'

'I know, and I am willing to give you time, but will you come and lie with me again? I don't mean to . . . well, just to hold me, to let me know you want me, and I promise I will do my best to recover. So that when our child is born we can – well, you know . . .' She smiled a tired, weak, unsure smile. He lifted himself off his haunches to reach her cheek. He kissed it, and then as she turned her head towards him he found her lips and his kiss deepened. The softness of her skin and the cushioning effect of her plump face stirred memories in him, and he knew it would be possible to get those feelings back. It would just take time. By his reckoning, it would be another three months before their child arrived, and then, as he understood it, another six or so weeks after that before he could even think about resuming their love-making. He would use that time to recover and to wean himself off his need of Lilly.

Sitting in the very well-sprung carriage on his way to Leeds the next morning, Andrew felt a sense of well-being settle over him. Today everything would be finalized as regards his new fortune.

He relaxed back and enjoyed the gentle rolling motion, a much pleasanter one than the jolting of his old carriage, whilst he went over in his mind some of the things he needed to make sure of during his visit to his bank.

Just over an hour later, as his driver drove him to his club, he reflected on how well the visit to the bank had gone. Armed with the knowledge he had from his solicitors after the very agreeable dinner of the evening before, he was able to sign all of the necessary papers. The extent of his wealth hit him in all its glory: he had over one million pounds in capital assets, property and land, and a further million in business holdings. Not to mention foreign assets, which he did not yet have a figure for, but he understood some of it to be in gold-bullion holdings in a Swiss bank.

So much had happened since the day his mother had told him of her marriage, and his worries at the time seemed paltry now. He entered the gentlemen's club of which he'd been a member for a number of years and found a quiet corner. He remembered sitting there with Jeremy once. A lot of the patrons then present had wanted to give Jeremy all their attention, and to bag some of Andrew's just to get in Jeremy's favour. Jeremy had been the richest member at the time. What the fawning bastards hadn't stopped to consider was what a nice man Jeremy was, rich or not.

Sipping the hot toddy the bartender had brought over to him, Andrew thought of how that part of Jeremy's character had shown itself in the last letter he'd received from him, when he'd told him not to feel guilt if – as had seemed imminent – he lost his life. That helped a lot, because without that assurance Andrew, the ultimate guilt-plagued man, would have felt terrible about the inheritance. Poor Jeremy! How very sad that he had met his death so soon after he'd written the letter, and doubly so because already there were rumblings of reaching agreement to bring about peace in Africa by early 1881, such a short time away; if only he'd remained safe until then.

The hot spirit warmed his stomach, taking some of the chill of the wintry weather out of him. He moved his chair to face the roaring fire. He had so much on his mind that he wondered if he'd cope with it all. For one thing he intended – very soon – to reinstate the stables at Hensal Grange, and for that he would need an excellent groom. He knew Henry Fairweather looked after the shire horses that remained, and he knew him to have far more skills than were called upon to do this work. But Andrew's dream was to have hunters and racehorses, as well as some good carriage horses and mounts, and Henry wouldn't manage all that. They would have to advertise for another skilled man to help him. But then, of all the inconveniences, he'd only just let the cottage that was usually reserved for a groom and his family! He'd have to find a way around it. Maybe if he got a single man, he could lodge him with one of the widows he hadn't yet moved out of the Miners' Row. Mrs Harman and Isabella – the very ones! Yes, that would do nicely. After all, two women would be a chaperone for each other to cover the impropriety of having a man living with them, and they could share and give the upstairs room to the groom. Besides, it wouldn't be for long, because Hadler could move into the first of the completed new cottages with his family, and then the groom would take possession of his rightful property. Well, that all seemed simple enough. He'd run it by Dvina and see what she thought, and then put an advert out.

Thinking of Dvina brought to mind their conversation in his study. He'd known something must happen soon, and was glad she'd broached the subject and got them talking about it all. Although she had charmed and entertained everyone at the dinner party with her social graces and her wit, he had felt a moment of embarrassment when she'd first entered. Jane had tried hard to fashion a gown to soften her outline. The silk material in the palest of lilacs had draped well from a band under her enormous bosom, but hadn't disguised her size; and the layers of fat had hidden any beauty he had once seen in her face. He didn't want to feel like this about her. He wanted to have the depth of feeling that could overcome everything, but he supposed he must have it, for it had devastated him when she'd suggested moving out. He tried again to remember how it had been in the beginning; how the pleasures of her had made it possible for him to fall in love with her and to contemplate giving up Lilly. He *had* given her up, in fact, for three whole months. He closed his eyes and imagined the softness of Dvina, how he loved to snuggle into her and sink himself deep into her . . . *God! I'm getting an erection!* He sat up straight; his reaction shocked him. There were things in his memory that he wanted to revisit with her – very much so – but in the meantime he would have to go and see Lilly.

His driver dropped him at the end of the street where the whorehouses stood. Not that he wanted it that way, but these houses were so close together there was no room for a carriage to pull along it. He stood a moment and looked towards the building from which Lilly plied her trade. A tenement block with few windows still intact, and tiles missing off the roof, it stood in a filthy street, the stench of which always necessitated him covering his mouth and nose with his handkerchief. Sewage ran down a gully on the pavement edge into a cesspit at the end of the road, and rotting vegetation and rubbish of all kinds lay in putrid heaps. As he came up to the door, the familiar cry of 'Watch out!' had him ducking into the alley as piss thrown from an upstairs window splashed onto the pavement where he'd been standing.

Lilly must have seen him approaching, as her voice bellowed out a tirade of abuse at whoever had been responsible. It seemed she was convinced they had done it on purpose. On his second attempt to knock on the door, it opened and she welcomed him in. 'Hello, love. I thought you wouldn't be coming for a while, as you said you had a lot to see to. Come on in. I've finished with me last one and I have a pot boiling, so I can have the wash-down you like me to have.'

The tinge of red on each cheek that he usually saw when he had finally done with her, and the glow she had about her that he'd seen on many occasions when she'd reached the height of satisfaction, made him feel rejected, as if he had somehow thought he'd been the only one who could take her there. *Stupid thought! Lilly was a sexual animal. She knew what she wanted, and how to get it . . .*

'What's up, love? You're not going to play up, are you? You know I have other customers. Look, go away and think about it. I'll have me wash, and if you want it – well, you can come back for it. Mind, don't be leaving it long; it's busy at this time of year. They're all trying to get a last good shag before they have to go and be good little boys over the Christmas season.' Lilly burst out laughing at this, showing her yellowing teeth. The sight turned his stomach. As she looked at him, her laughter ceased and a frown creased her face. She leaned forward, her breasts straining against the tight bodice of her frock. Her head nodded, causing her bedraggled ringlets to drape over the curve of her cleavage. She pushed them back, then ran her hand over where they had just been.

His mouth dried. He forgot her discoloured teeth and the obvious signs of latent pleasure on her face, saying, 'I think I'll come in and wait.'

Watching the water running off her creamy body with its beautiful curves and taut muscles made him impatient to lie with her, but he savoured the moment. Her long red hair fell forward as she bent to cleanse between her legs. When she lifted her head, her large liquid-blue eyes in her pink, well-scrubbed, pretty face invited him over. 'You can dry me, if you like. I'm all squeaky clean, so you can make me dirty again . . .' She laughed, a tinkling, provocative sound. 'But first, Mister' – she always called him that during sex, and he loved it – 'you had better take off your clothes. Your pants are that bulged and tight they look like they'll split open any minute.'

Discarding his clothes, he didn't stop to dry her. He lifted her damp body over to the bed and entered her, thrusting as deep as he could. All guilt melted away with the pleasure of feeling her long legs wrap around him, pulling him to her, writhing against him, yet accepting him and giving him sensations that sizzled through him. It was over in no time. He held himself still and taut. His breath laboured, gasps releasing and inhaling with each intense pulse pumping his very being into her.

After a moment he slumped down beside her. He didn't speak. The effort of trying to hold all the fractured parts of his deep inner being together left him shaken to the core.

'Is that it? I weren't for getting there. What's happened to you? You're usually in for the long haul, once you start.' She sat up, lit a cigarette and climbed off the bed.

Inhaling the remnants of the wisp of fresh smoke as it curled towards him, he smiled at her. 'I don't have an explanation. Except maybe . . .' *Yes, he knew now what had prompted him to take all she had, in that abandoned way.* 'Well, it was my last supper, so to speak.'

'Oh, we're onto that one again, are we? What is it? Fallen in love again with little wifey? Promised her you won't come and fuck your whore again? Well, I s'pose, if you try often enough, one day it will happen.'

'It's nothing like that, Lilly. I haven't promised anyone, and I never did fall out of love with her. I just know this is the end.'

'Ha, just like that? You use me and leave me . . . well, it happens. There are other cocks out there, so don't think for a minute as I'll miss yours.'

Although he couldn't see her face, he could hear pain in her voice. And he knew some of it to touch him, too. They had known one another for a long time now. She had been a part – a very big part – of his life, and she'd helped him when he'd needed her most. He knew she realized, as he did, that this really was the end. But suddenly he had plans for her, and he told her of them, making them up as he went along, but meaning every word.

'Lilly, you have served me well; and yes, you have been a

good friend when I most needed one. It is true I won't come to see you again, but I won't forget you. I am going to make a provision for you.'

'A what? Money, you mean? An allowance? Sommat as will get me out of this filthy hole?'

'Yes.' She had come right to the point, as always. He'd miss that: knowing exactly where he was with her. And he'd miss other things too: her body, her hair – her beautiful red hair – and he knew he'd miss the earthiness of her, the acts she'd perform on him and with him. But he would feel better knowing that she was well taken care of, without having to resort to this endless fucking with men. 'I haven't all the details worked out, but I am going to buy you a place of your own and settle an amount of money on you.'

'Tell me this ain't you taking me on. Tell me you mean it.' A huge sob stopped her saying anything more.

He stood up, pulled on his trousers, wrapped a scruffy blanket off the bed around her, then held her to him. 'I mean it. I'll leave you a good sum today, but keep it quiet. I don't want any of my cronies knowing of this. If ever they hint to me they do, I will invoke a clause that I mean to put on the gift. That clause will see you penniless and homeless in an instant.'

He had no need to say that to her. She had never betrayed his trust, but he felt he had to do so. He couldn't risk Agatha finding out. If she did, then it wouldn't be long before Dvina did, too.

'So, tell me where you would like me to buy a property for you.'

'I'd like to move reet away from here, to somewhere no one knows owt about me. Maybe the seaside? Yes, I could run a little cafe. All the girls say as me cakes are best ever, and even if I've only a smattering of tea leaves, I can make a decent pot. I could call it Lilly's Tea Room. I could make a go of it, I know I could.'

'Very well, I'll get my agent to find somewhere for you and to furnish it. We'll find one you can live above. How would that be?'

'It'd be grand – grand as owt.' She snuggled back into him. 'And I'll never give you any trouble, or owt like that. You'll never hear from me again, I promise.'

As she looked up at him, his resolve weakened for a moment, but just as quickly it strengthened again. He forced himself to move away from her and finish dressing, telling her as he did so, 'Lilly, I won't have direct contact with you again, but I promise you I will see to everything, and someone will contact you in due course about all the arrangements and the money. In the meantime, here is fifty pounds. I'd love to say use it so that you don't have to take any more customers, but you should carry on as normal as much as possible, so no one suspects anything. I'm sorry to ask that of you, but maybe with this it will make it possible to not have so many.'

'Oh, Andrew, it couldn't have come at a better time! Like I said, the customers go to ground for a couple of months now. They can't find excuses to get away from their wives when business closes. Look, Andrew . . . Well, couldn't I go now? I mean, leave it a couple of days, so it don't look like I went just after your visit, and then make me way to Scarborough. I went there once on the train with me mate. I could find lodgings and wait there, or I could look for places and let you know somehow when I find one.'

'Well, it's an idea. Look, I'll need to put some things into place. Yes, it would be good to know you don't have to carry on here.' *Not least because she will be out of temptation's way for me.* 'I'll visit a solicitor. Not the one I use for my legitimate business, but I've heard of a no-questions-asked gentleman whom my friends use at times of gambling debts and . . . well, anything really that they don't want family to find out. Once I have tracked him down and instructed him, he will call. I'll tell him to act like he's a customer. I don't think it will be a problem with him to do so, as I understand he does frequent these places. Anyway, he will give you his address, where you can contact me. Look, I'll leave you another twenty pounds, just to make sure.'

'Thanks, Andrew. Thanks for everything. I'll not forget you, and I'll turn out well – make you proud. And . . . well, you'll know where I am, if you ever need me.'

He couldn't trust himself to kiss her goodbye – not that he ever really kissed her. Just the odd peck. Mostly he indulged in heavy kissing of her neck and all of her body, anywhere except her lips.

A look of shock came into her face as he put out his hand. He laughed and said, 'We have a gentleman's agreement, and we need to seal it with a handshake.'

Lilly giggled at this and took his hand with surprising firmness. 'It's a done deal, love. I'll never be able to thank you for giving me this chance, but I'll say it anyway. Thanks . . .'

Watching the scenery bob up and down in time with the horse's canter, changing from drab buildings to suburban mansions and then to the crisp white of the frost-covered trees that led into the country, Andrew mulled over what had happened. *Where had it all come from?* But he enjoyed the feeling it gave him. Good fortune had smiled on him and he hadn't had to do anything for it, so sharing some of it was the least he could do. He liked, too, the easing of his conscience that came with the actions he'd taken. He just hoped it worked out all right and that no one ever found out.

21

Bridie and Issy

The bitter cold seeped into Bridie. As she pulled her cloak around her, she was for thinking the harsh March winds would cut her in two. Looking back at the cottage from where she stood at the half-open gate, she allowed her happiness to warm her and put her thoughts towards trying to justify her intended mission. The excuse of her past was wearing thin. It was true that the gin could help her forget everything that had happened with her da, and the life she'd been dragged into, but why was it that the life she had now wasn't enough to make her leave it alone? She knew it hurt Will to smell the drink on her. And, with Janet, wasn't it that any bridges they had built could crumble at the slightest provocation? Her dipping into the pot containing their savings – Janet's Holy Grail – would cause eruptions to fuel the fires of hell, she was sure of that. But she couldn't stop herself.

Maybe when they had a permanent home she could think more positively about breaking her drinking habit. She looked up towards the road running across the top of the lane. She could see the footings and partly built cottages, where once there had been fields. *To be sure, it would be lovely to live there. For wouldn't I be just minutes from here, but still able to walk down this lovely leafy lane and across the fields?* Memories of her home deep in the countryside in Ireland shot a pain through her. *Oh, away with you, Bridie! Just be remembering the happy times, as the other will drag you down, so it will.*

'Eeh, it's alreet for some, hanging around their garden gate looking for a bit of gossip, whilst others try to fit twenty-five hours into a day.'

This from Issy, as she turned into the lane and came towards her, brought Bridie back to the present. She loved Issy. It was good to have found someone so like Beth. She still had the heart-sore feeling of missing Beth, but Issy's kind ways soothed that. She called back, 'To be sure, I've been up since six and have all me chores done, so I have.'

'Ha, I'm only taking you on.' Issy looked concerned as she came up to her. 'By, you look peaky. Are you feeling alreet?'

'Aye, 'tis that I have been sick these last couple of mornings.'

'Eeh, Bridie, you know what that means . . .'

'I know, but I've seen me bleeding, so I'm for thinking it may be something else.'

'I don't know. It's not unknown. Me ma told me of a woman who saw it all the way through and just thought as she were putting weight on, until she was took with the pains. Should I ask her to come and have a look at yer?'

'No, don't be for worrying her. I'll be waiting to see how it all goes. I'll be fine, so I will. Would you be after coming in for a cup of tea?'

'No, ta. I'm on me way to meet Ma. She finishes about now, but I have to go back to Tarrington House later. Mrs Eastland is having some friends to dinner, so if I don't come and walk home with Ma, I'll not see her at all today.'

'I'm for thinking it's more like Tom you're hoping to catch a glimpse of. Isn't it as you have to walk through the stable yard to get to the servants' entrance?'

Though Issy laughed, Bridie saw her face take on a tinge of colour, so she knew she'd touched on the truth: poor Issy had fallen in deep for the new groom, who had only come to lodge with them a couple of weeks ago. But he seemed like the shy type, and even though Issy had said she thought he liked her, he hadn't given her any definite signs.

'Is it that obvious? By, I must have got it bad. But yer know, I find it hard to get through the day without seeing him, and I never thought I'd feel like this again after I lost Denny.'

'I'm for thinking he feels the same. Didn't you say you catch him looking at you, whenever you turn around? And the banter you have – that's for giving off a good feeling, so it is. You should give him some encouragement. Look at him from under your eyelids, hold his gaze, and put yourself in positions where he has to be pushing past you.'

'Eeh, Bridie, he'd think me a forward lass, and that might put him off. No, I'll just be patient. After all, I've only known him a short time. It might just be that I want any man, to fill the loneliness in me.'

'Aye, there's that. We women have our needs, though men are not always for knowing it. But then 'tis little choice you have around here, Issy, and there's a few young widows and spinsters who'd like to get their hands on someone like Tom. You take care and don't be after letting him slip through your fingers for want of a few womanly wiles to catch him.'

'I won't. Anyroad, that's enough about me. What about

you? Have you heard how your new home is coming along? I see as they're not working on the site again today – afraid of freezing their manhoods off, no doubt!' This set them off giggling. 'Eeh, what a thought! But still, I suppose you're not in a hurry, as it ain't going to be easy having to uproot again. Even if it is only to the top of the road. You've made a lovely job of this place, thou knows.'

'Well, if you get in with Tom, then to be sure it will be yours, so that will make it worth it.'

'If only. Anyroad, I notice you go up to the Irish quarter regular. Have you made some friends up there?'

Bridie knew Issy was only trying to change the subject, but taking their chat in this direction made her own face blush. For she wouldn't want Issy to be knowing of the real reason she had taken to going to the Irish. 'Aye, 'tis that I have some friends up there, and 'tis nice to have the craic with them.' A thought came to her then: maybe Issy would be able to help her with something she'd troubled over – no, more than that: feared over. Perhaps Issy could dispel the impossible thoughts she'd had about the rumours she'd heard of a traveller in the area being Seamus. 'Issy, have you been for hearing tales of a travelling man from Ireland? He'd be about your age, so he would. Very dark, curly hair, and eyes as black as the night?'

Issy's reaction shocked Bridie: her face paled, her eyes widened and a tremble went through her body as she nodded her head. 'Aye, there is a man of that description. He came here regular a few years ago, then he disappeared, but he's started to visit again. Is it from the Irish you've heard of him? Only be careful, Bridie, he . . . well, he's dangerous.'

Bridie couldn't say anything for a moment. She felt certain now it was Seamus, for hadn't he told her he'd travelled this way when he'd first had to leave Ireland? *Oh, Jesus, Mary and*

Joseph, why? Why, when I am so happy? For as sure as God was in Heaven, Seamus could spoil that happiness, for couldn't he give me feelings I'd not be able to deal with or want?

It had surprised her as much as it would have done if she'd heard there were little people living on the outskirts of Breckton, to hear of the Irish living there. She had found out it was the mining company who had shipped them in, after the disaster that had taken the lives of Issy's father and fiancé. Cheap labour, the Irish were after telling her they were. The places they lived in were no more than hovels: one building on the edge of the town, with just a room for each family and shared kitchens and lav. But, as with all her fellow countrymen, they had the spirit, the love and the humour in them to keep them going, so they did.

They had their own way of getting hold of stuff, and she'd heard tales linking the traveller to that, amongst other things that she'd never thought Seamus capable of. What had happened to bring him back? And, if what folk said was true, why? Why had he changed so much?

'Bridie, are you alreet? That gypsy hasn't hurt you or owt like that, has he?'

'No, no . . . I . . . I – well, I was for hearing of him and . . .'

'Well, you believe all you hear, cos it's reet – well, most of it. I don't know about all of it as – no offence, Bridie – but your folk can stretch a tale. Anyway, when you know he is about, don't go anywhere near him on your own. Now, I must get on. Like I said, I'm due back at work later. Ta-ra, love.'

Issy hurried away, her head down not only against the cold, but against the onslaught of feelings at the mention of the traveller. She turned her mind to her concern for Bridie. Although they had only known each other these last few months, she liked Bridie – liked her a lot, as it happened – but she had a feeling there was more to Bridie. She'd met her a few times coming from the Irish quarter and had been sure she'd smelt drink on her. She was also very secretive about her past, and about what she did for work before she met Will, and that kind of thing. It was as if they were to base their friendship on the here and now only, with no background – at least where Bridie's was concerned, for Issy had told her all about herself.

When she reached the gate to the stable yard, all thoughts of Bridie left her and her heart pounded in her chest. *Eeh, Issy, give over, lass! Anyone would think you were a young girl, the way you're carrying on*, she told herself, then jumped as Tom called out, 'Hey, Issy, what're you doing round here? By, you've come to the reet place if you want to see how the other half have to work.'

'Oh, is that reet? Well, the way I see it, you stable hands don't know you're born. Look at Henry – he's still like a young 'un, he's had it that easy.'

'Well, that's sommat, ain't it? And you with a job as cook to a household of one! I reckon that takes some beating as a cushy number.' Issy laughed at this from Henry, and knew she deserved it, with the way she'd poked fun at him just to get back at Tom. She loved the easy banter that she and Tom had fallen into in such a short time, and hoped it boded well for the future.

'Ha, she's nowt to say to that, Henry. I could do with taking lessons from you in handling her. It'd be as valuable to me as what you teach me about the horses.'

'I think you're doing alreet without me interfering, Tom.

Eeh, look at her, she's blushing! Now that's sommat as you don't see our Isabella doing very often. Aye, I think you've got yourself a head-start with that one. You can't do better round here, lad, I'll say that.'

Henry moved off, chuckling to himself, leaving Issy wishing the ground would open up and swallow her. Tom had turned away and was making great play of forking some hay from the bale into the stable. She had to say something to break his embarrassment.

'Take no notice of Henry. That's country folk for you: they speak whatever comes into their mind without taking stock of others' feelings. Not that they mean any harm. They're just straight with everything.'

Tom turned and looked at her. She held his gaze, like Bridie had said to. His face broke into a smile. 'I wasn't embarrassed on me own account, lass – only as you might think I'd said stuff, like.'

'No, I didn't think that. I know Henry and his like. Anyroad, I have to go and see if Ma's ready. I'll be in late tonight, so I'll see you sometime tomorrow.'

'Do you know what time you'll be leaving work? Only . . . well, if you don't mind, I'd like to walk up and meet you – not, thou knows, for any other reason than I likes the air at night. And anyroad, it ain't reet for a lass to walk home late on her own.'

Issy could have jumped for joy. Despite his justifications, he'd blushed when he'd asked, and she felt sure this was a start. 'Aye, I'd like that, Tom. Ta. I leave around ten. Me head will rest easy knowing you're meeting me, as I have a fear of them lanes in the dark.'

As she walked away she thought: *Not just in the dark, but any time since* . . . No. She'd not think on that. She'd not let anything spoil the anticipation in her or the lightness of her heart. By, if she were a few years younger, she'd skip up the path to the servants' quarters.

And thinking on that, she couldn't believe how everything had changed. She never thought to be walking towards Hensal Grange to meet her ma. The Grange had only employed time-served staff in the past, and the likes of her, Ma and Jane – self-taught and rough around the edges – wouldn't have got a look-in. Now Jane and Ma both worked there! And she'd never seen her mother happier, working as she was in the job she loved more than anything: looking after people when they most needed her. It was grand to think of the difference she'd made in Miss Dvina. And she felt certain it had been Ma's doing, as Miss Dvina's babby was nearing full-term, and Miss Dvina herself looked well. She'd lost a lot of her extra fat and shone with happiness again. And, best of all, Jane had told her Mr Harvey seemed better with her mistress once more, even visiting her chamber and sleeping there all night two or three times a week! Now that was something, though she couldn't really put that down to her mother's influence, could she? The thought made her laugh. Cos if Ma had those kinds of powers, she'd be asking her to work them on herself and Tom. *Oh, Tom . . . Tom!*

'Will, I'm thinking it'll be a shame to move from here. But then, it might help us to be more accepted.'

'And how do yer make that out, Ma? Anyroad, I think we already are, by most.'

'Well, some, I know; but living amongst the other miners' families, instead of down this lane where the land workers live, is bound to make things easier. It'll help us get to know them more.'

'Aye, you're reet. By, it doesn't seem like six months since we arrived, does it? Mind, I've been up to the site and there's not much building going on with this weather.'

'I know. But thou knows: that young man as has taken the groom's position won't want to stay long in lodgings. And this is his cottage, by rights.'

'Oh, don't be worrying your head over him. Henry tells me he's got himself settled with Issy and her ma. Henry's hoping for a match to be made there, as he thinks Issy is a lonely lass.'

'Aye, and a nice one an' all. I like Issy. And her mother, come to that.'

'Where's Bridie, Ma? She is in, ain't she?'

'She is. She's been out a while and came back with the smell of gin on her. I think she's getting it from them Irish. Eeh, lad, it's a worry. She's upstairs lying down. She ain't looking well of late.'

Will went through to the back porch and peeled off his sticky, coal-black work shirt. A bowl of hot water waited for him on the side, and clean clothes hung on a peg behind the door. As he went about the business of cleansing himself of all the coal grime, he pondered on this last.

Bridie's need for the drink was the only thing marring their happiness. It wasn't that she got drunk – she could hold her drink, could Bridie – but he had a bad feeling about how she got it, and wished to his heart she hadn't the taste for it. He didn't like the thought of her going up town to the Irish. He'd heard stuff about them: about the things they got up to. And a lot of it they proved right, by the way they acted at times. Still, he didn't like to say anything, as it was her only fault, and he knew it helped her to cope with her past.

Pulling his belt to the last notch, he thought about the

news he had to tell her, and he couldn't wait. Ma should be pleased with it, too, but he wanted to tell Bridie first.

'Anyroad, it's all turned out alreet, despite a lot of them in the Miners' Row being a bit cautious of us.' His ma carried on the conversation as though no time had lapsed in between. 'But thou knows, these are good folk, and I don't want Bridie's antics to put us in a bad light. You should speak to her, Will.'

'Don't start, Ma. I've told you – it'll take time. She can't just come off it like that. You should have patience; she's come a long way as it is.'

'Time don't come into it, when it affects what we have in the pot. She should get some work. They're setting on at the big house, and Issy's mother told me they want a scullery maid . . .'

'Don't think for one minute you and your precious pot will come between me and Bridie, Ma. Now give it a rest. I'm going up to her. I'll have me tea in a bit.'

The stairs led off the kitchen and straight into the small room his mother used. Their room was at the end of the landing, and he lifted the latch as quietly as he could. For a moment he stood trying to get used to the darkness inside. He could hear Bridie's soft snores, some of them released on a snort as her lips flapped together, but he couldn't see her. He turned and picked up the oil lamp from the small recess at the top of the stairs. Now he could see her, curled up into a ball at the top end of their bed. The stale air in the room had a faint whiff to it. He ignored it.

'Bridie. Come on, sleepy-head. What's this carry-on? Your man comes in from his shift and you're away to your bed again.'

Bridie stirred and turned towards him. She had a mark on

her face. She said, 'Will, is that yourself, home from work already?'

'Aye, are you alreet, love? Look, you've lain on your locket and left an impression on your face.'

A smile lit the beauty of her as she took the locket from his hands. He must have read the words on it every day since he'd given it to her on their wedding night. Always it reminded him of the way her eyes had looked at it in wonderment, and how she'd read out the engraving on the back of the solid silver locket: 'To Catch a Dream'. She'd said, 'Oh, Will, me heart is singing for joy, so it is, because 'tis that we have caught our dream, my love. We have.' Since then she had never taken it off.

'You'll have to let me have it back one day, thou knows, Bridie, as I plan to have a miniature done of our wedding-day picture and have it put inside. Maybe for our first anniversary. How would that be?'

'I'm for not wanting to take it off ever, Will. Can't you get the pictures done, take a drawing of the size you want and then we can be after fixing it inside ourselves?'

'Ha, yes, of course I can. I'm glad as it means that much to you, me little lass.'

'Lie on the bed a while with me, Will. That's right, cuddle up to me.'

'Are you feeling alreet, love? Only Ma said . . .'

'Oh, take no notice of her. Sure she makes a powerful fuss over nothing. I'm for being grand, Will.'

She kept her head away from him, no doubt trying to hide the smell of drink on her. He knew it shamed her and she tried to keep it from him, but he had heard the slur on her voice and already caught a whiff of the alcohol on her. Still, she was trying to take less of it, and he'd do no good going on at her. Instead he'd try to love her away from it: make her feel safe and happy, so she'd have no need for it. 'Come on, back yourself towards me, let me feel you where you belong, lass.'

'Are you not for thinking that could be leading to other things, Will? And Janet with your supper on, ready to serve to the table?'

'Aye, I hope so, lass, as I have a need on me. I have good news, and I can think of no better way to celebrate than to have me wife wrap herself around me and reward me with the best thing in me life.'

She turned in his arms. 'Is it that you have done something deserving of a reward, then?'

'I have. I've got a promotion. Shift supervisor of the gang as is to work the new seam. We're nearly through to it now, and it's going to be a cutting separate from the others. Eeh, lass, we're on the up. And Mr Harvey has said we're to have that corner cottage when they finish building it, and he's seeing to it as the workers get it done as soon as the weather lets up. Thou knows the one, lass. The one you liked the look of, the day we took a walk around the site.'

'Oh, Will. That's grand as owt!'

They both laughed at her mimicking his way of speaking, until his kissing of her lips brought them to a different place, and he lost himself in taking all the pleasure she had to give him.

22

Andrew

March 1881
A chance encounter

'You can come up, Mr Harvey. It's wonderful news: everything is fine.'

'Oh, thank God. Is the baby born? Is it a boy? Is Dvina all right?' By the time he'd asked all these questions he was in the bedroom and could see the answer to the last one. Dvina sat up in bed, grinning more widely than he'd ever seen her do before. In her arms she held a baby swaddled in a white blanket. 'Your son, Andrew,' she said. 'Meet Jeremy Edgar Isaac Harvey.'

They had long since decided on calling their son after these three very important men in their lives. Andrew thought of each one: Jeremy, courageous and one of the nicest men he'd ever met; Edgar, who'd made his mother so happy and had generously provided for him; and Dvina's father Isaac, a man of principle and easy to love. All had contributed to the wealth they now had, and which their son would one day inherit. The only sorrow was that none of them would ever meet Jeremy Jnr.

A proud happiness warmed his whole body as he leaned over and looked into the wrinkled face of his son . . . *HIS SON!* It sounded so wonderful that he wanted to shout it from the rooftops.

Dvina's hand reached up to him, and he took it in his as he said, 'Well done, you clever thing. I knew you could do it.'

'The best mother we've ever helped, wasn't she, Dr Payne? Like she were born to it.'

'Yes, yes, Mrs Harman. Spare Mr Harvey the details and Mrs Harvey the embarrassment, please.'

Mrs Harman grunted at this, and both Andrew and Dvina laughed. He'd had the Devil's own job to persuade the doctor to allow Issy's mother to be present, and yet he remembered Isabella telling him how glad the doctor usually was to leave her mother with the non-paying patients. Because of this, he felt the need to stick up for Mrs Harman and said to her, 'I'm sure that was all down to your excellent care of my wife, through the pregnancy and during the birth. We are very grateful, Mrs Harman.'

'And to you, Dr Payne,' Dvina added. Andrew felt her hand squeeze his in a gesture of approval, which also showed in her smile.

'Yes, of course. Now I think the doctor and I will partake of a nice, strong celebratory drink. Doctor?'

Andrew floated on air as he glided down the stairs. *A son. A son! No matter how often I say it, I still cannot believe it.*

He showed the doctor into the withdrawing room. Not feeling inclined to share his news with the staff in the presence of the pompous doctor, Andrew resisted the urge to ring the bell to summon Jameson, but instead excused himself and went off in search of the butler. When he found him in his downstairs pantry, he asked Jameson to gather the staff together. As he waited to make his announcement, he had a longing for this to have happened at Tarrington House. How much more wonderful it would have been to announce it to the staff there, many of whom had known him since he was a boy! But he would have that pleasure later – he would ride over to tell his mother and would ask her if he could announce it to them then.

Having visited Dvina and his son again and found both fast asleep, Andrew changed and strode out to the stables. The new groom, Tom Grantham, met him.

'Good afternoon, Tom. Did you get my message to saddle a mount for me?'

'Yes, sir. Goldboy is ready and champing at the bit. Very lively, the lad is. He could do with having the freedom of his rein.'

'Well, he'll certainly get that, as I am feeling the same.'

'Yes, sir. I heard the news. Congratulations.'

'Thank you. How are you settling in? Mrs Harman seems taken with you, but what about Isabella? Is she making you welcome?'

'Aye, she is that. I'm very comfortable.'

A sudden idea came into his head: Tom and Isabella, now that would be a good match! Isabella could do with a good steady man in her life, and he wondered if she had healed from losing Denny. He hoped so.

Mounting Goldboy, Andrew looked down at Tom – not that he had to look far, as Tom stood six feet tall. He'd found him a pleasant fellow to deal with, and what he lacked in knowledge, Henry had said he picked up very quickly on instruction. Andrew would call him a handsome man, in a

289

rugged way. A widower with no issue, he had looked for a complete change of scenery, and had heard of the job they offered through the grapevine that runs from estate to estate. Yes, the more he thought about it, he was sure Tom was just the right man for Isabella.

'Well, I must away. I'm glad you are settled. The weather has delayed the work on the new cottages, but they are taking shape now, so it shouldn't be more than a couple of weeks before you can move into yours.'

'Oh, I'm in no hurry. I'm finding me feet at the moment.'

Andrew hoped that once Tom did *find his feet*, as he put it, he would think about getting them under the table – another saying they used around here. That would be a very good outcome for all.

Setting a good pace, he rode off down the lane. He had a feeling of being at one with his horse and his world. His promised abstinence from Lilly added to his sense of well-being. That he hadn't given in to making a visit to Bridlington – where Lilly had finally settled – to see how she fared added to his pride. He'd kept to his word, even when it came to the very strong sexual urges that he experienced, and Dvina would regain her health soon enough. In the last three months she had reduced her weight considerably, and when he cuddled up to her he could feel the old urges that she used to awaken in him. Though he wouldn't want her too thin – not nearly as thin as Lilly. Dvina didn't give him what Lilly had, but what she did give was very special, and he felt sure it would be enough for him once they could resume proper relations. Lost as he was in his thoughts and feelings, he didn't see the young woman coming out of the gate of the groom's cottage until it was too late.

The shock of her sudden appearance made his horse rear

up. The struggle to stay in the saddle took all Andrew's strength. Gripping the horse's sides with his knees, he found the rein tugging his arms till the sockets burned. He leaned forward, urging the horse down, calling in soothing tones and trying to calm him. But then his heart lurched . . .

The red hair tumbling down, licking the creamy mound of a perfect bosom, and the eyes so big – sinking into a deep blue like he'd only ever seen once before – made him think for a split-second that it was Lilly. But no, once the horse settled, he saw that this young woman was infinitely more beautiful, and more graceful, like a dancer. She had a magnetism about her. Once he'd fixed his eyes on her, he could not look away, and when she spoke – though her tone was cross – her voice had a musical lilt.

'For sure, you nearly knocked me to me maker! You should ride with more care, so you should.'

'I'm very sorry. Are you all right?' His words barely left his tight throat. His mouth dried. He swallowed, adding, 'You will be William's wife. We haven't met before. I . . . I hope you have settled in and are comfortable.'

'Oh, it is sorry I am to have spoken to you like that, sir, but you gave me a fright. I wasn't for realizing who you were. My man will be after having a fit at me – and deserved – if he finds out. He loves his job, so he does.'

'Don't worry – I had it coming to me. I should have taken heed of the fact that it's likely someone could come out of one of these cottages. I haven't lived here that long. I am only glad you are not hurt.'

She smiled up at him. Her smile lit her face and held a promise of the pleasures of her. *Good God! What am I thinking?* He steadied himself enough to take his leave in a dignified manner. 'Good day to you, and once again I apologize for giving you a fright.'

'To be sure you are forgiven, sir. I . . . . I was after wondering, would it be too forward to ask after your wife? Issy told me this morning that her mammy had been up at the house since very early. And, well, 'tis as I am curious as to how everything went for you.'

'It has gone very well, thank you for asking. I have a son, and he and my wife are both fine.'

Why was he lingering, telling this woman his private business? Time to go . . .

He touched his hat and rode off. In a short space of time he'd gone from being at one with his world to being at odds with it. Familiar feelings gripped his groin. He fought against the yearning to turn around and take what he knew that she offered in her smile. A memory came to him of William Hadler sitting before him, telling him his wife had lost her way. Will had excused it by saying that others had led her to take that path, but Andrew doubted this. Apart from Lilly, he'd never seen any woman who exuded her inner need in such a way that all men would see it, feel it and – yes – want it, in the way he himself did at this very moment.

Issy heard the latch of the door. Her heart jumped. *Tom?* Oh, she hoped so, for as much as she wanted Ma to come home and give her good news concerning Miss Dvina, she yearned to have just a few moments alone in the house with Tom. Three months had passed since he'd moved in with them, and though he'd shown many signs of his interest in her, he'd not made a move other than to meet her from work, if she was late home.

She'd had a lift in her spirits and her longings this morning.

As soon as the messenger had knocked on the door, asking for her ma to go up to the big house, Tom had looked at her in a special way. Knowing it was her day off, was he trying to give her an indication that he'd come home during his break?

'Hello, Issy. Is it all right that I came home for me snap? Only with Mrs Harman out, I wouldn't want to embarrass you. Thou knows, set folks' tongues wagging, like.'

He stood filling the doorway, holding his cap and looking at her with puppy-dog eyes. To stop herself running to him, she made a quick retort. 'They can wag all they want to, Tom, cos if they ain't wagging at us, they will be at sommat else. No, I wanted you to come – I mean . . .'

'I'm hoping you mean what I want you to. I don't want to speak out of turn or have you think me a womanizer, but I have feelings for you and . . .'

'Eeh, Tom.'

He crossed the room and held his arms out to her. Issy went into them.

'Tom, I've wanted you to do this for so long.' She looked up into his face, and saw the longing there as his lips came down on hers. Every cold fibre of her that had shut down with Denny's passing – and she had forced closed after her encounter with the gypsy – jumped back into life, sending feelings she couldn't deny rushing around her body.

'Issy, Issy . . .'

Her name was a longing on his lips. She clung to him, saying, 'And here was me thinking you a shy one! Oh, Tom, I'm glad as you're for me, as I have loved you from the moment I opened the door to you. I was for asking you today, as I were getting fed up with waiting.'

'No, I'm not shy, just wary of frightening you. And, well,

I've been hurt bad. I suffered a big loss, and I didn't know whether I was ready or not.'

'We're the same in that, Tom. Tell me about your wife. You've never spoken of her, and you can, thou knows. I'll understand.'

They sat down, their hands joined across the table. Tom took a deep breath. 'I know as you will, Issy, and that helps, though I'm sorry you've been through the same as me. Alice was a lovely-looking girl. You have the look of her: your hair a bubble of curls, just like hers, and your eyes – your laughing eyes – so joyous to look into as hers were. She had a nature similar to yours an' all. Giving and fun-loving, though you have a way of saying things, Issy . . .'

'I know. I can be coarse and I try not to be, but it comes out before I can trap it.'

'Well, I'm getting used to it now. I know it's part of you and you never mean any malice. Anyway, my Alice died having our first babby. Babby died an' all. It were three years back now and, though I grieved hard, I found a peace when I came here. I hadn't thought to speak up yet, but I were seeing to Mr Harvey's mount and thinking of his wife up at the house giving birth, and all sorts of feelings came to me. It was like Alice was saying to me to get on with me life. And then you came into me head, like as if she had put you there.'

'Oh, Tom, I hope so, cos that would be a lovely way to think of us coming together. With her blessing, like.' Then she told him about Denny, and he sat listening quietly, holding her hand and rubbing his thumb up and down it in a soothing way.

A silence fell at the end of her telling, but then Tom said, 'I know we haven't known each other long, but would you think on becoming me wife, Issy?'

'Aye, I would, and I'd not even make you go down on one knee for me, cos I'd not be responsible for meself if I got you anywhere near a position as I could take advantage of you . . . Oh, bugger, there I go again. Sorry, love.'

'Ha, well, you make things easy for a man, I must say. Cos it can get awkward at first. I take it you and Denny – well, you know the way of things, like?'

She knew a moment of indignation at him for even thinking that, but then a fear set up in her. He'd know. He'd know she wasn't a virgin, and she'd never want him to find out why, so it would sit better with her to let him think it was Denny who'd taken her down. 'You're not for letting that worry you, are you? Only we . . . well, we were very much in love and only weeks from getting married.' The lie stuck in her throat, and she sent up a silent prayer asking for forgiveness.

'No, of course not! We're none of us in our youth, and I had sort of guessed anyway. Someone up there knew we should come together, Issy. We both need a healing, and we both know what having a real love is, so I reckon that gives us a head-start on others.'

Standing up, he came round the table to her, tugging on her hands as he did, and pulling her to her feet to meet him. Holding her against him, he kissed her hair, her neck and then her lips. Longings she'd tried hard to suppress, since the gypsy had first tapped into them, stirred inside her and she knew a joy at not having to deny them any longer.

His breath fanned her face as he murmured, 'I love you, Issy. I love you.'

She didn't know how they reached the bed. She could only recall later the swish of the curtain gliding back and a frenzy of kisses, touches and caresses, taking her to a place where every part of her wanted to take Tom into her and to give him all of her.

Lying in his arms afterwards, she found the blossoming of herself that she had so wanted. Only this time it wasn't tainted, and the fears inside her since hearing the gypsy had come back into the area were calmed. She had her Tom to protect her. No one could hurt her again.

'I love you, Tom. I love you more than I have ever loved anyone before. I'm not belittling me love for Denny by saying that, but I was a different person then. The person I am now can only have this one love, and it is yours.'

He moved onto his elbow and looked down at her. She saw a tear glisten in his eye, and his voice was heavy with emotion as he spoke softly, saying, 'Well, lass, I didn't think I would ever again feel as I do now. Only, like you, it is more so. And, like you, I'm not tainting Alice's memory, as I'm different an' all. And this different me, loves you with everything I am.'

As they came out of the kiss that sealed what they had pledged to each other, Tom made her laugh by tweaking her nose and saying, 'You're lovely, and you're all I thought you would be. That were grand, and thou knows – with practice – we could reach sommat unheard of. Eeh, marry me, Issy! Marry me as soon as banns can be read.'

She took on his way of lightening the moment and answered him in the same way. 'I'll have to, cos I can't see us getting much space to get the practice you're on about, until we do. Mind, there's conditions. You have to promise to come home for the kind of snap you did today, every day as I'm off work.'

'Ha, you've reminded me. I've had nowt to eat yet! Come

on, lass, what kind of wife are you going to make, if you don't think on feeding your man, eh?'

They both laughed at this, and the laughter brought them to a place where they could cope with all that had passed between them. But it was cut short when the sound of the latch had them scrambling for the curtains, swishing them shut, grabbing clothes and doing all kinds of funny man-oeuvres as they tried to present themselves as decent.

'Tom Grantham, I leave me house for five minutes and you take me Bella down! What kind of a man are you?'

Issy froze. Hearing her mother call her by the pet name she always used ground a shame into her. She looked at Tom kneeling on the bed, his arm stuck in mid-air as he tried to get back into his shirt. His face was a picture of horror. Issy didn't know how to help the situation, but then they heard a cackling laughter.

'Ha! I were beginning to think as you weren't a man proper, Mr Grantham, but I see as you are. Well, you'd better do the right thing by my Bella, or you'll have me to answer to.'

Her ma laughed again, and Issy poked her head out of the curtain, saying, 'Eeh, Ma, you gave us a fright!'

Tom pulled it further back. 'I'm sorry, Mrs Harman. I . . .'

'Give over, lad. It ain't reet, an old woman finding her unmarried daughter at it – and on me own bed an' all! – but if she were going to, I couldn't think of anyone better for her to choose than you. I hope you do have good intentions, though, cos she's a lovely lass and'd make you a good wife.'

'Ma!'

'And she has consented to be just that, though she hasn't promised the "good" bit yet.' Tom swung his long legs off the side of the bed. Somehow he'd managed to get his trousers back on, though Issy couldn't think for the life of her how. Not that it mattered at the moment; first she had to stop them talking about her as if she wasn't there.

'I did say yes to his asking, but now if he's going to be in league with you, Ma, and act like I'm invisible, then I might think again.'

'Issy, don't say that. I was in shock, that's all, and thought to have the banter with your ma to ease the situation.'

'I know, I'm only taking you on. Look, Ma, I'm sorry. We shouldn't have. I mean, it hasn't happened before – just . . .'

'Aye, when the cat's away. Look, I ain't angry. I'm really happy for you, lass. Now, can't a hard-working nurse get a sup of tea around here?'

'Oh, I forgot the babby! Did it arrive? Is Miss Dvina all right? Is the babby . . . ?'

'Yes, yes, I'll tell you all about it. But hadn't you better be getting back to work, Tom?'

Issy turned her attention back to Tom. His eyes held so much love for her that she had to turn away. She busied herself getting a pie out of the pantry and wrapping it in muslin, calling out to him as she did, 'I won't be a mo, love. I'll just get you some snap to take with you, and I'll see you out.'

At the door he took her hands in his and made as if to say sorry once again, but she put her finger on his lips. 'Don't. It happened, and that's that. I'm not going to think on it. I'm only going to think of what happened before Ma came home, and all the practice you promised me.' He kissed her in a quick movement, looking around before he did so. She shoved him, saying, 'Go on with you! You've ruined me standing with me mother, and now you're after ruining me reputation with the curtain-twitchers in the Row!'

Tom laughed as he went on his way. She watched him until

he turned into the lane, then went inside to hear all the news on Miss Dvina. Issy just hoped it was all good, though she had a mind it was going to be, by the cheerfulness of her mother. Eeh, to find out Miss Dvina was happy would just top the day off nicely.

Andrew rode slowly back across the fields. He'd seen smoke curling up out of the woods and had heard from his farm workers that Seamus was back. He thought to have a word, see where he'd been these past few years and how he was faring. He crossed through the stream, lingering a while to let Goldboy cool his feet. The thought of taking his boots off and dangling his own feet in the water appealed, until he saw the traces of ice on the banks. Happiness had shielded him from the cold, but as he looked around he realized how wintry it really was. The patches of white frost that the sun had missed, and left clinging like cobwebs to the branches and hedgerows, told of it.

Turning Goldboy out of the stream, Andrew allowed him time to become sure-footed, before setting off at a canter onto the road, until he came to the woodland. As he dismounted to steer the horse through the trees, he heard a high-pitched voice shout, 'I am not for believing you, Seamus. The bastard you are took everything I had. I am for hating you with everything in me, and if you come near me and me man, so help me I'll kill you, so I will!'

Andrew stopped and listened. Seamus's tones – deep, sarcastic and menacing – answered the person he thought must be Hadler's wife. 'So, you'll not be after wanting the gin I have for you, then? Oh yes, it is me that has kept you in it since you came here. I have been following your trail this last while. I saw what you had become, and thought I could wash me hands of you. I would have done meself a service if I had.'

'Were you not for thinking you had a hand in me downfall? You left me no choices. I had no money, nothing. I had to . . .'

'Aye, 'tis that you had to. All right. For isn't it the way of it as you were built to give the pleasure to men? But to sell yourself – you, Bridie O'Hara. I thought better of you.'

There was a silence. Andrew held his horse, still unsure what to do. To show himself would embroil him in whatever situation these two were in, and that was the last thing he wanted.

'Bridie, I never stopped loving you. I've told you me reason for going, but I've come back a different man. Some of me reason for coming back was to look for you, but me situation and the stuff I got mixed up in forced me hand as well. I have business interests around here. You've met the Irish community. You probably know what I'm talking about. Supplying them with the cheap liquor is only half of it.'

''Tis as I know. And I am for believing all of their tales. I came here to ask you to leave me and Will alone. I'm happy with him. We have a decent life. I don't want that spoiling, please, Seamus.'

'Well, 'tis as I was packing up anyway. But I'll be back, Bridie. And when I do, I'm for having you. No matter that the way you turned out sickens me; I can't cut meself off from you. You belong to me. You know in the heart of you the truth of that. Here.' Andrew saw a bottle fly through the air, its contents glistening in the sun. 'Take it. I've left a good stock with Paddy for you, but you have to pay like the rest of them. And make sure you do.'

The woman bent and picked up the bottle, then turned and ran towards the field at the back of the wood. He watched her lithe body move with the grace of a deer. Her hair billowed out like a flame behind her, and once more Andrew felt a stirring. A clenching of his muscles sent messages to his heart that he did not want to hear.

Turning back to watch Seamus caused his horse to snort. Seamus picked up his gun and aimed it in his direction. Not wanting to, but knowing he had to, Andrew called out, 'Good afternoon, Seamus. I heard you were back.'

'Is it yourself, Mr Harvey?'

Seamus glanced in the direction Bridie had run. Andrew did the same, but she was out of sight. He steered his horse out into the clearing and, trying to keep his voice steady, asked, 'So, where have you been these last few years? We thought you had gone for good.'

'Oh, here and there, as takes a man's fancy, but I'm not for staying. I've been here a few days and I'm ready for the off. I didn't make meself known to you as I wasn't looking for work.'

'Well, I won't keep you. I just thought I would drop by this way on my way home.'

''Tis Hensal Grange you are living at now, I hear. I was glad you had such good fortune, sir.'

Something had changed. Andrew couldn't put his finger on it, but Seamus had an arrogance about him. It was an air that struck a chord of unease in him. The sooner he left the gypsy's company, the better he would feel. He mounted Goldboy and, feeling less intimidated looking down on Seamus from the saddle, said, 'Yes, though at the expense of others' misfortune, sadly. Good day, and I hope your travels are prosperous for you.'

Setting off at a trot, Andrew had the feeling that Seamus watched him until he went out of sight. Something stopped him from turning back to look. He just felt the need to get home and to do so as quickly as he could.

23

Issy and Bridie

December 1981
The Lord giveth and the Lord taketh away

Issy clung onto Tom's arm. For such a wonderful year to end like this! The earth hitting the lid of her mother's coffin rattled like thunder. A gentle hand touched her. She turned to see Miss Dvina standing close, tears running down her face. Issy acknowledged her, wishing inside that she could cry, too, as she was sure it would be a relief to do so.

Mr Harvey stood just behind Miss Dvina, and his protective gaze on his wife bore a bitterness into Issy. Her mind still gave her the scene that had horrified her on her wedding day.

Held a week into June, just three months after meeting Tom, some had said it had been too soon, but they knew it wasn't, and that's all that mattered. It had been a wonderful day. Like all the estate workers' weddings, the venue had been the large barn in the meadow behind Hensal Grange, which had been cleaned and decorated by the household staff, with fresh bales of straw to sit on. There had been oceans of food and drink supplied by Mr Harvey, as was the custom for the master of the household to do.

The weather had been perfect: a lovely, warm, early summer's day. Everyone had had a really good time dancing to the music played by the local musicians: fiddlers, mouth organists and a drummer.

Miss Dvina hadn't recovered from the birth of her son enough to attend; it took her five months to fully recuperate as a weakness had settled in her and she'd tired easily – the cause had been a heavy bleed two days after the birth, when for a time it had been touch and go. But Mr Harvey had kept the tradition of attending the festivities of one of his workers' weddings.

She'd seen him watching Bridie, and had worried that his look held more than admiration.

Bridie, who at the time had no inkling there was a babby growing inside her, had looked beautiful. She'd danced longer and more daringly than anyone else, often on her own in a free and abandoned way, her skirt twisting and twirling around her, while the other guests clapped and egged her on, none more enthusiastically than Will, though his ma had had a face on her.

But, when Issy had gone around the barn to the makeshift lav, she'd happened across the pair, their bodies close and their lips sealing the feeling between them. Slipping away unnoticed, she'd taken it up with Bridie the next day.

'To be sure, I didn't want it to happen, Issy,' Bridie had said. 'Wasn't I for just going to the lav, when he came around the corner and grabbed me, before I could do anything? But when I pushed him off – which is as sure as Mary is Baby Jesus's mother I did – he was heart-sorry, so he was. And mortified at his actions. Don't be for saying anything,' she'd begged. 'I daresn't tell Will, for fear of his reaction losing him his job and, well – isn't it the way of things as I will be the one in the blame? Everyone will say it was me enticing him, and I didn't. I swear on the Cross, I didn't.'

Understanding this last more than she could say, Issy had held the sobbing Bridie in her arms and soothed her. She'd been shocked to hear all she'd been through, as Bridie's fear had tumbled her past out of her. From that day on she'd vowed to protect Bridie from those who would take advantage of her. And, too, from the harm she could do herself, though she'd had little progress in this. She'd tried to keep Bridie off the drink, and, knowing Bridie wanted a babby, had resorted to telling her many times how her ma had found that those women who took the drink often had problems with getting pregnant, and when they did, they often lost them before full-term.

'From ashes to ashes, dust to dust . . .' The vicar's words interrupted her thoughts.

No, not you, Ma. You could never be reduced to ashes or dust . . .

The cold, heavy handful of earth she'd taken from the tray offered to her by the vicar set the goosebumps standing out on her body. She didn't want to throw it, or hear the finality of it as it clunked onto the wooden casket. She stretched out her hand and let it trickle through. The harsh wind took most of it, but some fell in gentle splattering sounds. 'Oh, Ma . . .'

'Issy, she's at rest now. Come on, me love, say your good-byes. Let her go in peace, for no one deserves it more.'

'Oh, Tom . . .'

'I know. She'll be missed. It's like a hole in me, and me only knowing her a few months. But she'll live on in you, Issy. She'll live on in you.'

Miss Dvina spoke then. 'She will, Isabella. You have her

look and her ways, and Mr Harvey tells me you have her way with words, too, so you will ease all of our pain. I hope you can find peace and comfort in that. And remember, her failing health wasn't something she could live with. She wouldn't have liked not being the one to help everyone, and having to take help for herself.'

A tightening of her throat prevented Issy from answering, but she knew what Miss Dvina said had truth in it. Ma's health had troubled her these past few years, but in the last month or two her swollen, red-blotched legs would hardly carry her from her chair to her bed. They'd moved her into the cottage with them just two weeks ago. Tom had made a shake-me-down in the front parlour for her, which she never left. She'd hated the care she'd had to subject herself to, but on her last day all her grumpiness had left her and she'd lain peacefully, holding Issy's hand until she took her last breath.

'I have had some refreshments prepared in the hall at Hensal Grange,' Miss Dvina said, breaking into her thoughts. 'Please tell everyone they are welcome.'

'Oh, you shouldn't have. Oh, that's very kind of you, Miss . . . Mrs Harvey. Ta ever so much.' For some reason Issy wanted at that moment to seek Bridie out. She looked around, while Tom went to tell all those attending of Mrs Harvey's arrangements, but was shocked to see that Bridie, Will and Janet hadn't attended. A worry set up inside her. *Oh, God, don't let anything be happening. It's too soon. Bridie isn't due until at least another six weeks, if what they'd worked out together was right.* Unsure what to do, she waited until Tom rejoined her, then told him, 'Tom, Bridie isn't here. She wouldn't miss being here for me. Ask Gertie to go and check if she is all right, will you, love?'

*

Bridie's screams wrenched Will's soul. Helplessness and guilt burned into him, for hadn't he put her belly up and caused her this suffering?

Don't let it all be in vain, dear God. Let our babby live, and please, please take care of me little Bridie.

The prayer had hardly died on his lips before his ma came down the stairs. 'You'd better come up, Will. I know it's not a place for a man to be, but she's calling for you and I'll have to fetch help.'

'No, you stay with her. I'll go for Dr Payne. I'll be quicker than you.'

'No, Will, you can't . . . we – well, we haven't enough in the pot to pay him.'

'What? We must have! Me wages are twice what they were!'

'I told you, Will. I told you months back.'

'Oh, God! You mean, Bridie . . . Oh, Ma, what are we going to do?'

'I'll have to go along to Issy's.'

'But she's at her ma's funeral!'

'I know that, but I also know as she'll come. Or if she can't, she'll have an idea as to who I can fetch to help us.'

'Is Bridie going to make it, Ma? Will babby be all right? Oh, God . . .'

'Hold yourself together, lad. We've enough on our plate. Bridie needs the strength of you, and so do I. Lots of babbies make it after only being in the womb for eight months. Besides, it might be as it's been there longer, if it took first time. We've no way of knowing, but it's likely it did, cos Bridie were showing signs within three months. So let's not worry on that score.'

A scream almost drowned his ma's last words. He took the stairs two at a time. His stomach turned over when he entered the room. Blood painted the bed in huge patches of dark red. Bridie, demented with pain, clung onto the iron bedstead, her knuckles white with the grip she had on it. Her hair, wet with sweat, spread out like hundreds of coiled rusty springs.

'Bridie, Bridie, me little lass. I'm here, come on. I'll help you.'

Screwing up her face and groaning into her throat, Bridie didn't answer or acknowledge him. Between her legs a black bulge appeared, and she drew in her breath as if someone had given her a stinging slap. Her face swelled as she pushed with all that was in her, but the bulge didn't move. 'Don't be for just standing there, help me! Get it out, Will. For Christ's sake, will you help me?' The violence of the screamed plea shocked him.

The door opened behind him. 'Help's coming, Bridie, love.' Then, in answer to his unspoken question, his ma said, 'Gertie were at the gate. Issy had sent her. She's gone back to get Issy. They're only at the big house, so she won't take long to get here. Oh, Bridie, love, push. Push hard, lass. It's got to come out.'

'I can't, I ca—' But she did, her face bloated with the effort she put into doing so. The bulge still didn't shift.

'I think its wrong-road about. Oh God, Will!'

'I'm fetching doctor. I don't care if we can't pay him. He's got to come. I'll offer him payments – give him sommat each week.'

'Aye, it's worth a try. Oh, here's Issy. Issy, it's . . .'

'Out of me way, Janet, love. Let me get near her. Reet, Bridie, I'm going to try to get your babby out. When I say "push", push as hard as you can. Come on, love, we can do it.'

Issy knelt between Bridie's legs and placed her hands around the bulge. 'Reet, push, Bridie. Push.'

Bridie responded to Issy's commands with a scream that vibrated off the walls. She sank back, and the baby slid most of the way out.

'Hold it there, love. It's nearly here. Don't push. I have to release its leg. There, that's it.'

No one spoke. All eyes watched Issy cut the cord and begin to rub the tiny, lifeless body with the towel Janet had passed her. Will held his breath, and prayers tumbled upon prayers as he watched Issy lift the still form by its legs and shake it gently, before giving it a sharp tap on its bottom. Nothing happened. Issy tried again.

The room expanded with the silent fear held within it. Bridie sat up, her face red from her efforts, and her bloodshot eyes holding a horrific fear. Issy shook her head. 'I'm sorry. He's . . . he has no life in him.'

No one moved as she laid the babby down.

'I'm sorry, love – so sorry – but, lass, we have more to do. There's still the afterbirth. We have to get that out of you.'

Unable to take in what was happening, Will felt isolated, cocooned in a place where no one could reach him. An urge took him to hold his son. 'Pass babby to me, Issy, whilst you do what you have to do.' *Is this happening? Am I really holding the body of my son in my arms? Dear God, is there nothing I can do to breathe life into him?*

Issy passed him a small blanket from the pile on the chair next to the bed. Taking off the bloodied towel, he used it to wipe the little face. He swaddled the tiny body in the blanket, but couldn't cover his head. Looking into the cherub-like face with blue-tinted skin relaxed onto the bone structure, he wondered who his son would have looked like. Curls of matted, dark hair framed his face, and his half-closed, unseeing eyes looked the palest of blue. Like himself? Yes, his son had taken features from him. This warmed a small part of the ice-cold blood running through him.

Glancing up, he saw Bridie staring at him out of eyes that could have belonged to a mad woman. She didn't utter a sound, and her face had drained of all colour. Fear clutched him.

Issy's urgent tone shocked him. 'Will, you have to fetch the doctor, and hurry. Bridie is still bleeding, and I'm feared she might haemorrhage. She's torn badly and needs his attention.'

Nothing happened. He didn't move, and his ma just stood on the other side of the bed, her mouth open and her body shaking.

'Will, please . . . Janet! Janet – oh, for the love of God! I know you are shocked and saddened, and I feel your pain, but we must help Bridie. Look, she's taking with the ague. She's trembling all over.'

At this, Will knew himself to respond. His whole being wanted to hold Bridie, to make things right in her world.

Bridie's voice shook as she spoke. 'I . . . I want me babby. Will, let me be having me babby.'

'Pass him over, Will, then go. Go as quickly as you can. Tell the doctor as I sent for him. He'll come then.'

Just before he left the room, he looked back. The sight of his Bridie holding their dead son to her breast wrenched his heart from him.

'Me little lass, you're awake. You've slept for hours.'

'Where's . . . ?'

'I took him to the priest. He blessed him, but . . . Oh, Bridie.'

'Was it for being difficult, me wee love? Arranging the funeral and naming him?'

'I'm sorry, I – I couldn't do anything. It's as if our child didn't exist, Bridie. If he had taken a breath, then . . .'

'You mean, 'tis that he is nothing? Nothing! No, Will, no, no, no. I can't . . .'

'He'll never be "nothing" to us, Bridie: he'll always be our son. We just can't have anything official to recognize him. They wouldn't let me register his birth, nor even have a death certificate.'

'Oh, God, Will. What . . . ?'

'Don't, Bridie, please don't. Let's talk. Let's decide what to do. If we deal with the practical things, it will help us.'

'Where is it you have taken him to?'

'I haven't. He is wrapped up nice and snug. I made a box for him out of some of the wood hanging around the building site. Ma cut a lining for it from them curtains she didn't use – them blue ones from me bedroom in Sheffield. We cushioned it with the feathers out of one of her pillows, before I tacked it into place. I had to put it outside in the outhouse to keep it cold, but we left a candle burning in there. Oh, Bridie . . .'

He felt her arms come around him as her body was racked with deep sobs. He let her cry, letting her tears mingle with his as he kissed her face and held her close.

When she'd calmed, he told her of his plans. 'I thought to take him up on that hill at the back. Bury him near the beck, where he and me might have gone fishing one day. We can visit him on nice days, take a picnic up there and sit with him. What d'yer think, love?'

'Is it that he cannot have a burial in the churchyard? I'm for understanding he can't go in the consecrated ground, but back home there's a place for them who die without being baptized.'

Bridie seemed calmer now, and he was glad of it. 'No, they said he wasn't just one who hadn't been baptized. He—'

'No, don't be saying it. To be sure, he lived in the inside of me. Didn't I feel him moving around, kicking me for all he was worth? Well, then, 'tis that he must have a soul. And I'm not for believing what they say about this limbo place. Why would the good Lord abandon such a helpless creature and be at punishing him for something that was not his fault?'

The anger in her at the injustice of it all was helping her, he could see that. 'You're reet, Bridie. He has a soul, and that soul is flying around in Heaven causing as much mayhem as he did inside you. We'll hold onto that, but we won't taint his passing with taking the powers that be to task. Let's just have our own private ceremony. Put him to rest somewhere beautiful, as befits his precious soul.'

'Aye, 'tis right that you are. I would like that. What name shall we give him?'

'How about Eric?'

'But that isn't for being a saint's name. I've never been for hearing of a St Eric, so I haven't. What about Patrick, after the patron saint of Ireland? That would be lovely, so it would.'

'Eric is a name very dear to me. It was me da's middle name, and me granddad's name.'

''Tis Eric Patrick, then. Yes, 'tis for having a nice sound to it.'

Issy and Tom helped Will a couple of days later. The wind carried flurries of snow in it, chilling the tears flowing down his face. The hard and unyielding ground meant they could only use a spot where he and Tom managed to dislodge a large boulder. Underneath, the soil allowed them to dig a deep grave. They replaced the boulder and Issy arranged some heather around it. They stood in silence and prayed. Tom and Issy had the same belief: that Eric did have a soul and that it had gone to Heaven. Tom had brought some tools from the stables, and he took a moment to chip out Eric's name into the stone.

As they walked back, Issy talked of her concerns for Bridie. 'You must help her to come off the drink, Will. I'm afraid it is getting hold of her. Her body is all of a-tremble and only settles if I take her up a cup of gin.'

'I know I have it to do, but I was waiting a while. She's been through so much, and the drink helps her at the moment.'

'You shouldn't take that stance too long, thou knows. The more she depends on it, the worse it will be.'

Will knew Issy was right, but what could he do? When he'd left the house this morning, Bridie hadn't woken. At least, she hadn't stirred. Whether that was because she couldn't face what he was going to do or not, he didn't know. He'd sneaked out of the room and left her, rather than having to face dealing with her pain as well as his own. His ma had said he should buy a bottle of gin, as the one they had was nearly empty. There had been disdain in her voice, but even she seemed to have the mind to let it ride for now. He decided he wouldn't. He'd take Issy's advice and tackle it here and now.

Arriving home, he was glad that Issy and Tom refused his offer of coming in. 'No, Will, you just go and be with Bridie. We'll come by later. You've had enough for one day, we can see that.' Tom shook his hand as he said this, then Issy hugged him.

'Take care of her, Will. She's to face the pain of her loss proper. As yet, she's masked it. That can be dangerous for her.'

Promising her that he would, he took out his baccy tin. He'd only taken up the habit of late, and he found it soothed him. He drew in a deep lungful of smoke and, through the haze it made as he blew it out, he watched Issy and Tom until they turned into the lane. Finishing the last of his cigarette and stamping out the nub-end, he could delay no longer and went inside. He refused the tea his ma had made, then changed his mind and asked her to pour two mugs and he'd take them up with him.

The door creaked as he opened it to the darkened interior. The thick curtains pulled across the window stopped most of the day from coming into the room. He crept across to the bed and lay as close as he could to Bridie's huddled form. She moved, turning towards him. Concern seeped into him as he held her. 'Eeh, Bridie, love, you're shaking.'

'It'll be the shock as me body's been through. Issy was after saying it happens to most women. It's nothing to be worrying your head about.'

'I've brought you a nice drop of hot tea, love.'

'It's not tea I'm needing, Will.'

'No, love. I'm worried, Bridie, reet worried. I'm worried about you, and . . . well, lass, to tell the truth, I'm worried about your drinking. I can smell it on your breath and it's still morning. Have the tea.'

'Jesus, Mary and Joseph! Will you listen to yourself, Will? I've only just been after having a drop in me tea. Your own mammy gave it to me. She said it would warm me through.'

'Bridie, please, love. Your drinking the gin is getting out of hand. It's doing you harm and its taking all we have. There was nowt in the pot to pay the doctor with when I went for him the other day. I had to humiliate meself by asking for credit, and he wasn't good in his manner about it. The pot holds a good few pounds when it's full, Bridie, and that means a lot of bottles of gin.'

'Oh, Will, don't – not now. Haven't you just been laying our son to rest? I can't take any more. I can't!'

'Don't cry. Come on, Bridie love. I'm sorry. We can sort it. Bridie . . .'

My God, without meaning to, he seemed to have opened her wound up so wide there didn't seem a way back for her. The noise of her sobs brought his ma rushing upstairs.

'What's to do? Eeh, Will, what's to do? I could hear such a racket coming down the stairs to me.'

'We were just talking about her drinking, Ma, and the empty pot, and she took on like this. Come on, Bridie, it doesn't matter – none of it matters. Come on, love. Aw, Ma, what can I do? She'll be ill if she carries on.'

'Don't worry. Happen it's the shock coming out of her, and she stands need to cry, poor soul. It happens after a birth in the normal run of things, and it don't take much to trigger it. Let her cry. All women do it and it generally lasts a good few hours an' all. Try to get her to drink that tea.'

'I . . . I don't want tea, Will! I want . . . I'm in need of a drop. Oh, Will! I've got to be having a drink, please! Please, Janet, tell him. Tell him!'

Will couldn't speak for the shock that her begging rendered in him. What had he been thinking? He'd fought his ma to let Bridie have her gin. Oh God, why hadn't he noticed what it was doing to her? Well, there'd be no more of it. He had to be strong.

'No, Bridie. It stops now. Come on, lass – me and Ma'll

help you. Do it for little Eric, eh? Don't let his little life be for nothing. Hang onto how it would have been for him to have a ma whose life were about supping, and where she'd get her next one from.'

'Don't, Will. Don't be for putting that onto me. I can't, I can't. I need the gin to help me cope. Me body won't stop the shaking. I'm not for standing it. I . . . I'll kill meself, so I will.'

'Christ! How can you say such a thing?' At that moment all he could feel in him was disgust. Disgust at this woman he loved and had given his all to. Anger shook through him as he replied, 'Didn't I take you on, no matter what? Haven't I stood by you, tried to give you a decent life? Worked long shifts to keep us going? And this is how you repay me. You take all we have to feed your lust for the drink and you killed—'

'Stop it, son! Stop it now!'

The room closed in on him. He peered into the distraught face of his ma, then looked over at Bridie huddled up in the furthest corner of the bed, fear and horror masking her face. He turned on his heel and walked out of the room, every limb trembling with the emotions searing through his body. Leaving the house, he walked back towards the hill. He climbed until he saw the boulder in front of him. Reaching it, he sank down, rested his head on it and sobbed.

Bridie looked at Janet and saw hatred in her face. She recoiled as the vitriol spat from Will's ma. 'You bastard whore. You drunken, sneaky whore. Your drinking killed your babby. Brought him on too soon, and he didn't have a chance. Now you're trying to kill my son. Well, you're not going to get the chance – bitch!'

Janet's body flew at her, hands clawing and gouging

Bridie's face. Spittle sprayed from her as she ground out the filthy words through gritted teeth.

Fighting back, Bridie grabbed Janet's hair. With her strength low, she could only flail out with her fists in an attempt to defend herself from the renewed onslaught, as Janet escaped her clutches. 'For the love of God, stop, Janet! Why is it you're fighting me? I haven't done anything more than you already knew of me.'

Drained of energy, Janet at last slumped on the bed. Bridie stared at the blood seeping from the split in Janet's lip, and watched her tears water it down as they ran over her blotched-red, angry face.

'Oh, Janet, I only defended meself. I could do no other. Isn't it that we are all upset? I'm sorry to the heart of me. I am. Janet . . .'

'Shut your mouth! I wish Will had never met you. Never come under the spell of you. Aye, for in your own way you are a witch. To men you are. And you use what you have in you to get at them.'

'No, Janet, don't say that. I'm not claiming to be a saint, but I'm not what you put on me, either. You both knew me failings from the beginning.'

'You're right there. And I tried to live with them, for me son's sake, but you threw me efforts back in me face.'

Bridie watched Janet lift her weary body off the bed and leave the room. *Jesus, Mary and Joseph, what have I been after causing?*

Never in all his days did Will expect to see his ma in such a state. Tufts of her wiry grey hair had loosened from the pins that always held it in place, and blood ran down from her lip. Her tear-filled eyes stared out at him, giving him the feeling she wasn't seeing him, only someone she once knew. The chair he'd made for her rocked back and forth as her body heaved in a deep breath. On its release, her head sank onto her chest.

Will leapt forward, saying, 'Ma, Ma! Oh, Ma, what have I done to you?'

Looking up, she whispered, 'Sommat has to be done, Will. She'll be the death of us both, if not.'

'Naw, Ma, she'll be reet. You said yourself she'd been through a lot. I should have thought on. Aye, it's reet we have to tackle her drinking, but what possessed me to do it today – the day as we buried our firstborn? I've had time to think. I called in on the Irish and bought her a bottle. We're going to let her have a small drop and get her off it, bit by bit.'

'Aye, if you say so.'

'I'm sorry, Ma. There's nothing more I can do. But I'll not stand for you being hurt. I'll make that clear. Now, rest your head back. I'll just take this up to calm Bridie, then I'll get some water and bathe your wounds and make a nice drop of hot tea, eh?'

She didn't answer him, but she did smile. As he went up the stairs, he tried to dispel the feeling that the smile had held triumph. That he could take, for he'd been brought up on it, but what Bridie had done to her – to them – could he ever forgive that?

Opening the door to their bedroom, he knew he could. And at that moment he loathed his ma. His ma's injuries had broken his heart, but they were nothing to what Bridie had suffered.

'I was only at defending meself, so I was . . . Oh, Will.

Can you forgive me? I never meant to hurt your mammy. I . . .'

She spoke through lips swollen to twice their size. Her face was unrecognizable. Ripped as it was, he wondered if it would ever recover. No words came to him in answer.

'I'm going to be after trying to give up the drink. I promise.'

'Aye, I'll help you, me wee love. But, here, I've bought you some. Just a sip now and again, eh? We'll count how many you have, and cut it down over a time, eh?'

'Ta, Will. I want you to know I love you, and if it's in me power, I'll do it. For you and your mammy.'

'Alreet, lass. Sup that now, and I'll be up in a minute to help you get sorted. There's nowt we can do about today, except learn from it. It'll mend. Me love for you will make sure of that.'

24

Five years later –
late May 1886

Evil is as evil does

Andrew folded his paper and put it down with the precision of a man with something on his mind. 'Dvina, dear, I think we should sort out Jeremy's schooling. If we want him to get into one of the good schools by the time he is seven, we need to put his name down.'

'I've been dreading this moment, Andrew. Do we have to talk about it? He is still a baby.'

'No, he isn't, and I won't allow you to look on him as such. He turned five years old in March, for God's sake! That's two months ago, and I had been hoping you would broach the subject yourself rather than me having to do so.'

'I know, I'm sorry, but I cannot bring myself to think of parting with him.'

'You will end up making him soft and Mummy-dependent. I am happy for him to have home tutors for a couple of years, as long as you leave his education and guidance to them, but after that he must go to school. He depends on us to prepare him for the world. That cannot happen if he remains around your skirts for too long.'

'Well, thank you for that. I thought I was doing a very good job with him. He helps out in the stables and is around Tom and Henry a lot, and he knows more about horses than any other child could hope to at his age. He takes his knocks. He isn't a cry-baby, I instil courage into him and, all in all, his enquiring mind has us researching all sorts of things. Not least the workings of the mine where his papa spends most of his time! I think, when his tutors arrive next month, they will find a well-advanced, well-balanced little boy.'

'Of course, dear. I didn't mean to imply . . .' Beaten by her logic and straight talking once again, he gave in. 'Well, maybe we could stretch it till he is eleven, then. Yes, perhaps I was putting too early an age on it. But we must still think about getting his name down.'

Talking about these mundane things had become the usual topic of their conversation these days. Andrew still loved Dvina, but he increasingly found his faithfulness to her very hard-going, and couldn't believe that five years had passed since his last illicit taking of pleasure with someone else. Not that he'd gone any further than a kiss, but by God he'd wanted to.

The impact of that one kiss remained with him today. Had it not been for finding out soon afterwards that Bridie was with child, he would have taken her as his mistress there and then, but her losing the child had taken its toll on her and there had been concerns for her health.

After that she seemed to lose interest and had avoided him. His own ardour for her had lessened, and he'd thrown himself into his commitment to Dvina. Not that that had been difficult at first, but of late the fascination with Bridie had rekindled and he'd become unsettled once more.

It had started within a short period of her little girl being born, in around February of '84. To his shame, this had coincided with Will's worsening condition. Obviously, Will couldn't have kept Bridie happy in a sexual way, and her being made as she was, she began to see others – well, himself, at least – as potential lovers. Though this sounded pompous, even to himself, the evidence was there to substantiate him believing it.

Whenever they'd met – which was orchestrated as being by chance, and often by her – her eyes locked into his, sending him unmistakable messages. And when no one was about, innuendo had passed between them. All of this had fuelled his desire and had him fantasizing about what it would be like to lay with her.

Then, a stroke of some sort had taken her mother-in-law down and left her bedridden, and with poor Will succumbing more and more to the blasted bane of the mining world – the fatal coughing sickness – the right moment had never presented itself. Andrew rarely even caught a glimpse of her these days, as Bridie always seemed to be cooped up taking care of her family. Maybe after . . . *No. For God's sake! I cannot allow myself to hope for someone else's demise so that I can satisfy a need I have – especially someone as good and harmless as William Hadler!*

As if inside his mind, Dvina shocked him by mentioning Bridie: 'Changing the subject, Andrew dear, I have a worry I'd like to talk to you about. When I was out riding the other day, I saw Will Hadler's wife. She was sitting by Seamus's campfire with him, of all things. She looked very settled and at home. I thought it strange, and as you—'

Shocked, he thought Dvina was going to take him to task on his fancy for the woman, so he cut in, steering the conversation in a different direction. 'Oh, is Seamus back? He hasn't been around for a while, and I had hoped he wouldn't be coming this way again. Something has changed in him. I think he could be dangerous. What did you make of it?'

'I couldn't make anything of it. It looked innocent enough. She sat a few feet away from him. They didn't see me.'

'Do you think they were arguing?'

'What a funny question! I have no idea. Why?'

He told her about the last time he'd come across Bridie and Seamus.

'So they knew one another before she came here, then? Didn't you say her husband had said she needed to get away from someone? I hope Seamus isn't the one. We don't need any trouble on the estate and, with what is happening already to them, neither do Will and his mother.'

'No, that's true, though his wife has a lot to contend with, you know, looking after both of them. Maybe she was just having a moment's respite. By the way, I've charged Dr Payne with looking after the mother while he is visiting Will, and I am picking up the bill.'

'That's very kind of you, Andrew. That's one of the things I love you for: your kindness and thoughtfulness, even towards your workers. They are very lucky, and I hope they know it.'

'Oh, you still love me then?'

'Of course, you know I do. Don't I show you enough?'

He laughed at this. The little minx was flirting with him. He liked that. He knew she often tried very hard to be the wife he wanted in all things, and the fact that she wasn't enough for him wasn't her fault. It was some despicable demon within him, and it was a demon he knew he'd not be able to keep down for much longer.

Standing up, he went over to her and kissed her cheek. 'And I'm very lucky to have you, my dear. And you know how much I love you, as I am always showing you.' They shared a smile; their conversation was often a friendly game of touché. 'Do you fancy a ride out? I could do with some air. I might try to find out how things are, with Seamus being around again. I'll stop and talk to anyone I meet, to see how the land lies.'

'I won't, if you don't mind, dear. I promised Jeremy he could have another riding lesson in the paddock this afternoon. I was going to ask you to join us, but I think it's important you go on your mission. I really am worried something may be afoot. You can sort of sense these things in a small place like this.'

Jeremy, Jeremy, Jeremy. Sometimes Andrew felt he himself didn't exist and that their son took precedence on her time.

'That was a big sigh. Did you really want me to accompany you? Of course I will. I can get Tom to supervise Jeremy. His nanny will be on hand, so there won't be a problem if he needs any attention.'

'No, no. It was a selfish sigh. I did feel a bit peeved for a moment. But, thinking about it, I'd probably get more out of folk on my own.'

'Full of compliments today, aren't you, Mr Harvey!'

'Ha! You deserved that. No, it's just that they are used to dealing with me in a straight way. They hold you in such reverence that you make them tongue-tied.'

'I think you had better go, before you put yourself in so much trouble you can't get out of it. You might find our connecting door locked for a few nights, if you carry on.'

He laughed at the look on her face. There was so much to love about her. *Why, why can I not be satisfied with that?*

The afternoon held the last remnants of the late spring in its air. There wasn't enough warmth to give it its early summer standing, but it was pleasant enough and ideal weather for riding the estate. Not all the trees and bushes were yet clothed in their full greenery, though very few bare branches remained.

Tom met Andrew with his mount. Every time he saw Tom, he wondered about him and Issy having no issue as yet. After all, neither of them was young, and they should really have had a family before now. He tutted at himself. Wasn't Dvina always saying he was like a mother hen where his workers were concerned? He was beginning to think her right. Just look at him now. The last thing he'd had on his mind earlier was to ride out today, and now here he was sitting high in the saddle ready to sally forth like a knight on a white charger, to make sure all was well with his charges. This thought had him smiling.

'You look happy, sir. It's nice to see. There seems so much gloom about. You'd not think it was the start of summer, when all expectation should be in the air.'

'Oh? What's afoot, Tom? I sensed myself that all isn't well.'

'No, there's one or two down in the dumps. My Issy was telling me of the Irish seeming to have problems. She's been up there a couple of times this last week delivering babbies, and she says as there's more than the usual black eyes and bruises amongst the womenfolk. She's in a real twist about it all. Then there's poor Will, coughing his heart up, and his ma hardly able to get out of bed. Then . . . well, all in all, it's a sorry state of affairs.'

'Yes. I know about Will, of course. Not much hope for

him, from what the doctor says. Poor fellow was down the mine from an extremely early age. It's very sad. He is such a nice man – one of God's natural gentlemen.' Anger, a familiar feeling on this subject, touched his heart. 'The damn coughing sickness! It is a curse in our line of work. I do all I can to protect my workers, but some seem more susceptible to it. I believe Will's father died of it, so he may have had a weakness. Still, it seems unfair it should get hold of him, just as his mother took ill. Of course, she's getting on in years and so this kind of thing is to be expected, but it isn't nice to hear of her suffering. Anyway, on the other subject, what does Isabella think is happening amongst the Irish community?'

'She won't say much. She thinks it's to do with that traveller. She's heard tell of stuff he gets up to, and some of it beggars belief.'

'Is it something we could get the law onto?'

'I think they should be involved, but Issy says everyone is scared stiff, so she don't think they'll say owt.'

'Well, if you hear anything that is factual, let me know, Tom. Nothing can be done on conjecture. If I have a whiff of there being any truth in what's behind the fear, I'll speak to the magistrate and get the Leeds police involved.'

'I'll do me best. I'll tell her you're willing to help. That might give Issy a chance to get them to talk.'

'Let's hope so. I don't like any of my workers feeling intimidated. Seamus has a cheek, and a rum way of repaying kindness. I expect Issy told you he used to drop in on us on a regular basis. We welcomed him, gave him work, shared any extra kills the gamekeeper made with him and generally looked out for his welfare, and this is how he repays us. Well, I am not standing for it, and I have a mind to tell him to leave my land and not come back.'

'I beg your pardon, sir. I don't mean to be bold, but I don't think that would be wise. At least, not for you to tackle him on your own. He's a villain. Some of what Issy hears is of him already on the run from the law, and from others. And it seems these "others" wouldn't just stop at moving him on to another county; they'd be more likely to dispatch him to face his maker. Which means he could be a desperate man. You could be in danger by taking him on.'

'You're right, of course, and please don't worry about having spoken out of turn. In fact, if that is what is going on, then I might speak to the police anyway, to see if they have any information on him. Well, I'll be off. I want to call in on my mother, as well as have a scout around the estate. I should be back well in time for you to see to Goldboy before you finish for the night.'

Bridie opened the door to Issy. Her heart felt the gladness of seeing her friend, for some days she knew she'd not be able to carry on without Issy's help. The tiredness ached in every part of her body, from coping with Will and Janet in their sickness, and from her lively little Bridget.

God had blessed her, so He had, when He'd sent little Bridget to them, but didn't He soon after smote her with sadness?

Pride swelled in her, banishing these thoughts, as Issy entered and said, 'By, Bridie, she's a bonny little thing. And look at her, talking away to Janet as if she were going on thirty instead of being just two year and three months old!'

'I know, 'tis as me little Bridget has an old head on her shoulders, and she's for having the intelligence of a much older child. And isn't she for being such a help too, keeping her granny entertained as she does? And her pappy . . .'

Oh, Will, her poor Will. The doctor's words came back to her, and it was as if she'd not been for understanding them when she'd heard them. But now . . .

'What is it, love?'

'How is it I am going to cope, Issy? Dr Payne has been after warning me about Will. He's – well, he's getting worse . . . His time is near.'

'You're doing very well, lass; better than most would. You have a gift. You're a natural at this nursing, and your inner strength amazes me.'

Issy's arm came round her and gave her comfort. Her tears threatened to spill over, but she knew she couldn't let them or they would never stop. Issy seemed to sense this. 'I'm here for you, thou knows, love. You can call on me day or night. Come on, lass, let's have a brew. I have a thirst on me as would rival the Devil's, and with him sitting in all that heat, an' all.'

'Ha, I wasn't for thinking of him like that. Well, I hope it is that he's parched. It'll serve him right for the evil he does!' It surprised her to know she could laugh when the tears were a constant threat, but then Issy was after being a real tonic. She could take you from your sorrows to laughing in one sentence.

'Aw, love, that's better. Now, let's have an update while I make the tea. How is Janet today?'

'She's about the same. There's still no use in her left side, but she manages well. 'Tis not having her speech as is frustrating for her. She was after throwing her cup at me earlier, but I gave her a telling. Sure, it could have hit me wee Bridget, so it could. Janet cried, and it broke the heart of me. It must be like living in hell, not being able to communicate, and yet 'tis as Bridget seems to understand her. Many a time she'll be after saying, "Mammy, me granna wants drinkies" or "Me granna's tummy's making noises," to tell me Janet is hungry. It's uncanny, so it is.'

'It must be all those saints' names you gave her. They're all busy passing things on to her. What were they all again?'

'Bridget, Mary, Janet and Megan. Though I'm not for knowing if Megan is a saint or not, but sure it is the name Will's grandmother had, and as it was after being an Irish favourite, we put it in. Besides, it's a powerful thing having the Mother of God's name, so if one of them isn't a saint, then that will be for making up for it.'

'Ha, that's a good one, if ever I heard owt. I thought it was only the fairies you all believed in. There's nowt like having every possibility covered, is there? Anyroad, enough idle chatter. You look worn out, love. Is Will lying down?'

'Aye. When I looked in on him a moment ago he was after being in a deep sleep, bless his heart.'

'Well, let's have this sup of tea and I'll help you with Janet's bath. We'll get her comfortable, and if Will's still at his rest by then, how about you go out for a walk, get some fresh air, eh? I can sit for the rest of the afternoon. I've done everything at home, and there's no one about to drop a babby, so I'll not be needed elsewhere. Besides, it's days since I last sat for you. You can't stay cooped up all the time.'

'That would be grand. For the rest of the afternoon, you say? Would it be as I could go up the hill to see Eric? I haven't been there since early spring. I could be telling him how things are here, and asking him to help his pappy and his granna. Oh, to stretch me legs that far and to feel the sun would be wonderful, so it would.'

'Of course, that would be no problem. It'll do you good.'

A warmth entered Bridie, and it wasn't all down to the tea.

Oh, to be going out on me own, and aye, maybe even seeing Seamus for a wee while, warms me heart, so it does. Though doesn't that be giving me a feeling of a powerful guilt?

Issy broke into her thoughts. 'Bridie? Tom asked me to ask if you've decided what you're doing about Will's allotment. Only, he said to tell you it's not too late to get some stuff planted on it. He has an abundance of plants he says are really hardy and will take well. He won't need them all, and there's a few others are willing to help him to set them for you.'

'That would be good – thanks, Issy. Will did all the ground-work at the back end of last year. It'll be grand for him to be knowing 'tis planted out for us.'

'Reet, come on then, lass. Let's get started on Janet, and then you can away to the hills.'

'I'll just be after putting Bridget down for her afternoon nap first. She'll be out of our way then. Only if she misses her sleep she can be in a mood like they say the little people get in, if they can't find a mushroom to sit on.'

Issy laughed at this. 'Eeh, and you say as I have some funny sayings! You can top me, lass, and would win any witty contest we might enter.'

They giggled at this daft notion, and Bridie thought it felt good to have the feel of merriment come into the drab atmosphere of sickness.

'I'll get started on getting everything ready while you take her up, love. Go on with you! Little people indeed! You Irish are sommat else in the tales you tell. Aye, and you tell them that often, I reckon as you come to believe in them as truth!'

Leaving the house an hour later, Bridie took a deep breath. She turned into the lane and for a moment had to stand still and just gaze at the beauty around her. Dog roses and blackthorn blossom clothed the hedgerows and filled the air with a sweet, subtle scent. Her mood, already lifted by Issy, soared, and hope seeped into her. Jesus Himself wouldn't be for taking her Will from her, she was sure of that. The doctor could be wrong. Wasn't Will a strong man? To be sure he could fight back from this.

These thoughts settled in her, giving her the truth of them and belying what others would have her believe. An urge came into her to skip over the stile and run across the field, to stretch out her limbs, which had for so long only known the short walk to the Irish for her gin. Not that she had to go often, for hadn't she cut down and only took a drop now and then?

Only once had she ventured further, when a few days ago Seamus had left a message for her to contact him. Hadn't he been kindness itself on that visit, sympathizing with her plight and saying how he would always help her? But then, didn't she know he would, and now she wasn't for believing what she heard about him.

It was warmer than she thought. Beads of sweat stood out on her forehead as she climbed the hill. She could see the boulder, lying just feet away from the beck. She ran the last few yards to it and fell against it, panting for breath. 'Oh, Eric, 'tis that Mammy is for thinking of paddling in the beck, so she is, just to cool her feet down. But I have some things to talk over with you, so I'll do that first.'

She sat beside the boulder, going through all of her worries. She felt them lighten with the unburdening of them to her little son. She didn't hear the tread of a horse until it snorted and its master called out, 'Well, well, you're the last person I expected to see up here! Are you all right, Bridie?'

She jumped up. 'Oh, Mr Harvey – yes, I'll be after being

fine. Issy was for looking after things for a while, so I could take the air and spend some time with me son, as . . .'

'Your son?'

'Aye, 'tis that he is buried here under this boulder. They wouldn't let us bury him in the churchyard, for they were after saying as he had no soul, with him not taking a breath.'

'I see. So you buried him up here. Well, for one, I am sure he did have a soul; and for two, you couldn't have chosen a prettier, more peaceful resting place for him.'

She watched him dismount, and her heart thudded. She didn't know if it was from fear or anticipation, for she was remembering the kiss they'd shared and the looks he'd given her over the years since, as if he was undressing her in his mind. He came over and stood near to her.

'How are things at home, Bridie?'

'Oh, they are after saying as my Will won't last to see the year out, but I'm not for believing them.' She went on to tell him of her real feelings on the matter of Will. 'Now Janet, to be sure 'tis her time. 'Tis only when, not if, and the poor soul is for knowing it. It is lucky I am to have the help of Issy – I mean, Isabella.'

'Yes, it's good that she took over from her mother in looking after the sick and delivering the babies. I hear she does a good job, and I am sure she does. Look, Bridie, I have to tell you: you really must prepare yourself. Will is very sick. Oh, I'm not saying there isn't any hope – there is – but you have to face the fact he may not recover.'

'I know, but sure it is you can bring things about if you dwell on them, and I'm not about to do that.'

'Well, that is a good outlook. Now what about you, Bridie? How are you coping with it all? I . . .'

The space between them shrank. She could feel the tension

surrounding them, and her breath became shallow as desire lit inside her. For hadn't it been such a long time since Will . . . ? She shook the thought from her mind. Trying to control the urges attacking her, she searched her mind to find something to say, something to break the spell. 'What is it you are doing up here, Mr Harvey?'

'Andrew, call me Andrew. I saw you running across the field. I watched you come up here, and I couldn't resist following, though I had to take the more slanting route. Do we have to talk, Bridie? I think we have more to do than that?'

'Oh, so you did expect to be finding me here, and you after saying I was the last person . . .'

He swayed towards her. She could feel his breath on her cheek. The touch of his hand on her hair further awakened her. He ran his fingers through it, and let it fall back onto her shoulder. Strands of it licked the heightened feelings of her as it brushed her breast. He followed the flow of it with the back of his smooth hand. 'Oh, Bridie, I have wanted you for so long.'

His lips reached her neck, and a shiver ran through her, lingering between her legs and lighting up that part of her as if a flame had touched it. She turned her head and his lips found hers. The soft kiss deepened. His tongue sought entrance to her mouth. She gave in to its urgent probing. He tasted nice, clean and fresh. Their tongues danced together. His fingers undid the buttons of her bodice and slid it off her shoulders. She couldn't resist. She knew in the heart of her she should, but didn't know how to. No one would be after knowing, she told herself, and wasn't she yearning to take a man to her, after her enforced celibacy?

The grass accepted her like a down mattress, its lush depths cushioning her naked body. The sun kissed every part of her, tingle-drying the moist parts where he'd licked and sucked her skin.

Kneeling, Andrew discarded his jacket and shirt. She helped him out of his riding breeches, feasting her eyes and hands on what he had to offer her, and trying to calm the anticipation that took the heart of her and denied any resistance.

Joy surged through her as he entered her, tentatively at first, looking into her eyes as if seeking approval. She gave it by wrapping her legs around him, pulling him into her and crying out with the ecstasy that took the very being of her into a place she knew she belonged, as wave after wave of intense pleasure seared through her.

His words and his cries told her of his enjoyment of her. She had so much to give and to take, and she gave herself into forgetting everything but this moment, allowing every peak to wash her whole body in sheer abandonment, until at last she had given her all and relaxed under him, letting him seek his own moment.

When it came to him, her name was on his lips in gasps of deep, throaty whispers as he plunged deeper and deeper into her. 'Bridie, Bridie . . .'

His sweat dripped onto her face. She put her tongue out to lick it, and giggled as the saltiness of it made her wrinkle her nose.

He laughed down at her, then rolled off. 'Oh, Bridie, what am I going to do with you? You are a very naughty girl.'

'Me? Wasn't I sure it was you who took advantage of me, when you followed me up here? And wasn't I alone and defenceless?'

'Bridie, I . . . Well, you wanted it – you know you did. You offered it to me with your eyes, your mouth. Everything about you screamed out to me to take you.'

'Ha, I'm only for teasing you. I was after wanting a man to make love to me this good while.'

'Oh, any man would have done, then? You little minx. Well, it happened to be me and I'm glad of that, and if you keep fondling me like that I'll take you again. Bridie, has anyone ever told you, you were made for loving? Come here . . .'

His second taking of her matched his first, which surprised her, for didn't she find it wasn't usually so? Giving herself up to the pleasure of it, she drifted for a while, then had a mind to take a more active part, doing things she enjoyed doing. This thought froze in the fear of her as, without warning, the sun disappeared into the shadow falling over them. Before the scream left her throat, the whip curled through the air like a snake. It cracked down across Andrew's back.

The sting of it, and the shock, caused him to take a breath that Bridie thought he would never release. She somehow managed to get his body off her and got to her feet. 'Seamus, no. No!' Her voice hung in the air unbidden.

Seamus raised his arm, his body magnificent, taut and strong. His horse-whip, knotted in many places, was ready to strike again. Jumping at him using her full body weight jarred the pain through her, but did nothing to stop him. He brushed her aside as if she were no more than a feather. The sickening crack and the agony-filled scream were drowned out by Seamus's words. 'You fucking bastard! I'll not rest until you are for taking your last breath, so I won't. To be sure you'll never touch my woman – or any other – when I've done with you, you dirty, thieving bastard!'

The whip came down for a third time, but mercifully Andrew rolled out of its way. He lifted his hand towards the saddlebag of his horse, but whatever he thought to find had gone. Bridie saw the barrel of it glinting on the ground behind Seamus. She flung herself at it and aimed it at his back. She cocked it ready, something she'd learned to do from Seamus himself, in another life. His body stilled. He sucked in his breath, and his anger switched from Andrew to her. 'Put that down, now, Bridie. 'Tis your man you should stand up for, as he tries to defend your honour.'

'You are not for being *my man*. Seamus, what is it that makes you think you are, and can interfere with me life? You have no claim on me, and if you are not for putting that whip down, I will shoot you and think nothing of doing so, for you are not the man I knew. You're evil, so you are, and even your grandmother – were she here today – would urge me to pull the trigger.'

Seamus turned to face her. Sweat ran down his face. Tears brimmed in his eyes as he said, 'You are mine, and one day I will have you. Whore that you are, I have to have you – and soon, Bridie, soon.' He stayed still for a moment longer, the space between them a bridge that neither could cross. 'I'll be back, so I will.'

She watched, crushed by the silence he'd left behind him, until he disappeared into the thicket.

'Oh, Andrew, Andrew, 'tis sorry I am. Oh, sweet Jesus, look at you . . .'

Andrew lay on his stomach. The jagged weals gouged into his back glistened under the sun. His voice leaked pain as he begged of her, 'Help me, Bridie. Help me.'

'I will, Andrew. Lie still whilst I put on me clothes, and I'll do what I can for you.'

'There's w-w-whisky in the saddlebag. Use th-that to bathe my back.'

Fear for Andrew shivered through her. He'd taken a good swig of the whisky and, though she was tempted to do the same, she was stopped by the need to do what she could for him. Soaking his shirt with the golden liquid, she dabbed the sickening gashes. Andrew hollered out his agony as she worked.

'Oh, Andrew, I am for being as gentle as I can. Should I fetch somebody, tell them I found you like this?'

'No, no, help me get my trousers on.'

Once she had done this, he edged his way back into the shadow of the trees, his voice trembling as he said, 'Look, I'm sorry about the situation I have put you in, but thank you for saving me. I believe he would have whipped me to death. What is the hold he has on you? No . . . leave that for now. We have to think how we can explain this.'

Bridie sat down beside him. 'Maybe you should put your shirt back on. The alcohol on it will ward off infection, so it will.'

He took it from her and shuddered his body into it. She could see his muscles trembling, and feared for him.

''Tis shock as is taking you. You have to get home and get the doctor, for 'tis that you could take with the sweating sickness. I have seen it in the old days in Ireland, when men were injured and me pappy brought them to our house.'

'Yes. I can't seem to s-s-stop my limbs sh-shaking.'

'Will you be able to ride your horse? I'm for thinking you should go home. Tell them you were thrown off of it when Seamus stepped out in front of you. That it reared, like it was for doing that first day I saw you. And say as Seamus reacted by whipping you. He is known for the temper on him, so he is.'

'Yes, I . . . I think something like that will cut it. T-t-t-tell no one, Bridie. I'll be in t-t-t-touch.'

She helped him over to the boulder, and he sat there while she brought over his horse. Somehow they managed to get him into the saddle by using the boulder as a stepping stone. As he left she leaned over the boulder and touched her child's name, which was now barely discernible. She let the tears she'd held back run over her hot cheeks. ''Tis bad that your mammy is, Eric,' she whispered. 'But don't be for letting that stop you praying for your pappy, for he is a good man and I am not for being worthy of him.' Brushing away her tears, she started to walk down the hill.

Shame wasn't often her companion when it came to taking a man to her, but now it ground into every pore of her. She had betrayed her Will, and caused Seamus to attack Andrew. Something in her wished she had pulled the trigger. It would have been a good day to see the death of Seamus, for hadn't he turned into the Devil? And didn't he put the fear into her, with what she knew him capable of, and with him saying she belonged to him?

Hearing the horse snort, she turned around. Mr Harvey was making his way down in the opposite direction from her, where the hill slanted in a more gentle descent. She hoped his horse would stay sure-footed. Tarrington House lay in that direction. She was glad he'd thought to go to his mammy; she would know what to do for him. Not that Mrs Harvey wouldn't, but it would be a powerful thing for Andrew to face her so soon and have to cover for what he'd done, as well as lie about what had happened to him.

This thought compounded her own deceit, and she hoped with all that was in her that Will would still be asleep when she got in. For it might be that he would know, and she couldn't bear for him to be hurt by her actions. She had meant to keep her promise to him: that once they'd escaped

Bruiser's clutches, no man would ever lie with her whilst he had breath in his body.

Breath in his body . . . She sank down onto the grass as if someone had punched her. Her insides splintered. Breath was the one thing her Will didn't have. His lungs, clogged with filth, no longer gave him the air he needed to live. *Oh, her Will . . . her Will . . .*

25

Bridie and Andrew

Consequences

Exhaustion dragged at every part of Bridie, and she didn't
know how she would make it home. The thicket loomed in
front of her, its shadowy paths holding a menace. The only
alternative took her miles out of her way. She had to go
through it. Fear fuelled her, helping her to move faster.
Branches clutched at her hair, claiming strands of it for their
own. Thorn bushes scratched her skin and tore her skirt as
she stumbled in desperation to get to the open meadow
beyond. Her heart thudded, and her breath came in short,
painful gasps. She stopped a moment, trying to tap into the
last reserves of her strength. The edge of the thicket, where
the trees opened up to a wider path and into the open field,
came into view, teasing her.

A twig snapped. Her skin crawled with trepidation, and the
blood in her body chilled. Seamus stepped out in front of her.
She shrank back, but he grabbed her arm.

'Seamus, don't . . . Let me go, Seamus.' His silence
unnerved her, and his face, set in anger, gave her no indication of his intention. The shock of everything had drained

the last ounce of her strength. She could do nothing. The glow of his campfire flickered ahead. His horse neighed, shook its mane and tapped the ground with its hoof, unnerved by her cries and by its master's mood. The Vardo that she'd loved, in all its painted glory, now held nothing but menace. Her pleas to Seamus to let her go went unheeded.

A vicious shove sent her reeling towards the flames. Its heat seared her body as she hit the ground next to it. Temper rose in her. She scrambled away from the fire and sat up. 'What is it you think you are doing, you bastard! I'm going home, Seamus, and you are not stopping me.'

Pushing her back down with his foot, his anger spat from him. 'You ask what happened to change me. *Me!* What, for the love of God, changed you, Bridie?'

'We have been after going over this, Seamus.'

'Aye, that's true, but didn't you say you had mended your ways? I could live with that. You, married to a decent man, having a family – that's the natural way of things. Then, with your man ailing, it seemed I only had to bide me time. When I saw you running up the hill and, a few minutes later, that high-'n'-mighty Mr Harvey making his way up after you, I took it on meself to make sure you were all right. And what did I find? You letting him fuck you. Enjoying it, begging for more. For sure, it was more than a man could take.' He slumped down onto his stool. His hands held his head as despair oozed from his every pore.

'How is it you can put yourself on such a pedestal? Are you not for thinking I wouldn't want the new you: the bastard that extorts money out of his own countrymen, keeps them in fear and takes their little ones away from them?'

'Bridie, you do want me. You want me, like I want you.

341

'Tis a burning need set up in us when we were children. I have kept true to the traveller code and not taken you out of wedlock, but you have tried me too far now. This is the way it is going to be. I have a plan as will get back at that bastard and be for giving us the life I want.' His voice steadied as he told her what he intended. ''Tis as we need funds, for we can't be at making enough for us both to live where I intend to take you. There will be none of the dealings I have here, as 'tis a remote place in the south of Ireland . . .'

'Will you listen to yourself? Seamus, is it celibate you are telling me you have been? But then, 'tis not for making a difference, for I am not for going anywhere with you . . .'

'A woman does not ask a man about his ways. 'Tis enough that I haven't taken you down, and meant to keep you that way until I married you, but you are for going too far, Bridie. And you *will* come with me, or you will see me put your man out of his misery before his time.'

'Seamus, no! What is it you are saying?'

'Just that. You do as I say or your man, his mammy and your wee one will—'

'No! Seamus, you have evil in you. Your granny would turn in the grave she must surely be in, if she could hear you. And anyway, 'tis you are forgetting you just attacked the master of this whole estate. He will get the law on you this very night, so he will!'

'I am for doubting that, with what I saw. And if he does, Bridie, you will stand as me witness. You will say he came up on you and raped you, and I was for only trying to save you.'

'Never . . .'

He stood up and bent over her. She couldn't speak. Her heart screamed out at what she saw, deep in his coal-black eyes. The fear that gripped her weakened her as she stared at him. His words bounced off her. 'Oh, you will, for I have a man ready to do my every bidding. He carried out some of the worst torture imaginable on traitors to the Fenians. He knew the truth of me story. If your pappy had not sent himself to the Devil, I had this man ready to send him there on a slow, agonizing journey. And that is what I will tell him to do to your man and your wee one, if you betray me in any way.'

Tears burned the sockets of her eyes. 'Please, Seamus. Have you forgotten who it is you are threatening?'

'No, it's seared into me soul with pain – the pain you have caused me. You have brought me to this place in your life. I have come to the point of no return with you. Now, listen to the plans I have for us. Tonight I'll be carrying out something that has been a long time in the planning: I'll break into the Harveys' place. They have a stash of money and jewels that will keep us going for the rest of our lives, and I know exactly where it is and how to get around the house. One of me little Irish lasses works there, and she has given me all the information I need. You, Bridie, are to meet me at the stile on the stroke of three. I will have everything ready and we will away into the night. I have a man waiting to take us across to Ireland in a few days' time. Not my usual route, so no one will know where we are.'

'No, Seamus. I am telling you, I am not going with you.'

'I have been after giving you the consequences for your family, if you don't. I will leave the decision to you. Now, away out of me sight. But, Bridie, in case it hasn't sunk in, let me tell you in more detail what will be happening if you let me down. Before your man goes to his maker, with you having watched him suffer all the torture he can endure and with your wee one tied to her bed, Paddy – the man I told you of – will take a torch to your house. And so it will be that the end of us both will happen, Bridie. Only yours will be slower. For if they are after catching me, I will take the rope they put round me neck and fall hard, so it is over in an instant. Me man will bar your exits, so even if you escape the ropes he ties you in, you and yours will burn. You will see the skin peel off your man and child, and feel the heat stripping your own from your flesh. You will scream and writhe and beg, but hell will have come to meet you.'

The tears she'd held back dripped over the rims of her eyes. 'Seamus . . .' His name sobbed from her, but his stance did not change. Realization came to her: he meant every word. Despair slumped her body.

'Come on, me little Bridie. I can see you have the knowledge in you of what you must do, and that is good.' She took the hand he offered her and, with his help, got to her feet. He pulled her close to his body. His mouth brushed hers, and his breath fanned her face with his words, 'We will seal our deal with a kiss, me Bridie.'

She tried to turn her head, but the movement seared pain through her. He had coiled her hair around his hand.

'I'll not fight for what you give willingly to others and yet belongs to me.' His lips pressed hard on hers, bruising them against her teeth. His mouth opened, softening the pressure, and his tongue prised her lips apart. She had an urge to bite down on it until her teeth cut through it, but visions of her Bridget and Will crying out in agony stopped her. Instead she yielded to him. He shocked her by not going further. As he came out of the kiss, his smile mocked her.

*

344

Every rut caused Andrew's wounds to throb, and shivers trembled through him. As if he knew, Goldboy took on a steady, slow pace, picking his way over the rough terrain. Through the mist brought down by his pain, Andrew saw his mother's house in the distance.

He'd never been so glad in his life to see his old home, but the usual comfort he experienced when coming up to his birthplace had deserted him. Through his agony he had to think and take steps to come up with some credible story, but everything he thought of had more ways to show his lies than a sieve had holes.

He rode into the stable yard. Peter, his mother's groom, came out to meet him. 'Sir, what happened to you? Have you taken a fall? Here, steady on, I've got you . . . Whoa, Goldboy, hold still.'

Andrew allowed Peter to manhandle him out of the saddle. He had no choice but to do so, as his body had given up on him and the ground seemed to come up to meet him. 'H-h-h-help me into the stable, Peter.'

'Shouldn't I help you into the house, sir? You're in a bad way. What happened?'

'No, n-not yet.'

Peter helped him to a bale of hay and sat him down. 'What can I do for you, sir?'

'Help me off with my jacket . . .'

'God Almighty, there's blood.'

'Use some clean water to wet m-my shirt. It has s-stuck to me.'

The icy water made Andrew wince as a stinging sensation shivered through him. He fought not to cry out, and bit his lip in the effort it took.

'Who in Heaven's name did this to you, sir?'

345

'I don't know . . . I went up to the stream. I was going to sw-swim . . . The first l-lash took me to my knees. The second one sent m-me head-first into the water. By the time I righted myself, he was gone!'

'Look, I have to go and get someone. You need the doctor. You're in shock. I'll not be long, sir.'

This time Andrew allowed Peter to go. At last he'd thought of something that held a modicum of truth to it. Peter hadn't questioned it. Thank God he'd thought of a robbery and had thrown his wallet away, and his flask. It was the finer details of how someone had whipped him with no shirt on that hadn't occurred to him before. He'd left the hunting gun he always took with him when riding where Bridie had thrown it. Someone might find that eventually, but if they did he'd say the robber probably discarded it, as it had his initials on it and would be difficult to dispose of. No one would find his other possessions; he'd thrown them into the undergrowth. They had fallen amongst the brambles growing on the hillside in a thick, impenetrable mass. He'd tell Peter to burn his shirt when he came back. That way no one would smell the whisky and disbelieve his story about the missing silver flask.

His head hurt from working things through. His body wouldn't hold him, and sweat poured from him – yet he felt cold.

'Andrew! Andrew, darling! Oh, my darling . . . Peter, fetch Granger, and send the boy who does the fires to Dr Payne. Oh, God! Andrew! Peter, send someone over to fetch his wife. Oh, why did Agatha move down to London?'

His mother's voice sounded as if she was standing at the end of a long tunnel shouting at him. It faded, came back at him, then was gone, and he felt himself sinking. He didn't want to resist. He let the envelope of darkness fold over him.

'Bridie?'

The whisper came from behind her. Shrouded as she was by the oppressive black night, every noise heightened her fear. The church clock had struck three ten minutes since, and still she had stood there by the stile, unable to penetrate the gloom. 'Seamus?'

'Aye, 'tis me. Come on, climb over. Hold your skirt; don't be tripping over it. I daren't light the lamp. Someone woke at the house, and I had to make an escape as they were for smooching around. But I have what I went for, and I'm here now.'

Her heart clanged her despair. She'd hoped, with everything in her, that Seamus wouldn't turn up. He tried to take her hand, but she wouldn't let him. 'What is it you have there, Bridie?'

'Just me clothes and a few bits.' *Please, Bridget, don't be after waking up!*

'It looks like a powerful big bundle. You won't be needing it. Dump it here – 'tis slowing you up, so it is.'

'No, and if you're for making me, I'll scream and scream and take me consequences.'

'You've not lost your spirit, Bridie, I'll give you that. Give it to me. We must hurry. Paddy is for having me Vardo tethered on the road, and we've to cross the field and get through the thicket to get to it. I'm feared they may discover evidence of me entrance and raise the alarm. I need time to get us a few miles away.' Grabbing the bundle from her without knowing what it contained, he stopped and stared at her as realization dawned. 'No! 'Tis your wee one! Wasn't I after telling you . . .'

'And I'm for telling you, Seamus, me little Bridget comes with me, or I will take meself home. I'm not leaving without her. I'm heart-sore at having to leave Will, but I have to accept 'tis as he and Janet are not long for this world. But then, what is it me little Bridget will be doing? I'm not having her in an orphanage, I'm not.'

No further protest came from Seamus. Holding Bridget to him, he quickened his steps. It was all she could do to keep up with him. The turmoil of emotions swirling around her drained Bridie. *Oh, Will, was it that I'll ever be for seeing you again?*

The note she'd left for him told of her love, but to make sure he didn't send for the police to come after her and thereby bring the wrath of Paddy down on himself, she had written:

Forgive me, Will. I couldn't be for taking the sickness in the house and watching you and Janet losing everything that I know is you. Remember me with love, for you will be forever in my heart, my darling. And hold onto my promise: one day we will be together in Heaven, with little Eric, so we will.

The thought of Will's despair shredded her, and sobs weakened her body. Seamus didn't stop, but his voice held hurt as he spoke of her distress. 'Is it that you hate me, Bridie? Are you so desperately unhappy to be with me at last, as we were meant?'

'Seamus . . . Seamus, why? We were in love many years ago, but 'tisn't as I am in love with you now. What I feel is near to hate, so it is. You're ripping me heart out by taking me from me man. I wasn't for facing living without him when

I knew he was going to die, but now I'll not be by his side when he is for taking his last breath. Please, Seamus. Please let me go back. I promise you, when Will passes on, I'll be coming to you. Please, Seamus . . .'

Branches sprang back as he passed through them. They hit her in the face and twigs tugged at her hair, but the pain gave her some relief from the suffocating panic rising within her. Never had she felt so helpless. A voice – a loud whisper – told her they were near to the Vardo.

'Is that yourself, Seamus?'

''Tis, Paddy. Good man. Now, you know what to do? Fix up for your man to meet me in Portpatrick on 20th September. Tell him to bring a thousand with him, cos 'tis as what I'll have with me will be worth double that.'

'I will, Seamus.'

Seamus helped Bridie onto the seat behind the horse, then passed Bridget to her. He turned to Paddy, handing him a package. 'Here, there's a good bundle there for your trouble. Keep low for a bit. Don't be flashing it around or they'll be for putting the robbery onto your shoulders, so they will. Keep your ear to the ground. And don't hesitate to carry out what I have paid you to do if you get the slightest whiff of the law on me trail.'

'I'm telling you, Seamus, it will be a pleasure, so it will. 'Tis rare I get the chance to use me skills. They'll fry, and folk'll see the fire back in Leeds.'

This shuddered through Bridie, swelling the sack of despair that she held within her.

'Good. Take care, Paddy. See you in September.'

Paddy spat on the ground. His face turned in her direction as he said, 'Aye. God bless you, and God bless the cause and keep it from bastard traitors, so one day we can all take ourselves back to our homeland.'

Weary to her core and with the bones of her aching, Bridie found it difficult to open her eyes. When she did, she thought it strange to see the canvas roof above her. *How is it that I got inside the Vardo?*

Her head seemed weighted down, aching with a pain she could hardly bear. The curtains hooked back from the doorway let in the sun, and the glare hurt her eyes. She turned her head, ricking her neck. *Bridget!* But she had no need to worry. Bridget, snuggled in a ball at the bottom of the bed, slept on as if still in her own little cot at home.

'Oh, Bridget, me Bridget.' The tears threatened again, but Bridie swallowed them back. The smell of something frying wafted into the caravan, and her stomach churned. Oh, God, she was going to be sick! Scrambling off the bed, she ran down the steps of the Vardo and managed to reach the hedge just as the vomit billowed out of her.

'Here, drink this. It will be for settling you.'

She recognized the nettle tea. Its familiar aroma brought back memories to her, as did the powerful taste in her mouth. Brushing the memories back into the safety of the place where she kept them locked away in her mind, she asked, 'Have you been for doing something to me, Seamus? I have a feeling on me I have experienced before.'

'Well, it was in me interest to keep you asleep . . .'

'Ether! You drugged me! Seamus, why? Oh, God – Bridget! Tell me you didn't!'

'To be sure she only had a wee whiff. I wouldn't have done, but she started to whimper when I took her from your arms.'

'You bastard, Seamus! There was no need; I came willingly. What is it you want from me other than that?'

'I needed to make good progress and thought it best to keep you both asleep whilst I did. It's been two days since we left . . .'

'Two days! Bridget, Bridget . . .' Her fear propelled her up the steps. She lifted her daughter off the bed. Her sunken, unseeing eyes opened, then closed, then opened halfway. White froth foamed around the corners of her mouth. 'Bridget! Oh, God, Seamus, you've near killed her! Me wee babby . . .'

'No! Didn't I only give her a little?' He grabbed Bridget from her. 'Away and bring me the tea. Hurry yourself!'

Her mouth stretched wide, but no sound came.

'Do as I say, Bridie – now!'

His sharp tone compelled her body to move. Grabbing the pot of tea from the brick on the side of the fire, she hurried back inside with it. Seamus held a white cloth in his hand, while Bridget lay on her back on the bed, her face ashen.

'Take off the lid. Bridie, do it!'

With trembling hands she did as he said, while her heart screamed prayers beseeching the Blessed Mother herself. *Holy Mary, Mother of God, if you've never been for listening to me before, listen to me now. Save me wee Bridget – save her . . . please!*

The cloth turned brown as it soaked up the liquid. Seamus prised open Bridget's mouth and squeezed a drop of the tea onto her dry, crusty tongue. It moved, just a twitch. He tried again, letting a little more drip further into her mouth. Patches of damp appeared in the white, furry coating. Bridie couldn't breathe. Still and mesmerized, the only active part of her was her pleading mind. Seamus dipped the cloth again and again, tilting Bridget's head back and letting drops of the liquid touch her throat. Although Bridget gagged, the tea disappeared. She choked, coughing and spluttering. He lifted her up and patted her back, his actions gentle and caring, his voice soothing and encouraging. 'Come on, me wee thing. When I do it again, you swallow.' She did. A few drops later she began to suck the cloth each time he soaked it. 'Good girl. Open your eyes, little one.' Bridget moaned and writhed.

'Mammy is here, me little Bridget. Come on, precious . . .'

This time Bridget opened her eyes, looked at Bridie and started to cry. 'Hurts, Mammy, hurts.'

'Where, darling?'

Bridget pointed to her head. Bridie shoved Seamus out of the way, hissing obscenities at him as she did so. Taking Bridget in her arms, she carried her outside.

'There, didn't I say she would be all right? Look at her. She's enjoying the ride. It was liquid she needed, though I wasn't for thinking that until I saw her tongue. She ate well after she'd had plenty of the tea. Are you not for remembering me grandmother, and her faith in the nettle tea? Sure she was right, for it has cured everything that ever ailed me, and now it has done the same for wee Bridget.'

'Seamus, don't be for making light of it, and I'm not for wanting to think of the past. You could have been after killing me wee child! If you ever do anything like that again, I'll take your own gun to you, so I will.'

''Tis as I shall have no need to. We travelled a powerful way the day. This time tomorrow we will reach Portpatrick. 'Tis a pretty harbour on the west of Scotland. At night you can see across the water to our country, as the many candles flickering and oil lamps burning light it up. 'Tis a sight you will not want to miss. Me man will meet us with his boat.

It'll be calm waters we will be needing, but 'tis that the Irish Sea doesn't lie quiet for long. He has a steam engine to power his boat, but even so it will take us two days to reach the south of Ireland.'

'Seamus, won't you be for changing your mind? If you let me go, I'll not be telling anyone where you have gone . . .'

'No, Bridie, and whish asking. Your whining is driving me insane. I cannot think. I have me mind on looking for a field – 'tis marked by a line of stones across the verge, just before the gate. There is a clean stream running through it, where we can get water and bathe ourselves. A row of high pine trees shields it, so we could camp for a few hours, make a fire, cook food and rest our bodies.'

The brick of despair inside her took on more weight. The hopelessness of her situation ground her down. She could not escape, as where would she go? They had passed a few crofts set back off the road, but what if they wouldn't give her shelter while she sent a message? For miles and miles there had been only wilderness and mountains, making for spectacular scenery, just as she had heard Scotland had, but barren of life and of hope.

'Bridie, I have a mind to take you to me tonight. You wouldn't be fighting me off, would you? We cannot be man and wife till we hear God has made you free by taking your man to him, but after all that has happened between us, I am not for waiting for that.'

'No, Seamus. No. And don't talk of Will in that way. My heart is breaking with missing him, and I cannot . . .'

'Oh, in the way you couldn't with Mr Harvey, is that what you are saying, Bridie? To be sure, I'd like to be tasting some of what you gave to him and every man who asked it of you. But once I make you mine, you will never lie with another – never, Bridie. Is it that you are for understanding that?'

She didn't answer him. He turned the Vardo into the next opening, and it rocked and swayed over the uneven surface. Pots and pans clanged together. Seamus fell silent, concentrating his mind on getting them across to the water.

Left with her own thoughts she wondered, *Did I ever love him? Yes, I can remember him being the world to me. Could he be so again? Could I lie with him, want him, find with him the deep satisfaction my body craves, and which is a curse on me?* She didn't know, and her weary body gave her no sign of the fire that usually burned within her at the mere mention of a man's interest. But for her own safety, and Bridget's, she could pretend. She'd had a lot of practice at that. Hadn't she had to do so many a time when there was money involved and the customer had repulsed the heart of her? What would it matter if she had to do it again?

26

Two weeks later

Lies upon lies

Issy had her own thoughts on the goings-on, but she couldn't voice them to Will. She had a mind no one – except Tom – would think her account had any merit. Tom might listen to her. But no, she couldn't talk it over with him; she might have to tell him things about the traveller that she didn't want him to know.

Everyone blamed and despised poor Bridie. But they hadn't seen the love and devotion she'd given to Will, or her heart breaking at the thought of losing him. Nor had they seen her patience and loving care with her difficult ma-in-law.

And then, what of Mr Harvey? What part had he played in it all? The story of his attack being a deliberate ploy to disable him, in order to facilitate the robbery on his house, seemed credible, but why was he up on that hill? The very place Bridie had said she was going to? Issy had long since forgotten the kiss she'd seen them share, but what had taken place had brought it back to her mind. It haunted her every waking hour as she tried to make sense of everything.

The only thing that didn't fit her theory was how Bridie had returned home. She'd been agitated, and in a state that she'd tried to cover up, but she had come back, and nothing about her had suggested she was about to run off. But it did seem that her leaving had been her own choice. The note said so, and kidnap didn't fit with that.

Issy finished putting the last of the clean linen in the bottom drawer of the chest next to Will's bed, saying, 'There, that's done. Can I get you anything, Will?'

He'd lain still and quiet while she'd worked around him, too weak to do any other. She'd dreaded him questioning her. He tried to speak, then nodded towards the glass of water on the side. Holding his head, she helped him take a sip. Once he'd swallowed, he tried to talk again, and this time managed to whisper, 'Issy, thou knows me Bridie wouldn't have left me. She loved me. Sommat must have happened. I don't believe her note. I don't . . .'

'Neither do I, Will.' Mentally she crossed herself as she spoke the lie she'd prepared. 'I'm for thinking she had a breakdown of some sort. Happen in a few days she'll come home.'

'You mean – she might be sick in her mind?'

'Aye, I do. It's horrible to think of, but I think that's the most likely reason she's gone. She had a lot on her plate.'

'I know. And I couldn't lighten her load.' A coughing fit racked his body. Issy supported his frail frame until it passed. His breathing laboured as he continued, 'Tell her . . . Tell her I – I believe in her. I know she . . . she didn't . . .' His eyes, dark masses of blue sinking into hollow sockets, held a desperate plea as his skeletal, yellow-skinned face dropped forward. A rasping, gurgling sound like none she'd ever heard before came from him as he collapsed onto her.

She lay him back down onto his pillow. Blood and filthy slime clogged his mouth. In desperation she tried to clear it away, all the while calling his name, but he'd gone. 'Oh, Will, Will . . . If only you could have hung on till we got her back. Oh, poor, poor Bridie.'

Her legs gave way. She slumped back onto the bedside chair as tears soaked her face and ran down her neck. Prayers didn't come to her often, not pleading ones. She always berated God, as she couldn't understand how he could let happen the things she saw in her dealings with people. But now she gave way to begging of Him, *Please, God, bring Bridie back to us. Let her and little Bridget be safe. And help her. And help me in telling Janet that You've taken her precious son.*

She thought to add a plea for Mr Harvey, what with him nearing death's door with pneumonia, but she couldn't. For even though her mind hadn't dwelt on it, she'd never forgiven him for what he'd done to Bridie on her wedding day. And, more than that, what he'd done to Miss Dvina. She didn't like people who weren't what they seemed, and Mr Harvey had more than one side to him.

The sea mist swirled around the boat. Bridie sat below deck, unable to see out of the portholes, and feeling the dense isolation clawing at her. Carrying her to her doom, some would say – her just deserts. All morning she'd had this tugging sensation, like someone trying to pull her very soul from her. It intensified to a pitch until she wanted to scream and scream. She clutched Bridget to her as a presence surrounded her. At the same time she felt her terror melt into a comforting peace, before an emptiness left her exhausted. She lay down on the bunk, still clinging onto Bridget.

'Mammy, Pappy's here.' Shock held Bridie silent. In a tearful voice, Bridget said, 'Mammy, where's Pappy? I wanna go to Pappy and Granna now.' At Bridie shaking her head, Bridget demanded, 'Yes, Mammy.' Her tears broke and she sobbed, 'Want Pappy, want Granna.'

Bridie buried her face in her daughter's soft, wispy hair. Her heart bled tears, but she couldn't have the release of crying. Everything had died within her.

'Mammy, I wanna go home. I want me Pappy . . .'

'Whish, little one.'

'Don't want Seamus – he's bad. Want Pappy.'

'Seamus loves us. He is after taking us to the land where I was born. You will be happy there, so you will.' *How the lies trip off me tongue! But then isn't it that I have to protect me wee child?* Just as she thought this, a cold certainty came to her. 'Bridget, you are for knowing how sick your pappy was. Well, the Baby Jesus couldn't bear to see him like that, so he has sent his angel down with a lovely gold carriage to take him to rest with him in his beautiful garden. One day we will meet up with him again, but until then Pappy will look after us from his place in Heaven.'

Bridget looked up at her with anger in her face. 'No! Pappy not go! Pappy not say goodbye. Pappy wouldn't . . .'

'Bridget, Bridget, me wee love. He did say goodbye. He came onto the boat just now, so he did. Were you not for seeing him here yourself?'

A calm settled over her as she gave voice to this. *It is for being the truth – me lovely Will has gone. I know as he was for coming to me and Bridget to say goodbye. I shouldn't have been afraid. Will must go to the resting place that is for him, and go with her love.*

Smiling down at Bridget, she saw a frown crease the little face that was so like Will's. There was the same slight slant to her eyes, and the colour of them mirrored his. Her skin had the tinge of olive to it, and her hair was the exact match: black and shiny. With the logic of a child, Bridget couldn't leave it there. 'Didn't *see* him. Pappy was in me head. I wanna see him, Mammy.'

'That was all he could be managing. To be sure, we can't transport our body to another place, not when we are sick and can't travel. So he was after letting his spirit come to us. Sweetheart, Pappy was for being very sick. He had so much pain. Are you not for remembering how it felt when you fell over and your knees were scuffed and bleeding? Well, your pappy had more pain in him than that. Pain he couldn't bear, no matter how the heart of him wanted to stay with us. Baby Jesus was for knowing it, and took the pain away. Now, go to sleep for a wee while and soon you will see green fields, gentle slopes and a beautiful land just like the one Pappy has gone to.'

Andrew tried to lift his heavy eyelids. He couldn't understand the weakness in his body. When at last he managed to open his eyes, he saw his mother standing with her back to him looking out of the window. His mind wouldn't give him a reason for him to be lying in his old bedroom.

'Mother?'

'Andrew! You're awake at last! How are you feeling, darling?'

'Ill, but I don't know why. What am I doing here? And please may I have a drink?'

'You were attacked, don't you remember? Two weeks ago. Oh, my dear, so much has happened . . .'

Memory nudged his fogged brain. He sipped his water, giving himself time to adjust. Time to let all the pieces knit together to give him a picture – and, dear God, what a picture! Bridie, beautiful Bridie, her creamy body . . . her hair . . . Him drowning in the pleasure of her, then his world fragmenting into unbearable pain. The gypsy; the gun; the lies . . . He blocked them out. 'Where's Dvina, Mother?'

'She's – well, she is at home. She's very upset. Agatha is here. I'll send her to you. She will tell you everything. But don't overdo it, darling. You have been very ill. You had pneumonia. It was the shock, Dr Payne says.'

She left before he could protest. Agatha! God, she was the last person he needed right now, and he didn't have to ask why Dvina was upset, now that he knew his sister was around!

'Oh, who's been a naughty boy, then? As usual. In fact it takes one quite a time to think of when you were ever a *good* boy, Andrew.'

'Please, Agatha. Don't. My head aches, and so does every other part of me. Just tell me what has been going on, and how you have upset Dvina.'

'Me! I think that accolade goes to you, dear brother. First of all, you go somewhere you gave no indication you would. Then you come up with some ridiculous story about being robbed. Then you spend two weeks in a coma, calling for someone I have since learned is the village trollop!'

Andrew winced. Had he really called out for Bridie? Oh, dear Lord! In desperation he tried to sort out the facts from the swirly dreams he'd had, but wasn't able to separate them.

'Nothing to say, have we? Well, try to digest this then: your house was broken into and burgled – for real – that very same night. Dvina is mortified to have lost some very precious sentimental items. Stuff that had belonged to her mother and grandmother and, oh, generations of Portlands, it seems.'

'Oh, no!'

'Oh, yes, and that's only half of it. The gypsy you have welcomed to your estate over the years is thought to have been responsible. It seems he left his calling card – a red band he often wore around his head. They found it on the stairs the next day, but he had long gone by then. Taking, by all accounts, your floozy with him.'

'Bridie? I . . . I mean . . .'

'I know exactly what you mean. Andrew, you are disgusting. You take on that frump—'

'Don't you dare call Dvina that! She is a very beautiful lady – yes, a lady. Something you have no idea how to be. And your conjecture is all wrong. If I called out Bridie Hadler's name, it will have been because I had nightmares about her. She has something to do with this. I saw her. She called to me. She stood on the opposite bank and she had very little on. She came from nowhere and started to flirt with me. It flattered me for a moment, then I asked her what she was doing . . .' *God, where are these lies coming from? The more I lie, the easier it gets!* 'She told me she'd escaped for the after-noon away from the sickness of her husband and her mother-in-law. She'd seen me riding up the hill and thought to have some fun with me, if I was willing. Said she could show me a good time. She stepped into the water and came towards me, then seemed to nod to someone. I went to turn around, but that's when the whip lashed me . . . I assume now it was the gypsy. Maybe she kept my attention while that blackguard rifled through my clothes and saddlebag.'

'Bravo! A wonderful story, and all so plausible. So why didn't you tell it before? Needed time to work it all out, eh? Little brother, you take the biscuit and eat it!'

He kept his eyes down, amazed at his own ability to come up with such a tale on hearing that Bridie had gone with

Seamus. He'd thought there was more to her knowing that bastard. Well, good riddance. He'd sensed she was trouble; he should have left well alone.

'Well? What are you thinking about? Trying to conjure up more lies?'

'Oh, shut up, Agatha, you bitch! I didn't mention her because of Will Hadler, her husband, who is very ill and doesn't deserve to hear the truth about his wife. Though the poor bugger must know by now, if she has left him.'

'Ha, name-calling will not hurt me, Andrew. You, the man who always falls on his feet, shouldn't have need to resort to it, but a guilty conscience will out. You sicken me, do you know that? Here you are, the richest man in the county – in several counties – and how did you achieve such a status? Through hard work? No! By prostituting yourself, that's how.'

'Don't be ridiculous. So I sold myself to Edgar, did I? Well, I bloody well didn't. And though my marriage was that kind of arrangement, it turned out well. I love my wife very much. Ours is a happy union . . .'

'Oh, so why isn't your wife here at your sickbed, instead of at home weeping and thinking of leaving you, because she cannot take any more!'

'Go away, Agatha. I don't need this. I can't argue with you. Please ask Mother to send for Dvina and Dr Payne. I need Dvina here, and I need something to stop the pain.'

She walked to the door, where she turned, the look of triumph making her face ugly. She bloody well enjoyed making menace. Yes, he had his faults, but he tried, didn't he? He fought his weaknesses as much as he could, but what did she do about hers – her need to sow poison whenever and wherever she could, especially into his life and his marriage? Nothing! Sometimes he hated her.

His mother looked round the door a few minutes later. 'You two been fighting again, dear? I'm very cross with Agatha. I sent for her because it was touch and go with you on the first night and now, the minute you come round, she upsets you.'

'Oh, don't worry, Mother. I can handle her. Have you sent for Dvina and the doctor? I'm in sore need of them both.'

'Yes, dear. You know, Agatha came as soon as she could, and it's no mean journey from London. She broke her heart when she saw you. There was no consoling her. What is it with you two? I don't mind telling you as a mother: having two warring children is devastating.'

'Don't worry, old thing. We love each other really. God, if anything happened to her, I'd break my heart, too. It's just a clash of personalities. It can't be easy being the eldest and yet having no rights just because you are a woman, especially for someone as forceful as Agatha. I appreciate that, even though she annoys me at every chance she can get, and tries her best to put my marriage in jeopardy.'

'From what I hear, you do that on your own. Though you have been very good for a long time.'

'Christ, Mother! I still am. I explained to Agatha . . .'

'Yes, I know you did, but it still doesn't account for you calling out endearments to this . . . what's her name? Oh, I don't know, some Irish peasant name.'

'Bridie. And I don't see why it doesn't. Good God, am I to be hanged for having delirium? Oh, Mother, leave me alone, please. I have a terrible headache and I can't stand having my integrity called into question by two people who have no business doing so. You are both meant to love me, and yet you attack me the moment I come out of a coma that nearly took my life!'

He now had the satisfaction of seeing his mother hang her head in shame. Pity Agatha hadn't done the same – nor ever would. His mother's voice held anguish as she said, 'I'm sorry, darling. We have all become concerned for dear Dvina. That first night she stayed by your side till you started rambling on about that girl.'

'What did I say?'

'Well, dear, it isn't easy for me to say. It's embarrassing.'

'Oh, come on, Mother, you weren't born yesterday. At least give me a chance. I can probably explain it all. I have nothing on my conscience.'

'Well, you made several sexual references. You said she was the best – the very best you'd ever had. You said you would die if you couldn't have her again . . . that sort of thing.'

His dismay must have shown on his face.

'Yes, I know; rather difficult to get out of, isn't it? I hope you find a way, dear. If you lose Dvina you will lose your son, and that – if nothing else – would be a bad show.'

'Mother! I hate all these insinuations that I am not happy. I love Dvina. I adore her. She makes me very, very happy. I don't pretend. Surely you have seen our happiness over the past years? I didn't fake that. It is real.'

'I'm glad to hear it, Andrew. Maybe you can convince Dvina yourself. She is here now.'

Agatha swanned into the room, followed by Dvina.

'Dvina, darling, please don't listen to them. My God, this is a nightmare. Well, I am not taking any more of it. You stupid women! How can you judge a man on his delirium, when he's in a coma? Does everything that has gone before mean nothing? For Christ's sake, get out of my sight! I have never felt so let down in all my life. Where is that bloody doctor?'

The outburst had done the trick: Dvina was by his side, begging him to calm down, telling him she hadn't taken any notice, and that she loved him and trusted him. But it had cost Andrew dearly. What little strength he'd had ebbed away from him, and he flopped back on the pillow. The veil he'd fought so hard to remove from his brain floated back over it. His mind began to swim in and out of clouds. When he was in a clear patch he could hear Dvina screaming, 'What have you done? How dare you speak of personal things concerning me and my husband's life together, just to triumph over him, when he is so ill? None of it is any of your business. Get out! Get out, both of you. I am having him removed to Hensal Grange. You are not fit to call yourselves a mother or a sister. I will never forgive you for this, never!'

The words travelled around the room, and when they came to him they hurt. This was not what he wanted – his dear mother and sister becoming estranged from his wife. God, he'd known there would be consequences, but not this. Not this!

'Bridie, Bridie, will you rouse yourself up? We're here.'

Seamus carried Bridget to the beach. He stood on the shore looking back at her.

'Come on, Bridie, hurry, for it's grand to feel Ireland beneath your feet, so it is.' His smile, a boyish grin, told of his joy. Some of it seeped into her, but the cold sea lapping around her legs tempered it, as did the heavy feeling in her heart.

The sand tickled her feet and the fresh, cooling breeze played with her hair, sending strands across her face and blurring her vision. Brushing them back, she let her gaze take in the intense green pastures and the rolling hills dwarfed by the magnificent mountains. The sight lifted her, for wasn't she thinking this is how Heaven looks, and her Will was at this moment enjoying his peace there? The enormity of this hit her in the gut, shattering her spirit. She doubled over and her legs gave way. The sand accepted her, shifting into folds around her as if trying to comfort her.

'Bridie!'

'Mammy!'

The cries of anguish carried over her head. She had no tears to cry, but the splintered pieces of her heart pierced her whole body with pain. *'Tis that the wickedness of me has come home to haunt me. How can I bear not seeing me Will ever again? How could I ever ask him for his forgiveness?*

'Bridie, me little Bridie, what have I been after doing to you?'

The fear in Seamus's voice softened it, so that she could remember the way he used to talk to her. The years rolled back, taking her to the happiness she'd felt, just to know he rested across the fields from her house. How many nights had she looked out of her bedroom window to see the outline of him cover and uncover his lamp to let her know he could see her? Three flashes meant *hello*, four *goodnight*. He once asked her what she meant by hiding behind the curtain, then popping out again three times. She'd had a shyness on her, an innocence, which prevented her from telling him that this code was her secret way of saying *I love you*.

Could she love him again? She'd been ready to accept him to her on their last night in Scotland, as he'd told her she must, but he hadn't kept to it. Instead he had sat by his fire drinking whisky until he'd keeled over. To drown the shame of her disappointment, she'd taken a good drop of the gin he'd brought along for her.

'Bridie, please . . .'

'Mammy, Mammy . . .' Bridget's voice held fear. 'Mammy, want Pappy. Want Pappy . . .'

This plea put courage into Bridie. If she was to prevent her little Bridget from suffering, to the point of scarring her life, she had to accept things. She had to make light of her own pain and concentrate on giving Bridget the best she could of herself. This gave her the strength to reply, 'No, don't be afraid, me wee one. Mammy is just for being exhausted. And what did I tell you about Pappy? He *is* here. His soul is in Heaven, and this is as near to that as we can get. Isn't Seamus for being wonderful, for bringing us here and promising to take care of us?'

'Don't want Pappy in Heaven . . .'

'Would you have him in pain? Would you keep him by you when he had not the strength to do so? No, sweetheart, we have to let him go. Granna will go with him. She will be there, so she will. She'll take care of him. Now won't that be nice for him?'

'Mammy sit up . . . Mammy . . .'

'There, isn't it that you've made your mammy better?' Bridget looked up at Seamus as he said this. Her look held the same wariness that she had shown, but something had her listening to him instead of cowing away from him. 'Now, it is that we have to go. Your mammy isn't for knowing where, as she hasn't been before. It is a surprise for you both, and it is for being the loveliest spot in the world. Let me carry you, Bridget. Come on, Bridie.' Bridget lifted her arms to him, and Bridie felt a warming of her heart.

As Seamus helped her up with his free arm, he addressed the boatman, 'I have a horse and trap tethered on the shore waiting for us, is that not right, Sean?'

'Aye, it will be. I told Joseph to make sure to get it here for the day. He won't let me down.'

'Good, so we only have to climb up those rocks and then we can take it easy for the rest of the journey. Leave your things, Bridie. I'll help you both up there, then come back for them. This is a grand day, so it is.'

She had to let herself think it was. That was the only way to cope, and if she didn't cope, Bridget wouldn't stand a chance. There was nothing to go back for. Without Will, there would be no point in living back in England. She'd rather live here, for wasn't she at last back home? Back home, in Ireland.

27

July 1886

The injustice

'Aye, it's right what I say: he is coming back over the water on 20th September. That gives us a good while to be putting our plans into place. 'Tis my thinking, if a gang of us lie in wait for him, sure we could overpower him.'

'We'll have to be doing more than overpowering him, so we will. Someone has to be willing to kill him, for 'tis the only way to rid ourselves of the evil that is Seamus Finney.'

A draught caught Issy's legs. Fear shot through her. She waited, holding her breath, thinking herself in danger of being exposed.

She'd come to the pub to find Paddy, after delivering his wife of her fifteenth child. Paddy Docherty wasn't a man to cross. If he knew she'd heard what he and his cronies planned to do . . . She turned round. The door leading to the street had swung open, but no one had come through it. She must have left the latch off.

The haze of smoke coming through from the snug where the men sat made her eyes smart and caught in her throat.

She swallowed, trying to clear the tickle it had caused, as she strained to hear more of what they were saying.

'Aye, killing him is our only option, but he will be carrying all the jewels he robbed from Hensal Grange, so . . .'

'How is it you know this, Paddy?'

''Cos I helped him. Whilst he was in the big house doing it over, I got his Vardo on the road for him, ready for his departure.'

'Is it true Bridie Hadler went with him, then?'

'Aye, but not willingly. But that's no concern of ours.'

'I'm for thinking it is, Paddy. She's one of us.'

'No, she ain't. Her father was Michael O'Hara, the traitor to the cause and pilferer of its funds, and she took those funds, knowing where they came from. Seamus is a bastard, but he remained loyal to the Fenians. Oh, I know, 'twas for a long time we didn't think so, but we know now that Michael O'Hara betrayed him, just as he tried to do to us. Seamus was for following Bridie O'Hara to try to get the funds back, but she had been through the lot by the time he felt safe enough to return to these shores. Now, will you whish with your women's gossip and listen?'

Issy closed her eyes. *My God, Bridie! Eeh, lass, she had a more chequered past than what she admitted to!* Forcing herself to put this to one side, she concentrated on hearing everything they said.

''Tis me instruction from Seamus to set up a buyer to meet him. I've made contact with a bloke I knew back in the day. He knows of the stuff and where it came from, and is willing to take it on. What he doesn't know is the arrangement Seamus told me to have in place for him. He's for thinking I am to bring the jewels to him, which I intend to do.'

'So what is it you are planning, then?

'Is it thick you are, Martin? 'Tis that we go to Portpatrick, fully armed, and wait for Seamus. When he docks, I lure him towards the inn, where I say the buyer is waiting. You will all be hiding in the shadows. You jump him, so you do. Once you have him down, I'll be for finishing him off. I'd like to be using some of me torture skills on him, but we need to get the job done – and get out of Portpatrick – without anyone knowing we've been there. So, though deserving of a slow death, Seamus Finney will come to a swift end and we'll dump the bastard in the sea.'

'To be sure it will be like our Fenian days, Paddy. Well, you can count me in.'

'Thank you, Neil. Now, what about the rest of you? There'll be a good payday to come, once I've shifted the stuff. It'll be like a year's pay, so don't be worrying if any of you have to miss a shift or two. We'll have to invent a sickness to take us all out of action. I've to arrange funds for the train fare for us, so anything you can chip in would be a help. So, are you all in?'

'I am, but 'tis as I think we should go further. You know where Seamus has set up in Ireland, Paddy?'

'I do. What are you thinking, Neil?'

'That Bridie O'Hara should pay her just dues to the cause. Exposed as the traitor she is, like her father before her.'

As the 'ayes' went around the room, accompanied by cries of 'Let's rid ourselves of the vermin that is Seamus Finney and Bridie O'Hara!' and like comments, Issy crept back along the passageway. The shock of what she'd heard tightened the muscles in her throat. Somehow she had to draw on her inner strength and see this through. If she didn't, she'd have no chance of saving Bridie! Leaving the pub wasn't an option, because Paddy's wife might berate him for not coming home and tell him of Issy promising to fetch him; and he knew of her loyalty to the wives, so Paddy would wonder if she had set out to fetch him and then heard more than she should.

The fear of this happening made Issy's mind up about what she had to do. When she reached the open door, she banged it shut. Calling out to Paddy, she approached the snug again, hoping they would believe she'd just arrived. If they knew she'd heard, her life would be in danger – there was nothing as sure as that.

Paddy came to the door. 'Isabella, is that yourself? Is it good news you bring me?'

It was easy to give her reply, as Paddy showed no sign of concern at her being there. Once she'd told him of his seventh son's safe arrival, she turned away to leave. 'I'll come by later, Paddy, just to make sure Margaret is all right.'

'Aye, 'tis a debt I owe you, me wee lass.' He followed her out, telling his men he'd be in later. Trepidation caused sweat to stand out on her forehead, but when they were outside, his manner gave her no cause to worry. 'Ha, is that you still riding that old boneshaker, Isabella? Sure it will rattle your teeth loose one of these days! It must be twenty years old if it's a day. I'll tell you what I'll do for you. If ever I make me fortune, I'll buy you one of the new safety bicycles, so I will.'

'Aw, Paddy, I'll not hold me breath. They say as men will grow wings one day and'll fly around like the birds do. And thou knows what? I reckon that day will come afore you keep that promise to me.'

As she adjusted the pedals of her bike, he walked away, and she could hear him laughing at her retort. If he'd suspected her, he'd have said something – threatened her even – but surely he wouldn't just have walked away?

'There, didn't I tell you how lovely it was?'

Bridie gazed down at the little croft in the deep valley that

Seamus pointed out. County Kerry held many such places. It was sad to think of them being abandoned. The fight to change the Land Act had come to nothing, and many had deserted the area in despair, seeking a better life in America or across the water in England.

'The landlord was powerfully glad to get someone willing to take it on, so he was. We're going to take to the land as farmers, Bridie. Oh, I know we won't make much and 'tis hard work, but we'll be having the benefit of the money I have and the jewellery as I'm going to sell, so our life won't be marred by the poverty.'

''Tis beautiful. Just look at the lovely views around us. But I'm thinking there is a lot to do to make it habitable.'

'No, you're wrong there, Bridie. I've been back and forth this good while and have fixed it up inside. The outside doesn't show signs of that, but that's all we have to do to complete the job.'

Seamus steered the pony and trap down the gentle slope, his skill ensuring they didn't hit any of the many boulders strewn along the way. Bridie thought of all the years he'd done this with his Vardo and asked, 'Will you not be for missing your travels, Seamus?'

'No, for I've been wanting to settle this good while. I have friends around here from me days attached to the Fenians. Sure it is all out now about what went on back in the day, and everyone knows your pappy stitched me up. I've not been for telling them who you are, Bridie, as some would be for bringing down the sins of the father onto you. We'll keep it that way. It is for the best.'

'So, the tide has turned and 'tis me who is in hiding now. Well, I never expected that, so I didn't.'

Seamus unlocked the huge chain keeping the heavy gate

closed. Once inside, the clang of the gate shutting behind them planted a dread in Bridie, and the jangling of the chain as Seamus relocked it only increased her trepidation. The walls on each side continued on from the farmyard buildings – barns and a stable – forming an enclosure all around the croft. The walls hadn't looked this high, when she'd looked down from the top of the hill. Here and there new stones stood out amongst the old ones where Seamus had made repairs, and these too marked a layer of at least three feet, extending its overall height. To Bridie, the yard resembled a prison. The thought sent a shudder down her spine.

'Why did you think to build the wall so high, Seamus? Won't it block the light and our view from our windows?'

'I was for thinking it would be useful to protect you while I am away.'

He helped her and Bridget down. The oppressive aura seemed worse from ground level, although the croft belied this. Her heart lifted when they entered it. The door led them into a kitchen. Its stone walls, newly whitewashed, reflected the light from the two windows – one facing the entrance, the other opposite and looking out onto a smaller yard, where she could see a small brick building near to the wall.

'That's the lav. It drains into a cesspit on the other side of the wall. It works well and it's easy to keep the smell away from the house. The well is out the front, by the side of the barn. I've a chicken run there. The hens, a cockerel and other livestock are all on order.'

'It's busy you've been, to be sure, and it all looks lovely.' Everything shone like new, which she supposed it was. Gleaming pots and pans hung on iron hooks next to a large cooking range. Paper and sticks lay ready in the grate. Seamus crossed over to it and lit it. Eager flames licked the kettle standing on the iron stand, as he swung it over them. Shadows danced around the room. He waited a moment, then added a log from the pile on the floor, which splintered the flames into a million sparks that cracked and spat a warm welcome. Bridie looked around. Shelves on the other side of the pans held earthenware jars that she assumed contained jams, flour and other provisions. Plates and mugs made a colourful display on a dresser on one wall, and next to it another shelf held all the ornamental jugs and painted pottery she remembered from Mrs Finney's Vardo. And there, amongst it all, the tea caddy! The sight of this had her swallowing hard to dispel the sentimental feeling it conjured up in her, jeopardizing her resolve to stay brave for the sake of little Bridget. She looked away from it.

A scrubbed table stood in the middle of the room on a floor of painted red-brick, the sheen on which spoke of many hours of polishing them. A high-backed wooden chair had pride of place on one side of the range, and a stool on the other. All the room lacked was some finishing touches, and she looked forward to putting them in. Didn't she know now, through Issy's tuition, how to make a rag rug? And the chairs needed cushions, and the windows and table needed curtains, a tablecloth and a vase of flowers. To be sure, she'd have the prettiest kitchen in Ireland.

A door across from the range led through to the bedroom, where she found a large bed. And, like the old Miners' Row where the Irish now lived in Breckton, this room had a loft space reached by a ladder. Seamus saw her look up at it. 'There's nothing up there, and 'tis in need of a lot of work, but it can be made ready for Bridget when she is older. In the meantime, we can make her a shake-me-down. There's some dry hay in the barn, and I have some hessian sacks. Sure, 'tis as she'll be warm and cosy next to our bed, and 'tis best she is by your side till she gets used to her new home. Whenever I'm after going into town, I'll buy her a crib.'

The way he was with Bridget didn't fit with the tales she'd heard about his abducting children. Nothing about him these last few days spoke of the Seamus he'd become. Instead, the Seamus of old seemed to have made his way back inside the mind of him.

But seeing again the tall, grey wall so near to the bedroom window shook this theory. The wall held a threat, and the confidence that had started to grow in Bridie since coming into the croft began to fade.

She looked away. Her eyes fell on the bed, awakening her mind to the thought of her and Seamus cuddled up in it. As if reading her mind he said, 'I'm after thinking you're having the same thoughts as I am, Bridie?' He moved nearer to her and took her hands. 'I haven't been for touching you yet, Bridie. I've a powerful need to do so. And, like I was for telling you, I no longer feel we have to wait till we wed.'

Resigned now to his assumption that they'd spend their life together, she tried to reach into herself to touch the feelings awoken in her when she remembered the past. His eyes drew hers to him, and in them she saw his desire. It fuelled her own need, and left a promise inside of her. He smiled as he said, ''Tis happy we are going to be, me wee Bridie. We'll put everything that has gone before away from us. We'll be after having a new beginning. No one can hurt us here. No temptations can lead you astray from me.'

Indignation lit her temper. 'Is that you saying again I am a whore, Seamus? Well, I am not. Sure, the likes of Mr Harvey turned me head when I was at me most vulnerable, but before him I stayed faithful to Will. I'm heart-sore me body let me down, and wish I could wipe the incident out of me life.'

''Tisn't a fight I am looking for, Bridie. 'Tis true you have to build me trust, but it will come.'

'Is that why you've been after building a fortress? Because you don't trust me? Are you thinking to keep me prisoner here?'

No answer came. Turning, he walked towards the kitchen. She followed him through, ready to take him to task again about the wall, but she caught sight of Bridget sitting under the table, her eyes red from rubbing them.

'Will you see to your child and leave the talking? We can straighten out everything later. And a drop of tea would be welcome, so it would.'

The door slammed behind him. She watched him cross the yard and start to unload the cart. Bridget crawled out, saying, 'Mammy, I'm wet . . .'

This made her smile. 'Oh, is that all? Well, then it is a christening for our new home.' She took Bridget in her arms and held her to her. 'Come on, let's find some dry things for you. Did you hear about the chickens Seamus has brought for us? Sure, it will be your job to feed them, so it will.'

'But, Mammy, I don't know what they eat, and I can't cook. I'm not big enough yet, am I?'

'No, but you won't have to. Seamus will give you a bowl of food for them. You'll just have to scatter it in their run. Oh, and fill up their water, but it's easy, so it is. I used to do it as a little girl with me mammy.'

'Granna is Pappy's mammy? Where's your mammy?'

Oh, Bridie, you've started something . . . 'Away with such talk, and let's clean you up. We've tea to make for Seamus, and all our things to unpack. We've no time for gossip. I'll be after telling you of it another day.'

With Bridget's needs seen to, and the kettle boiling so hard it lifted its own lid in protest, Bridie reached for the tea caddy. Opening the cask gave her a moment of clarity. The filigree at the top of the little key, with its delicate interlaced lines, symbolized all the twists and turns in her life since she'd first seen it all those years ago. Some of the happenings she knew she could have handled differently, but others had been inflicted on her, and they were the ones responsible for shaping her. They and the insatiable need she had in her.

Everything had fitted in well; for a small cottage, it had plenty of storage. A cart had pulled up and Seamus had helped the man unload provisions – enough, Bridie thought, to keep them going for weeks. But then it was likely there weren't many tradesmen who would come out this far on a regular run. Seamus didn't let the delivery man anywhere near the front door, carrying it all through the yard himself. Now, with the last of it away and Bridget asleep on her shake-me-down, they sat on the bench in the yard. The sun of the late July evening held a pleasant warmth. Seamus outlined his plans for the farm, lulling her into a sense of security. 'But first I have to make me trip back to England,' he said.

'Seamus, I'm afraid of that time. Afraid of not having you here to protect us, and afraid of the news I know you will bring me about Will.' She told him of the presence that had visited her on the boat.

''Tis sorry I am to have dragged you away from your man afore he had his last days, but in the end I had no choice. I wasn't for coming without you, Bridie, but your own action caused me to do it sooner than I had planned.'

She didn't take him up on this. They could go over and over him finding her with Andrew, but wasn't the whole thing causing her pain enough, with the guilt of what the consequences had been?

'Would you mind if I made a little garden for Will? I think it will be helping Bridget – and me – to come to terms with it. A little place we can plant flowers for him and talk to him, like . . . a grave.' The word choked from her as she lost her battle against the tears. Her body crumpled.

'Bridie, me little Bridie, 'tis right you should let it out, for the pain of grieving is a powerful one.' His arms enclosed her. 'Wasn't I for having the pleasure of meeting your man long before you did?'

'Will? You met my Will!'

'Aye, sure it was, he was grieving for his pappy . . .'

Bridie listened to the amazing tale of how Seamus had come across Will in the ginnel; but even more incredulous to her was that they had discussed Bruiser! Somehow the story calmed her, and it was nice to think of them in that other life, chatting and helping one another. For didn't he say as Will told him how he should tackle Bruiser, if he came up against him, and Seamus had been for stopping to talk when he'd found Will in his darkest moment?

'Did you like that little snippet then, Bridie?'

'Aye, I did.'

'Well, I held a respect in me for Will from that day, and more so when I found out what he'd done to save a young woman's life. Are you knowing of that?'

'Yes, Will told me.'

'So it will be grand – and an honour – to have a remembrance garden for him. But I am thinking we can section it and dedicate areas to all those we want to think of, like me grandmother and your mammy.'

'And me little Eric.'

'Aye, I mind the time you told me of him. You've had your share of troubles, Bridie. Maybe I shouldn't be at blaming you for how you have run your life.'

''Tis as you have run yours like a saint, then? As from what I have heard, you are cousin to the Devil himself!'

''Tis true. I'm not the one who should stand in judgement, but wasn't you for knowing me character? You started out with such purity and beauty in yours.'

'Sure, but I didn't know you, Seamus – not the you that is before me now, I didn't. 'Tis as I can accept most of what I hear about you, but the abduction of wee children! Why did you do that, and what happened to them?'

'I wasn't for abducting them; their fathers sold their wee ones to me. They had to have some way of explaining it to their womenfolk.'

'They *sold* them?'

'Yes. Sure enough, they had plenty of them. And I delivered them to a life they would never have known back there in Breckton. A good life, with rich folk who would love them. Childless folk in America, who thought they were Irish orphans, and that the payment they gave for them would help others in the same situation.'

Bridie didn't know how to react to this. It was for sure a better life those little ones would have had, but if she tried for a year and a day she'd not get Seamus to see the wrong in it. 'Is that the reason you came back?'

''Tis. That, and me need to find you. I have a friend out there, a pastor of some religion or other – there are many in America. He worked as an adoption agent. I told him of the

380

large Irish families and the poverty of them, and 'twas he as suggested offering them money to part with one or more of their brood. His wife would pose as a nun and sail over here, so all I had to do was take them to her. 'Twas easy for her to take them on board, as they all took her to be one of those Sisters of Mercy, so they did.'

Bridie could see no mercy in the actions of this pastor's wife, nor in what Seamus had done to introduce this form of prosperity to the men of Ireland and the Irish community in Breckton, but when she thought of those callous fathers . . .

'Let's leave it now, Bridie. We can rake over the wrongs and rights of it for many a day and not justify any of it. Are you thinking you would like a drop of gin?'

'Haven't I been longing for some this good while? Where is it you keep it?'

'I'm not for saying. 'Tis as you need to have your consumption of it tethering stronger than a horseman would have to tie a stallion when there's a mare on heat in the next stable.'

'So, 'tis me all the rules are to apply to, is it?'

''Tis. For haven't I given up everything I was, of me own accord? Sure, I need no rules, as I haven't any vices left to temper. Today marks a new beginning for me, with the woman I love by me side.'

He got up and went into his barn. She hadn't yet been in there, so had no knowledge of where he might hide her gin, but when he was away on business in the town she would be having a good look. This thought died in her when Seamus emerged and snapped a huge padlock into place.

They settled back down with their drink. Soon a red glow clothed everything around them, lighting up the windows of the croft and the barn as if they were licked by flames, as the sun edged its way behind the mountains. Shadows formed, sending a shiver through Bridie.

'Are you feeling the chill? Hold on a minute while I light the brazier. It's all ready, so it is. And I have me mouth organ, so we can have some shenanigans to celebrate our new life.'

Bridie went in to fetch her shawl and check on Bridget, and when she came out a few minutes later the fire spat and crackled its presence. Seamus swigged from his whisky, wiped his lips and began playing an Irish jig. Fuelled by the gin, the music, the flickering of the flames and the fresh smell of the countryside, an excitement grew inside her. As it washed away the last of her sadness, she began to dance.

Seamus joined her. Holding his mouth organ with one hand and her with the other, he reeled her round and round until she fell against him. His closeness burned a memory into her. Feelings she thought she'd never again conjure up exploded inside her. He dropped his mouth organ and kissed her.

His hands caressed her, but he halted any advances she made. 'Let me take you as an innocent, me little Bridie . . .'

Sensing the importance of this to him, she let him take the lead and knew a deep awakening – something not marked by urgency, or by the need to take all she could, as she allowed him to explore her. He was for making her feel like a young girl in the hands of a caring lover. This was what Seamus wanted: her – not as she was now, but the her he felt he'd missed out on. The girl he'd fallen in love with.

Letting her mind go back to those days, she saw them running through the fields, climbing the hills, laughing and enjoying each other, and she knew that although he would never take Will's place, he was at this moment the other half to her broken soul.

'Me Bridie, me little redhead girl, I love you.' He took her hand, picked up his keys and ran with her to the gate.

'Where is it you are taking me, Seamus? What about Bridget?'

He unlocked the gate and pulled her through. ''Tis right I should take me bride under the stars on a carpet of Irish grass.'

She didn't question him any further. He had his fantasy, and her being his bride was part of that. And though she wanted to take hold of him and pleasure herself with the feel of him, she stayed in her role. She let him undress her, savouring the touch of his lips on her breasts as they tugged at her nipples. She waited while he shed his own clothes. She lay with him when he bid her to, shivering as he parted her legs and gently stroked her thighs, before kissing his way to the heart of her, and then she cried out with the ecstasy of the sensations his probing gave her.

When at last he blocked out the glittering blanket of stars with his body, she could hardly breathe. 'Oh, Seamus, Seamus. My love, my dearest love.'

His cries joined hers, and their tears and sweat mingled, as the world they had known all those years ago became whole. Bringing the two halves together to make one.

Andrew sat up in bed. His man worked around the room, checking things, putting them in drawers, brushing lapels and poking the fire that everyone insisted he needed, but was totally unnecessary on such a lovely day.

'Open the window, Wilson. It is stuffy in here. Remember what my old nurse used to say: "Fresh air, Andrew. That's what you need. Never mind the weather. You can wrap up against it, but you can't get goodness from stale air."' Wilson had been with the family in various posts for as long as Andrew could recall. He'd started as a young lad making up fires, and that was when Andrew was just a boy.

'I do, sir. She was a good soul. Can I get you anything, sir?'

'Yes, actually, you can. Do you remember that basket chair my grandfather had? The one with wheels on. What became of it?'

'I think it is in the attics. I know it came with you from Tarrington House.'

'Have someone dig it out and get it working. I have a mind to go outside today for a walk. Once you have organized that, come back and help me to dress.'

'Yes, sir.'

Wilson's smile held approval. Andrew hoped Dvina would feel the same way. She seemed to love having him as an invalid and molly-coddling him, even more than she did Jeremy. As if he had conjured her up, she walked into the room. 'Are you alone, darling?'

'Yes. I've sent Wilson on a mission.' He explained his idea.

'That sounds like a good plan, dear. Do you think I would be able to push it? I would like some time with you where we won't be disturbed. I have news.'

'Good or bad?'

'Both.'

'Oh, blast! And here I was thinking of a nice, peaceful day. The first I've felt like enjoying for a long time. You know, old thing, I'm so happy the women in my life have sorted out their differences. I felt very torn.'

'The women in your life will always have conflict, Andrew. Oh, don't take that personally. I am ready to talk about what really happened. I'm not a fool, you know, dear, but the years have taught me I am more than a puppy waiting for the crumbs from your table and a pat on the head to make me happy. I know I am the most important woman in your life – sometimes the only one. Those are our happiest times. But I also know others may usurp my position from time to time. I love you, Andrew, and I take you as you are. I just need you to be honest with me.'

'Well, that was a long speech. Have you been practising it? Look, why don't we leave it? Talking only makes things worse, and nothing can punish me more than seeing you hurt. But there is one thing I want to take you to task on: no one – and I mean no one – ever takes precedence over you in my affections. I do slip up. I don't know why, but I suffer for it, Dvina. I suffer more than you can know. I'm sorry, my darling. Really, so sorry.'

She stood looking over at him. Her dress flowed over her body, telling him she'd sought comfort in food once more. This compounded his guilt. Her stance softened. 'You're right. We shouldn't talk about it. Tell Wilson to let me know if he is able to get you into the garden. I'll order us some tea and cakes for lunch. We can have it in the summerhouse. I still have things to talk over with you – not about you and your ways, but other, very important things.'

The basket chair proved too rickety, but, not to be put off, Andrew had Tom fetched from the stables. He and one of the footmen helped him downstairs and out to the summerhouse. It felt good to take a lungful of sweet air and to feel the warmth of the sun on his face, and he found he had more strength than he thought, even though the damned complications he'd suffered had weakened his heart. Which, according to the doctor, would severely limit him. Well, doctors could be proved wrong. God, the stupid man had even said Andrew might have to be celibate, as the strain of having sex might prove too much! How would he live like that? It was impossible, and was not going to happen, even if he did deserve such a fate.

Dvina had changed her frock and now wore one that she called an A-line dress. The shape suited her far more than the layered style. It slimmed her, and there was a glow about her. She came over to Andrew as soon as the men had settled him and made him comfortable. Sitting at his feet, she put her head on his lap and said, 'Darling, we are pregnant again!'

'Good Lord! That's the last thing I expected you to say. How far?'

'Oh, four months at least, the doctor says.'

'That's wonderful, darling. How are you feeling? Is everything like it was with Jeremy?'

'Yes. It's all going fine. I'd like to ask Isabella to help. Her mother gave me such confidence.'

'Of course. I don't think she dabbles in all those herbs and things, but her mother must have handed down a wealth of knowledge to her, and no doubt she has picked up some of her own along the way. Well, well. I suppose that is your good news, but what is the bad?'

'It isn't all of my good news, but I will give you the bad first. Mrs Hadler passed away last night.'

'Oh dear. Poor thing, the last few weeks of her life have not been good. Is someone seeing to things? She'll go into the same grave as Will, I expect, but we should take care of everything.'

'Yes. I have done what is necessary and will attend the funeral.'

She stood up with some difficulty, and pulled a chair up close to him. A knock on the door prevented her from saying anything further. They sat waiting while the staff filled the table with much more than they would need. As one of the servants went to pour the tea, Dvina dismissed them, saying, 'Thank you, that all looks very nice. We will look after ourselves. Just open a few windows at the back, will you, Wilson? But close the door after you leave. I'll come for you when we have finished.'

'Yes, Ma'am.'

Andrew watched with growing impatience as Dvina served up lunch. He was annoyed at how much she piled onto her plate, but said nothing. Isabella would get that in hand, as her mother had done before her. He just hoped she agreed to take the position. She'd been out of sorts with him for a long time, although he had no idea why.

'I'm really rather excited about my other news, Andrew.'

'Don't keep me in suspense any longer. What is it? Tell me or I'll throw one of those cream buns at you.'

'There is news on the traveller. Isabella overheard a conversation, and has entrusted me with it . . .'

Andrew didn't know how to take the tale she unfolded. Obviously he now understood the need for all the secrecy, but it involved many of his men – trusted men, albeit from the Irish community, who never gave him the impression they held any loyalty to him. But he didn't blame them for that, as they always got the rough end of the deal. It had to be like that, no matter what Dvina said on the matter. He had to put his old workforce's needs first or there would be hell to pay. But to think many of the Irish had connections to the Fenians! Well! Then there was the other aspect: what about Bridie? He'd hoped he'd seen the last of her. Was this why Dvina had gone to so much trouble to give him that speech this morning, leading into it as if it had been between them since it had happened? *This woman of his worked in mysterious ways. I am never quite sure of her.*

'Well, what do you think?'

'I think we need to inform the police, but it has to be handled with care. I will talk to the sergeant myself. And to his inspector, too, if I have to. I know him; he's a good sort. I think he will agree with me that the Irish involved need to be arrested as well. God! Look what they are planning! A double murder and a robbery – that is, if you can rob a robber of his spoils. The Irish must never find out who informed on them, though. That is vital. We are not dealing with your average rogue here. Good God, to think there are men of that calibre in our midst. I'm regretting ever going to Ireland to recruit now.'

'Yes, I thought you would say that, but they're not all the same. We have a lot of decent, hard-working families in our employ. That apart, what about Will Hadler's wife?'

'What about her?'

'Oh, Andrew, I told you. Apart from the fact that she is in danger, Isabella told Tom that Paddy Docherty suggested Bridie hadn't gone willingly! We need to help her to come home.'

He had heard that part of the tale, of course, but had ignored it. It hadn't suited him to react to it. He'd compartmentalized Bridie Hadler, and put her in a place where everything had happened because of her.

'Andrew, are you all right? Darling, you're sweating. Oh dear, that news has upset you . . .'

'No, no, I'm all right. Don't worry. It's just that – well, oh God, what if my assumptions were wrong? After all, I can't *know* that she was in league with Seamus. I may have stopped everyone looking for her, or caring about her. They may even have damned her!'

'That's ridiculous, darling. How it happened . . . anyone would have read the same into the situation. No one would have thought she was there by chance, although Isabella is now saying that she knew Bridie meant to go up the hill to visit her son's grave. That's a very touching story, which I will tell you sometime, but that apart, there was the note, remember? The note was the reason everyone accepted that she'd left willingly with Seamus, and not anything you supposed from the situation. Anyway, why should you think you were wrong now? How you told it, it was obvious that she had something to do with it.'

'Was it? Didn't you doubt my story? You as good as told me earlier you thought I had given into her and committed adultery with her—'

'Andrew!'

'I'm sorry, but that is what you think, isn't it? Oh, why do I always end up feeling like the accused? I'm fed up with it!' He'd long since learned that attack was his best policy with Dvina. She always capitulated, but she surprised him this time, by retorting: 'That's unfair, Andrew. I haven't accused you. I had an understandable moment when I could no longer listen to my husband's ramblings about another woman, and left you to come home and get my thoughts together. But once you explained, I believed you.'

'What was all that about this morning, then? Come on, Dvina, you had heard all about this and you needed to tear a strip off me. That's the truth. All your talk about you being no fool, saying you understood. Making a martyr of yourself: "Oh, as long as I am the main woman in your life" – that kind of thing. What did you mean by all that?'

'As I'm now the one answering my judge and jury, I can only say in my defence that I'm only human. Anything related to this incident is going to bring back the things I heard you say. None of what you rambled on about whilst delirious fitted with your story. This morning I was trying to let you know that I will stand by you, no matter what. That I had come to know the place I hold in your affections. That it is a very big place – far bigger than I ever expected out of our marriage. That I hold it precious and would forgive your indiscretions.'

'In other words, you don't believe me, but it doesn't matter because you have forgiven me. Well, thank you, Dvina. Thank you for nothing.'

She put her head down. He'd left her no argument, no way of getting out of it all, and he knew he had done her a massive injustice by doing so.

How could she believe him? As she said, she was only human. If he'd gone into any detail or called out the things his mother had told him – and he probably had – then she was bound to think them true. Notwithstanding the fact that they were. But what could he do? He couldn't come out and tell Dvina, his mother and Agatha, for God's sake – not to mention all of his friends – that it had been a pack of lies!

'Andrew, are you sure you are all right, dear?'

'Of course I'm all right. Why do you keep asking?'

'You're very pale, darling. You're really not well. I should just have contacted the police and left it at that. It's up to them to do what is necessary. I shouldn't have worried about that woman . . .'

He wanted, with all his body and soul, to let Dvina off the hook. To tell her he'd lied and seek her help with how to get out of it all, but he couldn't. He couldn't do that to her, to himself or to his mother. He had to find a solution. 'I am a bit tired, to be truthful.' He sought to make light of it, bringing them back to even ground again by saying, 'God, what is wrong with me? I can't even enjoy a good fight with you any more. I haven't the strength. Besides, I need you as a friend. Sorry, old thing, and I can't say fairer than that. Because I am: very sorry.'

'Oh, no doubt you will regroup and come out the winner in the end. You just need a rest. Time to think.'

He laughed, but he thought that an odd thing to say. He used to know exactly where he was with Dvina, but the subjects in question had been easy then. Now he had complicated things – unnerved her, made her afraid to be straight-talking with him. He was beginning to think he wasn't a very nice person.

He watched Dvina walk across the lawn. Despite her bulk, she had a natural grace. She was a good person. He didn't deserve her, for now he had knowledge of the evil that he harboured and could tap into whenever it suited him. It had been apparent when he'd told the lies, but only now did he recognize it, as he realized he was willing to perpetuate those lies to save his own skin.

Even though there was a strong possibility that Bridie would be wrongly accused of aiding and abetting Seamus, and that she might face a prison sentence because of his testimony, he knew he would do nothing to stop that. He couldn't.

28

August 1886

Survival

'Right, sir. I've taken down all you have told me. It does seem like this is a very good lead, but to my mind it's too big for my force to handle. I will need to involve the chief inspector, but we have plenty of time to sort everything out. It's doubtful our friend will escape again. I'll be in touch.'

'Sergeant, I know Richard Nelton; we were at university together. In view of the secrecy surrounding this, and the fact that I'm not well enough to travel to his office' – Andrew sat at his desk, scribbling an invitation – 'would you give him this? I am inviting him and his lady wife to dinner. Explain to him that a man calling once in uniform is fine, as we have occasions to call on your help to deal with poachers and the like, and of course you were all here over the robbery. But after your visit tonight, any further contact must be in plain clothes. A dinner party will not arouse any suspicion. I can't imagine anyone would recognize the inspector.'

'Very well, sir. I'm sorry, I hope I don't arouse suspicion.'

'At the moment I am sure you won't – just curiosity, as no one knows any of us has any knowledge of what is planned, so don't worry.' He extended his hand. 'Thank you for coming.'

Once on his own again, Andrew gathered some papers that he needed to go over concerning the mine. Steadying himself by holding on to the furniture and walls, he made his way to his high-backed brown leather chair. He'd had it moved from its usual place by the fire to near the window, so that he could enjoy the peace of this room – his own little sanctuary – and the view over part of the town and the fields to the east. Some would say that the chimneys he could see rising from the ground spoiled the picture of tranquillity made up of hills, streams and clumps of trees, but to him they represented the life-blood of the town. And his own bank balance.

He tried to study the papers – new legislation over working conditions, et cetera – but couldn't put his mind to it. *When would he return to normal health again?* Although he was left with ugly, red, angry-looking scars, his wounds had healed, but any exertion, however small, left him feeling exhausted. *Damn and blast bloody Seamus Finney!*

A week later Richard Nelton and his lovely, petite wife Anna arrived early for the dinner. Andrew hadn't seen him since his stepbrother Jeremy's memorial service, and both that and Jeremy were the opening topics of their conversation as they sipped an aperitif.

'Never had Jeremy down as a military man, but he turned out a good one, by all accounts. His medals and citation testify to that.'

'Yes, I have them here. Dvina and I had them encased in a glass cabinet. Come and see. They are along here, on the wall of the hall.' Wilson stepped forward and offered his arm and, despite the humiliation of it, Andrew took it. He knew that if he gave in to small amounts of help, he could last a lot longer at whatever occupied him, and he needed to get through tonight. Richard didn't comment, but carried on as if nothing out of the ordinary had happened. He nodded at the display and said, 'A fitting tribute.' And then, raising his glass to Jeremy's picture to the left of the case, he toasted Jeremy. 'Well done you, old boy.'

They stood in silence for a moment.

Richard broke it. 'So, how are you? Since your invitation I have been down memory lane. We had some good times in the old days. It's good to see you, Andrew.'

'You too, Richard. I have tried to keep in touch, but it needs us both to make the effort, you know.'

'I know. I had reasons not to accept your invitations, and then you stopped sending them and knocked me off your calling list.'

'There just didn't seem much point. I took it your wife didn't want you to keep up with your old friends.'

'Nothing could be further from the truth . . .'

The dinner gong resounded around them. They rejoined the ladies, finding them engrossed in conversation about horses. It pleased Andrew to find they had common ground – not that Dvina needed one. She was an attentive host and always relaxed her guests. Dismissing Wilson, he proffered his arm to Anna, saying, 'May I?'

Anna linked in with him, with a light touch that put no pressure on him, and looked into his eyes as she said, 'It is very nice to meet you and your charming wife.' Had he detected a slight query in her tone? 'Richard and I tend not to socialize enough. I am almost a stranger to society. I can't think why we have never met?' And was there a flirtatious innuendo in her question?

They followed Richard and Dvina through to the dining hall. When Andrew felt confident that they were out of ear-shot, he said, 'It is remiss of Richard never to have accepted my invitations before. It has meant I missed out on having a chance to get to know you, Anna – something I am sure I would enjoy.'

'You're too kind.'

Andrew laughed at this. She had a way of saying things that implied more than her words. 'Well, we shall have to make up for it. You are always welcome, and I will make sure you are on our guest list in the future.'

Dinner over, the women retired to the withdrawing room, leaving the men to their brandy. Richard Nelton wasted no time in broaching the matter in hand.

'Well, we had better get down to business. My sergeant relayed to me what had happened here, and about your own mishap. I am sorry to hear it has left you unwell.'

Tiredness ached in Andrew's bones, but he felt determined to get through the next half an hour. 'Please ask all you have to.'

'I don't have questions, not yet. First, I think it important to get all the players around the table, and I have a plan to reel them all in. I am in touch with my colleagues in Scotland and have their full cooperation, which is something I hoped for. They are organizing officers to lie in wait for the gang and arrest them, once they are in position. Now, Seamus Finney will have a tail on him from when he is two miles away from shore. The police have commandeered fishing boats to surround him. Once he steps ashore, we will arrest him. He is wanted for a great deal more than your robbery, Andrew.'

'What about the woman – Bridie Hadler?'

'Yes, a tricky one. I had thought to leave her there, but if she is involved, we can't. And then, there is the possibility of her kidnap.'

'But she went willingly – at least partly. I mean, she left a note for her husband telling him she couldn't cope.'

'I've seen that, but don't forget: the young lady who reported all of this to you is certain she overheard the leader of the Irish lot saying Mrs Hadler didn't go of her own accord. What if threats were made – to her family, say?'

'Yes, I know, but I haven't put much store by that. So what will happen? Will you fetch her back?'

'That looks likely. Would that pose you a problem, Andrew?'

'Well, I haven't said, but . . . Oh, this is awkward.'

'It won't go beyond this room.'

'She flirted with me once before. At one of my workers' weddings – I have to attend these things. It's tradition. Anyway, she waylaid me and—'

'Bloody hell, Andrew, you never could keep your cock in your trousers! Still, I suppose one can't blame you; you were rather saddled. Didn't do badly out of the whole deal, though.'

'No, and in more ways than you can imagine, because I have found love with Dvina . . . Yes, yes, I know, and I don't expect you to understand, but I haven't the strength in me to defend her at this moment. You should visit more often and get to know her for yourself. Those who have – they have seen for themselves and know what I mean, and how truthful I am being.'

'I would, but I don't like to think of you being within a mile of my wife. She is known for her flirting, and men fall over her. I happen to have a jealous nature. Anyway, back to the point: what happened with the Irish girl?'

'We kissed. It was four or five years ago, but since then

there had been a sort of flirtation going on whenever we met. When I saw her up on the hill, teasing me, as she was from the other bank of the stream, I had every intention . . . I – well, I did suggest it, just before the first lash. What if they conjure up a story about me having fucked her? If they both say it . . .'

'Andrew, we won't take their word against yours. Whatever they say against you will go down as them trying to save their skins. Don't worry about it. Seamus Finney won't get out of this alive. It's the noose for him. And she's looking at a good stretch in prison, I shouldn't wonder. The rest of the gang – I'm not sure. Without the testimony of the woman who overheard them, we haven't got a great deal, and that is too risky. We will arrest them on suspicion in the first instance, but I don't think we can bring a case against them – not enough evidence, and what there is could be shown to be hearsay.'

'Is there no other outcome than prison for Bridie Hadler?'

'Possibly. The workhouse might be an alternative. There is no actual sentencing to send her there, on a criminal level, but there is still the Poor Law. I could sort something out. I have an influence over most things. How would that suit?'

'Better than prison; it isn't so final. Nor is it beyond the realms of any help I might give her.'

'Be careful, Andrew. Maybe she deserves your help – I don't know and don't want to – but don't do anything traceable; it won't look right, for you or me. Now, I think you owe me a few shooting parties? I'm not one for balls and such, but for Anna's sake – yes, I wouldn't baulk at some invites, as long as you promise not to dally with my wife.' He laughed, but Andrew knew he meant what he'd said. 'Anyway, I would especially like to attend events where I can further myself in my work. Not all of us landed on our feet, you know.'

'Of course, Richard – anything. Look, don't be short of funds, not ever. I have enough to look after you.'

'Very generous of you, Andrew. My own position on that score isn't good. Anna has a small inheritance, which along with my very good salary keeps us going, but if we socialize . . .'

'There will be a letter delivered to you tomorrow.'

'I'd rather not – not that way. You never know. Don't forget, I am surrounded by detectives, and more than a few of them would like to bring me down.'

'Well then, let's go into my office before we rejoin the ladies.'

Four weeks later

Bridie paced up and down. Seamus had left five days ago. She'd missed him with a passion, but now her anger at him washed away those feelings. Where was he? And why had he insisted on locking them in? She'd eked out the water from the full buckets that he had left her outside the back door, but now they were empty. Her mouth dried with fear. What if he didn't come back? Oh, God!

'Mammy crying . . . Mammy?'

Bridget touched the tear that had run down Bridie's face. Once more Bridie pulled herself up for her little one and soothed Bridget, telling her, 'I have a powerful lot of things to cry about, my wee one, but I'll stop now. There, isn't that a smile I have on me now?'

Bridget laughed.

'Go back to what you were doing. Mammy has to think.'

Bridie stood in the small yard and looked up. No sign of rain, but she placed the buckets away from the wall and out from the shelter of the eaves, just in case.

Looking around the high wall filled her with despair. It had many crannies in it where each stone rested on the other, making it possible to climb it, but she couldn't do so whilst carrying Bridget and she couldn't leave her here. If she climbed it, and then back over the one into the yard and managed to get water, how would she get it into the house? The chain on the front door held it fast, and the windows were far too high for her. And what if she fell? What of Bridget then?

Back inside she pushed two potatoes and a small turnip – the last of the vegetables – into the fire burning in the range. This morning they had toasted the remains of the batch of bread and eaten it with jam. It had kept them going. Bridget hadn't complained of being hungry, only of her thirst. Quenching that had emptied the last bucket. Her own throat burned; her tongue was heavy in her mouth. Bridie found it hard to gather enough spittle to dampen it.

The potato wouldn't go down, no matter how hard she tried to swallow it. Her body retched in protest and choked the remnants onto the floor. Hunger pains gnawed at her, but she'd trade all the food in the world for a sup of water. She was grateful for Bridget having eaten her potato, and she looked at her daughter curled up asleep on the bed. She would lie down beside her and rest a while, for wasn't she tired to the bones of her?

How much time had gone by when she came to? One moment the light poured in through the windows, and the next the black night crowded in on her. No fire lit these hours; its flames had died, leaving dry, grey ash in its wake. Bridie rolled off the bed. Bridget didn't move. Her cracked lips were open, and her tongue – yellow and crusty – protruded from them. Her eyes had sunk into their sockets. Dried blood caked the corners of her mouth, but still she breathed, deep, sighing breaths. *Oh, sweet Jesus, be after helping me.*

Too weak to move, Bridie flopped back onto the bed for a moment, before trying again. The room spun around her. In her confusion she thought the door had moved – it should be in the other corner. Her vision blurred. What was happening? *Help us . . . help us . . .*

The light above Seamus flickered. He blinked his eyes to wakefulness, and the worry in him increased with that awareness. But had they at last believed him and sent a boat over? *Please let them be after getting there in time.*

How long would the water have lasted? Jesus, what had made him lock Bridie in? Wouldn't it have been enough to lock the gate? At least then she would have had access to the water. He looked at the chalk marks on his cell wall: ten days since he'd left. Prayers tumbled over prayers. *Dear God, let them be in time to save her. And while I'm at it, I'd be asking Your forgiveness, for I have a mind I'll be visiting You soon.*

He thought over the questioning. Strange it was how they seemed to think Bridie had a hand in the robbery. And not only that; but the accusation of her having lured Mr Harvey up the hill, so that Seamus could rob him? That would be Harvey saving his skin. Sure, Bridie would tell them the truth of it, and when her story matched his, wouldn't they realize she was innocent? They had to, for robbery carried a long prison sentence, and she wouldn't bear that.

'Richard, how are you? How's the investigation? Have they found Bridie Hadler?'

'I hope so, Andrew. If not, they will find a corpse. As it is, the little girl is surely dead.'

'That bastard! How could anyone do such a thing? My God, it doesn't bear thinking about.' To his shame, he had held out a small hope that Bridie would die. Everything would be resolved then: no open questions, only his version of events ever heard.

'I came to tell you what Finney's side of the story is, Andrew. I'm afraid your worst fears have been realized: he *is* saying he came upon you fucking the woman he refers to as "his future wife" and that he flipped. He denies having stolen anything. He says Bridie will tell the same story.'

'And you believe him?'

'I prefer your version. It is more lucrative.'

His smile sickened Andrew. *How did I stoop so low? Bad enough going with that damned Bridie Hadler, but to pay this slime of a man to cover up for me? God! But I'm in too deep now, and I've no choice but to keep going with my story.* 'And it will remain so, as long as you continue to keep things in my favour. I won't testify to her being involved, though. I do think she was, but how can I be sure? What if she wasn't? My making a definite allegation of that would surely send her to prison, and you know that isn't what I want.'

'Stop worrying, Andrew. We are not thinking of charging her with aiding and abetting – not of robbery anyway. Problem is, we can't get Paddy Docherty to confirm that she didn't want to go with Seamus. He's hiding something. So she may have to face a charge of "helping with the disposal of ill-gotten goods".'

'Will that save her from prison?'

'In the normal run of things, no, but the solicitor I have lined up to defend her will come up with some good arguments. As part of us not charging her for the robbery, she will have to agree to put herself into the workhouse, say that she is repentant and wants to work off her sins. Have faith, Andrew. It will all go to plan.'

'I hope so.'

'Anyway, there is more. One of the gang has told us quite a lot. He says Paddy Docherty carried out torture for the Fenians, and did so for Seamus, too. He also expounded on that snippet your informant told you about Bridie Hadler. It seems she was right: there is a question vexing the Irish over some funds her father pilfered from "the cause", as they call it. They believe that after his death Bridie spent the money, which should have been returned to them. They are passionate about it, and the squealer confirmed that the talk was of one day getting their revenge.'

'Good God!'

'Yes, a nice lot, aren't they? But you can rest easy on that one. Seamus Finney – I suppose because he realizes his own fate, and that the Fenians can no longer get at him – has told the truth of what really happened to the money. But that doesn't alter the fact that Mrs Hadler planned to benefit from it, so we are not sure if that threat will be lifted from her.'

Andrew listened to what had really happened, including what Bridie's father had done – both to her and the Irish people. A part of the cold place he had in him for Bridie melted. *Poor sod! She never did stand much of a chance, by the sound of things. But I'll leave things as they are for now. I have to. There will be something I can do in the long run, though. But raped! And by her own father!*

When Richard had finished Andrew asked, 'Is there no end to this? I'm beginning to rue the day I ever brought the Irish over here, though my wife chastises me for saying so. And though she's right in saying there are a lot of decent families amongst them, this is shaking my faith in humanity.'

'Well, it would have saved us all a lot of trouble if you hadn't. But you weren't responsible for bringing Seamus Finney here, and he is our main criminal. His charges include murder, rape and child abduction, as well as robbery. Oh, a whole list of things, and for most of it we are gathering damning evidence. The Irish are coming forward in their droves. They hate him more than they hate you.'

This shocked Andrew. He knew he wasn't popular amongst them, but he hadn't realized they had that much venom in them for him. Still, that was as may be; the worrying thing was how this whole case looked as if it would have a high profile, even without his name attached to it. Who knew what stones would turn over, and how people would judge each incident – true or not, proven or not – or who would jump on the bandwagon to damn him?

'But,' Richard continued, 'one good thing has come out of all of this, and I expect Dvina is thrilled to know she will get all of her jewellery back. How is she keeping?'

'She is very happy about it, and doing very well, thanks. She is planning a dinner party to celebrate. Not until we know Bridie is all right, of course. She is very worried about her. You will come?'

'Delighted to, as always, but tell me: how do you do it, Andrew? You amaze me. No one else I know could have their wife worried sick over someone their husband had inter— Sorry, fancied having intercourse with.'

They both laughed at this, but Andrew felt a trickle of trepidation run through him. Richard had moved from friend to blackmailer, and he didn't know how to bring it all to a halt. How would he manage things when all this was over?

Because he felt sure the end of the trial would not be the end of Richard's preying on him.

Bridie's head ached. Each loud bang increased her pain and dragged her further to wakefulness, but she couldn't open her eyes or fight through what felt like a veil of spider webs clogging her brain. Voices shouted her name. Her lips cracked as she opened her mouth. She closed it against the pain and tried to swallow. Something cold dripped onto her. *Water, oh God, water* . . . She forced her tongue out to let the icy nectar fall onto it. It moistened her mouth.

Still her name resounded in her ears over and over. 'Bridie, will you open your eyes? Come on now, it is safe as you are. You're going to be fine.'

The Irish lilt soothed her, but it wasn't Seamus. Where was Seamus?

Her throat moistened enough for her to swallow. Sore as it was to do so, she took a bigger sip, but her body wasn't of the same mind as her and retched it back.

'Just a wee drop at a time. Keep it in you, Bridie. We have to get you to take the water.'

She tried to speak, tried to say her beloved child's name. Her brain wouldn't give her the information she needed. A tiny baby came into her mind. *No, not Eric, though her heart would like to see the wee fellow, but who . . . ?*

'She's mumbling, sounds delirious. 'Tis distressed as she is. What shall I do?'

'It's the dehydration, Sergeant, it causes confusion. Bridie, 'tis Dr Feeley. You are all right, so you are. And your little girl is doing better than you: she is already awake and taking the water like it was honey. Now you be at doing the same.

You'll soon be in the hospital. Once you have taken a drink, we can start to get you there.'

She took another sip, forced it down and made it stay there, swallowing hard against the threat of retching it up.

''Tis a good girl you are. Now just be having a wee drop more. That's right.'

The whiteness surrounding her took her back over the years, and the soft tread of the nuns gliding around as if floating compounded those memories. If only she could look to one side and see Beth sitting there, and all of this had been a dream. Parts of what had happened since that time she wouldn't be able to wipe out, but most of it she would. Heavier footsteps strode towards her – a black menacing figure amongst all of this purity. 'Bridie Hadler?'

She nodded.

'I'm Officer Walter Haines. I'm over from England – Leeds. They have Seamus Finney under arrest there, and in custody awaiting trial. I have to tell you that I am arresting you on suspicion of helping him to dispose of his ill-gotten gains.'

Dear God!

She couldn't make any protest. Her mind hadn't yet processed everything that had happened. All she could do was beg for information. 'Where is me wee Bridget? Is she to come with us? I'm not for leaving without her.'

The Sister, who had somehow reached the bed, answered her. 'Wee Bridget is doing fine. We will be keeping her. She is safe with us, so she is.'

'No! No . . .' The pain searing Bridie's heart ripped it in two. Her cries fell into sobs, then to screams. 'Not me wee babby! No, don't take her from me, no! No!'

''Tis us having no choice, Bridie. You can't be taking her. Where will she go whilst you and her pappy are in prison?'

'Seamus isn't her pappy. Her pappy died. Please, please . . . I have friends. They will be after caring for her, please.'

'Sister, I was told to bring them both back home. If there's a doubt concerning the young 'un's welfare, then the authorities in England will take care of her. She is English and is our responsibility.'

'Very well. I will be after talking to the doctor, to see when it is we can release them both.'

Bridie grabbed the policeman's hand. 'Thank you, thank you. It is a saint you are.'

'I don't know about that. Just doing me duty. A Yorkshire lass belongs on Yorkshire soil, and your young 'un is a Yorkshire lass through and through, so I had to say sommat. Now, let go of me hand and don't worry. I won't leave without both of you.'

It felt good to hear the familiar dialect again, though she never thought she'd be admitting that. She looked up at him. The exhaustion holding her in its grip only allowed her to say, 'I didn't do it. I wasn't for helping him.'

'Well, whether you did or didn't ain't for me to decide. It's a case as has more witnesses than ever I've known, so truth will out. If you did nowt, you'll not have owt to worry over.'

Witnesses? What witnesses? Who knew the truth? Only Paddy and Seamus, and she couldn't see Paddy coming forward – not to say he was willing to torch her home. And as for Seamus, would they believe anything he said?

29

One year later –
October 1887

Trial and punishment

The cells beneath the court held no comfort. Water ran down the brick walls, rats scurried around the floor, and the cold stored up over hundreds of years seeped into Bridie's body. But worse than all of this, the fetid stench of the bucket in the corner and of the latest inmate – who had a tinge on her of Dilly May – clogged her mouth and throat, making her retch. Swallowing hard, Bridie wiped her mouth, chafing her face with the coarse workhouse pinafore.

Hadn't living in the workhouse for a whole year since she'd recovered in the October, and committing herself to that hell-hole, closed her mind? To allow herself to feel would have meant giving in to the death of her. And didn't she have to live, for her Bridget?

But then it had all been to follow a plan, for the inspector had told her at the time that if she was to put herself willingly into the workhouse until her trial, and earn herself a good report from there, it would help her cause. It'd seemed like a good day when the officers had arrived to bring her to the courts, but not getting bail had meant she'd to endure life cooped up in this cell. If prison was anything like the conditions she'd had to put up with in this place over the last six weeks – the time the trial had taken – she hoped to Jesus the judge would be for letting her go back to Deanhouse – something she never thought to wish for.

She hadn't taken Bridget with her. Issy and Tom were taking care of her, and Issy brought Bridget to see Bridie once a month. Sure, it wasn't nearly enough, but it was better than having her in Deanhouse. Many a wee child died in there. Disease took them – anything from measles to whooping cough, as the place was a breeding ground for infection. Although Deanhouse was less than fifty years old – and, they said, designed for purpose – it was a warren of foul-smelling, overcrowded rooms. The stench came from the water closets, built in such a way that the putrid air from them came back into the building.

Those who'd been there a lot longer than Bridie were always telling her she was lucky, as things were a lot worse in the early days. Back then, they'd had to convert the vagrant wards into men's sick wards, the female-receiving ward into a bathroom for mentally ill females, and use the male-receiving ward as an infirm ward. Now at least they had the newly built infirmary attached to the north of the building. Bridie had tried to imagine the overcrowding they talked of as being worse than it was now, but couldn't for the life of her. Sure it was, she thought, the life of a prostitute had many merits compared to the lives of the inhabitants of a workhouse, and it made her sick to the stomach that it might be her lot for years to come. *But wasn't the alternative much worse?*

The clanging of the outer door leading to the cells meant

that her time had come to face the jury. Bridie knew a relief at this, but sent up a prayer as to the outcome. *Holy Mary, Mother of God, don't let them be for sending me to prison!* The plea had only just died in her when she remembered that Seamus was to face his sentence the day, too. She added a prayer for him, even though what she'd heard about him over these last weeks had sickened her: the taking of wee ones from the Irish as a payment for debt they couldn't honour – when he'd lied to her, and said the menfolk had sold them willingly – the raping of young girls as a punishment to their parents for stepping out of line, the vile threats of murder, and the actual murder carried out in one case, to make folk swear an alibi for him. Then there was the robberies, and having folk steal to order for him. And yet, despite it all, she held a feeling for him.

The warden clamped the irons around her wrists and took her through a maze of draughty gangways, passing by other holding cells from which men leered at her. As she passed the one that the Irish lot were in, a treacly glob of spit hit her face. Disgust shuddered through her. She pulled against the warden, forcing him to stop. Her eyes met the evil eyes of Paddy Docherty and she hissed at him, 'You bastard! You're for being more of a bastard than Seamus is, as you are a traitor, so you are. A traitor to your own. Isn't it true that you know I didn't go willingly with Seamus? That I had nothing to do with—'

'Shut your mouth, whore, and keep moving.' The warden yanked the chains linking her to him, and the Irish laughed as the pain cut into her wrists.

'Aye, you're right there, Warden. She is a whore, and 'tis as she was spawned by the Devil himself.' Paddy's voice followed her down the passageway. 'They say as the Devil takes his own, but he won't be for having you until we've finished with you, Bridie O'Hara. Every Docherty in the land will hunt you down. You're a dead woman, d'yer hear?'

They turned a corner and went out of earshot, but his words quivered through her. *Weren't the Dochertys known for violence, and weren't they known for bringing revenge down on anyone who crossed them?*

They reached the last familiar door. When the warden opened it, she saw the steps leading to the dock in the courtroom. A court usher standing at the top gave them an angry '*Shush!*'

The warden stayed his progress and leaned against the open door. A heavy, thick silence bore down on Bridie. She couldn't for a moment make out if the usher was the only person in the court above her. A cough told her he wasn't.

'The prisoner must remain standing.'

A shuffle indicated a lot of people sitting down. Bridie's breath caught in her lungs.

'Seamus Patrick Finney . . .'

Oh God! She wanted to be anywhere but here. *Jesus save him, save him . . .*

'You have been the cause of many people committing crimes, by exerting the power of fear over them. I want all the crimes admitted by these named witnesses struck from the record.' Bridie's heart warmed at the roll call, as she knew most were decent folk and had been driven by fear. As he came to the end of his list the judge said, 'I accept their crimes were committed under the pressure of extreme duress, and a real fear for their families and their own safety. The court thanks them for the courage they showed in coming forward, even though they knew their testimonies were incriminating.'

A cheer went up.

410

'Silence in court!'

The oppressive curtain of stillness and utter hush came down again. Something that Bridie couldn't see broke it, as a mass of gasps and excited chatter cluttered the space over her head.

'SILENCE!'

The see-saw of noise and quiet increased the tension in her. *What was happening?* She looked at the warden. He had a smile on his face as he patted his head and mouthed, 'The black cap.'

Holy Mother, no! Her throat constricted. She swallowed hard. The judge's voice boomed down to her: 'Seamus Patrick Finney, you have been found guilty of one count of murder, and are guilty as charged of rape, child abduction, robbery and intimidation. It is my duty to pass sentence upon you. You will be taken from this court and held at Her Majesty's pleasure until one month from now when, at twelve noon, you will be hanged by the neck until you are dead. May God have mercy on your soul.'

The bile gushed to her throat, and this time she couldn't stop it billowing from her mouth. The warden grabbed her hair and yanked her head back. His fist smashed into her chest. Her head swam. She couldn't draw in her breath. He dragged her body to a bucket of water standing a few yards away – kept, she assumed, for swilling away the mess made by frightened people awaiting their fate. With brute force, he dunked her head into the icy-cold water. Taking some of it into her mouth, she swilled out the taste of her vomit.

'You filthy bitch!'

The water splashed her feet as he threw it. She watched the water run the contents of her stomach down a drain. As her ears cleared, a ripple of applause started above her, and then a loud cheer went up. The elation only deepened her own despair. She held her body as if clamped in a vice, until the clanging of chains told her they were bringing him down. When Seamus came into sight, she kept her eyes on him. His eyes showed surprise at first, then twinkled, just how they always used to.

'Remember, it is that I love you, me wee Bridie. And don't be for thinking all of what you heard was the truth. We took our paths, you and I. They weren't the ones we should have taken, but they met in the end. That short time of happiness will go with me to me grave, so it will.'

'Move on, scum.' His jailers pushed him forward. He tripped and nearly fell.

Bridie leapt towards him. Although her warden jerked her back, he could not shut her up. 'I love you, me Seamus . . . I love you . . .'

She kept her eyes on him as they led him away. Her heart wept tears of pain until his whistling echoed around the corridor. The strains of the tune played all those years ago, and recently too, filled her. They nudged the pain away and gave her the joy of the campfire, the bright colours, the laughter, the fiddles and the dancing. The wonderful, carefree dancing.

'Bring her up now.'

She didn't mind the shove, or the climb up the stairs. She was ready. Seamus had given her courage.

The courtroom buzzed with whispers. It seemed that a million eyes were on her. She looked around and saw Issy. Dear Issy. Encouragement shone from her smile, and it helped to know she believed in her.

To Issy's left, a little way away, sat Andrew Harvey. Bridie lifted her head, shook her wet hair back from her face and stared back at him. She hoped the lies he'd told would rot his insides. Of all the men she'd lain with, he was after being the vilest! Hadn't he condemned her by saying she tried to seduce him? Oh, he'd tried to get out of it, by saying he couldn't be sure of her involvement with Seamus, but he was still saying it seemed that way. If she could reach him, she would give to him the same humiliation that she had suffered from Paddy and would spit in his face, so she would.

'Bridie Bridget Mary Hadler, I find the case against you as to your being an accomplice to Seamus Finney insubstantial, and the prosecution has withdrawn the charge. On the second count of helping to dispose of ill-gotten gains, I find the case proven.'

Her legs crumbled, but she remembered Seamus's bravery and held herself together.

The judge's voice droned on, telling her he believed there were mitigating circumstances and that he had listened to the plea of her solicitor. 'I therefore agree with him that your present circumstances should prevail, until such time as you can pay a fine of fifty pounds. Can you pay this fine?'

She could only shake her head.

'In that case, until such time as you are able to, you will be judged a bankrupt and will therefore be committed to the workhouse under the pauper law.'

The hope she'd held in her that maybe Beth could help, by paying the fine, died within her. *Fifty pounds! A fortune, which it would take a working man ten years to earn*. She couldn't name a soul who could raise such a sum.

Try as she might, she couldn't hold back the tears. Someone shouted something, and she heard the familiar tag to her name: *Whore!* Then another voice said, 'Whish, leave the girl alone, you skite. Hasn't she paid enough?'

'No, she hasn't. No O'Hara will ever be for paying enough. We'll get you, Bridie O'Hara, so we will.'

'Silence in court! Until I have left this court, it is still sitting, and those present remain bound by its rules. This is a court of law, and I will not tolerate threats of that nature. Sergeant, arrest that man and hold him in the cells for forty-eight hours for contempt of court.'

A rumble of voices followed this, but they quietened as the judge looked across at the public gallery once more. With order restored, he stood and left the room.

The warden pulled Bridie down the steps. At the bottom, Paddy Docherty stood with all of his co-accused behind him. His eyes stared into hers. She gathered the spittle in her mouth and repaid his insult. His jailer hustled him away before he could react. A small feeling of pleasure trickled into her. She only wished she could stay to hear his sentence. She'd cheer louder than any of the others.

The heavy doors swung open, and fresh air rushed into her lungs. She closed her eyes, taking deep breaths of it. When she opened them, Issy stood in front of her.

'Bridie. Oh, Bridie . . .'

They clung to each other, their tears mingling as they kissed cheeks. Issy seemed to be the only person in the world to believe her, and her support meant a lot.

'I'm sorry, Bridie. I'm sorry for everything. I know you love Seamus, but he's a bad . . .'

'Is it after being obvious how I feel? Does it show?'

'I hadn't guessed, no. I thought you felt the same way I do, but we all heard you shout it to him.'

'Do you hate him, Issy? I know you're not for liking him,

but if you got to know him – really got to know the heart of him – you'd not be for hating him.'

'I . . . Oh, you're reet love, happen as I wouldn't.'

As always when they talked of Seamus, Issy seemed on her guard, as if she knew something she couldn't share. Instinct told Bridie not to press the point, so she said, 'Anyway, how is me little Bridget? Is she asking after her mammy?'

'She is, and she's grand. I'll bring her across next week, eh?'

'Oh, Issy, 'tis that I'll never be for leaving that place.'

'Never say never, lass. Eeh, that knight on a white charger still might come over the hill.' They laughed at this. 'Anyroad, love, it's better than prison – at least I can visit, and if you get one of them tickets as lets you out for a day, we can go for picnics and walks. There'll be lots for you to look forward to, I'll see to that.' She took Bridie's hand, adding, 'By, love, you've some calluses since we last met! What's caused them?'

'It's the new job they gave me. I do oakum-picking now, but I am thinking, as I'm long-term, they will be taking me in to work in the infirmary. I told them I have a way in me for caring for the sick.'

'Aw, that'd be grand for you. But what the Devil is oakum-picking when it's at home?'

'We sit for hours shredding fibres from old hemp rope. They are after saying as the material is used in shipbuilding – they mix it with tar and use it to line the wooden boats.'

'See, you're getting yourself an education. You know all about shipbuilding already.'

'Oh, Issy . . .' Bridie's giggle verged on the hysterical, but she didn't care. It felt so good to laugh her fear and heartbreak out, instead of weeping. There'd be many hours for doing that.

'Well, enough funning. What happens now?'

'They said I'm to be back here to catch the cart as takes everyone where they are to go, at around five. They said I had time with me friend, arranged for me by someone of influence, who had been after guaranteeing I wouldn't run away.'

'Oh, well, we know who that was.'

'Aye, the bastard who was for putting me here in the first place. Oh, Issy, I hate him, I hate him with everything I am.'

'Come on, love, at least he sent me to you. He told me to wait for you and spend some time with you, so he sorted that. Keep your energy for getting through this; don't waste it on scum like him. There's a cafe down the road. Let's go and have a cuppa, eh?'

Sipping the steaming hot, sweet liquid brought a calm into Bridie. She wasn't yet ready for a bite of the huge cream bun; she wanted to savour it, look at it, be really ready to enjoy it and remember the experience of it. 'You know, Issy, it seems a shame that the punishment that is rightfully Andrew Harvey's is meted out to his wife. Has she recovered yet from the loss of her babby?'

'She'll never get better from that, not really. She were seven months, and the babby were formed proper, like . . . Oh, God, I forgot for a moment, Bridie! I'm sorry, love.'

'No, away with you – I'd never be for taking anything you said as hurtful, Issy. It's a fact as little Eric was like that, but that is for making me feel for Mrs Harvey even more. And for you, love, for you are in attendance when it happens, and you care.'

'Ta, love. I let me tongue have its own path more than I should. Poor Miss Dvina . . . Eeh, that's another thing: I can't stop thinking of her as that. Anyroad, she's not well. She's taken to her bed, and Dr Payne is worried something sinister is ailing her. The weight has dropped off her. Her skin has yellowed, and she can't eat without it coming back up. I'm feared for her, Bridie.'

'It's not for sounding good. Me mammy went that way. It should be him, not her.'

'Well, he ain't in good health, not since the whipping. They say he has a weak heart. He has to take it easy.'

'At least that's after some justice coming down on him, then.'

'Aye, though I don't think he deserved that whipping. The lowest of the low don't deserve owt like that. And he suffers over Miss Dvina. In his own way he does love her.'

Wanting to change the subject, Bridie said, 'Thinking on little Eric, it's his anniversary soon. Will you take Bridget up with some flowers for him? And I know as you'll keep Will's and Janet's grave tidy. One day I'll visit it, Issy, but I always have Will in the heart of me, so it won't matter if I don't.'

'You will, love, and of course I'll take care of them. Now eat that bun afore I pinch it off you.'

'I've been saving it, enjoying thinking of eating it and what it will taste like, making the pleasure of it last, but I will eat it now. Tell me about me little Bridget whilst I do. Anything – anything you can think of – so that I can picture her and what she's getting up to.'

'She does wonderful drawings. Here, she sent one for you. It's a cat playing with a ball.'

'Would you look at that? That's grand, so it is! Isn't she for taking after her pappy? He loved to draw, so he did. Oh, Issy . . .'

'I know, love. I feel your pain. Let's leave it, eh?'

'No, don't let me tears put you off. Tell me more. I can cope. I need the thoughts of her to get me through, so I do.'

Issy went on to say how Bridget loved the doll's house Tom made for her third birthday last February . . . *and now, here she was, my little babby, just four months off being four years old!* Issy's voice penetrated Bridie's thoughts once more: 'She likes swapping and changing the rooms around and living a little life in it with the corn-dollies.'

'Oh, bless the heart of her. Maybe if you have time you can start to teach her her letters, so that she can write to me?'

'I were coming to that next. Look on the back of the picture. She's written her name.'

''Tis clear as well! Oh, love, you are for doing a wonderful job. I can't find the words to thank you.'

'She is thanks enough; she brings us so much happiness. And you putting faith in us to take care of her; that means a lot.'

''Tis as you and Tom will make wonderful parents.'

'I know, and it's not for the want of practising that we're not as yet. It just doesn't seem to happen.'

'It will. One day it will surprise you. Just keep trying. Every dream is worth waiting for, as long as you're ready to catch it when it comes to you.'

'That's like the saying on your locket as I keep for you, ain't it? They're lovely words. Maybe one day they'll come true for you, love.'

'At times it's been for being a reality, but the curse that is in me has always destroyed it. Maybe it's right I should take me punishment. Maybe after that – if ever there is an end to it – things will be right for me.'

'You don't deserve punishment! You've been sinned against

and that has made you make some bad choices, but yes, love. It will come right, I know it will.'

Bridie bit into the bun. Even though it tasted like Heaven, it didn't dispel the dread in her that her life would never come right again.

Exhaustion, his constant companion of late, hit Andrew when he arrived home. The last six weeks had drained him, but now it was over. Not a bad result, all in all. The death sentence passed on Paddy Docherty had shocked him somewhat, but then – if he thought of how the bastard had done a lot of the dirty work for Seamus and of his involvement in murder, as well as the child abductions – he knew the man had received his just deserts.

Jameson took his coat. 'May I ask, sir, how it all went?'

'Of course.' Andrew gave a short account of the events, ending with, 'I think a whisky would go down well, please, Jameson, and will you let Wilson know I am home? Tell him to run a hot bath for me and prepare my morning suit. And ask Mrs Harvey's nurse to come to me, will you?' He took the letters off the platter offered to him. 'Thank you.'

As he waited for the nurse, the heaviness in him seemed to take on extra weight. He just didn't know how he would face losing Dvina. The doctor had warned him he should prepare himself for doing so, but, Christ, how did one prepare oneself for such a thing as that? How did you face losing the love of your life? Somehow, he knew this was his punishment.

Bridie came to his mind. It had been a shock to hear her call out her love for Seamus. She must feel like he did, having lost someone she loved – and for the second time, too! In that, he felt sorry for her, but her admission had confirmed that he'd been right: the two were in cahoots with each other, even if not on the day he'd suggested they were. And now he had no doubt that she'd gone willingly, despite what Isabella had heard.

Nothing about that afternoon had come out in their testimony. Just as Richard had said, neither the questions asked by the prosecution, nor those asked by the defence, had allowed it to. The jury had taken his version of events as the truth. It had shocked Andrew that the barrister for the defence hadn't pursued it. He could have made something of it in Seamus's favour, so there must have been some oiling of palms. And that probably accounted for Richard asking for more money. He'd said it was a one-time thing, and they could go back to their usual arrangement after the trial.

This was an arrangement that he must address. He couldn't go on making these regular payments. It wasn't that they hurt him financially, but he had to account for them somehow. He'd offer a settlement – a very generous amount; or maybe buy a house for Richard and Anna and put it on a long lease, then leave it to them, or their next of kin if they didn't outlive him. Yes, that could be the thing. They could sell their present home, which he knew they owned, as it had been part of Anna's inheritance. That would provide them with adequate funds to continue the lifestyle they'd taken up.

These thoughts settled him. It seemed he could put this whole sordid affair behind him at last. He sipped his whisky and thought of his beloved, Dvina. After losing their fifth child at seven months, Dvina had deteriorated before his very eyes. The weight had dropped off her and her body had been racked with sickness. A tumour in her womb had been diagnosed. A dread settled in him, but no. There was hope. *There had to be!*

A tap on the door made him jump. Jameson stood there announcing the nurse.

'Come in, Nurse. Please take a seat. How is Mrs Harvey?'

'She is comfortable, sir. She has slept most of the day.'

'Oh, that's good, very good . . .'

'No, it isn't, sir. Sorry, sir, but in my experience this peace does come just before . . . before . . . Anyway, I took the liberty of sending for the doctor earlier. He came, and he says the same. I'm sorry, sir.'

'Good God! Are you saying she is dying? Now? But I thought . . . I thought she might get better . . .'

'No, sir. I've never seen anyone get better when this takes them.'

'But the doctor said he thought the tumour had reduced.'

'It is difficult to say, but it's possible she has others inside, where we can't see them. She is fighting, trying to stay with you, sir, but . . .'

'Thank you, Nurse, I understand. I'll come up later and sit with her. You can take a break then. If she wakes, tell her I am home and will be with her shortly.'

'Yes, sir.'

Somehow he made his way to his bathroom. Once undressed, he dismissed Wilson. He resisted the hot water for a moment, dipping one toe in, then taking it out, and it took him a while to get fully in. When he did, he let the heat soothe him. When he relaxed his head back on the pillow Wilson always hung over the end of the bath, a huge sigh left his body. With it came the tears. And not just tears: huge sobs choked him, giving him no time to breathe in between. It felt to him as if his whole world was weeping, and everything had either tumbled or was about to tumble around him. *Oh God, Dvina really was going to die. She really is going to leave me. How am*

I to bear it, how? His body trembled with the exertion, but he couldn't stop. Didn't want to. The cathartic effect gave him some relief. When at last the wave of agony subsided, he rang his bell. Wilson came through the door in an instant. 'Have you been standing out there, Wilson?'

'Yes, sir. Forgive me, sir. I was worried about you. I heard you as I was putting your clothes away. I didn't mean to pry.'

'No, of course not. It was good of you to think of my safety. And to allow me that time to let out my grief. I suppose you and all the staff are aware of how things are with Mrs Harvey?'

'Yes, sir. I am deeply sorry.'

'Thank you. I'll just put on some pyjamas and my dressing coat, please, Wilson. Not the morning suit. And will you tell Cook I won't want dinner tonight, but if she could leave some soup ready for me and anyone who might arrive, perhaps you will serve us later.'

'Yes, sir.'

'Oh, and Wilson, I will need a letter delivering to my mother. And I don't want any callers, not tonight – only my mother if she is well enough to come over, and any medical people. Anyone else, just inform them that Mrs Harvey's death – well, it is imminent and only family should be here.'

'Very well, sir.'

Dealing with the practical things made him feel a bit better, giving him a sense that he could cope. Once he'd accomplished everything, he went through to Dvina.

She lay in a peaceful sleep, her hair spread over the white pillow. The care it had received over the last years had rendered it less wiry and had put a sheen on it. The sight of her gaunt face cut into his heart.

Telling the nurse to take an hour's break, he climbed onto

the bed and lay as close as he could to Dvina. Her eyes opened, and her voice was weak as she said, 'Is it done?'

'Yes, darling, the trial is over. Everything happened as Richard said it would.'

'And Br-Bridie?'

'She surprised us all by declaring her love for Seamus, though she didn't jeopardize the verdict, as it was just prior to her sentencing. She has been officially declared a pauper, so is committed to Deanhouse until such time as she can come up with fifty pounds.'

'P-pay the sum – clear the slate, darling.'

This shocked him. Had he never fooled her? Did she know what really went on?

'I can't do that, my dear. It will look so bad on me.'

'Pay it . . .'

'All right, now, don't worry. I'll see to it, as long as Bridie agrees to move away from this area. She should do so anyway, as there were threats made against her.' He had no intention of paying the fine, but he couldn't distress Dvina by not agreeing. A smile formed on her dry, cracked lips. It tore him in two. 'Dvina, my darling, I love you.'

'I . . . I love you, too.'

'I can't bear to lose you.'

'I know. Talk about something. T-talk about that day . . .'

He knew which day she meant, so he gently held her hand as he said, 'The sun was shining, and we had nothing particular to do. So we had a picnic sent to the riverside and rode our horses. We travelled over the fields, jumping small hedges and discovering routes we didn't know were there. Over the terrain we rode, laughing and calling out to one another. On the edge of the wood, where the stream runs across the road, we dismounted and walked hand-in-hand through the trees while our horses refreshed themselves, drinking from the clear water. We came across a clearing under a huge oak tree. We kissed. Then we made love. The sun dappled through the branches and danced on our naked bodies. It was a magical moment. Afterwards we rode the horses to the picnic site. We drank champagne and ate cucumber sandwiches. When we had finished, we swam naked in the cold water. It was a wonderful day and one I shall never forget, darling.'

She sighed. It was a happy-sounding sigh. Andrew waited, but she did not draw the breath back in. Her face relaxed, and the hand in his went limp.

'No, no! No, Dvina, don't go – please don't go . . .'

The door opened. 'Come on, Mr Harvey. Come along. She's no longer in pain now. That is something to be grateful for.'

'Yes, yes, it is, Nurse. Oh, God, Dvina . . .'

'Your mother is downstairs, sir. She'll help you. The doctor is with her. Will you have him informed?'

Getting off the bed, he walked round to the side where Dvina lay, and stroked her hair. In his mind he said, 'Goodbye, old thing. I'm sorry for the many times I hurt you. You rest in peace now. Rest in peace, my love.'

Outside the door, his body gave way and he slumped to his knees. His face was soaked with tears that he couldn't even feel coming from his eyes. How had it come about, this love he had for her? Hadn't she repulsed him in the beginning? Hadn't the marriage been just a convenience? Despite his questions, he knew how. He'd seen beyond the plain frumpiness; he'd seen the beauty of her, and he'd been given that beauty, the serene grace that was truly his Dvina. Many times he'd nearly lost her, but now he really had. He had lost something so precious. The love of his life . . . of his very soul.

30

Six years later – June 1893

The escape

Issy's concern for Bridie over the last six years had grown. Bridie had taken a while to accept her fate, and trying to help her do so had been a strain. The time after Seamus's execution had been the worst, but the following year Bridie began to settle, and conditions improved for her as she took on the role of nursing the sick. She loved the work, and the nature of it helped her to cope with how her life had turned out. But the drink had caused her downfall. How she got it, or afforded it, Issy dared not think, but – when caught – Bridie's punishment didn't fit her crime. Put on latrine duties, she had to sluice the buckets and the pans that the staff used at the hospital, as well as laundering the soiled linen from the wards, which was sometimes caked in excrement.

Working near the cesspit caused her to suffer bites from the vermin and insects around it. Her food rationing had dropped to the minimum level: workhouse broth twice a day.

The thin, sloppy stew contained no goodness, and the weight dropped off the bones of her.

Looking at her as she came through the door, Issy's heart lurched. Walking in small, shuffling steps, with her shawl wrapped around her, even though it was a warm day – the Bridie who was approaching her had aged. Her body was bent forward, her hair frizzed out in some places, but matted in others. Bridget, now nine years old, fidgeted by her side.

'Here she is. Here's Mammy.' Though it had been nearly a year since they had last visited, due to the restriction on the number of passes Bridie could now get, Bridget hadn't forgotten her mother. Issy felt grateful that her efforts to keep Bridie in the little girl's mind had paid off. The little hand tugged in hers. 'Can I go to Mammy, Aunt Issy? Can I?'

'Aye, you can, love, but don't rush at her. Hug her gently, as she's poorly at the moment.'

Watching them hold each other brought the tears to Issy's eyes, and she waited a while before she approached. When she did, shock held her rigid. Open sores covered Bridie's gaunt face, and her lovely eyes held pain. The lids, red and swollen, wept yellow matter, and her eyelashes were thick and crusted.

'Oh, Bridie, love.' Bridie didn't speak, but her head nodded and her dry lips formed a little smile. Issy took her arm. 'Come on, love, let's get to the cafe and get you a drink and something to eat, eh?'

They walked in silence, and Issy found it hard to think of something to say. Settling them both down in the cafe helped to give them a distraction. She picked up the menu. 'What would you like, Bridie love? They have a meat pie on. How about that, eh? It'll lie in yer, if their other stuff's owt to go by, and they don't skimp on the filling of pies.'

'Just a cup of tea will be doing me for now.'

'Alreet, love.' Issy ordered the tea from the counter. 'I got you one of those gingerbread men, Bridget – you like them. And a glass of milk.' Bridget didn't reply. Her eyes stared at Bridie and she clung on to her hand. This put a fear into Issy. *What if what Bridie had was catching?* She decided to leave it be. It would be cruel to do otherwise. Instead, she turned her attention to Bridie. 'Eeh, Bridie, you're not looking well, lass. Are you not eating? I know it's slop as they give you, but you need sommat to give you strength.'

'I can't eat. When I try it just comes back up.'

'Does a doctor come round?'

'Aye, the one who works in the hospital. He holds a surgery once a week, but 'tis the wrath of the matron you bring down on yourself if you line up to see him with complaints that could have been brought on by the conditions. She's a vixen, so she is. I'm after having enough on me plate without—'

The banging down of the tray on the table cut into Bridie's words. The waitress had a look of contempt in her eyes as she said, 'Scum! Drink your tea quick and get yourselves gone. We don't want the likes of you in here!'

This shocked Issy to the core. She felt her mouth drop open, then an anger came into her, but before she could speak Bridie said, 'No, Issy. No, don't be saying anything. It'll not be you she's wanting out. 'Tis because of me coming from workhouse.'

With the uniform Bridie had to wear, and the look of her, there was no mistaking where she came from. But that didn't give them the right . . .

'You've taken our money, and we're going to drink our tea as fast as we can, but not cos you say so; cos we don't stay in places where those as serve are kettles calling the pot black.

427

Look to yourself, lass, cos with a face like you've got, no one else will!'

Red in the face, the waitress stood there for a moment huffing and puffing, until she realized she had no retort. She turned and stomped back to the counter.

'Jumped-up little rat – how dare she? Her knickers must be too tight for her, is all I can say. Why else would she have such a pinched-up face?'

A pitiful sob came from Bridie. Issy was mortified. 'Eeh, Bridie, don't let it upset yer, love.'

'I have to get out, Issy, I have to.'

'No, love, drink your tea first. Sod Lady Muck. She can't hurt yer.'

'No, I'm meaning the workhouse. I have to get out, or me death will come sooner rather than later. I'm not for standing it any longer, Issy. I'm going out of me mind with it.'

'But how, love? I've tried talking to Mr Harvey, but he's a bitter man. He says all the things that you said about him killed his wife. Oh, I know that's not rational, and those who take on like that after a death of someone they love are just shifting the blame for their own guilt. Anyroad, he won't listen. And . . . well, I know it sounds cowardly, but when he said sommat to Tom about me asking, he indicated as he'd see the back of us if I said owt more on the subject. I can't risk it. I can't have Tom lose the job he loves.'

'Oh, Issy, I'd not want that. You and Tom have been for the saving of me, and me little Bridget. If you hadn't taken her in, she'd have not lasted in that place, and that would have ended me life, so it would. But would you help me, Issy? It has to be today. I have to take me Bridget and get a train to Sheffield. Beth is doing well now, so she is. She has a little business. She will take care of me. I was after asking her to visit me in me last letter, but I dare not tell her the truth of how I am, as those beggars are for reading mail before it leaves the place.'

'What are you asking of me, Bridie?'

'I'm just in need of the train fare. After you see me on the train, 'tis that you can go home. And when they come calling, tell them I never showed, so you were thinking they weren't for letting me out.'

'But what if they want to see Bridget?' Panic hit Issy. This was all so sudden that she couldn't think straight. Something inside of her told her she must do it, and that she was to find a way to, because as sure as the sun rises each morning, Bridie wouldn't last another year in that place. 'Look, I'm not saying no, Bridie. I just need time to mull it over. Let's go for a walk. Are you up to that, love? Maybe it will give you an appetite and we can find another cafe and have something to eat, eh?'

With the streets busy, they walked at a slow pace. People carrying shopping, others in their gardens hanging out washing, mothers calling out to their young 'uns and gossiping at gates – all of them had a look of disdain as they passed along, pulling young 'uns away from them. Some said 'Scum!' in low voices, and others just looked away. A gang of lads went by riding in an old pram. Their squeals of delight mixed with fear as it gathered pace down the hill, to the sound of a woman cursing and swearing at them. Bridie and Issy laughed at this, but Bridget remained quiet. Her eyes never left the ground.

'Are you for me, Issy? Will you be helping me?'

'Aye, I will. I just want to do it in a way as won't bring trouble down on my Tom.'

'I have another idea, and one as won't be after looking like

429

me disappearance was anything to do with you. I've had it a while, but I wasn't sure to put it to you or not. Sure, the last thing I want is to cause you problems, Issy.'

'Tell me of it and let's see, shall we?'

''Tis as I know this fella. He took his leave of the workhouse when his brother died. It seems in life his brother wouldn't help him, but in death he was for being generous and left the fortune he'd made in America to him. After he'd had his freedom, he went over the water back to Ireland, but there's only me knowing this. He always said he would, but then he had many plans that he was for doing with the money. That he actually went isn't something others know. He . . . he – well, he was for taking advantage of me and had a notion I'd be for going with him, so didn't he try to have me hand in marriage? I was sure tempted, though I wasn't for liking him. He showed me the tickets he had for us both. 'Tis that he would have paid me fine, but when I said I'd not go without me Bridget, he wasn't for having that. And I wasn't for going without her.'

'What are you thinking, Bridie? How can this man help us today?'

'You could be telling them as he waylaid us. They're after knowing the attraction he had for me. They punished him once. So if you were to describe him, tell them he snatched us and took us into a waiting cab, they'd be for believing you, Issy. They trust you. And they would never be after finding him, so it wouldn't matter that we're for incriminating him.'

It seemed Bridie had thought this plan through, but Issy had so many questions. 'But, Bridie, how would he know you had a day out today? I mean, he'd have to know that to plan his attack.'

'Cos it was arranged before he left. Sure, they will know

that and will think I was in on the planning, but they won't care. Yes, I'm committed there, but at the end of it all, it's not a prison. They'll report me for non-payment of me fine, and the law might think on doing something, but it isn't likely. Not if they think we have gone to Ireland.'

'Would they think that?'

'Sure they will. That or America. 'Tis as he never gave over talking of it. "The day of me release will be the day I buy me ticket out of this country," he was always telling them, and they would take him on, telling him it wasn't that easy; how he had to have papers and it would take a time. They're not for realizing money buys anything, and if you have it, you don't have to take the legal route to anything you need.'

'But won't they check? See if he has papers now and where he was going to? Or they might send a search out straight away to stop you – I mean, him – I mean, both of you, from leaving the country.'

'No, those who've gone before without release have just been left to their own luck. Their punishment is that the doors to every workhouse across the country are closed to them, which means very few are after leaving. Despite the hardship of the place, 'tis better than having to sleep rough and starving to your death. That is what folk in there are for saying, and I can relate to that. There is a sense of being secure in there.'

Issy's insides tore her in two. On the one hand, she wanted Bridie out of there; but on the other, she'd have to say good-bye to them both. Especially Bridget. How could she bear that? How? The child had filled a need in her – the void of a deep longing to have children of her own. It was a need that increased every time she helped to bring a babby into the world.

Dr Payne had examined her and found no reason why she

shouldn't conceive. And he couldn't put the blame on Tom, as he'd proved himself with his first wife. It just didn't happen. And it wasn't for want of trying: she and her Tom had a good time together. Their love was complete in every way, and a great source of comfort to her.

But she had to give thought to another worry niggling away at her and disturbing her thoughts – one she couldn't put on Bridie's shoulders, and one that had her and Tom between them watching Bridget every hour of the day and night. The Dochertys. They had made threats. It seemed to have taken a while for it to dawn on them that Bridget was an O'Hara. This coming into her head now made her mind up.

'I'll do it, Bridie. Come on, lass, I've some money on me. You sit there whilst I go into that shop over there. I'll buy you some decent clothes, then we'll go to that cafe next to it and I'll pay them to let you use the washroom and tidy yourself up. You'll only attract a lot of attention like you are.'

''Tis as I will never be able to thank you, Issy. You will stay in me prayers till me death, so you will.'

The train disappeared into the cloud of smoke swirling around Issy. She stood for a good five minutes after it had gone out of sight. An empty space opened up inside of her, threatening to fold her into it.

Never to see either of them again, because to do so would put them in danger of discovery; and never again to care for Bridget – wipe her tears, kiss her hurts better, cuddle her and play with her, tuck her up in bed and read to her. All of it gone. She'd known it must happen one day, but that day had seemed so far away that she'd not even thought to prepare herself for it. And how was she to face Tom? He'd never think of her doing something like this. Losing Bridget would rip his heart out.

She turned away. With her head down to hide her tears, Issy walked off the platform and made her way back to the workhouse. All the way there she prayed they would believe her story.

Andrew sat back in the carriage as the waiter served him a glass of champagne. He sipped it, savouring the flavour as he watched the countryside flash by. The noise of the train disturbed him somewhat, but he let it sweep over his head. Two hours to Bridlington.

His hand tapped his breast pocket. The crinkling sound of the letter reassured him. He'd had it so long without opening it – years, in fact. Coming as it did on the day Dvina died, it had been amongst some letters handed to him when he arrived home from the trial. He hadn't even attended to any of them until after her funeral. One of them came from his *other* solicitor. Inside, he'd been shocked to see an envelope with his name and address written on it in an uneducated hand He'd known it could only have come from one source: Lilly. He'd felt nothing other than a fear, caused by his predicament with Richard, of her possibly wanting to blackmail him. He'd even had to stay his hand from putting the letter in the bin. With pain attacking him on all fronts, he hadn't wanted any more. Instead, he'd dropped it into a drawer, and there it had lain for six years – years in which he'd suffered as he didn't know it was possible to do. *Dried-up* is how he'd describe himself. Functioning, but not taking part. Gnarled by guilt, cut in half by sorrow. Until a few weeks ago, when he'd gone for a long ride and the dawning of spring around him had touched his senses. Nothing had done that for so long. Clumps of golden daffodils, blossom on the hedgerows, budding trees, and birds busy collecting foliage to line their nests – the new life around him had infused him with new spirit.

On his return he'd had what the housewives would call a *spring clean*. He'd tidied his office – a domain none of the staff were allowed to enter, other than to flick a feather duster around and brush the carpet, under the scrutiny of Jameson.

It was then that he'd come across the letter. The thought of it containing blackmail seemed a silly idea now, because surely he would have heard from her again. Something – a spark more defining than the life infused by the signs of spring – had run through his veins as he'd scanned the short note. He'd read it so often since then that he knew every word, and how they were all written, bad spelling included:

> *Dear Andrew,*
>
> *Forgive me. I know I shuldn't write, but I had an urge to say thanks. Wot you did for me, I never thout anybody wuld do. I am doing well. Me busness is floudoing good. I have me reglar customers and I earn me money from it.*
>
> *I miss you, Andrew, and think of you a lot. Hope you can visit sometime, love Lilly xxx*

He'd written to her to ask her if the invitation still stood. His solicitor had taken the letter to Lilly and had waited for her reply. And so, here he was, with an excitement in his belly of the kind he'd forgotten the feeling of.

The thought of the possible blackmail that he'd tagged to Lilly's letter when he'd first received it brought Richard Nelton to his mind. The man's name conjured up disgust in him. The extortion had continued after the trial, as he'd supposed it would, despite Andrew being in mourning. Richard had even tried to force the settlement deal he'd proposed, and had managed to get a residence far superior to the one Andrew had in mind when the idea had first occurred to him. Now Richard and Anna held grand dinners and balls, living off his wife's inheritance and the proceeds of selling their not immodest previous home. Richard's career and social standing had risen in profile, leaving Andrew having to make polite overtures to them both, whilst seething under the surface. The worst was the knowing smile Richard always gave him whenever they met. Or maybe it was his conscience interpreting things that way. He didn't know.

Taking a good swallow of the champagne, he sighed. This train journey was turning from a pleasant experience of antici- pation into a nightmare of memories that he could do without raking over, as one thing led to another and Bridie Hadler now floated into his thoughts. For the first time ever, he felt a pang of guilt over her. He tried to bury it under the 'She killed my wife' heading, but it wouldn't go – not comfortably, as it always had before. Why now? Why had all these things come back to him, after lying dormant inside him for so long? All he wanted to do was to see Lilly and taste the pleasures of her once more, not relive moments from the worst phase of his life.

Perhaps it was time he helped Bridie leave that place. Oh God, he didn't want to feel like this! He didn't want to face the truth. He wiped the sweat from his brow. He'd sort it. He'd set Bridie up somewhere, like he had Lilly. But with a difference: he'd never, ever visit Bridie. Never, ever have her within his sight. He couldn't cope with that. He'd get all he needed from Lilly. If these few days he would spend with her went well, then he would make it a regular occurrence.

*

The sight of Lilly standing on the platform warmed him through. His surprise at how *normal* she looked must have shown on his face – normal in the sense of her dress, for she could have been any young woman waiting for someone to arrive. The old 'look' had gone – he hoped not forever. Her beautiful hair, so like Bridie's – *God! stop thinking of that woman!* – sat in a neat chignon on the back of her head. Her dress, of the kind ladies wore to travel, had a good cut to it. Grey in colour, its bustle was neat and not too big, and over it she wore a black velvet cloak fastened at the neck. Her smile pleased him. Gone were the yellowing teeth; she now sported clean, healthy-looking, gleaming white ones sitting evenly in pink gums.

'Andrew! Eeh, don't look at me like that, like you don't approve. I dressed special for you.'

The laugh left him before he could stop it. Her face fell, and he took hold of her and kissed her. 'I'm not laughing at you. More at myself, for expecting you to stand on this none-too-warm station in your corset, which is how you were used to greeting me.'

The soft giggle coming from her made him feel good. As did what she said next. 'Oh, Andrew, I still have some. I have one on, and it is much prettier. You'll get your treat later. In the meantime you must be hungry, love. I've booked us a table at one of the best places in town.'

This sounded so unlike Lilly. He'd never thought in a million years to do such a thing with her, but when they reached the venue – a beautiful hotel overlooking the sea, of a class that told of the kind of visitors it was used to – her reception there put him at ease. Everyone greeted her, and all treated her as if she was a lady. Lilly knew them all by name and had a word for each, asking after family and health, and introducing Andrew.

Sitting opposite her in a window seat, he didn't know where to begin, so many questions formed. 'Lilly, this is a surprise. I never expected . . .'

'I know you didn't, love, but this is what you did for me. I'm respected – one of the business folk of the town. I have a large tea shop here, and another in Scarborough. I don't pretend I'm sommat I'm not, and these folk appreciate that. And I've put sommat back an' all. Helped the community from me good fortune.'

'What about – well, your old business?'

'There ain't no *old business*, not to this lot there ain't. They think I had a bed-and-breakfast house in Leeds and made me money with it, and moved here to better me prospects. They also think I'm a widow. I've told them that you're a friend of me late husband's, on a visit.'

'Oh, I see. No renting a room then?'

If he could have snatched the words back, he would have done. Her hurt showed on her face, and he apologized quickly.

'Lilly, I'm sorry. I . . .'

'I know that's what you think of me, and why should you think different? But I've changed. I haven't been with a man since you. I'm waiting for someone who'll love me and give me a good life. Don't look so downcast – I'm still yours, and I want to – well, you know. In fact I can't wait, but I don't want you to think of me in that way only.'

'I promise I won't. I need you, Lilly, more than you can know. I need an uncomplicated love, like we had for one another in the old days. Oh, I know it did get complicated when I had to marry, but the feeling I had for you then is still in me now.'

'Thank you. I wanted to hear you say that, cos we did have sommat between us. I was sorry to hear about your wife. I didn't know until after I'd written. I was devastated when the solicitor came and told me. He works for me, you know, but he never discusses anything to do with you. He just told me that.'

'Well, there is a lot more that he could have told you. I think, Lilly, you may be shocked at some of it. But I need to talk it over with you. A lot happened, and I didn't behave well through it. I hope you won't mind listening, as I have no one else. No one I trust, like I do you.'

'Of course, love. Let's eat, then we can go back to my place. I'm set up nice, in me flat above the shop. It's reet big an' all, since I took over the two shops adjoining mine and had it all knocked through.'

After enjoying their lunch, they walked along the sea front. The breeze whipped around them. This small town had a beauty of its own. Its sandy beach, stretching to the sea, looked inviting. Andrew would have liked to take off his clothes and run along it, splashing into the water with the new feeling of abandonment he felt inside him.

Her apartment did take him aback, as did the tea rooms below. They stood on the promenade, their white frontage immaculate. The windows were draped in cream lace tied back with ribbons, and the red door had a shiny brass knocker. It all charmed him. He hadn't expected such a tasteful place.

They reached her apartment by way of stairs at the side of the building. And, as she'd described, it was large for the type of residence it was. Two reception rooms (a sitting room, a dining room), a kitchen and two bedrooms – not to mention a bathroom of the kind he'd only expect to see in houses of his own calibre. Everything shone, as though she'd spent hours preparing it. But she put paid to this notion when she said, 'I have a lady as does for me. I've no time for polishing and stuff – too much to do downstairs. Make yourself at home, love.'

She stood next to him, helping him out of his coat. Something held him back from taking her in his arms and drinking in the pleasure of her. He wanted to, with every fibre of him, but this was a different Lilly and he felt the need to let her take the lead. She did. She didn't immediately move away with his coat, but stood looking up at him. He held her gaze and saw the longing in her beautiful, huge, liquid-blue eyes. His face drew closer to hers, without him being conscious of the movement. Their lips met. He had no knowledge of this sensation with her, having never wanted to try it in the past. Now he savoured the sweet taste of her as he explored her mouth.

She melted into him, dropping his coat to the floor. They kissed until his lips felt tender. He eased her away from him. She parted her lips once more, her eyes half-closed. 'I knew that would be Heaven. Oh, Andrew, my love.'

The endearment shook him for a moment, but something kindled inside him: a strong feeling he couldn't deny. 'Lilly, Lilly, I've missed you.'

She took his hand and led him through to her bedroom. He had a feeling he'd not make it in time, as his veins rushed with the excitement of anticipation and his groin ached for release. That release came the moment he entered her. Nothing had gone before – no touching, no sensuous play. Lilly had recognized his need. She'd only taken the time to dispose of her ringed petticoat and bustle, before slipping off her bloomers and lying on her bed. They stayed locked together, clinging on as if they would never let go.

'I love you, Lilly. My own Lilly.'

Coming out of her, he undressed and slipped between the sheets. Lilly did the same, only more slowly than he had, playing the game she used to, of pretending to be an exotic dancer. Each item of clothing she peeled off revealed more of the beautiful, creamy, freckled skin he remembered. When she came to him and snuggled up to him, she had a softness about her. He hadn't noticed until she'd undressed, but she had put on weight. Now her limbs and stomach were rounded and no longer ribbed and bony. He snuggled into her. With the touch of her came a remembered feeling. Something he'd had with Dvina. He could think about her now without hurt or guilt. He could remember the divine contact with her body, how it cushioned him and enveloped him inside her. Lilly could give him that. She was already exploring him, heightening his expectation. This time there was no hurry. This time he could savour all of her.

The days had gone by too quickly. They were some of the happiest Andrew had spent in a long time. The only thing marring them had been when his heart suddenly went into a frenzy and he thought it would come out of his chest. Lilly had held him, soothed him, calmed him, and it had passed. Since then she had insisted on taking the active part in their lovemaking. Skilled as she was, this had enhanced his time with her, but the worry over his condition reared up in him once more. He vowed to see a specialist when he returned home.

'You will get that girl out of that place, won't you, Andrew? I can't bear to think of the poor lass, and didn't know you were capable of such a thing. But then again, I forget sometimes as you're one of them top-drawer types. You're not like us.'

They were taking a stroll along the sea front again, their last before he left. 'What does that mean? "Not like us." We do have feelings, you know.'

'Yes, but not like ours. Us common folk know how things *feel*, and it makes us care more. You have no idea. You're only wanting her out to ease your own mind, not to save her. How you could have put her in there in the first place beats me.'

'I wish I hadn't told you now.'

'No, don't wish that. Don't ever go back to having secrets and covering things up. It's not good for you. Everything about your life is in the open now.'

He knew what she meant, as he had unburdened himself to her and felt better for doing so, but he wouldn't agree everything was in the open. He'd still have to keep Lilly to himself. He couldn't be seen in public with her, or introduce her to his mother and sister. Come to that, he couldn't even introduce her to any of his friends, most of whom were more than acquainted with her in the old days. But they had sorted that out, too. He would come down every month to stay with Lilly for a few days.

To all of her friends, he'd be the shy man she had fallen in love with. And she had said they would allow for that. They wouldn't press her to introduce him. They'd just be happy she had someone at last. They'd accept that it couldn't go further for her, when she told them her story of him being a widower and having a small family and a business he couldn't leave. It was true, of course – at least the business part. As for not leaving his son, that didn't come into it. Now twelve years old and at boarding school, and spending most of his holidays with friends, Jeremy's routine wouldn't be upset by his father's comings and goings.

The fact of his own schedules being disturbed pleased

Andrew very much. He'd forgotten what it was like to look forward to something, and to have that something be time spent with the woman he loved made it very special. Because he did love Lilly. He loved her with an intensity that shook his emotions with the violence of a thunderstorm. It was a feeling he had thought he'd never experience again.

Issy trembled as she waited for Mr Harvey to speak. Her limbs had started to shake the moment Tom had told her that his master wanted to see her, and could she come to the house at two that day? Questions by the dozen had gone through her. Had the police contacted him? Would she be done for aiding and abetting? Oh, God, the implications of that!

Mr Harvey looked up at her. 'Isabella, this is awkward. I have had a change of heart over Bridie. I wanted to tell you, before I did anything. I have decided to pay her fine and set her and her child up. Will you act as intermediary between us? I have a solicitor who could do it, but I know you take her little girl to see her and have a good relationship with her, so you might be better suited to sort out what she wants or needs.'

Unable to speak, Issy swallowed hard. With him having been away, it seemed he hadn't heard yet that Bridget had gone. She hadn't expected him to come back a changed man, but she knew he had, as a certainty. Sitting before her wasn't the detached, despicable Mr Harvey, but the approachable, caring one she remembered from before everything happened between him and Bridie.

'Well, this is something new – Isabella Grantham having nothing to say!'

'I have plenty, Mr Harvey, but I can't say it, with the restriction of our positions.'

'Just relax, Isabella. I know you would love to give me a wagging of your tongue, but there are always two sides to every story. Very few people were innocent in this one, least of all Bridie Hadler.' He put up his hand to stay her protest. 'But that is as it may be. The fact is, I have had second thoughts and want to put right anything I did.'

'It . . . it's too late, sir!' She blurted out all that had happened on her visit last week, and his expression grew more incredulous with every word she uttered.

'Good God, Isabella! You could be in very deep trouble if they found out.'

'I know. I'm worried out of me mind, but I did it for the best. She'd have been dead soon if I hadn't, and then there were the threats on Bridget an' all.'

'Of course. That part of your story is appalling. I hadn't realized the state of things, nor am I going to tolerate the behaviour of the Dochertys any longer. But Bridie was committed there under the Poor Law. A law, Isabella – and a law you have broken by helping her to escape.'

Issy's stomach lurched. 'Please help me, Mr Harvey. I did it out of the goodness of me heart. I never meant to commit a crime.'

'Leave it with me. I have favours I can call in. I'll get my solicitor to look into it. Maybe if the fine is paid, that will be the end of it. How will Bridie live? Can you get help to her?'

'No, we parted for good. I don't know where in Sheffield she has gone, but I know she has a friend she sets great store by, and this friend will look after her. We thought it best that way. If I was to keep in contact, it might lead to her being caught. Best for Bridget an' all, as she can start a new life.'

'Yes, that must be heartbreaking for you. I'm very sorry. The child had been with you a long time.'

'Near on six years, but she'll forget. She's young enough to, so that's a good thing.'

'Yes.' He looked as if he wanted to say something else, but he didn't, other than that she should leave it with him. He would sort it out so that there would be no recriminations for her. Issy thanked him and left. She wished that was the end of the matter, but it wouldn't be. She'd never fill the hole left by little Bridget.

31

Two weeks later

Full circle

When Bridie opened her eyes and saw Beth sitting next to her bed, the intervening years were stripped away. 'Is it a correction convent I am in?'

'Eeh, Bridie. That was a long time ago. No, you're in hospital, love. You've been here a few days. You knocked on me door, after me not seeing you for years, and collapsed at me feet. They say you have sommat wrong inside – sommat they say as rat-bites cause. You're on the mend now, though, love.'

'Bridget?'

'She's at mine. She's a lovely little lass. She keeps talking about Aunt Issy and Uncle Tom, saying they did this and they did that, and how she were to sit down to her meals and eat proper. She's that old-fashioned with it.'

'Is it that she understands where her mammy is? I'm feared she may think I've run out on her.'

'No, she knows. She said she wants the doctors to make you better.'

'Thanks for having us, Beth. I had it in me that I could come to you.'

'Of course you can, love. But you might have arranged it!'

'It wasn't the way of it.' Bridie told her what had happened. 'Did you not get me letter? I hoped you would be visiting me and I could have sorted it out with you.'

'No. Last one I got were over a year ago. By, you've been through the mill, love.'

'I have, but 'tis as I had a lot of happiness with my Will.'

'I'm glad to hear of it. So, what plans have you? You know I still work at prostitution?'

'I'm not thinking of taking up the game again, Beth. I'll find something, so I will.'

'Aye, happen you will. Mind, it's not like the old days. We have clients come to the house now, me and a few other lasses. There's a room going, but it ain't reet for a young 'un. I'm onto a good thing, as I take a commission on every client the girls service. Well, me and Bruiser do.'

'Bruiser? You're not after associating with him, are you?'

'He's mellowed. He runs a good place. He has about five girls, same as me, and he has a nice house separate to that. If he sends me clients, he takes a cut, and the same other way around. It's business. Agnes has gone back to work for him. She says it ain't the same working for me, because we're mates. Besides, you wouldn't be here if it weren't for him helping me pay for it – you'd have been taken to the workhouse hospital up the road.'

'Bruiser helped me?' Bridie had forgotten the loyal friendships in the world that Beth and Bruiser still inhabited – the looking out for one another – but she hadn't forgotten the other side of it. In the workhouse she'd had plenty of the sick feeling of trading your body for your needs. Thinking of which, she asked,

'You haven't got a drop of gin on you, have you, Beth? Only I know you used to have a flask, to help you through it all. I've a powerful need of some. And I promise I'll think about the other, when it is as I am stronger.'

'Aye, I have. Not that I need it, but I thought on how it was in the days I did and knew you'd be suffering. You always mentioned your lack of it in your letters. But I'll tell you sommat, Bridie: you should think about giving it up. It's taking a toll on you, love. You're not half the woman you were. Here. But just a sup.'

Bridie lay back. The large gulp of gin heated her stomach and burned her throat. She swallowed hard as she felt a rejection of it rising, then her head swam into the hazy bliss she craved. 'Don't be saying that, Beth. You haven't the idea what it was like. I'll be getting better, putting flesh back on me bones, then sure enough I will think on giving up the gin.'

'I doubt you'll be here to do that by then, love. Listen to me: you have to stop. It's rotting your insides. I can tell by how yellow the whites of your eyes are. I've seen the signs many a time. And it's making you weak, so that you're not fighting off infections . . . No, Bridie, don't even try to protest. Have you looked in the mirror of late? Aw, don't cry, love. That was harsh of me, but you know I'm only thinking of you. Here, have me lace hanky. Oh, aye, I'm posh when I want to be, thou knows.'

Bridie dried her tears and smiled. Beth was so like Issy that when she was with one of them, it felt like being with the other. She was going to miss Issy. It made her heart-sore not even to have contact with her.

'Well, love, I have to go. A girl has to work, thou knows, and I have three appointments tonight . . .'

'Appointments? 'Tis a high world you're in, Beth.'

'I told you, it's all different now. No waiting on street corners. No hanging around outside bars to fleece the drunks. And if you have sommat about yer, you can make a packet. You'd do well, Bridie, if you could just get back some of what you were made of. Cos you were made for it in them days, love. Made for it.'

Beth laughed as she left, waving her hand until she reached the door. But Bridie didn't laugh. How often had she had those words said to her, and wasn't she for knowing they were her downfall?

Walking out of the hospital on legs that shook beneath her, Bridie couldn't believe it had been two weeks since she'd arrived there. She'd spent most of it asleep – a sleep through which she'd still felt her pain, so she didn't feel rested. Most of the infections on her skin had cleared up, but she had a weakness inside her. She hoped Beth would be waiting with the cab she'd promised her, and she hoped to God little Bridget would be with her. She didn't know if she could stand any more days without seeing her. Even though at times it had been a year in between visits in the past, just knowing they should now be together all the time made it more difficult.

As the doors closed behind her, Bridget dashed towards her. The silver locket swung from side to side around her neck, and her breathless little voice shouted, 'Mammy! Mammeee!'

For such a wee child, Bridget coped well with always meeting her mammy coming out of big buildings like this, and not knowing when she would see her again. Bridie supposed over the years she'd become used to it. She bent down and clung onto her. 'It's over now, me wee one. Mammy won't be for leaving you again.'

'Are you all better, Mammy?'

'I am, love, I am. Where's Aunty Beth?'

'She's not come. She had business. Mr Armitage brought me. He—'

'Bruiser!'

'Mammy . . . ?'

'Oh, don't be for taking any notice of your mammy. It was after being a surprise, that's all.'

'I bet it was. Well, well. Bridie O'Hara.'

'Hadler now, Bruiser. And that's not the only change I have in me.'

'I can see that. You're not half the beauty you were, but you'll do. We'll soon build you up. Come on. Cab won't wait all day.'

'Are you taking me to Beth's?'

'No, you're coming back to my house. A new girl started with us yesterday and took the last room we had in that house.'

'I'm not, Bruiser, I'm not for staying with you. Take me to Beth's – she'll be after sorting something for me.'

'Look, Bridie, Beth won't have yer. Not if you're not working. Them rooms mean money to her, and she likes to keep her pot full, so forget it. I've got a nice place – a big place. There's nowt goes on there, so the young 'un will be safe.'

'This isn't you thinking we can be together again?'

'Ha! Look at you! You might have had me heart at one time, love, but I go for something a bit classier these days. For old times' sake, well . . . I may have stepped over the line with you and owe you, but there's rooms at me house, food, warmth and somewhere for young 'un to play. That's all I'm offering. By, I'd not even put you out to earn money for me, the state you're in.'

Bridie cringed. What a mess she must be, to have the likes of Bruiser say something like that. Bridget cuddled up closer to her as she asked, 'Mammy, don't you want to go to Mr Armitage's house?'

The question gave her a pang of guilt. Did it matter what she wanted or didn't want? She had to put her wee Bridget first, so she replied, 'Yes, 'tis only me having a feeling we will be in the way.'

'You'll not. Me house is big enough for us not to meet, if we don't want to – and I'm of the mind not to, so you've nothing to worry over. I live on the outskirts in one of them posh houses – the suburbs they call it – and this cab is mine an' all. Ha, me and Beth have come a long way since your day, Bridie!'

'You and Beth, is it?'

'Business-only arrangement. But yes, we are partners, and it's working out well for the both of us.'

So much had changed. Fancy Beth letting this be the way of things, after what she knew Bruiser did! And Bruiser seemed different, too. She couldn't put her finger on how – kinder perhaps, with him thinking of Bridget, and sorry to the point of wanting to take her in. It didn't add up, but what choice had she? She had nowhere else to go, and she knew no one else who would take her in.

The house surprised her. Bruiser had told the truth of it being in the suburbs of Sheffield, but she hadn't expected it to be so grand. It stood on a hill, and when she stepped out of the cab she could see the town spread out below, with its smoking chimneys and dense array of buildings. Trees lined the street, and the houses stood back from the road. A three-storey building enclosed by a brick wall and a large, clanging gate, the house had a porch over the front door. The driveway, wide enough to accommodate the cab, had lawns on either side of it, and Bruiser told her there was a stable out the back for the horse.

The front door closed behind them, and they stood in a hallway with many doors leading off it and stairs to the right, with an ornate mahogany balustrade and a deep-red carpet. The house smelt of polish, giving her the idea that Bruiser must have staff working for him. She soon found she was right, as he explained, 'Your rooms are at the top. I've made you a bedroom each, and a sitting room. There's a bathroom up there – aye, and it has hot running water! I had it all put in last year. I have a lot of problems with the pipes still, but it works most of the time. There's a cook and a woman who does the cleaning, but besides that I do everything for meself. I'll show you round before I take you up.'

Each room had the style she remembered: elegant pieces of furniture at odds with each other, and at odds with his character. He pointed out his sitting room and his library, though she remembered he hadn't been able to read. Maybe he'd learned?

'Here is where I eat. It's not the room those who had the house before me used, but I like it. It's cosy. You can eat in here if you want, or you can have your meals upstairs. You'll see as you have a table in the sitting-room part.'

The room they stood in was much more like the kind she was used to, with its less-grand fireside chairs, scrubbed table and open fire with a kettle on the grate plate.

'That door there leads to the kitchen, so when Cook isn't here I can nip in and fill me kettle and have a pot of tea. I sometimes hold a fork with a crust on it over the fire and

451

make some toast. It's grand. Reet, let's take you up . . . Eeh, lass, are you all right?'

The dizzy feeling – her constant companion of late – made Bridie's body sway. She put her hand out to steady herself and caught hold of Bruiser's shirt. ''Tis as I am weak still. I'll just be sitting a minute . . .'

'Mammy?'

''Tis all right, wee one. Mammy is to take it easy for a while, that's all.'

'I should have thought on. Come on, I'll help you to the chair and make one of them pots of tea I were just telling you of.'

His strong arm came round her. It wasn't what she wanted to feel, but sure enough the strength of him protected her and trickled a warmth through her.

'Eeh, Bridie, lass, you're all skin and bone. Sit there and I'll look after you.'

The kindness of this spilled a tear down her cheek. Had she misremembered him? Blotting out the qualities he had in him, and thinking only of his bad traits?

The hot, sweet tea tasted good, but she wasn't for eating one of the buns he'd brought in. Her stomach couldn't take it.

'Cook makes these most days for me – she knows as I'm partial. Here, Bridget, you have one. It's a few hours till dinner.'

'Yes, me wee one, you be getting it down you,' Bridie said, in answer to Bridget's unspoken question.

'If I know you, Bridie, you'll be wanting a drop. Well, I've got you some. It's in your room. Only don't tell Beth; she's put me under a sentence of death if I give you more than a small sup a day.'

'Bruiser . . .'

'Leave it, lass. I know we need to have words. Clear the air, like. I did bad stuff to you, but I were provoked. We'll talk another day. We've plenty of time.'

'But 'tis as I cannot stay here, not for good. I'll be finding meself a job once I get me strength, and a room for me and Bridget, so I will. You need to be understanding as I'm not legally out, and if they have a mind, they may come looking. They're bound to find as I was once living in Sheffield and come looking here . . .'

'Well, I know different, lass. I went to pay your fine to the court in Leeds, but it had already been paid. There were papers there for you, releasing you of your pauper status. You have to pick them up if you want them, as they wouldn't let me have them.'

'What? Who . . .'

'Well, it must have been someone with a fat purse, cos not many could afford fifty quid.'

Andrew Harvey! It must have been him. But why?

'If I were you, I wouldn't give it much thought. It's done, and that's that. Anyroad, are you up to seeing your rooms now?'

'Yes, but is it there are two flights of stairs I have to go up?'

'Aye, come on. You can rest on the landing if you need to; I've some chairs there. Just as ornaments, usually, but they'll be of use to you.'

He took her arm and helped her up. Bridie couldn't be sure if its effect on her came from his closeness or for the want of someone to show her some kindness, but whatever it was, it felt good.

Each room showed signs of the thought he'd put into them:

nothing too posh, but everything to make her comfortable. He must have worked hard this last couple of weeks. The furniture looked new. He opened the wardrobe, and inside it hung various outfits. 'You'll find the chest over there has other items you need, and there's stuff for Bridget in her room an' all. Beth did the choosing of it all, and she chipped in to pay for them. She said not to get you too many, as she's a mind you'll fill out. Some of them might be on the big side as it is.'

How is it that the spirit can take cruelty better than kindness, she wondered, as this thought brought her to tears once more.

'They're what Aunt Issy calls joyful tears, Mr Armitage. Me mammy often sheds them.'

'Well, that's good then, Bridget. Now, you go along to your room and see what Aunt Beth has done for you. She listened, thou knows, when you told her about all the stuff you had – the toys and cuddly rag dolls. She said she hopes this makes up some for having to leave them behind.'

Bridie let Bruiser help her to the bed. He unlaced her boots and took them off, then eased her cloak from her. 'Here, I'll do that,' he said as she'd stayed his hand at her bodice. 'There's nowt I haven't seen before.' With everything but her shift removed, he lifted her legs onto the bed and pulled the cover over her. 'You get some rest, Bridie. I've to go out, but I won't be long. Bridget has plenty to occupy her. Oh, I hid the doings at the bottom of the chest. Shall I get you some?'

'Yes, please. 'Tis as it will help to rest the bones of me. And, Bruiser – thanks. I'm not deserving of all this.'

'Well, if I'd known of your plight before, I'd have done sommat, but as it was, Beth weren't for telling me as she even knew where you were. I'm mad at her for that. She only mentioned you after you turned up, cos she had no choice then.'

'Don't be mad. She was only for being loyal to me.'

'Well, that's sommat, you forgiving her. Cos she kept you in that place longer than she needed to. She could have coughed up the fine herself – well, at least asked for a loan or sommat. It beggars belief she didn't.'

When he'd gone, Bridie thought about this. *Why – why hadn't Beth been for doing something for me? Her saying she hadn't got many of me letters didn't seem excuse enough, and why wasn't she been for visiting me, even?*

She didn't like these thoughts and decided to leave them be. Instead, she took a large gulp of the good gin that Bruiser had left by her bed and tried to take in her new circumstances, for as sure as it was that the little Jesus lived in Heaven, she'd fallen on her feet. But then, why was it she was for thinking that, when all she'd done was come back near to the beginning again?

EPILOGUE
Life Does as Life Did
1899–1900

32

Early May 1899

Issy's news

Issy lifted her head. Her body shuddered. She hadn't been able to stop the vomit from billowing from her. The air she'd come out for hadn't helped, and the dizzy feeling persisted. But none of it – not even the vile taste in her mouth – could stop her smiling. *At last! At last I have Tom's babby inside of me.*

Going inside, she picked up the bucket and went back into the front garden to swill away her mess. The time for her bleeding had passed three weeks ago or more, and then, what with the morning sickness and the swelling of her breasts – well, all the signs were there. She just needed a couple of months to go by before the doctor could confirm it, and then she would tell Tom. She couldn't wait. In the meantime, she had to hold down the nausea until after he'd gone to work each day – not an easy thing to do.

Gertie turned into the lane, her little lad clinging onto her hand. No doubt she'd be looking for a brew and a good gossip, but there didn't seem anything to talk about at the moment. Not anything to do with her own news, that was certain, but she could give her a few snippets from the big house that Tom had told her of. Funny how most of their entertainment these days centred on what happened up there. Even the Irish didn't give them much to gossip over any more – they had all settled down after the hanging of Seamus Finney and Paddy Docherty, especially after Mr Harvey got rid of the rest of the Docherty clan. She was glad about this, as the Irish were lovely folk and had at last found their place in the community.

The news from Tom, though, centred on Master Jeremy being in conflict with his da about his future: Jeremy wanted to go into the Army, and his da wanted him to go to Oxford.

Jeremy had turned into a fine young man. At eighteen he stood as tall as his father and almost as tall as Tom. And handsome! Eeh, she'd never seen one better. He took after his father in his looks, though she thought Jeremy had the edge. But his nature was all Miss Dvina's – she shone through him. Jeremy loved to spend time in the stables, helping Tom do his chores and asking him for advice about his future. Tom had tried to make him see his da's point of view, telling him to listen to his father and try and come up with a compromise.

Mr Harvey wanted to hand over to his son, as his heart condition made running the mine very difficult for him. He tired easily. Though, she thought, Mr Harvey always seemed to have the energy to go to his fancy woman, for over the years she'd become certain that this was the reason for his regular trips away every month.

Tom loved Master Jeremy, and had done since the boy had been no higher than his knee. It broke his heart to hear the lad still ask if Tom remembered when his mama had done this or that. 'She should be here, Issy,' Tom would say to her. 'It ain't fair; she worked hard to bring at least one of her children into the world, and for her not to see him grow up . . .'

Thinking of this put a fear into her. She'd seen so many lost in childbirth or taken with some disease or other – what if it happened to her? She could think of nothing as sad as that, and sent up a prayer for her babby's safe delivery.

'Look, Jeremy, I understand the need in you for a military life. After all, you will be taking after your great-grandfather and his father before him, not to mention your namesake – my dear stepbrother. But what about the mine? I really thought you would want to get into the workings of it. You will have to at some stage, and in the not too distant future.'

'I know, which is why I thought I could join up now, do at least ten years in the Army, then come home and learn the ropes from you.'

'But don't you need a degree to be an officer?'

'I wouldn't think so. I'd be sure to get a commission, especially with Great-grandfather being a general in his day. But all right, Father. I'll do it your way, but only a two-year course and something to do with engineering or maths. Something useful. I couldn't stand taking law, or reading any subject just to say I've been to the top university.'

Andrew was flooded with relief. 'Well done, my boy. Very sensible. Of course, you may be like me and do your engineering, then go on to do something else.'

'I won't, Father. I want a military career. It is in my blood. I was never happier at school than when I joined the boys' army.'

'Well, look, I don't want to make you unhappy. Let's

compromise: you apply for a commission and, if you get it, all well and good. If not, you go down the route I want you to take. I can't say fairer than that, can I?'

'Oh, Father, thank you. Thank you so much. Whatever made you change your mind so suddenly?'

Andrew took the hand his son offered, but a sudden rush of emotion had him reach out and pull the boy to him. The hug was reciprocated, but after a moment they drew apart. 'I don't know, I must have had a weak moment.' To cover up the awkwardness of it all, he sought to change the subject. 'Anyway, son, are you taking up the invitation to go and stay in York and attend the ball Lord and Lady Meriden are giving for their daughter, Laura?'

'I suppose I must, but I'm not keen on all of this social stuff. These balls seem more like cattle markets to me, with all the mothers trying to bag the best catch for their daughters. But this one should be fun. Gregory Thomas is going.'

'I used to feel like that, but you know I came round to thinking it isn't a bad system. It helps us to meet our own kind. I have an invitation, but you won't want me tagging along, so I think I will go to Bridlington for the weekend. Anyway, if Laura has turned out as pretty as her sister Daphne, you will have a treat and will bray with the rest of them, my boy.'

'Good Lord, Father, I'll do no such thing! I'm too young anyway, and not yet earning a living.'

'Don't think that will matter – your prospects are the best in this county, and all the surrounding counties, you can bet. This is a forerunner to next year. I hear Laura will have a Season in London, hosted by her aunt, and is looking at all the young men in this area whom she might think to invite. Why do you think you've been asked? Anyway, you can stay with your Aunt Agatha, if you have a mind to attend any of the events in London next year. I will write to her to pave the way for you for next Easter.'

'No, Father, please don't waste your time doing any such thing. I won't be attending any of these stupid coming-out parties; they are just not my thing. Besides, I'm not for sale, so they can go and fish elsewhere. I don't want to marry for at least another ten years.'

Just like himself, Andrew thought. *Even then I hadn't been ready, but when I think of the wasted years* . . . 'Well, we'll see. Whatever you decide, your mother would be so proud of you – as I am, Jeremy. Good luck with the Army thing, old boy. I was wrong to protest. You shouldn't put off anything that you want to do. I wasted a lot of years before I married your mother, and she lived only a few miles from me. I just didn't see what a gem she was. Don't put too much score on compartmentalizing your life. Just let things happen.'

Jeremy gave him a funny look, but didn't reply. *Was he thinking I am referring to my frequent sojourns away from the house and business?* Funny, but Jeremy had never asked about his visits to Bridlington, or ever asked to accompany him. The thought had often visited Andrew over the years: *Had he guessed or not? Had he picked up on any of the rumours that surely flew around their society?* One day he would tell him – not everything, but he'd want Jeremy to let Lilly know, if anything ever befell him. He supposed he'd also have to come clean about the other affair: *There was always someone gossiping about it all.* For a moment he thought of Bridie, and how she had fared in the end. Something in him hoped she had done all right.

33

Early May 1899

Heavenly Love

Bridget sat on the step of the terraced house, one of rows upon rows that were all the same. The houses were run-down, as the owners of the steel works did no repairs, but the proud tenants did their best: windows shone, curtains were pristine and steps were scrubbed every day. These were the steel workers – the folk who thought themselves better than those who mined the coal, although Bridget couldn't understand the difference. Bobby, her boyfriend, worked down the pit, and his mammy kept a lovely home, as did most of her neighbours. The steel men drank just as heavily as the miners, and their work rendered them as dirty and sweaty as each other. But there was a divide nonetheless, regardless of her feelings about it.

She looked up towards the end of the cobbled street. Soon Mr Armitage – as she still thought of him, even though he had been her mammy's husband for near six years – would be home. And where had Bert got to? At five years old, her little half-brother got into more scrapes than any lad she knew, and the beatings he took from his da only made him more stubborn. But she adored him and would do anything to shield him.

Today she held out more hope of Bert coming home first, this being a Saturday. Mr Armitage would go straight to the pub, and if he got into a card game he wouldn't be home until late – whereas Bert's empty stomach would lead him back long before then.

A noise – a familiar moan – had her standing up and going back inside. Her mammy, flat out on the sofa, had roused, calling, 'Will you pass me the bottle, Bridget? What is it with you, forever putting it out of me reach?'

'Mammy, you've had enough. Go back to sleep. It'll do you good to rest some more.'

'No, 'tis as I need it, Bridget.'

'Oh, Mammy, Mammy . . .'

The sight of her mother tore at her heart. Bloated to twice the size she used to be, her hair was now a wiry, dull ginger peppered with grey, and her face was blotched with swollen blue veins. Her eyes, once a turquoise-blue, were now lifeless dark pools in a yellow bed, and her teeth had decayed to the point where many had fallen out. As tears ran down the mottled skin of her cheeks, Bridget gave in.

'Just a sup, Mammy, no more. Then I'll give you a wash and make you a pot of tea, eh?'

'Aye, if that's you saying so. Oh, Bridget, will you ever be at forgiving me? I thought I did the right thing marrying him. Sure he was well set up, wasn't he? And he said his love for me hadn't ever died and . . .'

'Hush, Mammy, don't go over it again. It causes you pain. You didn't do wrong; you weren't to know he'd turn out how he has. Oh, I know you'd said this had happened before – him losing everything to his gambling habits and having to go back to the steel – but he had Aunt Beth this time, and that gave you faith in him.'

'Poor Aunt Beth, God love her. Is it that you can remember the fight we had? Me and Aunt Beth? I wasn't for knowing she'd carried a torch for Bruiser. I didn't ever think me and her could fall out over anything, but her feeling for him was strong and is the reason she wasn't for helping me out of the workhouse.'

'Don't think of those days, Mammy. Everything sorted itself out. In the end, how he turned out, Beth were reet glad as you had him and not her.'

'I know, and it's a shame altogether, her getting that poxy disease. Beth, of all people. Wasn't she for only going with the rich ones as well? But then, they're for having no conscience. The one as gave it to her knew he had syphilis, I don't have a doubt of that. Wouldn't go with his own wife, but put it up a whore without a second thought, so he did.'

'Don't talk like that, Mammy, I don't like it. I hate the business you and Beth were in.'

'No more than me, me wee love, but didn't Bruiser force me back into it? I couldn't take any more of his beatings, Bridget. Be for saying as you forgive me.'

'Mammy, there's nothing to forgive. I have your love and protection, and that's enough. Oh, yes, I've heard him saying I'm ripe and should be bringing in more than the shop work can give me, and I know what he means. No one could live around it all, like I have, and not understand. I may have only just turned fifteen, but I've knowledge them twice me age haven't got, so—'

A sob from her mother stopped her flow. 'Oh, Mammy, don't take on. Here, take another sup, then that's it for today.'

Once she'd gulped it down, Bridie showed some control again. 'Will you go and see Aunt Beth in that sanatorium soon, Bridget? Will you see how she is? I'm worried her time is near. No one is for living that illness out.'

'I will, but she didn't know me last time, though she looked pleased as there was someone especially for her. Now the kettle's on the boil. I'll fill a bowl and then I'll make a pot with the rest.'

As she went about the task of washing her mother, bathing her open sores, gently squeezing pus out of her ulcers, dusting her in powder and helping her to put on a clean shift, Bridget didn't pursue the conversation. She only murmured words of comfort and encouragement to help her mother through the pain of it all.

Some days she didn't know how she coped with it, but somehow she got through. She'd been of good intelligence in her schooling, and she'd done well in her exams, gaining high enough marks to have gone on to better things. But money was always tight and the needs of her mammy had held her back, so she worked in the shop on the corner, under the leering eyes of Mr Bartram – a man who wasn't what she had first thought. The impression he and his wife had given was of a wonderful, sweet couple who adored each other, but Mr Bartram was cruel in subtle ways. He'd undermine Mrs Bartram, make a fool of her, and she'd cover up by giggling, to make it look like it was just a joke. But when Bridget was in their company for such long hours, this smokescreen wore thin and the real threat behind it was laid bare. Because of this threat, she couldn't speak of her fear of being alone with him to anyone – they would never believe her.

A lovely but timid woman, Mrs Bartram had a gentle heart and a kindness in her ways. Bridget loved her very much, and it was shocking to her now to realize that as a little girl she had loved Mr Bartram, too. Now she feared him – not because she thought he'd be violent towards her, but because there was something else present that she couldn't put a name to.

Unbeknown to her husband, Mrs Bartram often slipped a few items into Bridget's bag. 'See you and young Bert eat these,' she'd say of the apples and berries. 'They'll give you some goodness.' And every day, when they had a minute, she'd make Bridget take a teaspoon of disgusting-tasting oily liquid, saying, 'Keep your bones strong, lass, this will, but don't tell him I give it you. He'd go mad.' The accompanying little nod told Bridget that Mrs Bartram suspected she knew the real situation, and somehow it seemed like a conspiracy between them. *Him going mad* meant her husband beating her, as Bridget had discovered he often did. She'd seen the bruises by accident on a couple of occasions, and she'd heard the odd muffled cry when she'd been in the shop while they were in the storeroom at the back.

When her mammy spoke, she felt disorientated for a moment and had to bring her mind back to the cause of it: her very real worry over her sick mother.

'Bridget, I have something I have to say. 'Tis to do with what you were just saying about him, and how he sees you. When I'm gone . . .'

'Mammy, no! I won't listen to you. You're going to get better. Please, Mammy, don't give up.'

'I'll stay as long as the good Lord allows, but I know in meself, me wee love, as he's getting ready to take me. Now, whish, don't take on. I have to say things to you. It is as you say Bruiser is for trying to make money off you. When it happens – the minute I let go of me last breath – get out. Take Bert with you, and go back to Issy. Don't be stopping for me funeral, or to take stuff with you. Both of you, get dressed in two sets of clothing, so you'll not be carrying bags, and say as you are wanting to go for a walk together. Will you do it, Bridget, will you?'

'Mammy, I can't talk of this . . .'

'Please, Bridget, let me go to me next life with a peace inside me.'

'What're you two cooking up? It don't smell like it's me dinner.' Bruiser Armitage suddenly appeared in the open doorway, looking at Bridget. 'You lazy cow, you'll feel the back of me hand one of these days! Look at this mess.'

Bridget held herself tense. *How much had he heard? Had he been standing by the outside, having a smoke before he came in?* She thought this likely, as he'd seemed to turn into the open door as if he'd just rolled off the wall.

'Will you be for leaving the girl alone, Bruiser. She's just finished seeing to me . . .'

'Shut your gob, you pus-ridden swine!' His hand was raised.

'No! No, don't hit her, Mr Armitage, don't.'

'Get out of me way, you scheming bugger!'

The edge of the table dug into her ribs as the shove he gave Bridget sent her flying. Her breath caught in her lungs as his vicious swipe brought blood spurting from her mammy's nose and mouth, and what he said told of him hearing everything. 'Plotting to leave me high and dry, eh? After all I did for you. Well, you can go to your maker any time you like. That's if he'll have you, cos I can't wait to get the smell of you out of me house. In fact, you can get out of it now!'

Bridget gasped. He'd grabbed her mammy's hair and dragged her off the couch. She ran at him, kicking and scratching him, tearing his shirt, biting his arm. He'd let go of her mammy and now hit out at her. Punches ricocheted through the very being of her. One landed on her jaw, and a curtain came over the pain, black and suffocating, taking her to the ground.

*

'Bridgee, Bridgee . . . Oh, Ma, Ma . . .'

Bert's sobs penetrated the haze. As she opened her eyes, Bridget became aware of the wet, sticky substance she lay in, and saw her mammy lying next to her with her eyes closed. Looking up into Bert's anguished face, she tried to keep her voice calm. 'Help me, Bert, help me up.'

Small as he was, he managed to get her to a standing position. Swaying on unsteady legs and with her vision making stationary objects seem to be made of jelly, she bent over her mammy. 'She's still breathing. Oh God, help us. Mammy, come on, Mammy . . .'

'Shall I get some water, Bridgee? That's how they bring the bare-fisters round.'

Nodding at him to do so, she wondered where he'd seen such things, but she hadn't the inclination to ask. 'Good, lad, be quick. You'll have to get it from the well, as I used the last to wash Mammy with.'

The strength of him showed in the way Bert heaved the full bucket back into the room. She smiled at him as he told her to move out of the way so he could chuck it at their mammy. 'No, Bert, the shock will kill her. Just get a cloth – that's right. Now soak it and dab Mammy with it.' She couldn't move her arm to do it herself.

A groan gave her hope. She grabbed the back of a chair and put all her weight on it, to ease the pain in her ribs, as she cried out, trying to get through, 'Mammy, Mammy! Open your eyes, Mammy . . .'

Another small sound gave further hope.

'Wipe the blood away from Mammy's eyes and nose, Bert. That's right. Gently, it's sore. Good lad. Open your eyes, Mammy. Come on.'

Bridie heard her daughter's voice echoing through what

felt like layers of silt coating her mind, saying, 'It's all right, Mammy. You're going to be all right.' Then she heard Bridget speak to someone else. 'Fetch Mr Stevenson. Go on, lad, run. He'll help us get Mammy off the floor.'

Bert? Was she talking to Bert?

Bridget's next words confirmed that she was. 'Don't be afraid, Mammy. Bert won't be long, and I know Mr Stevenson is in. I saw him come home.'

Bridie tried a smile to reassure Bridget, but her jaw seemed to just hang and wouldn't do her bidding. She felt cold, so cold . . .

Someone picked her up. Her body floated; her stomach heaved. 'There you go, Bridie. By, that brute! He'll have his comeuppance one of these days. Eeh, look at you, an all, Bridget, love. Has that bastard had a go at you as well? Eeh, lass, I should send Bert for the doctor. Go on.'

'I can't, I haven't the money. I have to tip up everything I earn to Mr Armitage, and Mammy hasn't any.'

'Don't worry about that. Mrs Stevenson has some jams, so we'll pay the doctor with them.'

'Ta, Mr Stevenson. I have some tarts in the pantry an' all. Some as I made from the jam Mrs Stevenson gave me yesterday. I'll see if he'll take them and not put anything on the slate as owing.'

It all went on without Bridie taking any part, but she was glad that Bridget had called upon their kindly neighbour. He would make things right. This thought swam away from her; she didn't seem able to hold onto anything. Everything hovered above her in a different place from where she was.

'Oh, Mammy, if you'll just get better from this, we'll get away from here. I'll make you better from the drink. We'll go back to Breckton, like you said me and Bert should, and we'll find Aunt Issy, we will. She'll help us.' Bridget's voice swirled into the mist rolling towards her.

When the mist enclosed her completely, Bridie was looking through it along the muddy lane leading to her childhood home. Her mammy stood at the door of their cottage, beckoning to her. She looked beautiful, almost transparent, with an aura around her. She held a baby. *Eric?* Her mammy nodded and pointed across to the field, where Will stood. *Oh, Will, me love.* He waved to her to come to him. She went to run, but there wasn't any weight to her body. The air swished around her, under her, lifting her and stopping her progress. Will's face faded into a curl of smoke. When it cleared, another face looked at her. *Seamus! 'Tis Seamus!* He sat on the steps of his Vardo, watching her. He smiled. She waved, and he waved back, but a sadness clogged her chest. A voice – not of the world she now inhabited, but in the room below her – came droning through to her. 'Bridie, Bridie, my child, is it that you repent of your sins?' She could only nod.

Tinkling like a soft bell, her name – 'Bridie, Bridie' – compelled her to look away from Seamus and once more into the loving eyes of her mammy. Still she held the babby. A shape behind became clearer. *Will!* A glorious light beamed down, lighting up the three of them. Ecstasy born of wondrous joy filled her. 'Oh, Will, Mammy. I'm coming.' Music filled the air, played on a mouth organ, and took her into its depth. She began to dance, twirling this way and that. Mammy and Will laughed. She looked for Seamus, but he'd gone. She didn't mind. She went into Will's arms and knew he was for being the real love of her life and her eternal partner in death.

'Aw, God love her, doesn't she have the peace on her at last? Look at her, Bridget. She looks . . . serene. Yes, that is the word

I would use. From the moment she repented and took the Host into her mouth, she was for resting. God is good, so He is.'

'Yes, Father.'

The doctor had sent for the priest as soon as he'd entered the house. Bridget looked into her mammy's face and saw what the priest had seen. Perhaps this was the most beautiful she'd ever seen her mammy look. She didn't look anything like her picture in the locket, or what Bridget could just about remember of years past, but there was a beauty in her expression. Father Patrick had got it just right when he'd said 'serene'.

Somehow, in the moment of her mammy's death, Bridget couldn't cry and call for her not to leave, as she'd imagined she would. Inside her, she held a calm that not even the pain of her injuries could penetrate. When the priest asked, 'Will you come and see me when you have things sorted, Bridget, so we can talk about the funeral Mass?' she just answered, 'Yes, Father.'

How is it I can behave as if nothing has happened? Why is nothing touching me?

'Well, Bridget, I'll leave you now. I'll be after telling Bert and offering him comfort on me way out, as I sent him outside before I started the Last Rites. And I'll call in on the undertakers on me way home.'

She hadn't noticed that Bert had left the room, or been aware of the priest getting him out of the way. 'Thank you, Father. What about Mr Armitage? Who will tell him?'

'The police, I shouldn't wonder.' This, from the doctor, was the first time he'd spoken in a while. He'd stepped forward and checked her mammy just after the last sigh left her, and had then busied himself scribbling on a form. Now, as he handed her the piece of paper, he said, 'There, that's the death certified. You will have to register it at the Town Hall tomorrow, Bridget. I will report what has happened to the police in Leeds. I'll send a message to them.'

'Do you have to, Doctor? Can't we leave it be? It will only make things worse.'

'Well, it's up to you. You will have to be the one who presses charges, as your mother can't. I can't really say whether the blow to her face brought her death on sooner, but I knew she was dying. I have certified her death now and put the cause, so they wouldn't look into it any further. Perhaps you're right. Best leave it as it is.'

Bridget felt glad at this. She knew the doctor hated his time being taken up at inquests, so he always tried to avoid them. Even when Jack Cooper died suddenly – and him only a middle-aged man – it was said that the doctor put it down to natural causes and told the family to say he had been treating him, if asked. Afraid of the cost of everything, they had accepted this. With him agreeing now to let things be, her mammy could lie in peace and no recriminations or police activity would disturb that. Besides, she had to think of herself and Bert. Knowing her mammy had tried to make a plan for them to leave him had made Mr Armitage angry enough, without him thinking she'd testify against him.

'Now, Bridget. Let me take a look at you.'

The examining and cleaning of her wounds went on without Bridget giving it her attention or taking heed of the extra pain it caused.

'Well, you're going to have a sore body for a couple of days, and you will no doubt come out in more than a few bruises, but there's no real injury. Nothing is broken. Your arm has taken the worst of it – keep it moving as much as you can, or you could have trouble with it. Now, don't worry about my bill. That is something I'll get out of Mr Armitage.

I have enough to threaten him with to make him pay a weekly sum. He deserves that at least.' Despite this, the doctor took the jam Mr Stevenson had left on the table and the tarts she'd put next to them.

After they had all left, Bridget stood with Bert. His little body shook with sobs. 'Can I touch her, Bridgee?'

'Aye, let's hold her hand, eh?'

They stood in silence holding their mammy's hand. Tears ran down Bert's face, and there was fear in his eyes when he looked up at her. 'You won't leave me, will you, Bridgee? I'll not stay here without you.'

'No. If I leave, I'll take you with me.'

The thought of them leaving and going to Issy hadn't died in her. She'd try to sort it. Maybe she could give a penny a week to Mrs Bartram to keep for her, until she had enough for the fare. But she would write to Issy – that would be best. A lot of obstacles presented themselves as she thought it through, but she remembered Issy saying, 'You shouldn't meet trouble halfway, as it may not be travelling your road.' In the meantime she'd have to stay and fight her corner. Stand up to her brute of a stepfather.

A knock on the door interrupted her thoughts. Two men stood there dressed in long black frock-coats. 'We've come for the body, Miss.'

As the door creaked shut behind them, the house took on the emptiness of a shell. Her mammy encased in a box, carried out to a cart – gone. *Oh, Mammy, no!* Her body gave way. She sank down on the settle and wept. Never had she felt so alone.

'Don't cry, Bridgee. You said as Ma wouldn't want us to cry.'

'No, she wouldn't. She always wanted us to be happy.' Somehow, having to be strong for Bert helped her to feel so many years older than fifteen. She'd get through somehow, she would.

34

May 1899

Promises broken

Jeremy held the letter to his heart for a moment. Two of the envelopes in today's post had his name on – both he'd waited anxiously for, but the pretty-edged one written in a feminine hand drew his immediate attention. He hoped it wasn't just an invitation. He so wanted to hear from *her*.

He'd attended the spring ball at her house. He'd walked in still feeling he didn't belong there, and had drunk a large glass of champagne to help get him through it. Then Laura was announced. He looked up out of curiosity, and something hit him in the pit of his stomach – nothing tangible, just a feeling he'd never experienced before. But then, he'd never seen anyone as beautiful before. Her perfect face stunned him. Her eyes – round, big and the deepest velvety-blue colour he could imagine – drew him into her gaze. There was a glossy sheen to her jet-black hair as it caught the light, and her creamy skin glowed. The room seemed to empty, and yet it was full of people. Their voices had taken on a distant hum. He waited, holding his breath as she glided towards him and offered her hand. Taking it in his, he held it to his lips. He hadn't ever wanted to let go of it. They had danced almost every dance, and he'd seen off those demanding their turn, even though they had her promise marked on their card.

All too soon it had ended, but they had written to each other ever since – at least ten letters each in the month that had passed. He opened this latest one with care, slicing the paper knife under the flap and lifting it, letting the anticipation grow inside him. It was an invitation, but around it she had wrapped a note. She spoke of her horse, her long days shopping for her outfits and the fittings she had to attend. How she longed for this year to come to a close so that all the formalities were out of the way and her mother and father would start to take the offers for her hand. How she hoped his would be amongst them, and how it would be the one – the only one she would even think about.

Smiling at this, he marvelled at how far they had travelled in their relationship with just pen and ink to help them along – even to the point that they spoke of marriage. Through her letters he'd discovered a very forthright side to her, and amid the frivolous feminine activities she described was a love of horses and hunting, and anything to do with them. She even spoke of one day owning a stud farm, of all things. But whatever she wanted or dreamed of was fine by him. He loved her to distraction.

If only he was a couple of years older. Twenty was a decent age to offer for a girl, he thought. But maybe they would accept him; after all, Laura was just eighteen and her parents were looking for a husband for her. They didn't actually have to marry until much later – that is, if he could wait. He'd talk it over with his father to see what he thought.

He slit the second letter open with much less care than the first. Yes! Sandhurst had accepted him. He read down the page. It seemed he had to report there on 1st September. Splendid! He could accept the invitation to Laura's debut ball in August, and then stay on in London with his Aunt Agatha until he had to report for duty. That would give him time to shop for his uniform and all that he would need – though he might have to go down for measuring and fittings before that, of course. He sat down at once to write his acceptance, and the love-letter he would wrap it in. But he couldn't wait until then to see her. Propriety might mean he had to, but he could try to find a way to see her sooner.

My darling,

I must see you again. How would a picnic suffice? I could bring friends and you could invite some of yours. That should give the occasion convention. Do you think your parents would allow it? Perhaps early in August, before the shooting season? We could easily arrange it if you could wangle an invitation for me and Simon and Teddy. And I will speak to Father about us holding a shooting party here, this year. He hasn't done anything like that for years, but I am sure he will host one for me. Then I will invite you and your family and some friends of your choice, and arrange a summerhouse party for us younger ones.

Oh, do say yes! It would be such fun, and we would see each other twice more before your debut ball. That would make the long wait a little more bearable.

Before signing off, he told Laura of his success in gaining acceptance for officer training and finished with: *This letter comes with my undying love, Jeremy.*

'Oh, there you are, Jeremy. I've been looking for you. I saw two letters for you on the sideboard. I could see who they were both from. What did Sandhurst say?'

Andrew had a moment of disappointment at Jeremy's news, but hid it well. He congratulated his son warmly, before giving him some news he'd just heard.

'I am over the moon, my boy. Tom has just given me the news I have waited years to hear. Isabella is going to have a baby! How about that!'

'Really, Father, you get so involved in the lives of those on the estate. You are funny. One of the many things I remember of Mama is her saying you were like a mother hen with them. Still, it is good news. Is Isabella well?'

'Tom seemed to think so. Can't see why she wouldn't be – she's had plenty of practice at seeing others through it.' A stab of pain reminded him that she hadn't been successful in doing so with his dear Dvina, but that wasn't for want of her trying. No, there were no recriminations to put on Isabella's shoulders – she had devoted herself to Dvina.

'Good. Father, I have something I want to talk over with you. What age do you think it proper for me to offer marriage?'

'Good God, Jeremy! You have only met the girl once!'

'That's of no consequence. I couldn't be more sure if I'd known her all my life.'

'Well, well, fancy yourself in love, do you?'

'More than fancy . . .'

'Then I had better speak to her parents and facilitate a few meetings for you both. She could come and stay here – we could hold a dinner party, and of course her parents would come, too. How would that suit?'

'Very well indeed, thank you, Father. And I thought, maybe a shooting party? I would love that.'

'Yes! The very thing. We'll speak to the gamekeeper, though I am sure we will have plenty of kill. We always have an abundance. I'll give it all my attention. Draw up a list of the guests you want to invite, and I will do the same. Yes, I'm looking forward to it already. A splendid idea!'

Listening to his son switch his excitement from the woman he loved to his delight at his Sandhurst acceptance, Andrew's heart sank. There had been a moment when he'd thought that Jeremy's love for Laura Meriden would change his son's mind about his career path. But no, his enthusiasm for the Army hadn't waned, and it looked as if Andrew's worst fears had now received the stamp of finality. He faced years of continuing to have full responsibility for the mine, and his visits to Lilly kept to once a month. This lay heavily on him. He was tired. But he couldn't do anything about it – he'd tried and hoped, and failed. His son's ambitions lay in a different direction, and he had no choice but to respect that for now.

Bridget closed the book with a slam and put it under her pillow, tucking the pen in with it. The front door creaking on its hinges had prompted her action. She doused her oil lamp and shrank beneath the covers. *Please God, don't let him come into my room.*

His leering face, vivid in her mind, made her body tremble. He hadn't touched her, in the week since Mammy's funeral, but he'd said things. Things she knew he shouldn't, implying that she should be making more money and that she had the body and face to coin it in for them. And on a couple of occasions he'd looked like he might try it on with her himself, but she'd stood up to him. This made him angry when he was sober, but when drunk – as he likely was now – he'd say she had the spirit of her mother in her, and he liked that.

In the short time since her mammy's death she'd put a plan into action. Mrs Bartram had promised to help her. She'd said that she would add a halfpenny to every penny Bridget managed to put away. She'd promised to keep it in a tin, hidden away for her. And she'd said that when it was enough for Bridget and Bert to travel, and if Issy had been in touch by then, she would help them get away – provide a way of covering for them.

The book she'd secreted away held her partly written letter. The envelope was already addressed to *Mrs Isabella Grantham, The Groom's Cottage, Honey Lane, Breckton, Yorkshire*.

As she closed her eyes, her prayer wasn't to God, but to her mammy and pappy. *Look after me till that time comes. Please, look after me and Bert.* Her hands went to the locket, but as she went to open it, to gain strength from the beautiful young faces of her parents, the door of her bedroom crashed open. Mr Armitage stood blocking the opening, his body swaying. His slurred words held a menace.

'What's your game? Away to your bed afore I get in? It's only just on eight and—'

'If you're worried about your dinner, I have it ready. It's in the oven, so you only have to get it out. The table's set for you. I'm tired. I . . .'

'Tired? You don't know the meaning of the word! Get up. You've to go to Bartram's.'

'Bartram's, at this time of night? What for? The shop's closed.' Even as she said it, she knew it meant nothing to him. He often sent her around the back of the shop late at night to get baccy for him if he'd run out, but he'd only just come from the ale house, so surely he'd have got some there.

'The delivery of veg and stuff has come, and he needs your help. That useless bag of shit he calls his wife has took to her bed again. Get out of yer pit and get yourself down there. I promised him I'd send you the minute I got in.'

As he left, he slammed the door and it rattled on its hinges. Something didn't seem right. Yes, there was a delivery at the shop most nights – it was the only time a dray could get near unhindered, and a lot of the fresh stuff for the next day came in on a nightly basis from the farmers. But never before had Mr Bartram needed her help with it. Bridget's nerves jangled as she dressed herself.

Walking past the table provoked nothing from Mr Armitage. That was unusual in itself – no insults, no leering at her. He just slurped his dinner down him and kept his eyes on his plate. The worry in her escalated.

A light shone from the shop window, but no cart stood outside. Perhaps he'd managed it after all and wouldn't need her. She'd better call anyway, in case he'd got it inside, but needed help displaying and pricing it. The tentative knock that she gave the door resounded down the empty street as if she'd banged on it for dear life. It opened immediately. Mr Bartram stood there, with something new in his smile.

'You've come then, lass? Good girl. Bruiser said as you were willing. Come in.'

The worry turned to fear. Her voice shook as she asked, 'W-where's the new stock? Is it in the back?' The lock clicked into place. Her heart felt as if it had dropped into her stomach and then rebounded, hitting the back of her throat and making it even more difficult for her to speak. 'Is . . . is Mrs Bartram . . .'

'Don't worry about her, lass. She won't hear nowt. I've made sure of that. Get yourself in the back room. There's some sacks in there as will do for us.'

'Sacks? What for? What's going—?'

'Eeh, don't play the innocent, I've no time for that. Get

482

in there and get your clothes off. I've a drop of gin ready for yer. Bruiser said as that'll loosen you.'

She shot back towards the counter as realization dawned. 'No . . . let me out of here, Mr Bartram! I'm not for doing owt with you. I'll scream if you touch me.'

'Look, I paid good money to Bruiser. He said as you were ready, so what yer doing here, if you ain't?'

'He said . . . he said as you needed help . . .'

'Well, I do. And I mean to have it, whether you're willing or not. You're your mother's daughter, ain't yer? I know as you haven't had it yet – Bruiser took more than his usual charges because of that. But once you have, you'll be onto a good thing. Now get in the back and let's get on with it.'

Frantic, she felt behind her, hoping the large knife they used for cutting cabbages and the like was in its place. Her fingers felt its cold steel. Working along it to its wooden handle, she grabbed it, and the blade of it flashed in the dim, candlelit room. 'You touch me and I'll ram this into you!'

'You little bitch! Put that down!' His face took on the hue she'd seen before, when his anger got the better of him. His body turned, his movement swift. The huge potato he'd picked out of the sack behind him hurtled towards her. Ducking to avoid its impact put her off-guard. His hands dug into her ribs. The breath squeezed out of her as his muscular arms encircled her and crushed her to him. As if she were nothing more than a bag of garbage, he dragged her into the back room and threw her onto the sacks. Her head hit the concrete floor. A searing pain brought a cloud down over her conscious thoughts. It zinged around her brain, before it turned black and blocked everything out.

*

483

The sound of a woman's screams pierced through her. A guttural groan in her ear brought awareness of the weight on her, and of the odd sensation and pain in her groin. As the heaviness shifted off her, she knew something to release from her private part, leaving it sore and very wet.

The hammering and screaming took over the space around them. There didn't seem any room for her thoughts. She couldn't sort them out. The glass in the connecting door to the living quarters splintered with the sound of a thousand windows breaking. Shards of it landed on her, but she couldn't get out of the way. The moving shadow took the form of Mrs Bartram, who looked like someone demented. Her hair – which Bridget had only ever seen clipped tight to her head – flew loose, and spittle frothed from her mouth. Her eyes bulged, foul language spat from her, and she held a huge piece of wood high above her head.

The sickening crunch as the wood made contact with Mr Bartram's head brought the vomit gushing from Bridget. Bits of it stuck in her throat, and she could neither breathe nor choke it away. Panic died in her as the blessed relief of her own death stared down at her.

'Bridget!' Her body shook as Mrs Bartram tended to her. 'Oh, love, that's it. Cough it out of yer. Oh God, oh God!'

Retching as if to bring her insides up through her mouth, the vomit cleared at last from her. A huge painful gasp brought the life back into her. She could only stare at Mrs Bartram, and register the anguish shaking through the features of the woman's face. Watch the tears running down her cheeks and take comfort from the hand stroking her hair.

'You're awake, then?' A strange face – yet one with familiar features – looked down at her.

'Where am I? What . . . ?'

'Well, I'm not surprised as you can't remember. Mr Bartram falling off that ladder and knocking you for six gave you a right bump on your head. You've been in and out of consciousness this past week. The cart driver said as you never opened your eyes the whole journey down here.'

Nothing around her was familiar. Confusion crowded in on her.

'Don't worry, you're safe now. That stepdad, as me sister wrote about in her letter, can't get to you. I'm Ethel. I'm Fanny Bartram's sister. She sent you here during the night over a week ago. Gave me a right fright, someone hammering on me door at that time of the morning! Can't you remember anything as happened, then?'

'No . . . I . . .' She could, but none of it fitted with what this Ethel had said so far. A ladder? Mr Bartram falling? Something told her to hold her tongue and let Ethel tell her the version Mrs Bartram had given her.

'Well, your stepfather beat you, me sister tells me. She said you arrived on her doorstep in a terrible state. Her old man was doing some repairs in the back. She took you through to take you upstairs, when he fell. You came off light, compared to him. That sod has his toes up and is six feet under by now, I should think. Though I ain't sorry to hear of his demise. He gave me sister a hell of a life. She said in the letter as came with you to take care of you, and she'll come as soon as the funeral is seen to.'

'Where . . .'

The woman had a way of not letting you finish a sentence. 'You're in my house in Leeds. I live on me own, since me husband passed on last year. I've never had young 'uns – me and me sister are the same in that. Don't seem made for having them. Anyroad, do yer fancy a pot of tea? All this talking is drying me throat.'

When she'd left the room, Bridget tried to make sense of it all. Memory hit her in painful jerks. Tears that she didn't know whether to shed for her mammy, for what had happened to her own body or for the murder she'd witnessed streamed down her face.

'If that helps, you have a good cry, lass. But listen. Things ain't hopeless. You need never go back to him as done this to yer. Me sister intends to take care of you. You can stay here, if that's what she has on her mind. I know she'll tip up the money I'd need to look after you, and when you're well again you can get a job and start a new life. Our Fanny'll give you a reference. So, apart from the sadness in you as she says you just lost your ma, and the shock you've had and the beating you took, you've nowt to fret over. Get them out of yer and, thou knows, the world lies ahead of yer.'

Bridget almost laughed. The list she'd reeled off had been enough for anyone to cope with, let alone saying things were all right apart from them! But she did stop crying, as she had another worry she needed to talk about. 'I have a brother. I can't leave him. I promised me mammy . . . he's only five.'

'Happen as he'll be reet. Lads can take more than girls. Anyroad, until you're on your feet there ain't much as you can do about his situation, is there?'

The realization of this truth helped. Ethel was right in all she said. She had to get herself settled before she could think about fetching Bert. In the meantime she had to find a way of living with the secrets inside her, because not to do so would damn Mrs Bartram and let the world know what had happened. And she couldn't do that. Ethel's next words put her mind at rest as to another question that she was about to ask.

'And don't think on what folk will say about you having gone. Me sister has put it all in her letter – though how she thought it all out after her tragedy and got it all dealt with, I'll never know. She were always the timid one. Anyhow, she says as she'll sort out your disappearance so no one comes asking. She'll tell the police she got you away cos of your situation. She says they know of Bruiser and will understand, as will the folk around her. So I'd leave it to her. Sounds like she has everything sorted, and will tell us anything we don't know when she comes calling.'

Bridget lay back. Everything hurt. Pain racked her body and her head throbbed, but most of the hurt clogged her heart, to the point where she could have torn it from her. *Oh, Mammy, Mammy, I won't break me promise. I won't. I'll go back for Bert just as soon as I can . . .*

35

August–December 1899

The future generation

Laura looked beautiful in every situation, Andrew thought. Jeremy had chosen well. He watched the small party of young people walk across the lawn to the summerhouse, on this beautiful August day. His eyes followed Laura in particular. He saw her throw her head back and could almost hear her lovely infectious laugh. Everything about her was focused on Jeremy, who had no doubt made a joke she'd found amusing. He hoped this love that his son and Laura obviously had for one another would grow and deepen.

Andrew's eyes looked heavenwards. *Our son has chosen our own favourite place for his first official entertaining of Laura. What do you think of that, Old Thing? But I don't have to guess, I know you will be as pleased as I am and think like me – that Laura will do very nicely.*

Moving away from the window, he rang the bell, and as usual Jameson appeared as if he'd been standing just outside the door. Yet whenever Andrew went looking for the butler, he was never there, but downstairs in his office. Funny, that.

'I think I will take tea now, Jameson. And let Wilson know

I'd like a lie-down before dinner. Ask him to prepare for me going up in an hour, please.'

'Very well, sir.'

Sitting on the comfy old sofa that Dvina had brought from Tarrington House, she again came into his thoughts. How she would have loved to be here today – to have seen her son grow up into such a decent, kind young man, though one with a strong will when he set his mind to something.

Like him, Dvina had loved this room. She had chosen the decor: silver-grey and soft green. She'd had this sofa covered in silver with a thin green stripe running through it, so delicate that it was hardly discernible. Other chairs were either covered all over in silver or with the reverse effect of soft green with a silver stripe. The silk drapes, in the same green, had silver edgings to them. With the occasional tables in rich mahogany, the effect was of restfulness and elegance. How often had they sat in here together, discussing all manner of things? He wished he could have that chance now – just to sit with her and go over his concerns. He'd ask her to persuade Jeremy to start his training to take over the mine. A laugh welled up in him, as he could almost hear her response: 'You're just being selfish, my dear. You want him to relieve you from the drudgery that your work has become to you. Well, he is a young person, not someone to do your bidding or make your life easier!' He knew that Dvina would have been right, but that didn't help.

A knock on the door paused his thoughts. Jameson served his tea, passing idle conversation about the weather. He remarked on how happy the young people sounded and how the staff were thrilled.

'Yes, I suspect the staff have had enough of nothing going on around here. And so had I, Jameson. It did me good – as

I know it did them – to have something like the shooting party to organize.'

'Yes, it has put a fire back into everyone. May I ask, sir, what time Lord and Lady Meriden are expected back from the visit to their friends?'

'Oh, I'd think around six. They know dinner is at seven, and will want to change, of course. How are their staff fitting in with you all?'

'One or two clashes – nothing we can't handle – as you find that those who serve the titled think themselves above the rest of us. Their butler wouldn't even condescend to tell me the expected arrival time of his master. But I have them in their place and following our routine, instead of us changing to suit them.'

Andrew would have liked to laugh out loud at this, but out of respect for Jameson he just said, 'Well done. You keep a good ship, and all runs very well. We can't have the toffs coming in and upsetting things.'

'Quite, sir.'

Talking about domestic arrangements, and his amusement at the hierarchy of the servants, had taken him out of what could have become a morose mood. Sitting back and enjoying his tea, he made himself stay in the present. He had to do something about his situation. If Jeremy's plans didn't change, then maybe he'd hire a manager? Yes, that would be the thing. In fact, he could do with two of them – an estate manager, as well as one for the mine. One thing was for sure: he couldn't keep up his current pace, or he'd never live to see his grand-children.

Now that the idea had planted itself, he let it really take hold. He even began to plan how he and Lilly would spend the extra time that he'd have with her. These were very pleasant thoughts – yes, all in all, everything could turn out very well. Laura would make a fitting and excellent mistress of this house, and Jeremy had promised he'd only give ten years to the Army. So, if he himself took semi-retirement in the meantime, and the managers could support Jeremy when he was ready to take over the mine, life in his dotage would be very pleasant. Very pleasant indeed.

The last night of 1899

Bridget shifted her heavy body. The babby inside her protested at the move by kicking hard into her ribs. She rubbed the area. Her babby wasn't due for another five weeks, end of January, Sister Bernadette reckoned. Tonight the new millennium dawned. A time that all and sundry said would bring new hope to the world, but she wouldn't be celebrating. Not after last night. What happened in the kitchen last night would be etched onto her memory forever and a day.

At first, after what Mr Bartram did to her, it had seemed everything would turn out fine. She had only to try to forget. That hadn't been too difficult, as she had no memory of what Mr Bartram had done to her. She only remembered how she got to the shop, and the last bit, when she'd come round. Sometimes she could still feel the weight of him and how it had crushed the breath from her. At such times she could hear the animal-like noises he was making. But the other – the killing of Mr Bartram – that never went. It came into her nightmares, but she was learning to cope.

She liked Ethel, and Ethel had taken to her. Mrs Bartram had got away with the story she'd made up and, free of her husband's bullying and the misery he caused, she'd begun to thrive. She'd paid Ethel to take care of Bridget, and had even told Bridget to look into lessons for her to improve her education. And not just reading and writing – she'd talked of her becoming an accountant, saying she was good with figures, and she'd mentioned something about speaking proper English, like the rich. But then the sickness had started and Ethel had asked when she'd last had her bleeding, and it had all come crashing down.

'I can't keep you, lass. Me name'd be mud, with an unmarried living with me, and me being upstanding in the community. I'll sort sommat out for yer,' she'd said. What she'd sorted out had been St Michael's, a home for unmarried mothers run by the nuns.

Meeting Lucy Grampton had made life bearable here. Even though Lucy was top-drawer, they'd got on as if they'd known each other all of their lives. And now Lucy was dead.

With both of them just five weeks off having their babbies, they hadn't been sleeping well. Last night Lucy had had a thirst on her, and they'd crept down to the kitchen. They'd giggled with the thrill of their out-of-bounds escapade, and it had turned into a right game. Bumping into things and making a clatter in the dark, they had dodged a Sister on the way to the lav, and then Lucy had accidentally trodden on the cat and made it squeal. But that giggling had turned to horror when they entered the kitchen: Lucy had slipped and fallen, hitting the edge of the worktable first, had then crashing onto the slab floor.

Bridget curled up now as best she could against Lucy's screams, which still reverberated around her head. They had pebbled the flesh on her arms last night, just as thinking of them was doing now. She rubbed her forearm, trying to dispel the shock of what had followed: the pool of blood, the draining of colour from Lucy's face, the awful moans, the agonized pushing, and the babby slipping out into a bath of her mother's life-fluid. It had been a relief when Lucy finally lost consciousness, because then she could no longer cling onto Bridget and stop her going for help. Wrapping her nightgown around the babby, she'd run naked through the corridors, screaming for someone to come. Help had come too late for poor, lovely Lucy, but her little girl had lived.

The door at the end of the dormitory creaked. The soft tread and the jangling of keys told her it was Sister Bernadette, whose gentle Irish lilt cut her heart with pain, it was so like her mammy's. 'Is it you in here all alone, Bridget, and that being the worst thing for you? Didn't I tell that Ruth to stay with you till I could come to you?'

'I just don't want to be with anyone, Sister. I have so much hurt in me that it's making me angry.'

'I am for understanding that. 'Tis as you have been through a lot before you came to us, and with what happened last night it can be too much to bear. But 'tis as they say: sharing a problem can be halving it, so let us have a talk.'

'How's Lucy's little girl?'

'Oh, isn't she the bonny little thing! We are having to take extra care as she is early coming into this world, but she will thrive, she is determined to, demanding attention at all hours. She's after having dark hair, and though her eyes have not yet settled on what colour they are going to be, they look as though they will be dark, too. Just like Lucy's, God rest her soul.'

'I can't believe it . . .'

''Tis God's will, and none of us are for knowing how He does his work or the greater plan He has for us. Now, Lucy's parents are here. They are wanting to see you, but 'tis as I have a powerful worry, as there could be trouble. What was it Lucy was for telling you of her circumstances?'

'She told me a lot. Did you know as she was tricked, Sister Bernadette? Tricked by her own aunt?'

'I am for knowing some of it, but I'm thinking we will need to tread with care. Let me sit next to you, wee one, as I am after wanting to know all you can tell me.'

Once she'd moved up to make room on the bed, Sister Bernadette took Bridget's hand. She looked into the nun's lovely, soft, twinkly eyes and thought what a pretty face she had. And, as she often did in her dealings with Sister Bernadette, she wondered how she came to take the Holy Orders. She couldn't have been more than about thirty, and with her looks and shapely, slender figure she would have attracted a husband easily.

'Go on, my dear. Don't be afraid.'

'Well, Sister, Lucy thinks – thought – her aunt planned everything. She told me her mammy had had her very late in life, and her mammy's sister still hadn't had a child and was approaching the time when it would be too late. She was desperate, as there were rumours her husband would leave her. Lucy said he had a mistress. Anyroad, the aunt invited Lucy to go on holiday with her – well, it were more than a holiday. She'd taken a place in the south of France, and it was to last a year. Lucy said as she were that excited, as her life had been so dull.

'Whilst she was there, a nephew of her uncle's came to stay. Lucy fell in love with him. She said as she came under the spell of him. She thought that was down to her thinking of herself as on the shelf, cos she'd had no coming-out Season. With her parents being so old, they hadn't wanted to bother with it all. So, she said, she did a silly thing and let this man's attentions go to her head, but she came to realize that he was using her love for him in a blackmailing way. As if she was only in his affections if she did what he wanted her to. She liked the feeling of having someone of her own at last, and he took advantage of that.

'One night he tried to go further than he should, and Lucy couldn't fight him off. But she said as she didn't try after that first time, as she loved him so much and he'd talked of marriage . . . She will go to Heaven, won't she, Sister? Even though she did things out of wedlock?'

'That is for the good Lord to decide, but I know Lucy attended confession and Mass, so it is likely she asked for forgiveness. In which case, yes, 'tis as she is with our Blessed Lady at this very moment, because I am for thinking our dear Mother in Heaven would take it on herself to greet all those who died trying to give birth.'

Bridget hoped so, because that sounded lovely for Lucy. She might have had money, but from what she said, she'd had very little love. To think of her with the Holy Mother put a joy in her.

Sister Bernadette interrupted her thoughts, asking, 'Why was Lucy after thinking it was planned?'

'Well, as soon as her condition was realized, her intended went off, and her aunt seemed to have everything sorted as to what was going to happen. She booked her in here and told Lucy no one would know, as she would take the babby as her own, and that would be that. Once Lucy had travelled back to France with the babby, she could return home with her uncle and aunt as if coming back from holiday and as if nothing had happened, other than her aunt finally having got a child of her own.'

'Oh, I see. Now isn't that cunning? Wouldn't it be easy for

the aunt to say she'd become pregnant, with her away from all of her usual companions? Yes, I'm thinking 'tis as Lucy thought, for hasn't the aunt this good while given money to the convent? Now this is for being a secret between us, Bridget. You are not to tell a soul.'

'I won't, I promise, Sister.'

'I know 'tis as I can trust you, and 'tis important for the future, so I can put things into place to benefit everyone. 'Tis as I am for thinking the Reverend Mother has the full knowledge of it all and has played her part. She was after telling us one evening that Lucy was very special and had to be treated as such, without the other girls realizing it. She said the girl was related to someone she had known at school. You see, it is as the Reverend Mother herself once came from money, only I understand her family lost everything they had. Sure, 'tis as what she did, she did to attract funds. But didn't she bask in the glory of finding a beneficiary of such generosity? 'Tis sad, but an institution such as this rarely attracts one, and the bishop is very pleased, and for that small accolade my superior has facilitated a dreadful act on a defenceless girl, so she has.'

Bridget didn't know what to say. It all seemed like something you'd read in a book.

'Bridget, 'tis a sad tale all round. Now, before I can do anything, I have to speak with you about the reason I asked you to meet me here. 'Tis as we have to discuss what will happen to your own child.'

'I don't want it taken from me, Sister . . .'

'Well, now, my wee one, have you something sorted where 'tis as you can take care of it?'

'No, but me friend Mrs Bartram will help me out with money.'

'Weren't you for telling us you used to work for her? Well, that is kindness itself. Will you live with her?'

'I can't, cos of the man as married me mammy. He lives near her and he is a bad man. Violent and—'

'Listen, Bridget, you are for being just off turning sixteen. You are not for having a home, and I know it is as you can't go back to the man who should be your guardian. I have been looking into it all, and you haven't a job or any prospects of one. So, my wee one, 'tis not possible for you to take on the care of your child, nor the young brother I have heard you talking of.'

'I have to . . .'

'Yes, one day in the future, when 'tis as your life is sorted out. In the meantime, 'tis as I will take care of your child, as I will of Lucy's . . .'

'What? How? But Lucy has a family!'

'Her parents are not for having anything to do with the babby. They say as they are old and the responsibility is too much for them, and I am for thinking they have guessed what their sister was up to. They asked to see you, because they are wanting to know if their daughter told you anything. Maybe it is as the aunt even wrote to them to say she was pregnant – I don't know – but 'tis clear they have suspicions, as they have a lot of questions as to how their daughter came to be here.'

'I don't want to see them. I can't, Sister. It's like none of them care about Lucy, and when I talked to her she seemed so lonely, and had no one.'

'No, 'tis as I am thinking you shouldn't. It will be too up-setting for you. I'll be for telling them you're not well, and I'll deal with everything. I am for thinking they are seeing their daughter as a sinner, and their main concern is to prevent any scandal. That is for sticking in my throat, now I know the truth of it, and I believe they are after seeking assurance of your silence.'

'You can tell them they'll have that, as I don't know anyone as would want to know it all. But the aunt – I know she did a bad thing, but couldn't she care for Lucy's babby?'

'It seems not. I am not for knowing why, but there is a lot of bitterness in Lucy's mother, and they are saying the child is not to be recognized by any of the family.'

'It don't seem right. Her own grandparents. There's a lot of wickedness in the world, Sister, and in me young life I seem to have met most of it.'

'You have, but 'tis a measure of the strength of you how you have been for coming through it all and are still a lovely, caring girl. That is why I am wanting to set you free from the shackles of trying to bring up your child when you haven't yet the circumstances in which you can.'

'But how can you take care of them? I mean, they don't have babbies here.'

'Because of what I know – I will be using that against the Reverend Mother. I will force her to let me go to the orphanage across the other side of Leeds. 'Tis as I cannot stay here under the direction of such a woman. I have thought about it all night. If it is as I go to St Benedict's orphanage, I can also be insisting I take Hattie and your child with me, and I can look out for them until a time when you can come for your little one. And I will do all in my power for them, so I will.'

'Hattie?'

'Yes, wasn't that for being my grandmother's name? And wasn't she a resilient old thing – a survivor, so she was – so I have given Lucy's child her name. We baptized her this morning. Now, what are you thinking about my plan?'

'I can't think on giving up me babby . . .'

'Bridget, my wee child, don't you know, 'tis as you will have no choice . . . Oh, wee one, don't cry. 'Tis sorry I am to tell you, but 'tis the way of it. The babies are taken away as soon as they are born from the girls who have nowhere to go.'

Bridget's heart wept inside of her, splitting her very being. The child was part of that being, and to take it from her would tear her world in two. Sister Bernadette let her cry for a while, but then beseeched her to stop.

'Sure you will do yourself and your baby harm, wee one. Are you not for seeing what a solution I offer you? You will have peace in your heart, knowing your child is with me, and knowing I will have the say as to what happens if there is to be an adoption.'

'No, Sister, please don't let me child be adopted. Please keep me babby at the convent until I can come to collect it.'

Sister Bernadette didn't answer for a moment; she just wrapped her arms around Bridget and held her. Some of the wetness caused by tears didn't come from her, for Sister Bernadette was crying too. ''Tis as I will be doing my best. Now, it is as you will have to agree to what I propose, because if they see your determination, they will be for taking the child from you to a secret destination and none of us will be having a say in it.'

A pain shooting through her caused Bridget to break away from the comforting hug. She grasped her stomach.

'What is it? Oh dear Lord, is that you going into labour?'

Bridget smiled at this. She knew it was the Irish way to ask questions in that form, as her mammy had often done so. The Irish seemed oblivious to how it sounded, and a picture of the astonished look on Jesus's face on being asked if *He* was going into labour tickled her sense of humour. 'Sister, how can the Dear Lord, as you call Him, go into labour?'

Aghast, Sister Bernadette looked at her, then her lovely giggle came from her and they both laughed together before she said, 'You are knowing my meaning, little one. Have you had another pain?'

'No, I think it was because I was bent ov— Ooooh!'

'Oh, me wee Bridget, 'tis as your baby is coming, I'm sure of that. Don't worry, 'tis early it is, but if Lucy's Hattie can make it then so can your wee one. Come on, let us be after getting you into the delivery wing. I'll not leave you. Once I have me nurse's apron on, I'll be right with you. We'll be for seeing this child into the world together, so we will.'

Issy sat up in bed, her heart bursting with pride and joy. Her little girl – her own little girl. She had a mind to call her Cecelia – a bit posh, but she'd loved it ever since a little girl with that name had come to stay at Tarrington House many years ago. Besides, everyone would call her Cissy, so she wouldn't get ragged for having a top-drawer name.

She looked up into Tom's eyes as he asked, 'Bridget?'

'No, there was only one Bridget. We don't want her to be a copy; we want her to have her own identity. We'll tell her of Bridget one day, though.'

'I often think of her, you know.'

'Aye, I do too. I'd love to know how they are, the pair of them. Do you think they're all right, Tom? It was a worry to me, them going back to where – well, thou knows, where Bridie had a different life.'

'We'll never know, love. I thought of asking you if you wanted to contact her once the Dochertys were gone, but I left it for you to say.'

'I know, and perhaps I will. I still have the address of that Beth, as Bridie put so much store by. Happen as she came good for them and took them in.'

'Well, it's a bit late to worry about it all now. Let's just leave it as it is, shall we? You never know what you open up, do yer? Now, can I hold me very own little daughter, or are you going to keep her to yourself?'

'Here you are, love. Meet Cecelia. Cissy to everyone else – well, and to us, I reckon, if other young 'uns are not going to laugh at her.'

'Oh, you settled her name then. Don't I get a say?'

'Aye, you can add some names of your own, but I'm set on that one, thou knows.'

'Eeh, Issy, she's beautiful. I wonder what life has in store for her?'

'Just happiness, if we have anything to do with it, eh, Tom?'

'Aye, love. If she is as happy as she is beautiful, she'll be reet, so she will.'

The crying wrenched Bridget's heart. A little girl – a beautiful baby girl, with curls that showed a hint of red on them, even though they were matted to her head. Her brief glimpse of her babby had planted her firmly into the very soul of her, and that's where she would stay. They could take her away, but they couldn't separate them. They would always be joined together, and one day she would find her. One day.

'There, aren't you the clever girl? Have you a name you are wanting to call her?'

'Yes. I want to call her Megan. It is one of my names – me pappy and granna gave it to me, as it was the name of me great-grandmother. From what I was told of her, she lived a happy life with very few troubles, and surrounded by her loving family. That's what I want for my Megan, too.'

'Well, 'tis a lovely name, so it is. And I will be adding Anne, as she needs a saint to take care of her. Now, is it that you want to hold her, now we have her all cleaned up? But only for a moment as we have to take great care of her. She is little, but isn't she showing a fighting spirit in her yells? She is going to be fine, so she is.'

Bridget froze. She'd thought they wouldn't let her hold her child, and now she wasn't sure she could. Letting go of her, after only a stolen look at her, shredded her to pieces. *Oh, Mammy, Mammy, help me!*

But she knew the answer – if she held her babby to her, it would destroy her. She refused. She couldn't do it. It seemed like an icy coldness had wrapped itself around her heart, protecting it from hurt. Somehow she could deal with the things she needed to do, and she could cope with not being able to do what she wanted to do. Her mammy was surely helping her.

'Sister?'

'What is it, wee one?'

'Will you give this to Megan – keep it with her at all times? It is a locket belonging to me mammy. There's a picture of me mammy and pappy inside – their names were Bridie and Will. And tell her about me, and about her having an uncle. His name is Bert. He's five now. And . . . and tell her I'll come for her. If it takes me the rest of me days, I'll come.'

'Lie back and give yourself time to rest, wee one. Sure 'tis a hard task you have just come through. Won't you take comfort from knowing I am with her? Because I am on my way now to the Reverend Mother.'

'Come back and let me know. Please, Sister?'

'To be sure I will.'

The crying of her babby stopped, but for Bridget it was just beginning. She couldn't imagine a time when her life would not contain tears. But then, what kind of life would she have? Where would she go? Would Ethel have her back? If not, she might find herself in the correctional convent, and dear God, she didn't want that.

'Bridget . . . is that me wee Bridget, with her sleepy head on?'

The sun streamed through the window opposite her bed. Her eyes cringed against it, and could barely make out Sister Bernadette standing over her.

'Sure it is a lovely day. Crisp and cold, but God in His goodness has chosen to welcome the new century by flooding His world with sunlight, so He has. And I am bursting with news and ideas for you.'

Sitting up, Bridget managed to shield herself from the glare. She looked into Sister Bernadette's excited face as she lowered her voice and said, 'Isn't it as I have found out things that could lead to a future for you? Now listen: this is just for you to know. I have been after speaking to the Reverend Mother. She has money belonging to you – it isn't for being much, but it seems your Mrs Bartram is sending it on a regular basis. Now, I have been for watching you, and I am thinking you will make a wonderful nurse. Reverend Mother agrees, and she says you can be staying here and can train under Sister Marie-Louise. There never was for being a more patient and kind person than Marie-Louise – she's a saint, so she is, and an expert in medicine. She thinks it a wonderful idea. Sure you will get your full board and will work in the infirmary where the poor are treated. Isn't that a wonderful solution for you?'

A trickle of hope entered Bridget. She rubbed her eyes, unsure if she was really awake or still in the land of dreaming.

'Now, 'tis as you have to sit an exam. If that is satisfactory, then there are enough funds to pay for one year's training; but if Mrs Bartram isn't for carrying on with the payments, I have it on a promise that the rest of your course will come out of what Lucy's aunt paid. This is for being a wonderful opportunity, so it is, as girls coming for training are usually funded by their families. So, what is it you are for thinking about it all?'

'I think it's a wonderful idea. Once I have me qualifications, I can look for paid work. I'll write to you then, Sister Bernadette. I'll write just as soon as that day comes, and make arrangements to pick up Megan.'

'Oh, 'tis glad I am! You are for having your whole life ahead of you, and who knows where it will lead you? 'Tis as you are the future, and I will pray for you every day I am living.'

Right now, Bridget needed all the prayers she could get. She looked heavenwards and asked her mammy and pappy to pray for her, too. Though her mammy hadn't taken care of her very well, she knew it wasn't because she hadn't loved her. Love had been in her mammy's make-up, but her love just hadn't had the strength of willpower behind it. Well, that wouldn't happen to her Megan, because nothing would stop her taking care of her own child. And Bert – she would keep her promise to go and get him, too. She just had to accept that it would happen in the future, and hope and pray life wasn't too bad for Bert in the meantime. At least she knew that Megan and Hattie would have the best care Sister Bernadette could give them. And she entrusted them to her. *Oh, her little Megan . . .*

As Sister Bernadette stood at the door and looked back at the young girl she had come to love, her heart filled with joy, for didn't Bridget's future look brighter than would ever have been possible before? And though Bridget wouldn't thank her now for what she intended to do – keep her away from her child forever – surely it would be that she would do so in the years to come? Because as Bridget made her way in the world, wouldn't she come to dread the sin of her past coming to light?

Well, she would see that it didn't, and in doing so would know the beauty of it all, for Hattie and this babby now belonged to her: a woman judged at birth as having no right to marriage, simply because a vital part of her – her most private part – hadn't formed in the way it should have.

Now, at last, she had her reward. And wasn't it justice that it should be so? For hadn't she for so many years endured the same longing for a child that other women had, without having it satisfied? And hadn't she tried to find release from that longing through the power of prayer?

What was happening to her this day was all meant to happen, she knew that. Besides, it couldn't be right, could it, that such a wonderful gift would be taken from her, only to spoil the life of wee Bridget?

Turning away, she thought: *Isn't it that they say as the good Lord is for working in mysterious ways? Well, to be sure, He has been for proving this to me this very day, so He has.*